Simon vs. Simon:

The Saint and the Sorcerer

Simon vs. Simon:

The Saint and the Sorcerer

An Inspiring Story Based on Historical Records

EDWARD N. BROWN

RESOURCE *Publications* · Eugene, Oregon

SIMON VS. SIMON
The Saint and the Sorcerer

Wipf & Stock
An Imprint of Wipf and Stock Publishers
199 W. 8th Ave., Suite 3
Eugene, OR 97401

www.wipfandstock.com

PAPERBACK ISBN: 978-1-6667-4914-4
HARDCOVER ISBN: 978-1-6667-4915-1
EBOOK ISBN: 978-1-6667-4916-8

The little-known story of Simon Peter and his battles with the greatest heretic and magician of the time, Simon Magus.

Already persecuted by Jewish traditionalists, Gentile pagans, and imperial Roman authorities, the early Christians are now troubled by false messiahs, phony prophets, sham sorcerers, and mystery religions.

Strong in faith, will, and determination, and empowered by Jesus Christ with the 'Keys to the Kingdom', Peter takes on the challenge of his life, and proves to all the believers that he truly is the 'Rock of the Church'.

CONTENTS

PREFACE

This book takes up where the New Testament of the Bible leaves off. In the Bible, nothing is mentioned about Peter's life after the events at the Council of Jerusalem around 48-50 AD (see Acts 15). But there are other ancient writings that do report on his life activities right up until his death in Rome as a martyr in 65-67 AD. The accuracy, sincerity, and trustworthiness of those writings vary immensely, but when viewed as an aggregate, certain scenarios stand out as common, and form the root core of probable historical events.

Now, I should make it clear that this book is not just a historical summary of those writings – it is not just a compendium of events. Instead, it is a weaving of plot elements, account fabrics, and event descriptions into a writing that comprises the crux of a historical non-fiction narrative tale.

And it is a narrative tale that has all the elements typical to the genre of a 'story'. The names, places, dates, and events are all accurate to the ancient writings, and told in a logical progression. But many of the nitty-gritty details of everyday life have been extrapolated by the author using the best values and characteristics of a 'good story'.

The characters, setting, plot, conflict, and resolution attributes of the story type are all present. The style is in the sense of a life-vs-death adventure story, but there is a strong temptation slant of the morality story, and a serious love-vs-hate slant of the romance story. What drives the story narrative is the value of human connection mixed with the value of 'going beyond yourself to discover a larger purpose' (illustrated throughout by the conflict between good and evil).

The theme follows the classic age-old tragic adventure script: the good likeable hero – Peter, in this case – defeats the bad despicable monster – Simon, in this case – but the hero perishes in the end. However, it is also a morality story – temptation vs. virtue – and a faith-based story – belief in an invisible God vs. belief in visible idols. In the final analysis, it's a love story – love of God, and His love for us, forms the basic formula for everlasting happiness.

So, is the story fiction or non-fiction? All the major events are as accurate as we know them, but much of the dialogue is reconstructed from the sporadic and imperfect memory of ancient scholars and scribes. Certainty in documentation is rarely 100%, and the best double and triple-checking will still leave an element of doubt as to what really happened. In addition, not all historical details are even recorded, so a storyteller has to 'fill-in-the-blanks' as best that he can.

But in general, a story thread must be deterministic (not random, unless it's a dream or fantasy setting) and that means the author must develop the narrative such that things are logical and tie together, just like they did in real life. This often necessitates some artful reasoning as to what was the most likely scenario or sequence of events, when concerned with small increments of time. And this thought process is manifested in the storyline herein. Note that there is no intention ever to alter history – just to make it as believable and realistic as possible. So, in a generic story, Jane may have coffee for breakfast on a dark and dreary morning, rather than tea, which she actually may have had in reality. That's just detailing for the sake of believability.

So, is the story fiction or non-fiction? It depends on who you talk to and what the venue is. To the scholarly academic community, it may be classified as fiction. But in my opinion, it can readily be considered as non-fiction, albeit with the caveats mentioned above.

The gist of the story is true to history. More-or-less, the significant happenings actually played out in the past as described in the story. So, for all practical purposes, the story is non-fiction.

In fact, the official category ascribed to this book is 'Narrative Non-Fiction'. Whether Jane had coffee or tea for breakfast is irrelevant to the big picture. In addition, there are valuable 'take-aways' from the story that just don't hold viability if it is considered to be fiction (inspiration and hope being the most powerful). The reader's imagination is stimulated – "if the real-live hero could do it, then I can do it also." When these subtle factors are taken into account, there is good reason for the reader to believe that the story is true – at least from the big-picture standpoint – the standpoint at which 'take-aways' matter.

With that in mind, read on and see where it takes you.

Edward N Brown
Chicago, April 2022

BACKGROUND

Samaria was both a region and a city in ancient Palestine that experienced many changes throughout biblical history. The hilly region extends for about 40 miles from north to south and 35 miles from east to west.[1] It is bounded by the region of Galilee to the north, Judaea to the south, the Mediterranean Sea to the west, and the Jordan River to the east.[2]

RELIGIOUS OVERVIEW

In Israel and Samaria under Assyrian rule (722-626 BC), the 'civilizing' colonization process of Alexander the Great was continued - called Hellenization. The people lived in a more cosmopolitan world than the people of Judah. This meant that the pursuit of the restless, inquiring, creative spirit of Greece – what might loosely be called today, the 'scientific spirit', based on human discovery and experience – was a normal way of life.[3] Cultural clubs called gymnasia, were introduced, in which people gathered to study, to learn, and to enjoy each other's company. After competing in various forms of athletics, prominent men and women would soak themselves in hot baths – delight in the body beautiful was a major preoccupation. To most of them, polytheism was a matter of civilized behavior. Many Samaritans believed in YHWH (Yahweh), but accepted Him as just one of several gods who had to be reckoned with.

On the other hand, in Judah, the Jewish view of life was totally in opposition to this. It was a way of life based on spiritual revelation. They regarded Hellenism as a form of nature worship. They saw it as the continuation of the pagan religion of the Canaanites, which they viewed as simply mythologizing the anger, hate, lust, envy, and greed of un-enlightened human hearts. Their belief was that it was Yahweh who chose Israel to be 'a light to lighten the nations'.[4] The reason for Israel's existence was to put the revelation of God into everyday life, by producing an ordered human society that was ruled by God's justice and love, and not by human desire, reason, and force.

Before the Assyrian exile of the Israelites, the Samaritans were mostly descended from ancient Semitic inhabitants of the region.[5] Religiously, they were adherents of an Abrahamic religion closely related to Judaism. Based only on the first five books of the Bible (the Pentateuch), Samaritans claimed that their worship was the true religion of the ancient Israelites prior to the Babylonian exile, preserved by those who remained in the Land of Israel and were not taken into captivity. Through the Pentateuch, they saw themselves as co-equals in inheritance to the Israelite lineage.[6] However, after the Assyrian acts of exile and immigration, the Samaritans were considered to be less fervent and less credible by the Jews of Judah.

Antagonism between Samaritans and Jews

Within the region of Samaria, in the historical city of Sychar (also called Shechem),[7] was the site of 'Jacob's Well'. This was the location of Jesus' conversation with the Samaritan woman, who asked, "Are you greater than our father Jacob, who gave us the well and drank from it himself, as did also his sons and his livestock?"[8] Later in the conversation, she brought up a centuries-old controversy: "Our ancestors worshiped on this mountain, but you Jews claim that the place where we must worship is in Jerusalem".[9] The 'mountain' referred to is Mount Gerizim in the central Samaritan highlands, the place where the Samaritans had built their own temple in the middle of the 5th century BC; what they considered to be the true temple of God.[10]

From the death of Herod onwards, the history of Samaria/Sebaste is part of the history of Judaea (although not because the inhabitants wanted it that way). There were religious tensions between the Samaritans and the Judaeans, economic differences between the urban and peasant economies, and the cosmopolitan city was culturally different from most towns in Judaea. Most Judaean Jews in Jesus' day disliked the Samaritans because of their questionable religious views and their mixed racial heritage – calling them racial half-breeds – spiritual heretics who taught a distorted faith based on a fusion of pagan belief and modified/condensed Jewish belief.

The antagonism between Samaritans and Jews is important in understanding the Bible's New Testament story of the 'Samaritan woman at the well' and the parable of 'the Good Samaritan'.[11] In the 1st century AD, Samaria was under Roman control and influence. The disciples of Jesus had nothing but disdain for the Samaritans, but in the apostolic age (after Pentecost), many Christians preached to them, marking the first transition in the extension of the church into the non-Jewish world.[12]

Samaria is included as one the geographical locations in Jesus' Great Commission to spread the Gospel.[13] Once the church was scattered after Stephen's martyrdom, many Christians fled to the surrounding areas, including Samaria, and continued to preach the 'Good News'.[14]

First Attacks on the Jesus Movement

Herod Agrippa was raised in Rome, but he was conscious of the role of Judaism in his territory. As a good politician, he publicly supported the religious leaders in and around Jerusalem. In order to gain favor with them, Herod Agrippa started a major attack against the Jesus movement. He arrested a number of people thought to be members of the movement, intending to persecute them. His first high-profile victim was the apostle James,[15] the son of Zebedee, who was put to death with the sword. James was a fisherman and brother of John. When Herod saw that this was met with approval from the Jews, he proceeded to seize Peter also.[16]

Peter was put in prison, guarded by four squads of four soldiers each. Herod intended to bring him out for public trial after the Passover celebrations. But the night before he was to come to trial, Peter was sleeping between two soldiers, bound with chains, and sentries standing guard at the entrance.

Suddenly, an angel of the Lord appeared, and a light shone in the cell. The angel tapped Peter on the side and woke him up. "Quick, get up!" he said, and the chains fell off Peter's wrists.[17] Peter put on his clothes and followed the angel past the guards and right out of the prison. He had no idea if this was a dream or really happening – it was like he was in a daze. They got to the main iron gate at the entrance to the prison, and it just opened by itself. Peter walked through the gate and down the adjoining lane – and then the angel disappeared.

When Peter came to his full senses, he thought:

Now I know without a doubt that the Lord has sent his angel to rescue me from Herod's clutches, and from everything the Jewish people were hoping would happen.[18]

Herod Agrippa died in 44 AD, while presiding over a celebratory festival at the port city of Caesarea.[19] Decked-out in royal garments made entirely of silver, he was a spectacle to behold – and the people cried out that he was a 'god'. However, just after being hailed as divine by the crowd, Herod was gripped by a sharp pain in his stomach – thought to be worms at the time. He died five days later because it was said that 'he had not given the proper glory to God'.[20]

Herod Agrippa's son, Agrippa II, would serve as the final king from the Herodian family. It was Herod Agrippa II that participated in the trial of Paul at Caesarea, after Paul had appealed his case to the emperor.[21]

NOTES

1. In Hebrew, the name 'Samaria' means 'watch-mountain' or 'watch-tower', which corresponds to its hilly features.

2. The city of Samaria, within the region of Samaria, was located about 30 miles north of Jerusalem.

3. This way of life was based on the assumption that 'man is the measure of all things' – a statement by the ancient Greek philosopher Protagoras – usually interpreted to mean that the individual human being, rather than a god or an unchanging moral law, is the ultimate source of value.

4. Isaiah 60:3

5. To this day, the Samaritans claim descent from the Hebrew tribe of Joseph (Ephraim and Manasseh). The heroic figure Gideon was from the tribe of Manasseh – Reference Judges 6:14.

6. Today, only about 800 ethnic Samaritans remain, divided among four broad families in two areas. Since men comprise most of the remaining members, the community must now rely on women from the outside world for survival.

7. The region of Sychar in Samaria was the place where Abram (Abraham) first built an altar after God had promised him the land of the Canaanites (Genesis 12:6-8). Later, Abraham's grandson Jacob bought some nearby land and also built an altar (Genesis 33:18-20).

8. John 4:12

9. John 4:20

10. The Samaritan temple at Mount Gerizim was later destroyed under the Jewish Hasmonean king John Hyrcanus of Judaea, around 129-110 BC.

11. Luke 10:30-37

12. The apostle Philip was the first (Acts 8:4-13).

13. Acts 1:8

14. Acts 8:1

15. James 'the Greater' – the only other apostle besides Peter and John who was present at the Transfiguration of Jesus.

16. Acts 12:1-3

17. Acts 12:6-7

18. Acts 12:11

19. The festival was celebrating a reconciliation and trade agreement with the cities of Tyre and Sidon.

20. Acts 12:23

21. Acts 25:13 – 26:32

INTRODUCTION

SIMON MAGUS

Simon was a man who achieved god-like status in the first century AD through his philosophy and his acts – through his preaching and his magic tricks. There were many prophets, messiahs, fortune-tellers, seers, and mystics roaming around at the time, but Simon was the most notorious. He had an uncanny talent for deceiving people to his own betterment. And he was not afraid to use religion as a tool for his masquerades.

At the time of the ministry of Jesus of Nazareth,[1] nearly all the people of Samaria were followers of Simon of Gitta.[2] The name of Simon's father was Antonius, and that of his mother, Rachel. He learned magic as a child from his father, but as a young man he traveled to Alexandria to study Greek literature. He was a bright young man. But during those years of schooling, he became ambitious – so ambitious that he wished to be considered as the highest power, higher even than the God who created the world. He hinted that he was the messiah, calling himself the 'standing one', a name used to indicate that he would stand forever, and not suffer from bodily decay. He did not believe that the God who created the world was the highest, nor that the dead would rise. And like all Samaritans, he maintained that Mount Gerizim in Samaria was the center of divine thought on earth, and not Jerusalem.[3]

Simon was also one of the most esteemed followers of John the Baptist. As Jesus had 12 apostles, representing the number of the 12 solar months in a year, John had 30 leading men following him, bearing the number of the daily cycles of the moon in a month. In addition to Simon, one of the 30 leading 'men' was a woman named Helena, who was also a 'friend' of Simon. In addition to following John, Simon was also the de-facto leader of the religious sect to which most Samaritans belonged.

But, on the death of John the Baptist,[4] when Simon was away in Alexandria honing his skills in magic, a man named Dositheus spread a false report of Simon's death – and succeeded in installing himself as the leader of the sect.

Upon returning to Samaria, Simon thought it best to pretend friendship with Dositheus, and temporarily accept his leadership role. However, it wasn't long before he began to hint to the others that Dositheus was not familiar enough with the doctrines of the sect – that he wasn't competent enough to be the leader. Fearing that his reputation would be damaged beyond relief, Dositheus then moved with rage and began to beat Simon with a rod. But amazingly, the rod seemed to pass through Simon's body as if it was translucent smoke. Seeing this, Dositheus was astonished, and said to him, "Tell me if you are the 'standing one', such that I may revere you."

When Simon answered that he was, Dositheus fell down and worshipped him, giving up his leadership position to Simon – and he ordered all the others to henceforth obey Simon. Not long after this, Dositheus died, and Simon was the unchallenged leader of the sect.

Having fallen in love with Helena, Simon took her about with him, saying that she had come down into the world from the highest heaven, and was his companion – inasmuch as she was Sophia, the 'Mother of All'.[5] It was for her sake, he said, that the Greeks and barbarians fought the Trojan War, deluding themselves into thinking that she was an innocent mortal, when in reality she was the 'Ennoia', the 'thought of god'.[6]

By such allegories, Simon deceived many, while at the same time he astounded them with his magical illusions.[7] He was often referred to as 'Faustus' ('the favored one' in Latin).

Simon was not afraid to plagiarize the words of John, or Jesus, or Paul, or anyone else for that matter, if it suited him. He appropriated everything that he thought would be advantageous, twisted it as needed, and used it to further his own personal agenda.[8] He was very smart, but not very wise.

Simon's Self-centered Worldview

Simon's philosophy has been likened to that of the Gnostics.[9] According to the Gnostic philosophy, this world of ours, and the material cosmos, is the result of a primordial error on the part of a supra-cosmic, supremely divine being, usually called 'Sophia' (or 'Wisdom', or the 'Logos'). This being is described as the final emanation of a divine hierarchy, called the 'Pleroma' (or 'Fullness'), at the head of which resides the supreme god, the 'One-beyond-Being'.

The error of Sophia, usually identified as a reckless desire to fully know the transcendent god, led to the hypostatization (attributing real identity to a concept) of her desire in the form of a semi-divine, and essentially ignorant, creature known as 'Yaldabaoth', or the 'Demiurge' (craftsman in Greek), who was responsible for the formation of the earth and the material cosmos.[10]

But in Simon's worldview, he himself, was part of the divine hierarchy. Some scholars have called Simon 'the father of Gnosticism'. But most scholars today believe that Simon's philosophy was unique, although some commonalities existed with the Gnostics that followed.[11]

In the Words of Simon:

The presumed words of Simon, as reported by early church scholars, are summarized in the following paragraphs:[12]

"In the beginning, god was one undifferentiated boundless essence outside of time and space – 'the arch-aeon'.[13] At some point, the 'arch-aeon' subsumed into left and right elements – begetting itself – being its own mother, its own father, its own daughter, its own son. God contains all sexes, and is unbegotten. The leftmost element controlled the essence of incorporeality (spirit), and the rightmost element controlled the essence of corporeality (matter/energy). In the beginning, the dualism of incorporeality and corporeality was confined to the 'arch-aeon'."

"The undifferentiated boundless essence took on form when it subsumed and became the 'aeon of Mind' (Truth) and the 'aeon of Thought' (Grace). The former was male in nature while the latter was female. The 'aeon of Thought', the rightmost element, the female principle, brought forth everything else into existence. She is the Mother of all, and is called the 'Ennoia'. Knowing what the 'aeon of Mind' willed in the beginning, she created all existence and being – upper and lower regions (except the uppermost, which is confined to the aeons) – time and space – body and soul. She then descended into a lower region, and generated (emitted) all the orders of angels. Following the design provided by the 'Ennoia', the lower order angels created the universe, the earth, and the human being – a majestic entity with both body and soul."

"But certain sinful angels rebelled against the Ennoia out of jealousy, and created the world, with the living human beings, in such a manner so as to be her prison – a 'fallen' earth. They were envious of her station – they did not wish to be considered as the progeny of any other – so they prevented her ascendance. She was held in bondage by the same angels that were generated by her, and they subjected her to every form of indignity in order to prevent her from hastening back to the upper regions."

"She ended up falling from the highest region to the lowest – from heaven into the cosmos, then down to the earth, and was embodied in human female flesh. Through the centuries, as from one vessel to another, she migrated into ever different female bodies. She was reincarnated many times – each time being shamed. She was once widely known as the suffering Helen of Troy, and then finally, as a slave and prostitute in the Phoenician city of Tyre, named Helena. In her wanderings across multiple personifications and associations, in which she continually endured ignominy, she lastly prostituted herself in a brothel – and that was her last incarnation until I arrived."

"And on her account, did I come down from heaven to earth; for this is what is written in the ancient writings. In every level of heaven I took on a different form,[14] according to the form of the beings in each heaven, such that I might escape their notice of my powers, and remain concealed from the ruling sinful angels – enabling me to descend to the Ennoia, the 'thought of god'."

"Yes, I am the divine spirit of god. And I have come to earth. Already the world is being destroyed by the wickedness of men. You are all condemned to perish because of your iniquities. But I am here now – and I wish to give you eternal salvation!

"I have come with heavenly powers, such that you will believe in me. Blessed is he who believes – and has worshipped me now! But know this: I will cast everlasting fire upon all the rest, both in the cities and in country places. And men who fail to realize the penalties in store for them will gnash their teeth and groan in vain. But I will grant eternal life to all those who believe in me."

The Philosophy of Simon

The 'aeon of Mind', the leftmost element – the male principle – has its essence in Simon, and is personified by Simon. Because of the sinful angels' act of imprisoning Ennoia in female flesh, Simon descended from the uppermost region (the highest heaven). His mission? To rescue her from the sinful angels and raise her back to the uppermost region – and to confer salvation to mortals if they believed in him – such that their spirit could have eternal life in an upper region. That was his story.

To do this, Simon said he had to appear in various forms. Because the angels were mismanaging the world, owing to their individual lust for rule, he had to come to set things straight. But he had to continually descend under changed forms, likening himself to the Principalities, or to the Powers,[15] through whose regions he passed. As a result, it was said that he appeared as a man among men, even though he was not a man; and was thought to have suffered in Judaea, although he had not actually suffered.[16]

Simon appeared in Judaea as 'The Son', in Samaria as 'The Father', and in other places as 'The Holy Spirit'. And he took on the messianic role of Jesus, mimicking his teachings without acknowledgement. He did not accept Jesus, except as a precursor to himself – the one who was the real messiah – the one who was god descended to redeem the world. As such, his teaching revealed that Jesus' suffering on the cross was not real. According to Simon, hanging on the cross was a phantom – a ghost, rather than a suffering human being.[17]

The one he had come to save, the Ennoia, was now called Helena, a prostitute in Tyre. He freed her from subjugation and she became his consort. While he himself did not suffer, Helena certainly did, as evidenced by her humiliation of imprisonment in human flesh and by her many transformations. Simon had compassion for her. His reasoning was that she caused the world to be made, and now she had to be saved.

Simon's doctrine maintained that the Old Testament prophets had delivered their prophecies under the inspiration of the world-creating sinful angels, and not the supreme deity – consequently, they were flawed and meaningless.[18] The only way to salvation was through him – that was the message he taught.[19]

But many of those who pinned their faith and hopes on Simon and Helena, began to drift away, minding him less and less. Being saved merely by belief in him, and not by good works, they reasoned that they then had freedom to do whatever they pleased on earth.[20] Consequently. they overindulged in sex, drink, and vice, fearing no consequences for their deeds [21]– for morality was only by convention – a convention in accordance with the enactments of the world-creating angels, who by their design precepts, wished for human beings to live in slavery to them, the gods.

To stem the tide of drifters, Simon promised that those who were his disciples – who consistently gave him tribute either financially or through enterprise – would be freed from the dominion of the world-creators, and would live forever when he dissolves the present world.[22]

SIMON PETER

He came from Bethsaida in Galilee, was married, and helped his father John and his brother Andrew in a small fishing business at Capernaum on the Sea of Galilee. They were in partnership with Zebedee and his sons James and John. He was just a regular average guy. His name was Simon (or Simeon).

Andrew, a casual disciple of John the Baptist, was referred by John to Jesus, to whom he then brought his brother Simon. Jesus later gave him the name Peter (or Cephas). At the beginning of his ministry, Jesus called Simon and Andrew away from their fishing work to follow him, promising that he would make them 'fishers of men'.[23] And they abandoned their nets and went off in his company as followers.

Simon soon became the preeminent leader among the group of followers, called apostles. He was the most frequent spokesman, and together with the brothers James and John, formed the 'inner core' that alone witnessed Jesus' raising of Jairus's daughter from the dead,[24] as well as Jesus' transfiguration,[25] and his agony in the garden of Gethsemane before his arrest.[26]

Near the town of Caesarea Philippi, when Jesus asked his followers the question, *Who do the people say that I am?*, Simon replied, "You are the Messiah, the Son of the living God."[27] And then Jesus said:

Blessed are you, Simon, son of John. For flesh and blood has not revealed this to you, but my Father who is in heaven. And I declare to you, you are the 'Rock', and on this rock I will build my church, and the jaws of death shall not prevail against it. I will entrust to you the keys of the kingdom of heaven. Whatever you declare bound on earth shall be bound in heaven, and whatever you declare loosed on earth shall be loosed in heaven.[28]

The word 'Rock' (translated as Cephas in Aramaic, Petros in Greek, Petrus in Latin, and Peter in English) is conferred upon Simon as a personal name, to indicate his role as the firm foundation on which Jesus intends to build his church. Simon Peter becomes the keeper of the keys to the kingdom of heaven (the power of administration of the household), the one who has the power/authority to allow and to forbid. The exercise of this responsibility is similar to the disciplinary and doctrinal authority of the rabbis who interpreted the Old Testament for the faith and life of the people. Peter becomes recognized as the prime authority figure and respected principal of the group of believers in Jesus (later called the Christian community) – the shepherd of the flock.[29]

Significantly, Peter is the first apostle to see the risen Christ,[30] who he had denied three times before the crucifixion.[31] He soon becomes the outspoken and active leader of the budding Jesus movement – and quickly gets in trouble with established influential figureheads.

NOTES

1. approximately 27-30 AD

2. Gitta was a village not far from the Roman town of Flavia Neapolis, supposedly originally settled by the Hebrews and not by earlier Canaanites.

3. Reference: John 4:20. The Samaritan woman at the well said that this mountain (Mount Gerizim) is where her ancestors worshipped God.

4. The story behind the death of John the Baptist is eloquently told in Matthew 14:1-12, Mark 6:14-28, and Luke 9:7-9.

5. Later critics were not very gracious. As one unknown detractor put it, "The liar was enamored of this wench, whose name was Helena – he had bought her, and taken her as his mistress – and it was out of concern for his reputation in front of his disciples, that he invented this fairy-tale."

6. a popular Hellenistic philosophy at the time

7. It is said that he once conjured the soul out of a boy and kept the boy's image in his bedroom.

8. As an example, when preaching to the Greeks, Simon utilized the words of Paul about the armor of God (Ephesians 6:10-17), and weaved them into his own identification of the 'Ennoia' with the goddess Athena.

9. Gnosticism (the Greek word for 'knowledge' or 'insight') is the name given to a loosely organized religious and philosophical movement that flourished in the first and second centuries AD.

10. Edward Moore, "Gnosticism", *Internet Encyclopedia of Philosophy*; accessed Oct. 2021 under https://iep.utm.edu/gnostic/

11. Simon's philosophy and the Gnostic philosophy have in common the place in the work of creation assigned to the female principle, the ignorance of the rulers of the lower world with regard to the Supreme Power, the descent of the female into the lower regions, and her inability to return.

12. Justin Martyr, Irenaeus, Hippolytus, Epiphanius of Salamis, and Cyril of Jerusalem wrote historical critiques of Simon. The text here is paraphrased from: "Simon Magus", *Wikipedia*; accessed Sept. 2021 under https://en.m.wikipedia.org/wiki/Simon_Magus.

13. In philosophical thought, an 'aeon' was a timeless spiritual entity.

14. There are seven levels of heaven according to mystical theology.

15. Principalities and Powers are two different orders of angels in the angelic hierarchy. Until New Testament time, there were only two orders of angels: the Seraphim and the Cherubim. Saint Paul extended the number by adding 7 new orders, bringing the number to 9. Listed in order of their importance, they are: Seraphim, Cherubim, Thrones, Dominions, Virtues, Powers, Principalities, Archangels, and Angels. Per modern theologians, orders range from 7 to 12, with 9 being the most common, although sometimes the Archangels and Angels are distributed among the higher orders. It was said that Simon gave barbaric names to the individual beings within the orders of Principalities and Powers, because he could not confront them directly, being in disguise.

16, a veiled reference to the Passion of Jesus Christ.

17. Per Catholic theology, Jesus Christ was 'fully God' and 'fully man' – and possessed two natures, one divine and one human, without confusion – the 'hypostatic union'.

18. Simon maintained that the 'Law' of the Hebrews espoused by the Old Testament prophets was not from God, but from 'sinister powers' (sinful fallen angels).

19. Simon's message was similar to the message of Jesus. Of course, Simon patterned his philosophy after Jesus', which is why he was considered so heretical by the early church Fathers.

20. Many early followers of Christianity fell into the same disgrace. Most of the Epistles of Paul were written to remind the Christians of their moral obligations, which were handed down by God at the time of Moses. Becoming baptized in the Lord, and assurance of salvation in heaven, did not mean that freedom to pursue licentious lives was allowed on earth.

21. The free love doctrine was held by many in its purest form. The names of Simon and Helena were often associated with images of Zeus and Athena.

22. In the doctrine preached by Simon, there is a large portion common to almost all forms of Gnostic myths. They have some things in common, such as the place in the work of creation assigned to the female principle, the conception of the supreme deity, the ignorance of the angels of the lower regions with regard to the supreme deity (the 'arch-aeon'), the descent of the female principle into the lower regions, and her inability to return. Unique to the tale of Simon is the identification of Simon himself with the 'aeon of Mind', the male principle, and of his consort Helena with the 'aeon of Thought', the female principle.

23. A metaphor meaning that in the future he will be catching men (people) instead of fish. Of course, 'catching' means 'converting' or 'bringing one to Christ'. Reference Matthew 4:18-22; Mark 1:16-20; Luke 5:1-11.

24. Matthew 9:18-26; Mark 5:23-43; Luke 8:41-56

25. Matthew 17:1-9; Mark 9:1-9; Luke 9:28-36

---

26. Matthew 26:36-37; Mark 14:32-34

27. Matthew 16:13-16; Mark 8:27-29; Luke 9:18-20

28. Matthew 16:17-19. This is Jesus' prophecy that he will successfully build a new Israel (the Church) on the shoulders of Peter.

29. This is illustrated in John 21:15-17, when three times Jesus asks Peter, "do you love me?" After Peter responds in the affirmative each time, Jesus says, "Feed my lambs", "Tend my sheep", and "Feed my sheep" respectively. This is the risen Christ's commission to Peter to shepherd His flock. The three affirmations cancel out the three denials Peter had made earlier.

30. Luke 24:34

31. All four Gospels contain the story of Peter's denial. Reference Matthew 26:69-75; Mark 14:66-72; Luke 22:54-62; John 18:15-17,25-27.

1 THE BEGINNING

On the day of Pentecost, following a riveting sermon by Peter, 3000 people are baptized in the name of Jesus Christ. The year is 33 AD.[1] The 'Christian' movement – at first known as 'The Way'[2] – has started, although it is not until a few years later that the believers are first called 'Christians'.[3]

PUBLIC DISCUSSIONS IN THE TEMPLE

Then, one fine day that was acceptable to all parties, many of the apostles go into the temple in the presence of all the Jewish priests and leaders – to bear witness concerning Jesus, and at the same time to charge the Jews with many foolish things which they were doing.

At first, the high priest Caiaphas encourages the people to politely listen to the apostles' testimony, such that they could judge for themselves the substance of it. But then, he immediately starts to praise the rite of animal sacrifice for the remission of human sins – and denounces the baptism of Jesus Christ, as being in opposition to their sacrificial rites.

But Peter refutes his argument, clearly showing that if one is not baptized with water in the manner of Jesus, then not only will he be deprived of the immediate kingdom of heaven, but he will also be in jeopardy during judgment at the time of the resurrection of the dead, even though he may have led a good life and had an upright disposition.

After a minute or two, Caiaphas glances at Peter, with a combined look of warning and accusation, and says, "You should refrain from preaching Christ Jesus – it could lead to your own destruction. You deceive yourself and are also deceiving others. After all, you are nothing but an uneducated peasant – a fisherman and common villager. You should not be assuming the office of a teacher."

But Peter is not about to be cowed by these haughty words. So, he replies, "It would not be dangerous for me to accept Him as a teacher of the law, if He were not the Christ, but it would be very dangerous for me to only accept Him as a teacher, if He, in fact, was the Christ – which assuredly He is – for He has appeared to me in heavenly glory, and I believe in Him with all my heart and mind. But if I, an unlearned and uneducated man, as you say, a fisherman and a rustic, have more understanding than all these wise elders gathered here, then you should be sorely afraid. For, if I did have extensive education, and won over your wise and learned men, it would be said that I had acquired this skill by longtime learning, and not by the grace of divine power. But now, when we uneducated men are able to convince and outdebate your 'wise' men, who with any sense at all would think that it is just lucky muttering, and not the work of divine will and gift?"

Thus, the apostles debated, argued, and bore witness to God that very day. Fishermen and uneducated peasants taught the priests concerning the one and only God of heaven – the Sadducees, concerning the resurrection of the dead – the Samaritans, concerning the sacredness of Jerusalem – the scribes and Pharisees, concerning the kingdom of heaven – the followers of John the Baptist, that they should not suffer John to be a stumbling-block to the faith – and all the people assembled, that Jesus is the eternal Christ.

Then, Peter advises them all to be reconciled to God, and believe on His Son:

"For it is only through grace that you can be saved. Baptism in the name of the Father, and of the Son, and of the Holy Spirit, and receiving the Eucharist of Christ our Lord, is the only way forward. It is utterly impossible for you to be reconciled to God otherwise, even if you should kindle a thousand sacrifices on a thousand high altars.

"The time of giving animal sacrifices has passed away – there is a new covenant here and now. But, because your hearts are hardened, you will not believe this. So I tell you now, that the temple will be destroyed, and an abomination of desolation shall stand in the holy place.[4] And then, the Gospel will be preached to the Gentiles, and they will receive it. Your unbelief will be matched by their faith."

After Peter had said these things and foretold the overthrow of the temple, the whole multitude of priests are in a rage. But Gamaliel urges calm, saying, "Refrain a bit from these men. If what they say is just human musings, it will soon be apparent and come to an end. But if it truly is from God, why would you want to sin and displease Him? For who can overpower the will of God?

"It is late in the evening. Let us reconvene tomorrow morning in this same place, so that I may openly oppose them and clearly refute every error." And with that reassurance, the people disperse peacefully.

SAUL RAISES A RIOT

The next day, under the leadership of James the bishop,[5] the apostles return to the temple and take a prominent position. A great multitude of people were already there, many having been waiting from the middle of the night, and all eager to hear the proceedings. When silence and order is finally achieved, Gamaliel gives an introductory speech that pleads for everyone to listen politely to what the apostles have to say, to meditate on it, and not jump to any hasty conclusions.

However, the high priest Caiaphas is not enamored with Gamaliel, and seeks to steer the discussion toward his own agenda. So, in his high and mighty way, he states that all the discourse henceforth must be drawn from the Hebrew Scriptures only. "In that way, we will know whether Jesus is the very Christ or not."

And so, with that, James begins a long exposition and history of the prophets and the law. When he has fully discussed everything in great detail, and brought into light all the biblical prophecies concerning the coming of the Christ, he shows by most abundant proofs that Jesus is, in fact, the Christ – and that in Him are fulfilled all the prophecies which are related to His humble beginning.

And he clearly illustrates how two comings of the Messiah are foretold: "one in humbleness and poverty, which He has already accomplished – and the other in glory, which we hope will be accomplished in the near future – when He shall come to give the kingdom to those who believe in Him, and who observe all things which He has commanded."

When he had plainly taught the people all these things, he reiterates what Peter had said yesterday:

> "That unless a man be baptized in water, in the name of the Father, and of the Son, and of the Holy Spirit, he can neither receive remission of sins nor enter into the kingdom of heaven. This is the prescription of the unbegotten almighty God. And just to be clear, do not think that we speak of two Gods, or that one God is divided into two. We speak of the only-begotten Son of God, not sprung from another source, but indescribably self-originated – and in like manner we speak of the Holy Spirit."

So eloquent is the sermon of James, that almost all of the people, including many of the priests, are ready to receive baptism straightaway.

But just at the height of the euphoria, Saul enters the temple with a few henchmen, and begins to cry out, "Men of Israel, what are you doing? Why are you so easily swayed? Why are you being led headlong into wholeheartedly believing this group of miserable, terribly confused, uneducated peasants? – a bunch that could easily be deceived by Simon, the Samaritan magician?"[6]

James tries to calmly refute him, but Saul begins to rile up the crowd with shouting and arm-waving. In short order, James is drowned out, and Saul starts to willfully instigate confusion and mass hysteria. He reproaches the priests, and enrages them with insults and abuse. Like a madman, he runs all through the crowd, inciting and agitating – trying to whip up a frenzy. Unabashedly, he begins to provoke the people to violence, exclaiming, "So, listen up! Stand up for your heritage! Resist these deluded malcontents! Why do you hesitate? Enough of sluggishness and inaction! Let us lay our hands upon them, and pull these disgusting unrighteous fellows to pieces!"

Then, seizing a sturdy fire-stoker from the altar, he begins to strike the apostles and sympathizers. Others, seeing him and following his example, also begin to beat the believers. Gamaliel is unable to stop the ruckus. Before long, a full-scale riot ensues, with people beating, and being beaten, on all sides. Caiaphas just looks on smugly.

In the midst of the confusion, James is beaten and thrown headlong from the top of the steps. Thinking him dead, the hooligans turn their ire on Peter, but he evades them and helps to rescue James and pull him to safety. He has a broken leg, but will survive.

When evening comes and the riot has died down, the priests board up the temple, and the apostles, nursing their wounds, return to the house of James, spending the night there in prayer.

The next morning, they all leave Jerusalem and go to Jericho for safety. 5000 believers make the trek.

Then after three days, one of the believers comes to the apostles with a message from Gamaliel – apparently, Saul has received a commission from Caiaphas, authorizing him to arrest and detain all 'Jesus believers' in Jerusalem – and to wreak havoc among the faithful using hooligans, zealots, and unbelievers. In addition, he is authorized to go to Damascus and do the same thing – because they believe that Peter, one of the top troublemakers, has fled there. Laying low, the apostles stay in Jericho for 30 days and then return secretly to Jerusalem.

On this day in the year 36 AD, the deadly persecution of Christians and the Christian faith begins – **and make no mistake about it, severe persecution continues actively to this very day.**[7]

In short order, Saul and the Jewish religious police (together with their lay confederates) start a round-up of believers, disciples, followers, and supporters by going house-to-house, dragging out both men and women suspects, sending them off to interrogation centers or prisons, and generally harassing their daily movements.[8] The persecution is harsh and relentless. Fearful of loss of life, health, property, or reputation, the ruthless violence and intimidation drive many good people out of Jerusalem. The apostles hunker down in secret rooms in private homes after returning from Jericho, but most other believers leave town altogether and scatter throughout the countryside of Judea, Samaria, and beyond.[9] But wherever they go, they take their new faith with them and proclaim the 'Good News' of 'The Way'. Home-churches are set up clandestinely, and very quickly, the teachings of Jesus spread all over the Roman Empire.[10]

THE APPEARANCE OF SIMON MAGUS

The first apostle to leave Jerusalem to evangelize is Philip. He travels to the town of Samaria (the main town in the region of Samaria) and begins to preach the 'Good News', in accordance with the final directives of Jesus.[11] He is well received by the people, performs many miracle healings and exorcisms, and many are baptized in the name of Jesus Christ.

In the town is a charlatan named Simon Magus,[12] who is very popular among the gullible, naïve, and unsuspecting, because of the phony magic and sham sorcery that he uses to bewitch them – he is, indeed, a master of trickery and beguilement. Simon claims to be the 'great divine power',[13] (which is another way of saying that he claimed to be God – or some part of the Godhead), but without coming out and proclaiming that he is the God of the Hebrews. He is so convincing that most of the Samaritans exalt him, saying: "This man is the 'power of god' that is called great".[14]

He pretends to believe in Philip's message, but in reality, he just wants to learn Philip's secret 'magic' so that he can benefit from it himself. He is even baptized,[15] and follows Philip around town pretending to be an ardent disciple.

When the apostles in Jerusalem hear that the Samaritans have accepted the 'Good News'; they immediately send Peter and John to assess the situation and pray that they might receive the Holy Spirit. And through their laying-on of hands, Peter and John witness that the people of Samaria are indeed filled with the Holy Spirit at this time.

When Simon sees that the Spirit is transmitted through the laying-on of the apostles' hands, he reveals his true unholy nature, and offers them a large amount of money if they will give him the power by which he could transmit the Holy Spirit to other people.[16] But Peter is sorely offended and rebukes him severely:

> "Because you thought that you could obtain God's gift with money, you are doomed to perish along with all your silver and gold! You will never share in God's Kingdom because your heart is not right before God. For I see that you have a heart of bitterness and are trapped in the chains of wickedness. Therefore, you must repent of this wickedness, and pray to the Lord God that your heart be forgiven."[17]

But Simon does not sincerely repent, although he pretends to do so by asking Peter to pray for him, such that he will not suffer the fate of which he had spoken.[18]

After Peter and John have returned to Jerusalem, Simon continues to practice his swindles, even incorporating some of the terms and sayings of the infant church into his snake-oil proselytizing. He professes that it was actually he who appeared among the Jews in Galilee and Judea as the 'son of man' – it was he who appeared in Samaria as the 'great divine power' [19]– and it was he who appeared in other places as the 'holy spirit'. Many people are sadly taken-in by his hocus-pocus bewitchery. He never forgives Peter for the public rebuke, and he becomes a real thorn in the side of Peter for many years.

A New Threat Emerges

This is the beginning of a new form of threat and persecution against the Word of God, separate from stalwart devoted Jews, resolute pagan Gentiles, and brash egocentric emperors. Imitators, false messiahs, self-proclaimed saviors, and purveyors of twisted Christian belief will plague the believers of 'The Way' for many years. Although usually not deadly, the net effect of such heretical movements is of great concern to the fledgling church.

Peter is especially concerned about phony doctrines, sham preachers, false messiahs, and people who misinterpret or misrepresent the correct teachings of the apostles. They are spreading around Judea alarmingly, twisting the words of the apostles, and teaching spurious doctrine, while pretending to be the truthful mouthpiece of the apostles. Belief is corrupted and souls are being lost. Heresies need to be dealt with forthrightly,[20] and Peter is the designated inquisitor.

In a letter to fellow Christians,[21] Peter exclaims:

"False prophets have arisen in the land, and there will be false teachers coming among you who will secretly bring in destructive opinions. Sadly, many of you will follow their licentious ways, and the way of truth will be maligned.

"In their greed, they will exploit you with deceptive words. Bold and skillful, they are not afraid to slander the preachers of truth. They entice unsteady souls, and their hearts are filled with malice. They promise freedom, but they themselves are slaves of corruption. They have left the straight road and have gone astray. For them, the deepest darkness has been reserved.

"These impostors of truth speak bombastic nonsense, and with licentious desires of the flesh, they entice people who have just escaped from paganism and turned to the one true God, to turn away again to false gods. For these poor souls, it would have been better to never have known the way of righteousness, rather than to have known it and then turn away from the holy commandments, embracing the darkness instead. Their souls are forever lost."

Simon is not the only heretic, but in the mind of Peter, he will become the most dangerous. And it will be Peter's mission to call him out, and expose him for the con-artist that he really is.

PETER GOES TO CAESAREA

After Peter and John had brought the 'Good News' of Jesus Christ and the blessings of the Holy Spirit to the people of Samaria, they return to Jerusalem in Judaea with feelings of great joy and satisfaction. They are little concerned with maverick charlatans like Simon. Besides, he had begged for forgiveness and they had prayed for him in passing.[22] Instead, their thoughts are centered around the Samaritans, and how the 'Good News' was positively received by the quasi-Jewish people. If the Samaritans could be converted over and baptized, then why not also the Greeks and Romans – and Gentiles throughout the world? After all, wasn't that the commission of Jesus? But there are details to work out – questions to be answered. Would the new believers be required to obey all the Jewish laws and customs? Would males be required to be circumcised? Was the eating of non-kosher food allowed? The apostles struggle with these issues for years, as do many of the new communities of believers.[23]

Reduced to despair in Samaria by Peter and John, Simon soon abjures the faith and embarks instead on the career of a sorcerer. In the following years, he will travel around the empire and become a real thorn in the side of Peter, and will never forgive him for the public rebuke. Eventually, he will travel to Rome where he will pursue a life of ambitious huckstering and mongering. There, he will perform amazing magical acts and give acclaimed speeches – becoming renowned throughout the city. So convincing are his performances, that he will become recognized as a god.

But before journeying on to Rome, Simon travels to the cities and towns of the Mediterranean seacoast (and then eventually on to

Jerusalem), thinking that he might be able to learn more about this power of the Holy Spirit that the apostles seemed to have mastered. Of course, he continues with his usual scams, swindles, and con-games.

Not long after the conversion of Saul and his short visit to Jerusalem, James asks Peter to travel to Caesarea in order to confront Simon, who is spreading lies and falsehoods about the faith, and stealing souls away from Christ. The faithful convert Zacchaeus had written to James about how he was subverting many of the believers,[24] asserting that he was the great power of the high God, superior to the Creator of the world – in other words, he was the Christ. At the same time, he was performing many dramatic miracles, and gathering disciples. Zacchaeus had told James everything he learned from two deserters who had left Simon and had been baptized to Christ by himself. And James explained all this to Peter.

"There are many souls in jeopardy," said James. "For the sake of our holy ministry, it behooves you to go and refute this magician – and to teach the Word of truth. Therefore, make no delay – and worry not that you go alone.[25] Know that our Lord Jesus Christ will go with you, and will help you – and by His grace, you will soon have many associates and followers. And by the way, please send me periodic reports in writing of everything that befalls you."

NOTES

1. Date is per many religious scholars – reference: Jimmy Akin, "National Catholic Register", 10 April 2020, https://www.ncregister.com/.

2. The Christians got this name for their religious movement because they believed that Jesus was the only way to the Father, as evidenced by when He said, *I am the way, and the truth, and the life. No one comes to the Father except through me.* (John 14:6). Refer also to Acts 9:2 and Acts 11:26.

3. The nickname 'Christian' (which may have originally been akin to an insult) started in Antioch, Syria, where Barnabas was the pastor of a church of Greek and Hebrew Jews, as well as Gentiles. Eventually, the new name stuck, and the former designation, believers in 'The Way', faded into obscurity.

4. Daniel 9:27; Matthew 24:15

5 This is James the Less, son of Alpheus, who was also present the previous day, but in a non-leadership role.

6. Saul knew about Simon, and assumed that the apostles would be bested by his trickery and glibness.

7. It is believed by many modern historians and scholars that in the history of the world, all in all, Christians have been persecuted more than any other religious or ethnic group. Deadly persecution still exists today in parts of Africa and Asia.

8. when thought appropriate – see Acts 8:3

9. There was an 'inner core' of 70 disciples (Luke 10:1-20) who maintained close affiliation with the Apostles, attending daily prayer meetings and services.

It is believed that most, if not all of the 70, along with their families, fled Jerusalem at this time. They went to Egypt, North Africa, Mesopotamia, Assyria, Cyprus, Asia Minor, Greece, and even to Rome, probably to stay with relatives.

10. The good roads and transportation systems set in place by the Romans undoubtedly contributed to the rapid spread of the faith throughout the empire.

11. Acts 1:8

12. A 'magus' was a word used to indicate a prominent religious figure.

13. or 'the divine Spirit of God'

14. Acts 8:9-10

15. Simon Magus was baptized by Philip (see Acts 8:13), but only in the Name of Jesus and not in the Name of the Holy Spirit.

16. Simon's attempt to buy the power of the Holy Spirit is the origin of the word 'simony', which means the buying and selling of sacred things. During the Middle Ages, 'simony' referred to the purchase of ecclesiastical offices and privileges.

17. Acts 8:20-23

18. Acts 8:24

19. another way of saying 'God the Father'

20. An unwanted by-product of the movement to spread the 'Good News', renounce pagan thinking, and counteract heretical beliefs, was the economic industry that surrounded the unholy practices. This could present a real physical threat. Physicians lamenting their lack of business, and idol-makers bemoaning their lack of sales, could present real problems, as the disciples and apostles would soon learn. (For example, refer to the story about the riot of the silversmiths in Acts 19:23-40).

21. For the entire biblical text of Peter's emotional appeal to turn away from false prophets, refer to 2 Peter 2:1-22.

22. Acts 8:24

23. The apostles and disciples in Jerusalem were divided on this issue.

Some thought that it should be mandatory for a new convert to be circumcised (not a popular choice for older men) and to rigorously follow all the Hebrew laws and customs (ordained by the Pharisees), including kosher food restrictions and not eating at the same table with Gentiles.

Others thought that physical circumcision was not required (their baptism provided a spiritual circumcision) and only a few basic Hebrew rules needed to be followed. Paul was the forthright leader of the latter camp of thinking. However, Peter wavered between the two camps. At first, he ate with Gentiles, and then he refused to eat with them (Galatians 2:11-13) – and for that, he was strongly rebuked by Paul. Later, he had a change of heart. His experience with the Roman centurion (and Jewish sympathizer) Cornelius and his family, when receiving the Holy Spirit (Acts 10:1-11:18), led him to firmly believe in the Pauline approach. This was solidified at the Council of Jerusalem (Acts 15:1-29).

24. This is the same Zacchaeus as the tax collector in Jericho, who climbed a tree to see Jesus passing by, and then received Jesus in his home. The conversion of Zacchaeus is recorded in Luke 19:1-10.

25. In actuality, Peter's wife accompanied him, and possibly a servant or two.

2 IN CAESAREA

Peter is scheduled to hold a discussion of words and questions – a debate – the next day with a man called Simon, a Samaritan. He has called together his friends and followers to review the issues and topics beforehand, and gain some encouraging support.

After pondering in silence for a bit, Peter starts to address the troubling issues of the day by explaining the causes of ignorance in humans, and then how Jesus the Christ and the Holy Spirit, the true Prophet and divine helper, can enlighten the souls of people, such that they can discern the way to eternal salvation. Otherwise, it is impossible to obtain knowledge of divine and eternal things.

Finally, Peter says, "I hope you will be present whenever debates and disputes arise in the coming days. For these will surely occur with those who contradict and reject my teachings. Since I am only a fisherman and a villager, it may seem that I have been bested at times by those with learned rhetorical skills. But I am not afraid that you will be led astray, for I sense that you are keen discerners of truth. Even if I shall seem to be beaten in debate, it is just oratory – those things that have been shown to me by Jesus, the Christ, and the Holy Spirit, whom He sent to us after His death, remain the overarching truth. Yes, I hope that we will not be overcome in debates, but if our listeners are reasonable and lovers of the truth – able to know what discourses are specious and artificial, and what are natural and guileless – I am hopeful that they will recognize that the real truth depends not on show and ornament – that is just a distorted image of truth – but on insight, reason, and divine revelation."

Then, after Peter has finished, Zacchaeus says, "I give thanks to God Almighty, because I have been instructed as I wished and desired. At all events, you may depend upon me for support. I will never come to doubt any of the things that I have learned from you."

To which Peter responds, "I also give thanks to God, both for your salvation and for my own peace. I am delighted that you understand the value of the 'Good News'.

"I hope that many of you will be able to be present with me at the spiritual debates with nonbelieving adversaries. For tomorrow, I am scheduled to have a contest with Simon, the magician and heretic. And I need all the backup support that I can get"

DELAY IN THE DEBATE

The next morning, Zacchaeus comes in to the breakfast table where everyone is gathered,[1] and after a brief "hello – good morning" says to Peter, "Simon has put off the discussion for seven days – he says that only then will he have the available time for the contest. But it seems to me that this delay can work to our advantage, such that we can have more time to prepare. So, if it seems proper to you, let us occupy the interval in discussing among ourselves the things that may come up in the debate, such that we can agree on the best strategy and answers. If the things that are to be spoken by us are clearly impregnable in every aspect, then we shall have confidence in entering into the debate."

To this Peter answers, "Tell Simon that we accept the delay, and to rest assured that, Divine Providence granting, he shall always find us ready.

"Yes, I believe that this can work to our advantage. In this interval of seven days, I can explain to you all the full aspects of our faith without any distraction.

"For it is God alone who knows the past as it was, the present as it is, and the future as it shall be. Even things that were plainly spoken

36

by Him, were not plainly written down, and cannot be plainly understood without a teacher – an interpreter and expounder. This is because human beings are finite in brain capacity and can only fathom God in a blurred hazy way. Furthermore, our sinful nature – a consequence of the Original Sin revealed by Adam [2]– warps our thinking process. But, if we put our faith in God the Father, God the Son, and God the Holy Spirit, we can have hope of a limited understanding – understanding sufficient to allow us to live according to God's plan, and be assured of everlasting life."

Peter Explains the Faith

With that, over the next few days, Peter explains point by point – event by event – everything that is related to our interaction with the Divine – from the creation of the world right up until a few days ago when a man named Clement arrived at the door.[3]

Near the end of this long explanation, Peter explains how the debate with Simon came to be:

"When I entered the city, our beloved brother Zacchaeus met me, and brought me to this lodging. He inquired about each of the apostles, and especially James, our leader in Jerusalem. When I told him that he was still lame on one foot because of the riot in the temple instigated by Saul,[4] he was deeply saddened.

"In return, he told me of the doings of Simon and why he wrote to James for help. The next day, Simon himself sent a message to me – how he heard of my arrival I don't know – which said, 'Let us debate tomorrow in front of the public.' When I answered in the affirmative, the debate quickly became news throughout the whole city. So, I tried to explain everything to you quickly, to bring you up to speed. Now what remains, beginning tomorrow, you shall hear from day-to-day in connection with the questions and answers raised in the debates with Simon."

In the days following his historical and spiritual accounting, Peter expounds on the foundations of faith and piety: "There is only one true God, triune in nature, whose work the world is, and who, because He is in all respects righteous, will render the future reward of eternal life to anyone who believes the faith and lives his life accordingly. To prove this, thousands of words can be brought forward to convince the doubters, but to those who believe with all their hearts and are baptized with water, all this forest of words is cut down. You simply cannot find truth through your own inquisitive desires. Everyone who has tried this in the past has fallen into the snare of philosophical meandering. For God, as caring for all, has made the recognition of Himself easy for all to attain. Neither the Greeks, nor the Jews, nor the barbarians are prevented from finding Him.

"Since God is righteous, it is fully evident that there is a judgment, and that souls are immortal.

"Friends, by the mercy of God, it is time to cease from the blood sacrifice of animals, intended for the remission of sins, for there is no longer any benefit from that practice. Instead, God has instituted baptism by water, and communion of bread and wine, transubstantiated into the body and blood of Christ,[5] as the pathways to absolution of sins.

"On the invocation of His name, and the sincere belief in our Lord and Savior, one can gain eternal life, being purified not by the blood of beasts, but by the purification of the Wisdom of God."

Peter then describes the scriptural prophesy of the coming of the Messiah, Jesus Christ,[6] his life and passion, and the success of the Gospel. And he talks about His second coming, when He will judge us all, condemn the wicked, and take the pious into a shared association with Himself in His kingdom.

He describes the schisms that have arisen among the Jews – the Sadducees, who think they are more righteous than the others, and deny the resurrection of the dead – some of the followers of John the Baptist, including Simon the magician, who assert that it is unworthy to worship God based on the promise of a reward (salvation) – the Samaritans, who deny the resurrection of the dead, and assert that God is to be worshipped on Mount Gerizim, and not in Jerusalem – and the Pharisees, who hold the word of truth received from Moses as the key to the kingdom of heaven, but hide it from the people.

He targets Simon as being particularly troublesome. "His background is not widely known. For if it was, he would not be believed. But now, not being known, he is improperly believed. And though his deeds are those of a hater, he is loved – and though an enemy, he is received as a friend – and though he be as death, he is worshipped as a savior – and though he is dark as night, he is esteemed to be light – and though he is a deceiver, he is believed as a speaker of truth."

Then, one of the followers interrupts, and asks, "Who then is this Simon, one who is such a deceiver? I would like to know more about him."

"It would be best to learn about him direct from the sources that provided me with the information."

And with that, Peter starts to tell the remarkable story of Nicetas and Aquila.

JUSTA, NICETAS, AND AQUILA

"There is among us a woman called Justa, half Syrian and half Phoenician, by race a Canaanite, whose daughter Bernice was very sick with an incurable disease. She came to our Lord Jesus Christ, as He was passing through her village,[7] crying out and begging for Him to heal her daughter. But we said to Him, 'Lord, it is not lawful to heal Gentiles, who eat unclean meats and engage in sinful practices. The table in the kingdom has been given only to the sons of Israel – only they are worthy of healing.' But Justa persisted, claiming that she was pure in heart and obeyed all the laws of the Jews. The Lord looked straight into her eyes and knew that she was sincere and humble – and Bernice was healed by a touch of His hand.

"Justa continued living cleanly and simply, following all the Jewish laws. But her pagan husband was incensed by this, beat her cruelly, and eventually threw her out of his house forever, along with their daughter. Although she was a 'non-person' now in social circles, she remained faithful to the vows she had given our Lord. She gave her daughter Bernice in marriage to a good man who was poor, but a true believer in our faith. She herself remained unmarried, but since she had some money saved up over the years, she purchased two young boys from the pirate slave market and raised them as her own sons, educating them and teaching them in the ways of the Lord. The names that the slave traders had given them were Nicetas and Aquila.

"Wanting the best for her sons, she placed them under the tutelage of Simon Magus, who had the reputation of being a godly man and was widely revered throughout the land. She was unaware that he was, in reality, a charlatan, a magician, and a swindler. Over the years, the boys learned everything that he taught, and became full disciples of Simon.

"But one day, the boys happened to come upon Zacchaeus, who was travelling in the area. They listened to his preaching, asked questions, and realized that he was speaking the real truth, and that what Simon had taught them was just incorrect nonsense. They repented of their former beliefs, and denounced Simon as being a pretender and uninformed of the real truth. Together with their foster-mother Justa, they left their home and followed Zacchaeus back to Caesarea, to this very house. Shortly after I arrived here, Zacchaeus presented them to me, and ever since they continue by my side, enjoying instructions in the truth."

The Truth about Simon

After telling this story, Peter sends for Nicetas and Aquila and asks them to accurately relate everything they know about Simon. Aquila, then, proceeds to rant on about all the false doctrine, wickedness, and deceit associated with the man.

"He is very powerful in magic, and being ambitious, wishes to be recognized as a supreme power, greater even than the God who created the world. He calls himself the 'Standing One', intimating that he will always stand, and not have any bodily degradation that would cause him to fall. He says that the God who created the world is not the Supreme God, and he does not believe that the dead will be raised. Regarding the law of the Hebrews, he regards it as corrupted because it was misguided. Worst of all, instead of our Lord Jesus Christ, he proclaims himself as 'the Christ'.

"He goes about in the company of a woman named Helena, sometimes called Luna. He maintains that he brought her down from the highest heaven to the world on earth. She is a queen; an all-wise and eternal being, for whose sake the Greeks and the Trojans fought a great war over. By cunningly explaining things of this sort, made up from Grecian myths, he deceives many – especially since he performs many magic tricks, such that if we did not know better, we ourselves would be deceived.

"He is a wicked man and has committed horrible acts. Once, by weird incantations, he differentiated the soul away from the body of a young child. By turning air into water, and water into blood, and solidifying it into flesh, he formed a new human creature – a boy – and boasted that he had produced a much nobler work than God the Creator. After all, God used the earth for creation whereas he used the air – a far more difficult task. Then, he unmade the creature and restored him to air. But not until he had placed the boy's picture image in his bed-chamber, as proof and memorial of his work and power. His arrogant bragging was believed by many, but my brother and I refused to be conned or duped. We denounced his chicanery, and withdrew from him."

After Aquila gives his account, Nicetas adds, "As God is my witness, we assisted him in no impious works – we only looked on as he did harmless things, and hyped them up. But when he said that it was through divine power that he did the things that were done simply by magic, we no longer could follow him, although he made us many promises – that there would be statues of us placed in the temple, we would be thought of as gods, be worshipped by the multitudes, honored by kings, given public acclaim, and enriched with boundless wealth.

"We counselled him to desist from such improprieties, but he just laughed. 'I laugh at your foolish suggestion, because you falsely believe that the soul of man is immortal,' he said. But I countered, saying, 'We are not angry, O Simon, at your attempts to deceive us, but we are confounded at the way in which you deceive even yourself.'"

After a moment of pensive silence, someone then asks about the 'miracles' that Simon performs. And Aquila answers, "It has been said that he makes statues walk – he rolls himself on the fire, but is not burned – he flies in the air – he becomes a serpent – he transforms into a goat – he exhibits two faces – he changes himself into gold – he opens locked gates – he melts iron – he creates realistic images of things – he even makes dishes float in the air to his table. Of course, I wondered about all this, but many witnesses have said that they have seen such things."

After listening to all this, Peter feels the need to speak: "This man Simon works theatrical wonders to astonish and deceive, not wonders of healing meant to convert and save. Whenever we think we witness a miracle being done, we should always judge the miracle-worker. What is the character of the performer, and what is that of the deed? If one performs unbeneficial miracles, he is the agent of wickedness; but if he performs beneficial miracles, then he is a leader of goodness.

"Those fancy 'miracles' that you say that Simon did – making statues walk, rolling himself on burning coals, becoming a dragon, changing into a goat, flying in the air, and all such things – are not for the benefit of people. They are of a nature to deceive people. But the miracles of compassionate truth are philanthropic, such as what you have heard that the Lord did, and what I have sometimes done after Him, through my earnest prayers."

"But there is one more thing, my esteemed Peter," adds Nicetas. "I am afraid that in this contest with Simon, it is possible that you could be overmatched. For it often happens that he who defends the truth does not gain the victory, since the listeners are either prejudiced, or have no great interest in the better cause. But over and above all this, Simon himself is a most skillful and intense orator, trained in the art of debating, and in the tangled logic of metaphors and allegories. To make matters worse, he is highly skilled in the magic arts. Therefore, I fear that because he is so strongly fortified in all these aspects, he could be thought to be defending the truth by those who do not know him, when in reality, he is just spouting falsehoods."

Peter sighs and laments, "You must have faith, my friend. Yes, I often wonder at the infinite patience of God, given the audacity of human rashness in people. How can one possibly persuade Simon into thinking that God judges the unrighteous, when he persuades himself that he employs the obedience of disembodied souls in the service of his illusions? In truth, he is deluded by the devil. I don't know if he is redeemable, but we have to remember the multitudes who have been hoodwinked by his overtures – we must try to reach their sense of reason and goodwill. After all, that is why we agreed to debate in the first place."

The assembled believers nod in silence, and then Peter continues, "If God permitted the devil to do whatever he wanted, all people's souls would have perished long ago. But because of His mercy, this has not been allowed. However, the devil has been permitted to exert great power. And now, unfortunately, most of the world's people have been made enemies of God. The devil has entered their hearts and turned them away from the innate affection that God the Creator had implanted in them. So how can we say that the devil is the cause of our sin, when this is done by permission of God? It is a great mystery! I don't have all the answers. It is just meant for us to know that everyone will be either saved or condemned on the 'Day of Judgment'. Those who have abandoned their duty towards their true Father and Creator, because they are allured by greater earthly promises, are doomed. Those who have kept the faith and the love of the Father, even with poverty and tribulation pervasive, will enjoy heavenly gifts and immortal dignity in His kingdom."

With that, everyone retires to meditate and pray.

On the scheduled day of the debate, Zacchaeus arrives at dawn and announces that Simon wishes to put off the debate for another day because today is his sabbath day, which occurs at intervals of 11 days. Peter agrees and the matter is settled. "Let us not allow Simon's postponement of the debate irritate us," he says, "for perhaps it has happened by the providence of God for our benefit."

So, they spend the rest of the day preparing for the debate – by discussing the topics that they think Simon will bring up. They have a spy in the camp of Simon, and he has reported back on what arguments Simon plans to employ. Of course, they suspect that Simon has also planted a spy in their camp, so the reverse is also likely. Alas, such is the life of an itinerant preacher.

NOTES

1. Sixteen believers were gathered at the table that morning: Zacchaeus (the early convert by Jesus), Sophonias (his brother), Joseph and his foster-brother Michaeus, Thomas [Phineas] and Eleazar [Eliesdrus] (the twins), Aeneas and Lazarus [not the same Lazarus as who was raised from the dead by Jesus] (the priests), Elisaeus, Benjamin (the son of Saphrus [Saba]), Rubelus (also a brother of Zacchaeus) and Zacharias (the stone masons), Ananias and Haggaeus (the sons of Safra), and Nicetas and Aquila (the twin brothers who deserted Simon).

However, it is understood that Peter had 12 core disciples on this trip: Zacchaeus, Sophonias, Joseph, Michaeus, Eleazar, Phineas, Lazarus, Elisaeus, Clement, Nicodemus (whether this is the same Nicodemus as the Pharisee who defended Jesus in the Sanhedrin, and then later assisted in His burial, is unknown), Nicetas, and Aquila.

2. Concupiscence is the natural tendency in humans to crave sensuous pleasure, and to think evil thoughts, which is the result of the 'Fall' of Adam and Eve. It presents a continuous struggle between the flesh and righteous reasoning.

3 This is the same Clement who is mentioned in Philippians 4:3. He eventually became the third bishop of Rome after Peter (the fourth Pope) and is renown for his ecclesiastical writings (especially the Epistle to the Church of Corinth, called 'I Clement').

4. The apostle James, named bishop of Jerusalem, had stood on the top of the temple steps, and enlightened all the people by reading the Holy Scriptures and explaining to them that Jesus is the prophesied Christ – and how they should all be baptized in the name of Jesus. But just when it appeared there would be a mass conversion, Saul and his henchmen instigated a riot and stirred up the people against them.

5. Transubstantiation is the conversion of the consecrated bread into the Body of Christ, and the consecrated wine into the Blood of Christ, the physical appearance of bread and wine remaining unchanged. Reference John 6:51.

6. The man who is above all other men is Christ Jesus. He is called 'Christ' because it is a certain rite of exaltation. Among the Jews, a king is called Christ, like Caesar is to the Romans and Pharaoh to the Egyptians. Although indeed He was the Son of God, and the beginning of all things, He came to earth and became a man above all other men. Metaphorically, He was anointed as a king with oil taken from the 'Tree of Life' (He was begotten of the Father). Because of that anointing, He is called 'the Christ'.

7. Matthew 4:23-24

3 FIRST DEBATE WITH SIMON

Mid-morning the next day, Zacchaeus enters the meeting room, saying, "It is time, O Peter, for you to go out and engage in the debate. A great crowd awaits you, gathered together in the courtyard – and in the midst of them stands Simon, like a war-chieftain attended by his warriors."

Hearing this, Peter says to his followers, "Brothers, let us pray that God, by His unspeakable mercy through our Lord Jesus Christ, will help me in striving for the salvation of those who have been created in His image." And after a brief personal prayer, he goes out into the courtyard.

THE CONTROVERSY OVER PEACE

Peter is first to speak to the crowd. He salutes them, saying:

"Peace be to all of you whose hearts and minds are prepared to receive the truth. For God is pleased with all who accept the truth – and they will obtain His greatest gifts. Therefore, the first duty of all of us is to recognize the righteousness of God, such that we can learn how to think and act rightly – and by doing so, reap His promised reward of eternal good blessings. But on those who have acted wrongly – contrary to the will of God – a worthy infliction of penalties, in proportion to their doings, is inescapable. Therefore, it behooves you while you are in the present life – while there is still the opportunity – to ascertain the will of God, and react accordingly. For the time is short, and the judgment of God will be composed of verdicts, not questions. Before anything else, we must learn how we should rightly act, in order to merit the gift of eternal life."

Peter then proceeds to explain what righteousness is, and how it is the pathway to eternal life in the kingdom of God. He finishes with "and if anyone has anything to propose which he thinks is better, let him speak – and when he has spoken, let him hear with patience and quietness. Indeed, I have prayed for peace with you all, such that this debate will be useful in your quest for answers."

But Simon is unwilling to let Peter woo the crowd with compassionate preaching. "We have no need of your peace," he exclaims, "for if there is peace and harmony, we shall not be able to make any headway towards the discovery of truth. In a debate like this, peace is not needed – battle is needed – such that errors in thinking can be identified and eliminated. When two fight with each other, there will be peace when one has been defeated and fallen. Therefore, fight as best you can, and do not expect peace without war."

Peter then proceeds to explain why he desires a peaceful discussion. "In the contest of debates, when some perceive that their error has been exposed, immediately begin, for the sake of making a good retreat, to create a disturbance and stir up strife, such that it may not be obvious to all that he is defeated. Therefore, I frequently ask that the investigation of the matter in dispute be conducted with all patience and quietness, so that if anything seems to be not rightly presented, one can go back over it, and explain it more distinctly. For it is not uncommon for a comment to be spoken in one way and heard in another. On this account, I desire that our conversation be conducted patiently, so that one side cannot snatch the conversation away from the other, nor use obtrusive contradicting speech to interrupt the other. Since the way of God is the way of peace, let us with peace seek the truth about God."

Peter attempts to continue and speak about the attributes of God, but Simon interrupts him, saying, "Why do you hasten to speak whenever and whatever you please? I understand your tricks. You wish to bring forward those matters that you have well studied, such that you may appear to the uninformed crowd to be speaking like an expert – but I will not allow you this subterfuge. Now, since you have promised to answer any point that anyone chooses to bring forward, please be prepared to answer my points of argument first without changing the subject."

To which Peter responds, "I am ready, provided that our discussion may be with peace."

Then Simon snidely says, "Don't you see, O simpleton, that in pleading for peace you act in opposition to your Master,[1] and that what you propose is not consistent with anyone who promises that he will overthrow ignorance?[2] Or, if you are right in asking for peace, then your Master was wrong in saying, 'Do you think I have come to establish peace on the earth? I assure you, the contrary is true. My mission is not to spread peace, but division.'[3] Either you say right, and he is wrong, or your Master says right and you are wrong. In either case, your statement is contrary to his, whose disciple you profess yourself to be."

But Peter is not flustered. He responds by saying, "He who sent me did not err in fomenting division upon the earth. Neither do I act contrary to Him in asking for peace among the debaters and their followers. Instead, you rashly find fault with what you do not understand. You have heard that He did not come to send peace upon the earth. But you have not heard that He also said, 'Blessed are the peace-makers, for they shall be called the very sons of God.'[4]. Therefore, when I recommend peace, my sentiments are not any different from those of my Lord and Savior, who dispensed blessedness on the keepers of peace."

"But Peter, in your desire to answer for your Master, you have brought a more serious charge against him. If he himself came not to make peace, but praised others who did make it, then this is inconsistent with the other saying of his: 'The pupil should be glad to become like his teacher, the slave like his master.' "[5]

"Not so," replies Peter. "Our Lord Jesus Christ neither contradicted Himself, nor instructed us to do anything different from what He practiced. When He said the things you have cited, He was inviting all to follow the path that leads to salvation, encouraging them to endure poverty and suffering, without coveting or acting unrighteously. On the other hand, He mourned over those who lived in riches and luxury, and bestowed nothing upon the poor, who they ought to love as themselves – they will have to render an account on the Last Day. He also said, 'Blessed are the pure in heart, for theirs is the kingdom of God.'[6] This was meant for all those desiring His promise, such that they should keep themselves from evil and polluted thoughts.

"By sayings such as these, He brought some people to follow Him, but others became hostile. He charged the believers and the obedient to keep peace among themselves. But for those who would not believe, and set themselves in opposition to His doctrine, He predicted that there would be strife and division: 'From now on, a household of five will be divided three against two and two against three; father will be split against son and son against father, mother against daughter and daughter against mother.'[7] For in every house, when there begins to be a difference between believer and unbeliever, there is inevitably a contest.

"Therefore, observing the commands of our Lord, we first offer peace to our listeners, that they may understand the way to salvation without any turmoil. But if they will not receive the words of peace, nor accept the truth of the Word, we know how to confront them in an argument, and to rebuke them sharply by revealing their confusion and exposing their sins."

THE 'CONTRADICTIONS' OF JESUS

Then, Simon smugly responds with, "I am astonished at your folly. For you promote the words of your Master, as if they were the accurate words of a prophet. However, I can easily prove to the audience that he often contradicted himself. And I can refute your statements using the same words that you have yourself brought forward. For you say, that he said that 'every house divided against itself shall not stand'[8]; and elsewhere you say, that he said that he would spread division, even within the same household. If, then, what is divided cannot stand – it falls – then he who causes divisions is the reason for the falling. As such, that person must assuredly be wicked."

Peter calmly responds by saying, "You should not rashly take exception with things you do not understand. When the Lord sent us apostles out to preach to all nations, He directed us to teach the things which He had taught to us. But we do not just reiterate the things that were spoken by Him. For our commission is not to speak, but to teach those things – and show how every one of them rests upon truth. Also, we are not permitted to interpret things on our own. As an apostle who is sent out to deliver a message from a sender, I must deliver the sender's message accurately. Otherwise, I would be a false apostle, not imparting the sender's message, but instead expressing my own predilections. Anyone who does this, just wants to show off – to make himself appear to be better than he really is. He is a traitor to the one who gave him the message. However, if he stays true to the message he is given, then he is accomplishing the work of an apostle. Therefore, blame me not because I bring forward the words of Him who sent me. If there is anything in them that is not true, you are at liberty to refute it. But you will not be successful at this, for He is the prophet of truth, and cannot be anything but truth."

Then Simon speaks up, saying, "What you say is just circular reasoning. I am only concerned with how these sayings agree with one another or not. For if he can be shown to be inconsistent, then it is proven that he is not a prophet."

"No one can be proved to be a prophet merely by being consistent," answers Peter, "for it is possible for many to attain this. Furthermore, no one can be proved not to be a prophet merely by being inconsistent. There are many things which to some seem inconsistent, but when given a more profound investigation, are found to be consistent.

"Therefore, the first thing to do is determine whether the one who has spoken things which appear to be inconsistent, is in actuality a true prophet. Then, those things which seem to be inconsistent must actually be consistent – they are just misunderstood."

Simon then says, "Tell us, therefore, how it is consistent when one who causes divisions in a house, which results in the falling of the house because of those divisions, can be claimed to be good, or to have come for the salvation of men."

And Peter answers: "By His words, the Lord has divided up the kingdoms of the world, which are founded in error, and every home in them, such that error may fall, and truth may reign. In any house, once error is introduced by anyone, the house is divided. And where error has gained a footing, it is certain that truth cannot stand. So, if you agree that everything which is divided falls, it just remains for me to show, if only you will hear in peace, that our Jesus has divided up, and thereby dispelled error, by teaching truth."

"But it is uncertain whether your Master divides up error or divides up truth," replies Simon. "And do not keep repeating over and over your talk of peace – it is annoying and extraneous – just expound briefly on what you think or believe."

"Why are you afraid of hearing frequently of peace?" says Peter, "for peace is the perfection of the law. Wars and disputes spring from sin – but where there is no sin, there is peace of soul. And when there is peace, truth can be found in debates."

But Simon shakes his head and moans, "You seem to me not to be able to clearly say what you think."

To which Peter responds, "I will speak according to my own judgment, and not under constraint of your tricks. I only desire that what is constructive and beneficial be brought to the knowledge of all. Therefore, I shall not delay to state it as plainly as possible: There is only one God – He is the creator of the world – a righteous judge – rendering sentence on everyone according to their deeds and faith. To prove this, there are thousands of words that can be called forth."

Then Simon calmly declares, "I admire the quickness of your wit, but I do not embrace the error of your faith. You have wisely foreseen that you may be contradicted, and you have even confessed that to prove these things, countless thousands of words will need to be called forth. And why is that? Because hardly anyone agrees with your faith. As to there being only one god, and the world being his work, who believes this? Not any of the pagans, certainly none of the philosophers, none of the crude and prejudiced Jews, and definitely not myself, and I am well acquainted with the Jewish law."

"Put aside the opinions of those who are not here, and tell us face-to-face what your own view is," says Peter.

SIMON'S EXPRESSION OF BELIEF

"I *could* state what I really think, but I am reluctant to do so in this setting. For if I say what is not acceptable to you, you will straightway shut your ears, such that they won't be polluted with what you think is blasphemy. You will throw up your hands, intimating that I am a kook, because you can't find an answer – and the unlearned folks here will take your side, thinking, albeit falsely, that you embrace the things that they commonly believe in. And they will curse me for professing things new and unheard of."

"Are you not making use of long preambles, as you accused me of doing?" states Peter. "Have you no truth to bring forward? If you do, please begin straightaway. Some people may leave and some may stay – it doesn't matter. Just tell us what you think is true."

Then Simon nods and says, "I say to you that there are many gods, but there is only one incomprehensible supreme 'God' [9]– and he is unknown to all – he is the 'God' of all the other gods."

"This god whom you assert to be incomprehensible and unknown to all, can you prove His existence from the Scriptures of the Jews, which are held to be of unquestionable authority, or even from the Greeks, where intellectualism is esteemed? asks Peter.

And Simon replies, "I shall make use of assertions from the law of the Jews only, for this law is of universal authority. Yes, I rightly declared that there are many gods, of whom one is more eminent than the rest – the incomprehensible 'God' of gods. The Jewish Scriptures clearly tell us this. Here are some examples:

- When the serpent speaks to the first woman Eve about the tree in the middle of the garden, he says, 'the moment you eat of it, your eyes will be opened, *like gods* who know what is good and what is bad.'[10]
- After Adam has eaten from the fruit of the tree, 'God' himself says to the rest of the gods, 'Behold, the man has become like *one of us*; knowing what is good and what is bad.' Therefore, it is clear that there were many gods engaged in the making of humanity.
- In the beginning, 'God' said to the other gods, 'Let us make man in *our image*, after *our likeness*.'[11]
- And after the 'Fall', 'God' says '*Let us* then go down there and confuse their language.'[12]

These verses indicate that there are many gods. Furthermore, there are many other verses, some obscure and some plain, which testify that there are many gods. For instance:

- It is written, 'You shall not revile the gods, nor curse a prince of your people;'[13]
- And the writing, ' 'God' alone was their leader, no strange god was with him,'[14] indicates that there are other gods in existence.

One of these gods was chosen by lot to be the god of the Jews. But it is not him that I speak of – rather, it is the 'God' who is also his god – the 'God' above him – the supreme 'God' – who even the Jews did not know."

Upon hearing this, Peter answers, "Fear not, Simon, I have neither shut my ears, nor run away. But I will respond to those things which you have spoken of falsely, with words of truth. First of all, there is only one God, the God of the Jews, the Creator of heaven and earth. He is the God of all the others who you mistakenly call gods. None are superior to Him – He is above all.

"Even if there were other gods, as you say, they would be subject to the God of the Jews. For it is written that Moses said, 'For the Lord, your God, is the God of gods, the Lord of lords.'[15] Although there may be many that are called gods, He who is the God of the Jews is alone called the God of gods.

"Of course, we understand that not everyone who is called a god is actually the God. Moses was considered a god by Pharaoh,[16] and it is certain that he was a man. The Roman emperors are called gods, and we all know that they are not.

"The Hebrew Scriptures record God as saying, 'I alone am God, and there is no God besides me. It is I who bring both death and life,'[17] and Moses as saying, 'The Lord is God in the heavens above and on earth below, and there is no other.'[18] This conclusion is supported by Scripture in many places – He who created the world is the true and only God.

"But be sure of this Simon, I will not allow myself to be deceived by you. Confessing beguilement will not help me at the Day of Judgment – it did not help Eve. That is why even if some prophet should arise who tries to persuade me to worship other gods besides the God of the Jews, even by performing signs and miracles, I will never believe him. For it is written: 'If there arises among you a prophet or a dreamer who promises you a sign urging you to follow other gods, then even if that sign comes to pass, pay no attention to the words of that prophet or dreamer; for the Lord, your God is testing you to learn whether you really love Him with all your heart and with all your soul.'[19]

"Now know this: My Lord Jesus Christ is the real God of the Jews – the God of all kings – the judge of all. Neither an angel, nor a man, nor any creature can be truly a god, since they have been created and are changeable. He alone is the true God – who not only lives Himself, but also bestows life upon others, and takes it away when it is fitting.

"For this reason, Jesus did not teach the Jews that they must seek God. They were supposed to already know Him. Instead, He taught that they should seek the rewards of His kingdom, through faith and righteousness. But the religious leaders shut Him out."

To this Simon replies, "Straight from the words of your Master, I can rebut what you're saying. Surely, Adam knew the god who was his creator, as did Enoch, Noah, Abraham, Isaac, Jacob, and Moses. But your Jesus said, 'No one knows the Son but the Father; and no one knows the Father but the Son.'[20] Therefore, even your Jesus admits that there is another 'God', incomprehensible and unknown to all."

And Peter responds, "If Jesus knew him, who you call the unknown 'God', then he is not known by you alone. And, if Jesus knew him, then Moses knew him also, since he prophesied that Jesus would come. Now, if it is the option of the Son to reveal the Father to whom He wills, then the Son, who has been with the Father from the beginning, must have revealed the Father to Moses. This being the case, it is evident that the Father has been known by others. But how could the Father be revealed to you, since you don't believe in the Son? Why would the Son reveal Him to you? The Son reveals the Father only to those who honor the Son as they honor the Father.[21]

SIMON'S UNDERSTANDING OF GOD

With that, Simon decides to change the subject. "Remember that you said that God has a Son. But how can he have a son unless he is subject to passions, like humans or animals? But on this point, there is not time now to show your profound folly. Instead, I wish to make a statement concerning the immensity of the supreme light – so listen carefully now:

My belief is that there is a certain power of overwhelming and indescribable light, the greatness of which is incomprehensible – such a power and dominance that even the maker of the world, Moses the lawgiver, and Jesus your Master, are ignorant of it."

Then Peter interrupts before Simon can continue. "Isn't it a bit presumptuous of you to assert that there is another god than the God of all creation, and then try to convince others of this? Who will believe that there is a power so mighty, that no one knows about it except you? Furthermore, if there really is a new power, why doesn't it confer upon us some new sense, in addition to the five senses which we already possess? Then, we might be able to understand this new power. But if it cannot bestow such a sense upon us, how come it has bestowed it on you? If it has revealed itself to you, why not to us also?

Now, if you can understand something that no one else can, or ever could, then please tell me what I, and everyone else here, is thinking right now. If there is such a spirit in you that you can know those things which are above the heavens, which are unknown to all and incomprehensible by all, then it should be easy for you to know the thoughts of the people standing here. But if you cannot know the thoughts of us who are here, how can you say that you know those things that are known to no one?

"And how could you know about a great incomprehensible light unless you have received both vision and understanding from that light itself? Rather, I think, you are merely framing it all in your imagination, as if dreaming. But, until you find a new sense beyond the five which we all enjoy, you cannot assert the existence of a new 'God'."

"Since all things that we know to exist are in accordance with those five senses, any power that is more excellent than all others, must be capable of being received by those senses," admits Simon.

"But that is false," asserts Peter, "for there is also a sixth sense – the sense of foreknowledge, a sense that the prophets possessed. How, then, can one know a 'God' who is unknown to all, without the prophetic sense of prescience, or foreknowledge?"

"This power of which I speak," replies Simon, "is incomprehensible and more excellent than all – even more so than the god who made the world. Not any of the angels, nor any of the demons, nor the Jews, nor any creature which was made by the creator, knows this truth. So, 'how could the creator's law teach me something that the creator himself did not know,' you ask me?"

But before he can finish, Peter interrupts again, saying, "Yes, I wonder how you have been able to learn more from the law, than the law was able to provide – how you can assert something, when neither the law nor He who gave the law – the Creator of the world – knows the things of which you speak! In fact, I wonder why you, who alone know these things, are standing here now in debate. Don't you already know the outcome?"

There is a brief chuckle among the crowd, and then Simon says, "Do you laugh, Peter, when such great and lofty matters are under discussion?"

"Be not angered, Simon, for we are just keeping our promise – neither shutting our ears nor running away – regardless of how preposterous your words are. So, please explain to us how, from the law, you have learned of a 'God' that the law itself does not know of."

"If you are done laughing," says Simon sarcastically, "I shall prove it by clear assertions."

"Please do," replies Peter.

Thereupon, Simon proceeds to elucidate his philosophy and beliefs.

Simon's Declaration

"Listen now to what I have to say. There is one 'God', who is better than all, from whom all that exists took its beginning. This is not just the result of reasoning, but also of intuition and instinct. All things that exist are derived from he who is the chief and most excellent of all.

"When I had ascertained that the god who created the world, according to the Scriptures, is in many respects weak and imperfect – and weakness or imperfection is totally incompatible with a perfect 'God' – I necessarily concluded that there must be another 'God' who is perfect.

"For the creator god who is described in the Scriptures, is weak and imperfect in many aspects. In the first place, why is it that because the man who he had formed was not able to remain obedient to the law he had given him, he had to be punished?[22] Why should he be forbidden to know what is good and what is evil? With that knowledge, he could shun the evil and choose the good. But god did not permit this. Because the man discovered what is good – and realized that he should cover his nakedness because it was bad to stand naked before his creator – he is condemned to death, even though he had learned to honor god. And the serpent, who had shown him these things, is cursed.

58

"If man is to be punished in this way, then why put the cause of the error in paradise at all? Shouldn't evil be outside of paradise, which is all good? Why place in paradise something that is not good?

"Therefore, according to what is written in the Scriptures, he who made human beings and the world must be imperfect. And if that is so, then without doubt, there must be another who <u>is</u> perfect. For it is of necessity that there be one 'God' most excellent of all, such that every existing creature keeps its rank – a 'God' more powerful and more gracious than the imperfect god who gave the law in Scripture.

"And in this way, Peter, I was able to learn from the law what the law did not explicitly say. But even without the law, it was still possible for me to deduce, from the evils that are done in this world and are not corrected, that its creator is powerless. And if he cannot correct what has been created wrong, or doesn't wish to do so, then he is evil himself. If he neither can nor will, then he is neither powerful nor good. And from this, it must be concluded that there is another 'God', more excellent and more powerful than all."

Peter's Rebuttal

Peter tries to answer tactfully: "People who conceive such absurdities against God, do not read the Scriptures with the instruction of learned experts – they think they can understand it themselves. Nevertheless, I will address your points:

"Inasmuch as you say that the creator of the world is not all-powerful, and is evil also, how is it that you cannot see that the greater power, who you say is superior to all, is subject to the same charges? For the very same thing can be said of him – that he is not all-powerful, since he does not correct the lesser power who has erred – and that he is evil, if he can but will not.

"It is even worse if others believe this greater power to be real, when in truth he is not. For He who created the world proves His existence by the very operation of creating the world. But this greater power which you say that you alone know, affords no indication by which we might perceive that he exists.

"What kind of creature would we be if we abandoned God, in whose world we live and enjoy all things necessary for life, and follow a power, or a 'God', who not only provides us with nothing good, but doesn't even let us know if he exists? In fact, this other 'God' does not exist. For when you call him light, you borrow that name from our Creator, and when you say that he is above all, it's just you making elaborate speech. In fact, you have nothing new concerning this 'God' – this power – you speak of. You don't even have a name by which to call him.

"But if, as you say, there really is some 'God' more benevolent than all, he could never be angry with us since he doesn't know us. Or if he is angry, then he must be evil. On the other hand, when our God is angry and punishes, He is not evil, but righteous. For He corrects and adjusts His own creation with wisdom. But he who has nothing to do with us, what could be his motivation? If he inflicts punishment on us because we have not been convinced by wild imagination to forsake our own Father and follow him, how can he possibly be good or just?"

Then, Simon says, "You are confused Peter. Although people's souls were made by that good 'God', the most excellent of all, you seem not to know that they have been brought down into this world as captives."

To which Peter retorts, "Then he is not unknown to all, as you said a little while ago. And another thing: how did the good 'God' allow his souls to be taken captive in the first place, if he is the power over everything?"

"He sent the creator god to make the world, and after it had been made, he let it be known that he was the supreme 'God'," said Simon.

"Then the supreme 'God' is not unknown to him who made the world – nor are souls ignorant of him, if they were stolen away from him. To whom, then, is he unknown? Furthermore, why didn't the supreme 'God' know that the god who created the world, would not do it right? For if he did not know, then he is not all-knowing – and if he did know, but allowed it, then he is himself guilty of not doing it right, and is not all-good. But if he did know, but could not prevent it, then he is not all-powerful."

Then Simon says, "He receives those who will come to him, and does them good."

"But there is nothing new in this," speaks Peter, "for he whom you acknowledge to be the creator of the world also does so."

"But the good supreme 'God' bestows salvation if he is only acknowledged, but the creator-of-the-world god demands also that the law be fulfilled."

"So, let me get this straight," says Peter. "He saves adulterers and murderers if they know him; but good, sober, merciful people, if they do not know him – because they have no information about him – he does not save! Wow! This 'God', who you proclaim to be great and good, shows no mercy to the upright, and is the savior of the evil."

But Simon is not rattled. "It is very difficult for man to know him, as long as he is in the flesh – for blacker than all darkness, and heavier than all clay, is this body with which the soul is surrounded."

Peter thinks for a bit and then responds, "That good 'God' of yours demands things which are difficult, but He who is truly God seeks easier things. Now, if he is so good, let him leave us with our Father and Creator God. Then, when the time comes for us to depart from the darkness of the body, we shall more easily know him.

"But that is not what I think will happen. I think that when the soul departs the body, it will better understand that God is its Creator, and will remain with Him. It will no longer be harassed with wild imaginations, nor wish to affiliate itself with another power, which is known only to Simon – and which is of such goodness that no one can come to it, unless he first be guilty of wrongs against his own brother! I'm sorry – I don't know how this power can be called either good or just."

And Simon calmly responds with, "It is not sinful, for the sake of greater benefit and reward, to flee to him who is of deeper and richer glory."

To which Peter says, "If, as you say, it is not sinful to flee to a stranger, then it should also be pious to remain with our own father, even if he is what you call the 'lesser god'. In fact, I think your 'higher God', if he really existed, would commend us for this; because if we had been his creatures, we would never have been seduced by the allurements of any other god to forsake him."

"But if souls are from him, and do not know him, then is he truly their father?" asks Simon.

"If, as you say, he is more powerful than all, how can one believe that the weaker wrenched the spoils from the stronger?" says Peter. "If the creator god was able to pull souls down into this world by force, how can it be that, when they are separated from the body, the good 'God' can call them to judgment? It was because of his weakness that they were dragged away in ignorance to this dark place we call earth, in the first place!

"It seems to me that you do not know who God really is. I could explain to you the truth about where souls are, and when and how they were made. But how can I disclose these things to you, when you are in such error regarding your knowledge of God?"

Then, Simon says, "A time will come when you will be sorry that you did not understand me when I spoke of the indescribable supreme power."

And Peter replies, "Then give us some new sense, by which we may know this new 'God' of whom you speak. After all, as being yourself a creature that has come directly down from him, that should be easy."

The Problem with Imagination

Simon starts to explain his worldview in greater detail: "Apply your mind to the things which I am going to say, and allow it to peacefully absorb the wisdom. Now, have you ever projected your mind into regions or lands situated far away, and remain so fixed in them, that you could not even see the people that were next to you? Or even know where you were, by reason of the delightfulness of the things in which you were transfixed?"

"It is true, Simon, this has often occurred to me" says Peter.

"Then, in this way, reach forth your mind into heaven – even to above the heaven – and behold that there must be some place beyond our reality, in which there is neither heaven nor earth, and where there is no shadow of things to produce darkness. Since there are neither bodies in it, nor dark shadows caused by bodies, there must of necessity be immense light. Now consider what sort of light that must be, never interrupted by shadow. For if the light of our sun fills the earth, how overwhelming must be that bodiless and infinite light? So great, that the light of our sun would seem to be darkness in comparison, and not light at all."

Peter, then, speaks to this: "I will address both matters – stretching out the senses and the immensity of light: Yes, I have sometimes in thought extended my sense, as you say, into regions far away, and have seen them in my mind just as clear as if I had seen them with my eyes.

"Once when I was fishing and was in a semi-dream state, I did not perceive that I had caught a large fish, which was attached to the hook and dragging down my line. However, my brother Andrew, who was sitting next to me, noticed that I was in a trance and almost ready to fall. He shoved his elbow into my side, as if to awaken me from sleep, and said, 'Peter, don't you see that you have caught a large fish? Are you dreaming or are you in a stupor of astonishment? What is the matter with you?' It's funny, but I was cranky with him for removing me from the delight of the things which I was day-dreaming. I answered that I was not suffering any difficulty, but that I was mentally absorbed in an idyllic experience. Although here in the body, in my mind I was wholly carried away to another place. And then Andrew uttered some inspired words of wisdom and truth:

'Peter, listen to me: those who are beginning to be possessed by a demon, or disturbed in their minds, usually begin in this way. They are first carried away by fancies to some delightful thing or place, and then they pour out all their emotions in vain on things which have no existence. This happens from a certain malady of mind – they see not the things that are, but the things that they long to see. This is because the soul is distressed, suffering a failure of its natural service – being pulled away from its natural state by excess of cold or heat, thirst or hunger, or other reasons. It is an ailment, but can be corrected by faith in God.'

"I told my brother about the places and the people that I had seen in my mind. But when I actually came, for the first time, to one of those places, it was nothing at all like what I had envisioned. I pictured that it had beautiful gates, walls, and buildings, similar to others which I had previously seen, but in reality, it had none of those things.

"Indeed, no one can imagine anything totally new, only things similar to what he has previously experienced. If you see a bull with five heads in your imagination, it is because you have already seen a bull with one head, and you just elaborate on the form.

"Therefore, if you try to look above the heavens and perceive what is there in your thoughts, then you will undoubtedly imagine it based on those things which you have already seen here on earth. If you think that there is easy access for your mind above the heavens, and that you can truly understand the things that are there – like comprehending that immense light – you are sadly mistaken. No mortal can comprehend these things. Of course, if you are not mortal, then tell us what this chap standing next to me is thinking right now."

To this, Simon snickers and replies, "You have woven a web of many frivolities, Peter, but listen now. It is impossible that anything that comes into a man's thoughts should not also exist in truth and reality. For things that do not exist, have no substance, and things that have no substance, cannot present themselves to our thoughts."

And Peter says, "If everything that can come into our thoughts has an existence, then what about that immense light which is outside of our world? If one man thinks in his heart that it is light, and another thinks that it is darkness, how can one and the same place be both light and darkness?"

Above the Heavens

Simon groans and changes the subject again. "Let's move on from what has just been said. So, tell us Peter, what do you believe exists above the heavens."[23]

So, Peter expounds a bit on immensity and the law. "A reading of the law, and keen observance of nature, is all that is needed to tell us what to believe regarding immensity. If the doctrine of immensity is known to the law, then nothing else can be unknown to it. Therefore, it is a false supposition of yours, that there is something that the law is not cognizant of.

"In any case, I cannot speak to you about immensity – of those things that are without limit – unless you accept our account of each of the heavens being bounded by certain limits, or else offer your own account of them. If you cannot understand things that are limited, how can you understand things that are without limit?"

To which Simon replies, "The simple man will simply believe that a god exists, and that the heaven which we see is the only heaven."

Peter reacts by saying, "Perhaps, but it is proper to believe in one God who truly <u>IS</u>, and in many heavens which were made by Him. One heaven is the visible firmament, and the highest heaven is eternal and infinite. The visible heaven will be dissolved and pass away at the end of the world, so that the heaven which is older and higher may appear to the holy after the final judgment."

To which Simon responds, "These things may appear to be so by those who believe them. But to one who searches for reasons of these things, it is impossible that they can be derived from the law, especially concerning the immensity of the light."

"Don't think that I say these things because I believe them by faith alone," says Peter, "but my belief is also based on reason – for truth cannot be without reason. He who has received these things through faith, and fortified through reason, can never be torn away from what he believes."

Then Simon replies, somewhat derisively, "It sure is a remarkable thing that you promise – that the eternity of boundless light can be shown from the law."

"I can prove it whenever you please," answers Peter.

However, Simon decides to adjourn the debate and continue tomorrow. "Since it is now a late hour, I shall debate with you again tomorrow. And if you can prove that there is only one god, and that souls are immortal, then you shall have me to assist you in your preaching."

Then, Simon departs the courtyard, followed by about a third of the gathered people.[24] The rest of the crowd bend their knee before Peter, and he blesses them. He cures some who are possessed by demons and others who are sick. Then, he dismisses the people, advising them to come again early the next day.

Privately, Peter laments to his close friends that many unclean spirits dwell in the bodies of people, compelling them to obey their own lusts, and turning them into willing vessels for demons. "Such a man is this Simon, who is seized with the sickness, and cannot now be healed – sadly, it has taken over his will. It cannot be driven out, since it is now inseparable from himself. I'm afraid that it has become his very soul."

NOTES

1. Peter's Master, that Simon refers to, is of course, Jesus Christ. But Simon will not acknowledge this by speaking His name.

2. Matthew 10:34-36

3. Luke 12:51 and Matthew 10:34

4. Matthew 5:9

5. Matthew 10:25

6. Matthew 5:3

7. Luke 12:52-53

8. Matthew 12:25

9. The word 'God' in single quotes, refers to the unknown highest supreme divine entity in Simon's theology, below which exist other gods, including the god who created the earth.

10. Genesis 3:5. Some translations leave out the words 'like gods who'. Other translations say 'like God who knows'

11. Genesis 1:26

12. Genesis 11:7. Some translations say 'confound their language'

13. Exodus 22:28. Some translations say 'God' instead of 'the gods'.

14. Deuteronomy 32:12. Some translations say 'The Lord' instead of 'God'

15. Deuteronomy 10:17

16. Exodus 7:1

17. Deuteronomy 32:39

18. Deuteronomy 4:39

19. Deuteronomy 13:2-4

20. Matthew 11:27; Luke 10:22

21. John 5:22-23

22. The given law here was that Adam could eat the fruit from all the trees in paradise except one – he could not eat from the tree of the knowledge of good and evil – and if he did eat from it, he would die. Reference Genesis 3.

23. The familiar doctrine of the Seven Heavens (or multiple heavens) is found in many ancient Mesopotamian religions. Usually, each of the seven heavens corresponds with one of the seven classical planets that were known to exist in antiquity. Peter and Simon were not concerned with defining all the intermediate levels of heaven – only in what existed in the lowest or visible heaven (the sun, moon, stars, clouds, and sky) and the highest heaven (the boundless domain of God).

24. Some sources say this was about 1000 people (mostly men).

4 SECOND DEBATE WITH SIMON

Early the next morning, one of the believers comes into the meeting room and shouts, "There is a great multitude of people waiting in the courtyard, and in the midst of them stands Simon, endeavoring to infuse the ears of the people with his sinful persuasions. He accuses you, Peter, of being the servant of wickedness, of having great power in magic, and of enthralling the souls of men in a way worse than idolatry."

And so, Peter goes out immediately, and stands in the spot where he did the day before – and many of the people turn to him in anticipation.

But when Simon perceives that the people turn to look at Peter, he says quietly, "I marvel at the folly of men – those who love Peter and call me a magician – whereas, having known me for many years, they ought to love me instead. I hope that those here who have any sense will understand that Peter is the real magician, since he seems to garner affection without having any acquaintance."

PETER TAKES THE OFFENSIVE

After having saluted the people in his usual way, Peter launches an immediate attack on Simon, saying: "Simon, if you wonder why those who are acquainted with you do not love you, then I will explain it: You profess to proclaim the truth; and on this account you have had many friends who desired to learn the truth. But when they saw things in you contrary to what you preached, being lovers of the truth, they began to love you no longer. But many did not forsake you immediately, because you still promised truth. As long as no one else could show them truth, they bore up with you. But now, since the hope of better instruction has dawned upon them, they turn away from you. For you are nothing but a fraud. At first, you thought that you could escape detection through the use of nefarious arts. But you are detected, Simon! You are driven into a corner, and made to appear disreputable – not only as being ignorant of the truth, but also as being unwilling to hear it from those who know it."

After Peter had spoken these words, Simon calmly responds by saying, "I did not come here to listen to undignified inflammatory and accusatory speeches, Peter. I came to hear the answers that you promised to give yesterday. You said that you could show that the law teaches us about the immensity of the eternal light, that there are only two heavens, and that the higher is the abode of that light – in which the indefinable father dwells alone forever – and that the lower visible heaven will some day pass away. You also said that the father of all is one, because there cannot be two infinites, else neither of them would be infinite. Since this is what you promised to show us today, please refrain from unbecoming rants, and set about doing this."

To which Peter replies, "If I were asked to speak of these things only to you, who comes only for the purpose of contradicting, then I would have nothing to say. But seeing that many in the crowd truly seek enlightenment, I will not delay."

"Peter, you seem to me to be upset today," says Simon. "If that is so; it is not necessary to continue the debate – you can be excused and the discussion postponed."

"I think you perceive that you are about to be convicted," replies Peter, "and you wish to politely escape from the contest."

But Simon retorts, "I shall force myself to patiently put up with your blatant unskillful attacks. The bottom line, Peter, is that I teach the truth, and it is you who wishes to seduce the people. So, to shorten this unproductive discourse, I will refrain from a discussion concerning the boundless light. Instead, answer me this: Since your god made all things, why did he make evil?"

THE QUESTION OF EVIL

"To put questions in this way is not the part of an opponent, but of a learner," says Peter. "If you wish to learn, admit it; and I shall teach you. But if you do not wish to learn, then I will set forth my beliefs, you can set forth your beliefs, and the listeners in the crowd can judge who is correct."

To this Simon answers, "This has got to be a joke – a peasant who offers to teach me! Nevertheless, I shall endure you, and bear with your ignorance and arrogance. So I confess, then, I do wish to learn; let us see if you can teach me."

"If you truly wish to learn, then first know this:" says Peter, "You have unskillfully framed your question. You say, 'Since god made all things, why did he make evil?' But before you ask this question, there are three questions that should be asked: 'Does evil really exist?', 'What exactly is evil?', and 'Who does the evil affect?' "

To this, Simon answers, "Oh you are a most simple and untalented man – is there anyone here who does not believe that there is evil in this life? When I asked about evil – thinking that maybe you had a hint of common sense – I was not wishing to learn – least of all from you who knows nothing. I already know all things. My purpose was to illustrate how you are ignorant in these things. And it's not because I am angry – it's because I am moved with compassion for those here who you are trying to deceive."

"There is no compassion in you for these people," replies Peter. "You are just trying to raise a smokescreen. And where there is smoke, there is fire. Nevertheless, I will address your statement. You say that all believe in the existence of evil, but this is false – the entire Hebrew nation denies its existence."[1]

"Those who say there is no evil, speak correctly," says Simon.

Then Peter continues, "Yes, the existence of evil is not universally admitted. But the other questions about evil need to be addressed, particularly 'where does it come from?' – from God? – from nothing? – has it always been, or was there a beginning? – it is it useful or useless? – and there are other questions."

"Let's look at my original question," says Simon. "Why did your god make evil?"

Peter is still dubious about Simon's motivation in asking the question, and tries to sound-out his thinking, but Simon is resolute. "Let's get to it," he says, "where do you begin?"

So, Peter responds, "I advise that the first inquiry should be whether it is in our power to understand from what place, or from what source, we are to be judged on the evil we have done."

But Simon says, "No, we should first inquire about a god, and how he relates to evil – everyone here is interested in that."

"You believe, then, that free choice is within the will-power of men, when it comes to obeying God?" asks Peter.

"By no means" replies Simon.

So Peter says, "If we do not have the will-power, then it is useless for us to inquire anything about God, since it is not in the power of those who seek answers, to find answers."

Then says Simon, "Now you are speaking double-talk – just re-stating the same gibberish in different words."

Peter tries to trap Simon with his argument. "See, my friends, into what absurdities Simon has fallen – who before my coming was teaching that men have it in their power to do what they will, but now, driven into a corner, he denies that men have the power to do the will of God!

"Tell me this then, how does your 'God' judge every person according to his acts, if people don't have it in their power to do what he wills? If this is the case, then trying to do good is folly – judges should not punish those who sin, for it is not in their power not to sin. People who labor to be righteous will be miserable, and people who exercise tyranny and wickedness will be happy. Accordingly, there is no righteousness, or goodness, or virtue – in effect, no 'God'.

"But I know why you have said this. You just wish to avoid honest inquiry into your views, so that you cannot be publicly refuted. But you have lost. I say, therefore, that man is under his own control."

Smiling self-assuredly, Simon then says, "What do you mean, 'man is under his own control'? Tell us."

"If nothing can be learned, why do you wish to hear?" asks Peter.

To which Simon says, "Just answer the question. Or do you not have an answer?"

Then, Peter answers, "For the benefit of the crowd, I will say this: The power of choice is the sense of the soul, possessing a quality by which it can be inclined towards doing the acts that it wills."

Uncharacteristically, Simon applauds Peter for his words, but then puts forth another question: "You have explained it well and succinctly – for it is my duty to bear testimony if you speak well. But now, please answer me this: Is it true that what a god wishes to be, always comes to be, and what he does not wish to be, never comes to be?"

Peter then responds, "I think that is a ridiculous question, but I will answer it anyway." He then expounds at length on how God is the author of 'good', and not of 'evil', which is just an absence of 'good'. He finishes by saying, "According to how their will leads them to action, and how the judgment of their mind inclines them to think, people cause either good or evil to occur – therefore, He has prepared rewards to those who do good, and penalties to those who do evil."

But Simon asks, "Why did he not make us all such that we could only do good, and not have it in our power to do otherwise? Didn't he have the power to do this?"

"That is another ridiculous question," says Peter, "for if He had made us of an unchangeable nature and incapable of not doing good, we would not really be good, because we couldn't be anything else. And it would not be because we purposefully wanted to be good – it would just be as a result of our nature. How can anything be called good if it is not done on purpose under free-will? There is no such thing as good without liberty!"

THE VISIBLE HEAVEN

Sensing that Peter is getting the upper hand, Simon changes the subject again. "Now, answer me this Peter: Since the visible heaven exists, and you say that someday it will be dissolved, then why was it made in the first place?"

"It was made for the sake of the people He created," answers Peter, "such that there would be a separation between the divine and the corporeal – lest any unworthy person see the habitation of the divine. For the abode of God Himself has been prepared only for those who are pure of heart. But, in the present time of conflict between the righteous and the unrighteous, the highest heaven has been made invisible, destined as a reward to the righteous."

Then Simon says, "If the creator is good, and the world is good, then why would he ever want to destroy that which is good? Indeed, if he does destroy that which is good, how can he be considered to be good? But, if he destroys the world because it is evil, then how could he be considered good if he made an evil world in the first place?"

To this Peter replies, "Since I have promised to answer your foolish questions, listen up: If indeed, the visible and transient heaven had been made for its own sake, there would be some reason in what you say. But, if it was made for something else, and not for its own sake, then by necessity it must be dissolved, such that what it was made for may appear.

"Let me illustrate this with an egg. However carefully the shell of the egg may seem to have been formed, it is necessary that it be broken and opened, in order for the chick to emerge from it. That is the reason why the form of the whole egg was designed as it is, in the first place. Therefore, in a similar way, it is necessary that the condition of this world pass away, such that the more magnificent condition of the heavenly kingdom may shine forth."

And Simon answers again, "It does not seem to me that the heaven, which you say has been made by the one god, can be dissolved. That is because things that are made by a corruptible one – a lessor creator god – are temporary and decaying, and worthy of dissolution. But things made by the eternal one – the higher supreme god – are eternal and cannot be dissolved."

"Not so," says Peter, "the Eternal God does not always make things incorruptible, nor always corruptible – but the things that He makes are according to the will of God the Creator.[2] For the power of God is not subject to law, but His will is a law to His creatures."

Simon then says, "I want to go back to the first question. You said that your god is visible to no one, but when the heaven is dissolved, and the superior condition of the heavenly kingdom shines forth, then those who are pure in heart will see the god – but this statement is contrary to the law, for it is written that God said, *for no man sees me and still lives.*"[3]

Then Peter answers, "It may seem contradictory at first, but it is actually not. God is seen by the mind, not by the body – by the spirit, not by the flesh. The angels, who are spirits, can see God, but human beings, as long as they are alive, cannot see Him. But after the resurrection of the dead, when righteous humans are made like the angels,[4] they <u>will</u> be able to see God. Therefore, my statement is not contrary to the law – and neither is what my Master said: 'Blessed are the pure of heart, for they shall see God.'[5] Jesus said that a time will come when righteous people will be made like angels, and in the spirit of their mind, they will see God."

After this, Simon begins to lose patience and seeks to escape the debate. But first he says, "Concerning one thing only, tell me why you think the soul is immortal. If your answer is satisfactory, I will accept your teaching in all things. But let it be tomorrow, for today it is late and I am tired."

With that, Simon leaves the courtyard with only a few associates. Most of the people in attendance turn to Peter and prostrate themselves before him in reverence. Then, Peter prays over the crowd and they depart rejoicing, for they have heard the doctrine of the true God.

NOTES

---

1. Satan occupies a prominent place in Christianity, which generally regards him as a rebellious angel and the source of all evil – and who will meet his ultimate demise in battle at the End of Days. In Jewish traditions, Satan is usually translated as 'opponent' or 'adversary'. He is often understood to represent the sinful impulse in man, or more generally, the forces that prevent human beings from submitting to divine will. Some Jewish scholars believe that he isn't real at all, but is merely a metaphor for sinful impulses.

2. Peter seems to be implying that God the Son created things according to the will of God the Father.

3. Exodus 33:20

4. Matthew 22:30

5. Matthew 5:8. Some translations say 'the single-hearted' instead of 'the pure of heart'. This is part of Christ's famous teaching on the mountainside, called 'The Beatitudes'.

5 THIRD DEBATE WITH SIMON

On the following day, Peter rises at dawn, as is usual, and finds most of his followers already up and ready to listen and learn. He summarizes the doctrines which were spoken of yesterday, but without the contentiousness of adversarial argument. Then, he expands on the doctrines in proper order and with understandable clarity.

Then, after his morning prayers and a quick breakfast, he goes out to the courtyard for the day's debate. Seeing Simon standing in the middle of the crowd, he greets the people in his usual way, and then says to them, "I confess that I am somewhat grieved with respect to certain people who come to me to learn something, but when I begin to teach, they profess that they themselves are masters – they ask questions like uninformed persons, but they contradict like expert ones. And the topics do not flow logically one to another, which adds to confusion."

THE ORDER OF LEARNING

"Now, let me say this," continues Peter, "the teaching of all doctrine has a certain order – there are some things that must be delivered first, others things second, others third, and so on, all in their respective order. For if these things are delivered in the proper sequence, they are much easier to understand. But, if they are delivered out of sequence, they may seem to be spoken against common sense. Therefore, we need to pay close attention to order, if we are to find the truths that we seek."

Simon then takes issue, saying, "From what you say, then, truth is not available to all, but only to those who are skilled in the art of rhetoric. This is absurd and simply cannot be. Any god is equally the god of all – everyone should be equally able to know his will."

"All were made equal by Him," says Peter, "and to all He has given equally the ability to receive truth. But no one is born educated already – education occurs subsequent to birth. Since all are equally capable of learning,[1] the difference is not in nature, but in education. In the trades, one must first learn before he teaches. Similarly, in the spiritual ministry, one must first learn and then teach – and in the proper order."

To which Simon says, "This is not true in the pursuit of knowledge – as soon as one hears, he has learned."

But then Peter responds, "Indeed, if one hears the truth presented in an orderly manner, then he will be willing to believe it. But if he hears in a disorderly manner – in bits and pieces, and out of sequence – then he will be confused."

"Should everyone believe that whatever they hear is true?" asks Simon.

And Peter answers, "Whoever hears an orderly statement of the truth, may want to believe it. But he can only firmly and totally believe the words if he can test them according to the rules of life that are inherent in his nature – his character and constitution – which are driven by both internal and external factors. For example, no one can be persuaded to become shorter or taller, just due to words alone, because the force of nature does not permit it. So, if one hears the truth in words and believes, and another does not believe, it is because of the nature of the person."

Simon then asks, "So tell us what one must first learn if he desires to know the truth."

To which Peter replies, "Before anything else, it must first be determined what is possible for man to find out. Because of our finite body and brains, we cannot know everything that God knows. But it is within our power to try to find out what is good, even if we can't or don't follow it. This is because the judgment of God depends on it. If a person is able to do good and does not, then for that he will be judged.

"Other than this, we cannot know the answers to the first primary questions. We do not need to know how the world was made. This would only be necessary if we were to enter upon a similar construction. It is sufficient for us to know that He <u>did</u> make the world, but how He made it is not a pertinent inquiry. We will not be judged for not knowing this. But we <u>will</u> be judged for not believing that the righteous and good God is the Creator of the world.

"Furthermore, just knowing that He is good, is not sufficient for salvation. For in the present life, not only the worthy, but also the unworthy enjoy His goodness. But if we believe Him to be not only good, but also righteous, and if we observe like righteousness in the whole course of our life, then we will enjoy His goodness for ever.[2] At the Day of Judgment, He will bestow eternal rewards upon the worthy, but the unworthy will be excluded."

Then, Simon asks, "How can one and the same entity be both good and righteous?"

And again Peter explains, "Because without righteousness, goodness would be unrighteousness. It is the part of a good God to bestow His sunshine and rain equally on the just and the unjust.[3] But this would seem to be unjust, if He always treated the good and the bad with equal fortune. But as the rain equally nourishes the grain and the weeds in the field, at the time of harvest, the grain is gathered into the barn, but the weeds are burned in the fire.[4] So it will be at the Day of Judgment, when the righteous will be allowed into the kingdom of heaven, and the unrighteous will be cast out. This is how the justice of God will be manifest. For if He remained forever alike to both the evil and the good, this would not be good and would not be righteous. It would be unjust for the righteous and the unrighteous to receive the same gifts."

IMMORTALITY OF THE SOUL

Then, Simon changes the order of discussion again. "The one point on which I really wish to be convinced of, is whether or not the soul is immortal. I just cannot take up the burden of righteousness unless I first know whether the soul is immortal. For if it is not immortal, then the whole profession of your faith is ludicrous and cannot stand."

To this, Peter replies, "Let us first inquire whether God is just. Once this is determined, the perfect order of doctrine will straightaway be established."

But Simon protests, saying, "With all your boasting of your knowledge about the order of discussion, you are now answering contrary to order. For when I ask you to show whether the soul is immortal, you say that we must first inquire whether your god is just."

"It is perfectly right and in proper order," says Peter. "Some men who blaspheme against God, and who spend their whole life in injustice and wickedness, die in their own bed and obtain an honorable burial. However, others who worship God, and spend their whole life in justice and goodness, die in deserted places and are thought not even worthy of burial. Where, then, is the justice of God, if there is no immortal soul to suffer punishment in the future for impious deeds, or to enjoy rewards for piety and uprightness?"

"This just seems incredulous to me," rejoins Simon, "because many well-doers perish miserably, and many evil-doers finish long and happy lives."

To which Peter says, "The very same thing that you are skeptical of, convinces me that there must be a final judgment. Since it is certain that God is just, it is a necessary consequence that there is another world – a world in which everyone receives favor according to his belief and deeds. If all people now received the same rewards, I would truly seem to be a deceiver. But the fact that in the present life, a reward is not made to every one according to his belief and deeds, affords indubitable proof that there shall be a judgment in the future."

"Then, why am I not persuaded of it?" says Simon.

"Because you have not heard Jesus, the Christ and the true Prophet,[5] say, 'Seek first His righteousness, and all these things will be given to you besides.'[6] "

Then Simon says sarcastically, "Pardon me if I am unwilling to seek righteousness, before I know whether the soul is immortal."

"I cannot say other than what the Prophet of truth has instructed me," says Peter.

"Then, it is certain that you cannot prove that the soul is immortal," says Simon. "That is why you resort to a 'he told me so' answer. You know, that if the soul could be proved to be mortal, then that entire religion you are attempting to propagate, will disappear into nothingness.

"I commend you for your passion, but I am not swayed by your persuasiveness. For you persuade many to embrace your religion, and submit to the restraints of pleasure, in the hope of receiving future good rewards. But these poor souls lose their enjoyment of life in the present, because they are deceived with false hopes of good things in the future. For at their very moment of death, their soul will be extinguished."

When Peter hears this, he is overcome with grief and emotion. He grinds his teeth and rubs his forehead, while uttering, "Armed with the cunning of Satan, you stand here trying to deceive souls. You profess to be a teacher, but like the wily devil and the pagan, you try to introduce many gods. But being refuted in that, you assert that there is no God at all.

"You deny that God is the Creator of the world, and instead say that it was made by a lesser god – one who is an evil being, or has many equals, or is not God at all.

"Now you assert that the soul is mortal, so that people may not live righteously and uprightly in the hope of things to come. Since there is no hope for the future, why should anyone be merciful? Why not indulge exclusively in luxury and pleasures, a behavior from which all unrighteousness springs?

"And while you introduce so impious a doctrine into the miserable life of people, you call yourself pious, and me impious –

because under the hope of future good things, I do not sanction men taking up arms and fighting, plundering and subverting, and attempting whatever lust may dictate. What kind of life is this that you would introduce? – where men will attack and retaliate, be enraged and disturbed, and live always in fear? For those who do evil to others must expect like evil to themselves.

"Don't you see that you are a leader of disturbance and not of peace, of iniquity and not of equity? I sigh in despair, not because I could not prove that the soul is immortal, but because I pity the souls which you are endeavoring to deceive.

"Therefore, I will no longer speak as compelled by you. Rather, for those who really want to learn, I will instruct as is suitable."

Then says Simon, "If you are angry, I shall neither ask you any questions, nor do I wish to hear you."

And Peter replies, "If you are now seeking a pretext for escaping, you have full liberty, and need not use any special pretext. For everyone has heard you speaking all amiss, and have perceived that you can prove nothing. They only sense that you ask questions for the sake of contradiction, which anyone can do."

PETER'S FINAL STRATEGY

"But you and everyone else should know, that I can prove that the soul is immortal in a single sentence. But first, I need to ask you a single question regarding a point that is familiar to all. Answer the question, and I shall prove to you in one sentence that the soul is immortal."

Although he had thought that he had found a pretext for departing, Simon stops short on account of the remarkable promise that is made to him, and says: "Ask me then, and I will answer you. I wish to hear in a single sentence, as you have promised, how the soul is immortal."

"So answer me this," says Peter, "which way is better to persuade a skeptical man, seeing or hearing?"

"Seeing," says Simon.

Whereupon Peter says, "Then why do you wish to learn from me by words – what can be proved to you by sight itself?"

"I have no idea what you mean," replies Simon.

Then, Peter goes for the knockout punch. "If you don't know, go to your house now, and entering the inner bed-chamber you will see an image of the figure of a murdered young boy clothed in purple. Ask him if the soul is immortal, and he will inform you, by showing you his presence. For what need is there to hear from him when you can see him standing right before you? For if he did not exist, surely he could not be seen. But if you know not what image I speak of, let us go to your house straightaway, with ten other men from those who are gathered here."

Hearing this from Peter, Simon turns pale and becomes fidgety and nervous. He is afraid, that if he denies it, his house will be searched – or worse – if he doesn't deny it, that Peter in his indignation will betray him more openly, and everyone will learn the truth about him.

And so he answers, "I implore you, Peter, by the good god who is within you, to cast out the wickedness that is in me. Hear my repentance, and for penitence you shall have me as an assistant in your preaching. For now, I have learned in all clearness that you are a prophet of the true god, and therefore you know the secret and hidden things of men."[7]

Not deceived by Simon's chicanery, Peter addresses all that are gathered, "Brothers and sisters, now you hear Simon seeking repentance, but in a little while you will see him returning again to his infidelity. Thinking that I am a psychic because I have disclosed his wickedness, which was supposed to be secret and hidden, he has now promised that he will repent. But I cannot really say whether this infidel can be saved or not! For as I call heaven and earth to witness, I spoke not as a psychic, but simply as someone who learned about what things he did in secret – such as this devilish act – from good folks who once were his associates in his mischief, but have now been converted to the one true faith."

SIMON'S BLASPHEMY

When Simon hears this, he becomes enraged, and assails Peter with curses and rebukes, saying, "Oh you most wicked and deceitful of men, to whom luck and not truth, has given an apparent victory in this debate. Of course, I sought repentance not for any deficiency in knowledge, but to convince you of my sincerity in wanting to become your disciple – hoping that you would entrust me with all the secrets of your magic – which after learning them all, I would be able to use to publicly rebuke and humiliate you.

"But you have cunningly understood the real reasons behind my pretense. And now you desire to expose me, in the presence of the people here, as unskillful and deceitful – knowing that I will of necessity be indignant. You hoped that I would confess to not being truly penitent – and you anticipated me returning to my infidelity after my penitence.

"Because I did not foresee your trickery, you appear to have conquered me on all sides. But, as I said, your victory is hollow – the result of luck, and not of logic or truth. I did not foresee your deception because during the time of this debate, I stood by you and spoke with you in good faith, and bore patiently with you.

"But now I will show you the power of my divinity – and you shall quickly fall down and worship me." With that, Simon works himself into a tirade:

"I am the first power – who is always – without beginning or end. Having entered the womb of Rachel, I was born of her as a person, that I might be visible to people;

I have flown through the air;

I have been mixed with fire, and made into one entity;

I have made statues move, and animated lifeless things;

I have turned stones into bread;

I have flown from mountain to mountain, and moved from place to place – upheld by angels' hands – and have alighted upon the earth."

"Not only have I done these things, but even now I am able to do them.

"Peter, your words are all in vain. You cannot perform any real miraculous works such as I have just mentioned.

"Listen to me now: By facts alone, I can prove to you all that I am the son of god, enduring for all eternity – and I can make those who believe in me, in like manner live forever.

"And finally, I say to you all that he who sent Peter is nothing but an amateur magician – one who could not even deliver himself from the suffering of the cross."

To this blasphemy from Simon, Peter responds, "Do not meddle with the things that belong to others. You are just a bedeviled magician, Simon. This is apparent by the very deeds that you have done.

"But my Master is the Son of God, and is the essence of good. This has been told to you, to everyone in the crowd here, and it will be told to everyone in the world in the coming days. Alleluia!

"Now, if you will not confess that you are a magician, let us go, with all this multitude, to your house, and then it will become evident who is the teller of truth."

Even before Peter has finished speaking, Simon starts to bombard him with curses and profanities. He tries to instigate a riot, hoping that it will obscure his refutation, and drive Peter to withdraw, making him look like the loser.

But Peter stands fast, and the crowd starts to reproach Simon more fervently.

After a few minutes, the people grow in indignation, and drive Simon from the courtyard, pushing him out the gate. Only one person follows him.

After the ruckus has subsided and calm reinstated, Peter speaks to the crowd: "Brothers and sisters, we must bear with wicked men patiently, knowing that although God could cut them off and cast them out, He permits them to remain until the day appointed, when judgment shall pass upon all. And as such is the way of God, we have to tolerate them in a loving fashion – we cannot allow ourselves to hate or loathe.

"If the wicked one had not found Simon to be his henchman, he would doubtless have found another – for it is of necessity that in this life transgressions will come. My friends, Simon is to be mourned over, because he has become a choice vessel for the wicked one, which undoubtedly would not have happened had he not received power over him for his former sins. Regretfully, at one time he was with us, and believed that souls were immortal.

"But now he is deluded by demons – persuaded that he has the soul of a murdered boy ministering to him in whatever act he pleases to employ it in. Sadly, there are some men very proficient in their crimes, who the wicked one is drawn to, such that once deceived, they will never revert and repent."

Then, Peter prays for the people, entreating them to repent and turn to the Lord. Looking towards heaven with tears in his eyes, he thanks God for His goodness, and asks for mercy on those who have come over to the faith this day.

Then, he dismisses the crowd, asking that they return the next morning for further instruction in the faith.

NOTES

1. Peter had no knowledge of modern psychology or neuro-science, so he did not dwell on the nuances at play here. All 'normal' people have the capability to learn, but not all at the same rate or in the same way. His point was that learning (not intelligence) was an acquired skill after birth and everyone could do it. But how and what they learned was a function of their inner nature as well as their upbringing and environment.

2. See Matthew 6:33.

3. Matthew 5:45

4. See Matthew 3:12.

5. Very often during his sermons, lectures, and teaching sessions with Jews familiar with the Old Testament Scriptures, Peter would refer to Jesus Christ as the 'True Prophet', the greatest of all the prophets from the past. It was thought that this would enable them to better relate to Jesus.

6. Matthew 6:33. Some translations say 'kingship over you' instead of 'righteousness'.

7. Once again, Simon is trying, through subterfuge, to get for himself the 'magic' power that he finds in the apostles.

6 FAREWELL TO CAESAREA

The following morning, while sitting around the breakfast table, Nicetas asks Peter, "How is it that Simon, who is the enemy of God, is able to do such marvelous things? For indeed he told no lie, in his declaration of what he has done."

And Peter says, "God's creation is based on the precept that no one can be good, unless they have inherently in their power, the ability to perceive how they can become good – that by their own intent, they can be what they choose to be. Otherwise, if they were kept in goodness by compulsion, and not by purposeful intention, they could not be truly good. Therefore, God has given to everyone the power of his own will, such that he can choose to be and do, what he wishes to be and do.

"This power of the will allows some people to choose good things and other people to choose evil things. Consequently, the human race is divided into two classes, those who are righteous and those who are not – the good and the bad. He has permitted each class to choose both a place and a king, as they wanted."

"But what is the reason that Simon, whose thoughts are against God, is able to do such great marvels?" asks Nicetas, still perplexed.

So, Peter goes into a long explanation of love, God's commandments, miracles, and truth. He finishes by talking about the ten important things:

THE TEN PAIRS

"In order that there might be a distinction between those who choose good and those who choose evil, God has concealed the beneficial rewards – the eternal possession of the kingdom of heaven – and has hidden it as a secret treasure. No one can easily attain it by his own power or knowledge. But a report of it, under various names and images, has been brought to the attention of all.

"Whoever is a lover of good, can ask He who has hidden it, to reveal the knowledge by which he can know it – and then pray that it might be given to him. This knowledge is only open to those who love God above all things in this world. In no other way can anyone understand it, however wise he may seem to be.

"He who perfectly loves the understanding of the kingdom of heaven, will undoubtedly cast away all practices of evil habit – neglect, sloth, malice, anger, and such like. Because, if you prefer any of these, loving the vices of your own lust more than God, you will not attain entrance into the heavenly kingdom. Truthfully, it is foolish to love anything, or anyone, more than God.

"Because of this distinction between the two choices, ten pairs of things have been prescribed as a test in this present age, corresponding to the ten plagues which were brought upon Egypt. For when Moses asked Pharaoh to let his people go, Pharaoh would not consent. And in spite of being shown ten heavenly signs, Pharaoh could not be brought to consent. He had freedom of will, and his own magicians seemed to do similar signs. He could believe that the signs brought by Moses were sent by God, or he could believe otherwise. He chose the latter, and the rest is history.[1]

"In a similar manner, I am now engaged with Simon. For when Moses pleaded with Pharaoh to believe in God, the magicians opposed him by pretending similar exhibitions, and so kept back the unbelievers from salvation. And now, when I have come forth to teach all nations to believe in the one true God, Simon the magician resists me, acting in opposition as the magicians did to Moses.

"Friends, God has not buried His truth deep in the earth, or heaped mountains upon it, such that it can only be found by those able to dig down deep. No - instead, He has surrounded the mountains and the earth with the expanse of heaven. He has veiled the truth only with the curtain of His love. Anyone can reach it, who has first knocked at the gate of divine love.

"As I have said before, God has created this world with things in pairs. Evil and good must always exist as a pair. And given to every person is the gift of judgment, regardless of intelligence, enabling him to freely decide one way or the other, at every step in life. He who decides to follow the evil path may work signs and wonders, but they are not useful for helping humanity to better find God. But he who decides to follow the good path, can work signs and wonders that <u>are</u> useful in helping humanity to better find God.

"So tell me, what is the use of making statues walk, stone dogs bark, mountains dance, or of flying through the air?[2] On the other hand, the signs of God are directed to be of help to people – like those which were done by our Lord, who gave sight to the blind and hearing to the deaf, cured the feeble and the lame, drove away sickness and demons, and raised the dead. Signs like these are for the benefit of people, and confer good in the world. Satan cannot do this, except at the time of the end of days."[3]

"Remember, I said that ten things have been prescribed as a test for discerning between good and evil. Indeed, there are also ten pairs of things which have been assigned to this world from the beginning of time, that are testimony to the conflict:

- Cain and Abel, the first pair after the 'Fall'
- The Nephilim – the giants – and Noah [4]
- Pharaoh and Abram (Abraham) in Egypt [5]
- Abimelech, the Philistine, and Isaac [6]
- Jacob and Esau
- Pharaoh's magicians and Moses, the lawgiver
- The Jewish traditionalists and Jesus, the Son of Man
- Simon and myself, Peter

- All the world's evangelists sent to preach the Word to those people in the unenlightened nations
- The Antichrist and the Christ

"The wise man so desires salvation of his soul, that he renounces all the affairs of the world, such that he can attend solely to the Word of God. He sells all that he has and buys the one true pearl.[7] He understands what the difference is between temporal and eternal, small and great, men and God. He understands that there is eternal hope when in the presence of the true and good God."

PETER RESOLVES TO FOLLOW SIMON

Later that morning, one of the disciples of Simon – the one who had followed him out from the debate – comes to the house in a wretched state. Groaning and moaning, he wails, "I beg you, Peter, have mercy on me – a fool who has been deceived by Simon the magician, to whom I pledged my loyalty by reason of the miracles which I saw him perform. But when I heard your discourses, I began to think that he might not be everything that he said. Nevertheless, when he left the debate, I alone followed him, for I had not yet clearly perceived his transgressions and irreverence.

"But when he saw me following him, he said that I was blessed, and led me to his house. Late in the evening, he said to me, 'I will make you better than all men, if you will remain with me until the end.' When I had promised him this, he demanded of me an oath of perseverance, which I gave to him. Then, he placed upon my shoulders two bags of secret things – things I now know to be illicit and accursed – that I might carry them for him. Then, he ordered me to follow him.

"When we came to the sea, he went aboard a boat that was docked there, and took the bags from me. A few minutes later, he emerged from the boat but had nothing with him. I thought that maybe he had thrown the stuff into the sea. Then he asked me to go with him on the boat, saying that he was going to Rome – and that once there, he would please the people so much, that they would

92

reckon him to be a god – and he would be publicly gifted with divine honors. He promised that if I then wished to return to Caesarea, he would send me back loaded with riches, slaves, and servants.

"When I heard all this, but saw nothing in him that would predict that any of this could actually happen, I surmised that he could only be a fraud. And so I answered, 'Pardon me, I pray you; for I have a terrible pain in my feet, and therefore I am not able to leave Caesarea. Besides, I have a wife and little children, who I cannot leave by themselves.'

"But when he heard this, he charged me with disloyalty, saying, 'You will be sorry when you hear about all the glory I will get in the city of Rome.' And after this, he set out in the boat – I know not where. But I decided to come back here straightaway and ask for forgiveness – and allow me to make atonement – because I have been deceived by Simon the sorcerer, and I am sorry."

By this time a large crowd has gathered in the courtyard, eager to hear more from Peter. And so, going out from the house, he stands in his usual place. But he asks that the man who has just returned from Simon, be seated close by. Motioning towards him, Peter begins his talk:

"Brothers and sisters, this man here has just come to me, telling me of the wicked practices of Simon, and how he has thrown the implements of his wickedness into the sea – not induced by repentance, but being afraid that his lawlessness will be detected, and he will be subjected to the public laws.

"And he asked this man to remain with him, promising him immense gifts. But when he could not persuade him to do so, he rebuked him and left him, setting out for another place, possibly Rome."

After Peter has said this to the crowd, the man himself stands up, and begins to tell the people everything he knows about Simon's crimes. The crowd is shocked by all the things they hear – things Simon had done by his magical acts.

Peter then says, "Be not distressed by these things that have been done, but give heed to the future – for what is passed is ended – but similar shocking works in the future are of great concern – they are dangerous to those unsuspecting souls who unwittingly fall for them. For sinful offences shall never be wanting in this world, as long as the devil is permitted to act according to his will.[8]

"As you have heard, Simon has gone forth to possess the ears of the Gentiles – who have been called to receive the faith. Consequently, it is necessary that I follow in his track, so that whatever heresies he may introduce, they can be properly rebuffed and the truth revealed.

"Therefore, in order that you may be more confirmed in the truth, and the people – or the nations – that are called to salvation may in no way be prevented by the wickedness of Simon, I have thought it good to ordain Zacchaeus as pastor over you. I will remain with you myself for 10-20 days, and then go after Simon. Otherwise, if I delay any longer, the crimes of Simon menacing in every direction, may become incurable."

That night, Peter assembles his core group of believers and announces, "I will soon be going forth to the Gentile nations that say there are many gods, to teach them about the one true God – the One who made heaven and earth, and everything on the earth – such that they may love Him and be saved.

"However, evil has anticipated me, and by the nature of the law of pairs, has sent Simon before me. He is telling them to disown the many gods on earth, and instead, to believe that there are many gods in heaven, he being the highest. Oh, the sacrilege of it! Oh, the poor souls who believe him and are fated to perish with eternal punishment!

"And what is dreadful, is that he forestalls me with slanders and persuades them with magic, warning them not even to listen to me. For he is afraid of being convicted of being himself – in reality a devil – and of having the truth of God and Christ be revealed. Therefore, I must quickly catch him, and confront him, lest his false accusations thoroughly influence the thinking of many people over time."

Zacchaeus Appointed Bishop

"Therefore, it is necessary to set apart someone to fill my place here in Caesarea. Let us all pray to God, that he who sits in the chair of Christ, may piously rule His Church. Who, then, shall be set apart?

"My friends, in matters of faith, the multitude of believers ought to follow one person, such that they can live in harmony and enjoy peace by means of good order.[9] To those who are thought worthy of eternal life, God appoints one universal King in the world, such that there may be unfailing peace. Therefore, it behooves all to follow someone as a leader, honoring him as the messenger of God – and the leader must be acquainted with the road that enters into the holy city.

"Of those who are present, I must choose Zacchaeus, to whom the Lord called and rested with,[10] judging him worthy to be saved."

And having said this, he lays his hand upon Zacchaeus, who is standing near, and urges him to sit down in his own chair. But Zacchaeus falls at his feet, and begs that he be permitted to decline the office.

"Whatever the ruler is supposed to do, I will do," he says, "but please do not give me this title. For I am afraid of assuming the title of rulership, as it teems with bitter envy and danger."

But Peter laughs and says, "Do not be afraid. You are not the ruler, but an 'Appointed One', the Lord having permitted you to be called this when He said, 'Blessed is the man who the Lord shall appoint to the ministry of his fellow-servants.'[11] You are not to rule as the ruler of a nation, but as a servant ministering to the needy, as a father to the oppressed; visiting them as a physician and guarding them as a shepherd – in short, taking care of everything needed for their salvation.

"Now consider this: In proportion to the work involved, and danger in ruling the church of Christ, so much greater is the reward. Knowing that you are the best instructed of my disciples, I pray that you use those noble powers of judging, which you have been entrusted with by the Lord – and that you may be saluted with 'Well done, good and faithful servant'.[12] The people are aware of the danger they incur by disobedience to you – because whoever disobeys your instructions, disobeys Christ; and he who disobeys Christ offends God."

Peter then goes on at length to talk about the duties of the church officials, the sanctity of marriage, the love of neighbors and community, and the various responsibilities of 'Christian' believers.

Having spoken this, Peter places his hand on the head of Zacchaeus, and says, "O Ruler and Lord of all, God and Father, I pray that You watch after this shepherd with his flock. You are the power, the helper, the physician, the savior, the life, the hope, the refuge, the joy, and the comfort. You are all things to us, and can do all things. For You are the Ruler of rulers, the Lord of lords, the King of kings.[13] I pray that You give power to the bishop to loosen what ought to be loosened, and to bind what ought to be bound.[14] Make him wise, O Lord. And by his name, protect the church of Christ. For You are eternal glory. Praise be to the Father, and to the Son, and to the Holy Spirit for all ages. Amen."

Twelve Sent on Ahead

Then, Peter proceeds to ordain 12 presbyters and four deacons, and says further, that in the next few days he will baptize all those who wish it and are prepared. "Whoever has the will and desire, let him come to Zacchaeus and give his name – let him hear the mysteries of the kingdom of heaven – let him attend to frequent fasting and approve himself in all things – and at the end of this time, he may be baptized in ever flowing waters, with the name of the Triune Beatitude being invoked over him [15]– anointed with oil and sanctified by prayer – such that once being consecrated by these things, he may partake of the body and blood of Christ."[16]

Peter then dismisses the people, and retires to his reading room accompanied by his 12 core disciples. "My brothers, let us consider what is right – it is our duty to bring the 'Good News' to the Gentile nations, who are called to salvation. Now, you have heard that Simon has already set out, wishing to anticipate our journey. We must follow him step-by-step, such that wherever he tries to subvert any souls, we might immediately confront and refute him. However, I think it right that I should remain here awhile with those in this city, who have been turned to Christ, and strengthen them. But I cannot neglect those who are still afar off – they could become infected with the power of pernicious doctrine, and become more difficult to recover."

Peter then suggests some substitutions:

- Benjamin, the son of Saba, for Zacchaeus
- Ananias, the son of Safra, for Clement
- Rubelus, the brother of Zacchaeus, for Nicetas
- Zacharias, the builder, for Aquila

"I wish for you to proceed to the Gentiles the day after tomorrow – follow secretly in the footsteps of Simon, and inform me of all his activities. Also, inquire quietly into the sentiments of the local people, and tell them that I shall come to them shortly."

Then, all of the gathered applaud him, saying, "We approve your pious judgment, and will fulfill the task as you think best."

On the morning of the day appointed, the 12 disciples stand before Peter, and collectively say, "We set out now, as you have asked of us. But we shall always retain in our hearts the remembrance of you. May God be with you and with us all."

Then, after pouring out a prayer to the Lord for them, Peter dismisses the 12 and walks out to the courtyard. A large number of people have come, all gazing upon him with tears – because they have heard that he was going to leave them on account of Simon. Seeing them weeping, Peter is emotionally affected, although he tries to conceal and restrain his tears. He has great affection for the people. But the trembling of his voice, and the cracking of his speech, betray his composure.

Rubbing his forehead and eyes, he mutters softly, "Be of good courage, my friends. Comfort your sorrowful hearts with good counsel, referring all things to God, whose will alone is to be preferred in all things. As friends of God, acquiesce to His will, but also judge yourselves on what is right. Above all, let us see to it that we do not, by an unreasonable affection, accomplish the will of the wicked one."

Over the next few days, Peter spends his time teaching and comforting – and when the last day of the Festival of Lights arrives,[17] upwards of ten thousand people are baptized.

Farewell to Caesarea

A few weeks later, a letter comes to Peter from the 12 advance scouts, stating that Simon has arrived in Tyre,[18] not Rome, and has set up his heretical movement there. It details the crimes of Simon – how going from city to city he was deceiving multitudes, and everywhere maligning Peter – so that, should he come there, no one would listen to him. He was saying that Peter was a magician, a godless man, injurious, cunning, ignorant, and professing ridiculous things. And he was proclaiming that Peter was teaching the crazy notion that the dead will rise again like zombies.

The letter reveals that if anyone attempted to confront Simon, he would be cut off by secret snares set up by his attendants. Furthermore, Simon was declaring the following lie to everyone in public: "After I had vanquished him in the debate, I fled out of fear of his sinister traps – lest he should destroy me by incantations, or arrange my death through deceptive machinations."

The letter also notes that he was staying in Tripolis,[19] the nearby port, and might be found there.

The letter is grim and Peter is saddened. But he orders the letter to be read to the people. After the reading, he addresses them, telling them to keep the principles of the faith and to obey Zacchaeus, the new bishop. He commends the presbyters and deacons, and then announces that he will spend the winter in Tripolis. After concluding with a benediction, he retires to the house for rest and meditation.

After a few hours, Peter summons Clement, Nicetas, and Aquila, and says to them, "I am going to set out for Tyre in seven days, but I wish for you to go there first thing tomorrow morning. You can stay secretly with Bernice the Canaanite, the daughter of Justa, who is with us. Learn from her whatever you can about Simon, and accurately write back to me what is going on. This is very important, so that I can prepare myself accordingly. Therefore, depart as soon as possible, and go in peace with my blessings."

And so early the next morning, Clement, Nicetas, and Aquila, leave Caesarea and head off to Tyre, as directed by Peter.

Seven days later, Peter sets out from Caesarea with his family and some faithful men who had resolved to accompany him.

The Letter to James

Having an excellent memory, a sharp mind, philosophical background, and skill in scripting, Clement had been asked by Peter to commit to writing whatever seemed worthy of record, and to send it to James in Jerusalem. Therefore, during the three months spent at Caesarea, whatever Peter spoke to the people in the daytime, and explained more fully in the evening, was carefully documented by Clement, and then sent off to James.

NOTES

1. Pharaoh ought to have understood that his subjects were not workers of truth, because they were called 'magicians' and not 'messengers of God'. Moreover, they seemed to maintain the contest only up to a certain point – afterwards, they confessed their limitations and yielded to their superior. This should have made Pharaoh realize the truth of the situation. But it didn't – he had the free will to resist, and he did. Eventually, the last plague was inflicted, the destruction of the first-born. Moses is then commanded to consecrate the people by the sprinkling of animal blood over their doorways – so enabling death to pass over the Jews. The Passover celebration commemorates this event. Reference: Exodus 8:19 and Exodus 12.

2. Peter is referring to the magic tricks performed by Simon.

3. At the end of the world, it will be permitted for Satan to go beyond his bounds – to mix up his fruitless signs with some good signs, such as the expelling of demons or the healing of disease. In this way, he will become divided and fight against himself. And in the end, he will be destroyed. Therefore, the Lord has warned that in the last days there will be such temptation. Even the good may be confused by this deception. This is sometimes associated with the second of the two beasts from the sea in Revelation 13 – the pseudo-lamb which speaks with Satan's voice. Some interpret this as state-sanctioned, state-dominated religion – a false prophet mimicking the real thing and misdirecting people's worship. Reference: Revelation 13:11-17.

4. The ancient Book of Jubilees narrates the genesis of angels on the first day of Creation, and the story of how a group of fallen angels mated with mortal humans, giving rise to a race of giants known as the Nephilim, and then to their descendants, the Elioud. The 'mortal humans' are considered to be the impious children of Cain. Their hybrid children, the Nephilim, in existence during the time of Noah, were wiped out by the great flood. However, God allowed ten percent of the disembodied spirits of the Nephilim to try to lead mankind astray after the flood.

5. The story of Abram's deceit – saying to the Egyptians that his wife Sarai was his sister – is told in Genesis 12:10-20.

6. The story of Isaac's deceit – saying to the Philistines that his wife Rebekah was his sister – is told in Genesis 26:1-11.

7. Matthew 13:46

8. Matthew 18:7 and Luke 17:1

9. Peter is proclaiming the foundations of the diocese, the bishopric, and even the papacy.

10. Luke 19:5

11. A related parable exists in Luke 12:42-48.

12. Refer to Matthew 25:21, from the Parable of the Silver Pieces. Some translations say 'industrious and reliable' instead of 'good and faithful'.

13. Reference: 1 Timothy 6:15, Revelation 17:14, and Revelation 19:16

14. Matthew 16:19

15. A reference to the Trinity – Father, Son, and Holy Spirit.

16. The Sacrament of Holy Eucharist, or Holy Communion in Protestant faiths

17. The Jewish eight-day Festival of Lights (Hanukkah, meaning 'Dedication') commemorates the cleansing of the temple, erection of a new altar, and reconsecration of the sanctuary, after Judas Maccabeus recaptured Jerusalem from the Greco-Syrian king Antiochus IV Epiphanes in 165 BC. Its distinguishing ceremony is the lighting of candles each evening, commemorating the rededication of the temple to the worship of the one God.

18. Tyre is on the Mediterranean Sea coast, about 137 miles north of Caesarea, in modern day Lebanon.

19. Tripolis was the maritime district in ancient Phoenicia, the commercial center of the confederation of Tyre, Sidon, and Aradus. Over time, it evolved to become the present Lebanese city of Tripoli.

7 ON THE WAY TO TRIPOLIS

Clement, Nicetas, and Aquila, arrive in Tyre, in Phoenicia, and according to the directions of Peter, obtain lodging with Bernice, the daughter of Justa. She receives them most gracefully, and Clement explains the reason for the visit.

"We understand that Simon the magician, being worsted in the debate with our lord Peter, has hastened here, and is already doing much mischief. He is slandering Peter, in opposition to the truth, and stealing away the souls of many people. He is a magician in reality, but he calls Peter a magician – he is a deceiver in reality, but he calls Peter a deceiver. And although in the debate he was beaten in all points, and fled in disgrace, he lies and says that he was victorious. And he is telling the people that they should not listen to Peter, for their own sake; else they be tricked by a terrible magician.

"Therefore, Peter has sent us to investigate the doings of Simon, and inform him of what we find, such that when he arrives, he can convict him face-to-face of the accusations he has made."

"These things are indeed as you have heard," says Bernice, "and I will tell you other things about this Simon, that you probably don't know.

"He astonishes the whole city every day, by making phantoms and ghosts appear in the midst of the market-place. When he walks around, statues move – and shadows go before him, which he says are souls of the dead.

"Many who have tried to prove him an impostor, have been speedily convinced otherwise. And once, under pretense of a banquet, he killed an ox, and gave it to them to eat. But it infected them with various diseases, and subjected them to demons.

"In a word, having injured many, and being believed to be a god, he is both feared and honored. I don't think anyone will be able to quench such a fire as has been kindled. No one doubts his promises, but everyone affirms the danger.

"Therefore, I advise you not to attempt anything against Simon until Peter arrives. He alone can resist such a power, being the most esteemed disciple of our Lord Jesus Christ. So much do I fear this man, that if he had not been overcome in debate with our lord Peter, I would counsel you to persuade even Peter himself not to attempt to oppose Simon."

Then, as evening had come on, they all take supper and retire for the night.

THE FLIGHT OF SIMON

In the morning, one of Bernice's friends comes and tells them that Simon, learning of Peter's imminent arrival, has departed in the night for Sidon – and that he has left in town three distinguished scholars as his defenders: Appion Pleistonices of Alexandria, an orator and friend of Clement's father, Annubion of Diospolis in Thrace, the astrologer, and Athenodorus of Athens, student of the doctrine of Epicurus.[1]

A few hours later, Appion, Annubion, Athenodorus, and 13 other men arrive at Bernice's house, their intent being to convince Clement, Nicetas, and Aquila of their erroneous ways.

The trio engage in debate with Appion, and all his partners, over the course of the next week. They discuss a wide range of philosophical topics, mostly revolving around morality and the sinful nature of the pagan gods.

But after many days of heated debate, no minds are changed or actions altered. Everything is as it was before – Appion's mission has partly failed, but at least he has delayed the three men from following Simon. However, it has become readily apparent that Appion hates the Jewish people. He has written many books against them, and has formed a friendship with Simon, not through desire of learning, but because he knows that he is a Samaritan and also a hater of Jews. He thinks that he might be able to learn something from Simon that he can use against the Jews in his philosophical arguments.

At the conclusion of all the discussions, Appion expresses his feelings:

"Ever since I heard that you were consorting with Jews, I knew that it would corrupt your judgment. For it has been well said by scholars that 'evil communications corrupt good manners.' "

To which Clement replies, "And also, my friend, it is said that good communications can correct evil manners."

THE TRAVELS OF PETER

Having set out from Caesarea on the way to Tyre, Peter's entourage make their first stop at a small town called Dora, because it is not far distant. Almost all the people from the area who had become believers because of the preaching of Peter, can scarcely bear to be separated from him – they walk along with his group, again and again gazing upon him, again and again embracing him, and again and again conversing with him, until they come to the inn, where Peter spends the night.

The following day, he arrives in Ptolemais, and stays ten days. After a considerable number have received the Word of God, Peter indicates that, if they wish, they can follow him to Tyre for further instruction.

In Tyre

Arriving in Tyre, he is met at the city gates by Clement, Nicetas, and Aquila – and they fill him in on what they have learned about Simon – his slanders, magic tricks, and the sickness brought about (from which no one was cured) – and their steered discourses with

Appion. Knowing now that Simon has already fled to Sidon, Peter decides not to linger in Tyre, and instead, to quickly move on to Sidon in pursuit. But he relents to staying on a few days to preach to the anticipated crowds, and warn them about Simon.

The next morning, a great many of the residents of Tyre gather outside, and someone shouts, "May God, through you, have mercy upon us; and God through you heal us!" So, Peter stands on a big stone and greets them in a godly manner.

He tells them that Simon has been given authority by Satan to do evil things to people who do not do things pleasing to God, such as sinning or not worshipping the one true God. But if they repent of their evil ways, and do those things pleasing to God, they may recover their health and save their souls. Then, he heals many in the crowd before retiring.

After a few days of teaching and healing, many people repent their sins and are baptized. And when the citizens of Sidon hear about the marvelous words and deeds, they immediately send word inviting him to come to Sidon.

So, after founding a church in Tyre, and setting up one of his followers as bishop, Peter departs Tyre for Sidon. But when Simon hears that Peter is coming, he straightway flees to Berytus,[2] a suburb of Laodicea, with Appion and his companions.

In Sidon

As Peter enters Sidon, many people follow along with him, and upon arriving at the inn, they sit down on the ground – many on couches – and beg him for healing.

But Peter says, "Do not think, I pray you, that I can work healing miracles for all maladies, for I am only a mortal man, myself subject to many evils. But I shall not refuse to show you the way in which you must be saved. For I have learned from the Prophet of truth – from Jesus the Christ – the conditions that have been pre-ordained by God before the foundation of the world. That is, the evil deeds that if men do, they will be injured by the prince of evil – and in like manner, the good deeds that if men do, they will have their bodies made whole, and their souls established in safety.

"Knowing then these good and evil deeds, I tell you that there are two paths, by which travelers on this earth are lost or saved. The path of the lost is wide and smooth – it ruins them without troubling them. But the path of the saved is narrow and rugged – in the end it saves those who have journeyed through it.[3] And these two paths are presided over by unbelief and belief. Those who journey on the path of unbelief, have preferred near-term pleasure over long-term happiness – they have forgotten about the day of judgment, doing that which is not pleasing to God, and not caring to save their souls by His Word.

"He who does wrong in his pursuit of what is right, will be saved after being slightly punished.[4] But he who has not resolved to pursue what is right, even though he has done many good deeds, will be severely punished.

"To pursue what is right, you must worship the one true God only, trust in Jesus Christ, the Prophet of truth, and be born again through baptism by saving water,[5] for the remission of your sins. In addition, you should not eat food offered to idols,[6] be sober-minded, and refrain from all wrongdoing while given to good works. With this in mind, you can ask our all-powerful God for everlasting life through prayer and continual supplication."

Such is Peter's counsel to the people of Sidon. In the following days many repent, believe, and are healed. A church is founded, and one of his followers is set up as bishop. Then, Peter leaves Sidon to head for Berytus in pursuit of Simon.

In Berytus

No sooner has Peter reached Berytus, than an earthquake rattles the town. People are frenzied and scurrying about in fright. A large group run up to Peter, pleading with him to help them. "Help us Peter – stop the trembling – we are afraid that we will all perish," they cry.

But just then, Simon and his companions see the fearful crowd beseeching Peter for help, and they shout out, "Run away, friends, from this man! He is a magician and conjurer! It is he who has caused this earthquake! Furthermore, he has sent diseases to terrify us, as if he were God Himself." And many other such false charges are brought against Peter by Simon and his friends.

But Peter quells the multitude, and with surprising boldness and a little sarcasm, says to them, "Friends, I admit that I can do all these things that Simon and his cohorts have charged me of – what's more, I am ready to overturn your city from top to bottom if you do not believe what I have to say to you."

Shaking with fear, the people promise to do whatever he should command. And so Peter continues, "Then let none of you talk with these sorcerers, or have anything to do with them anymore."

When the bulk of the people hear this concise command, they promptly pick up sticks and stones, and chase Simon and his friends until they have driven them completely out of town. And those who are sick or possessed with devils, cast themselves down at Peter's feet.

Touched by all this, and desiring to free them from their torment, he says to them, "Even if I could cause earthquakes and do everything else that I wanted – which I can't – I assure you that I would not destroy Simon and his compatriots. For I am not here to demolish them, but to have them as friends, so that they may no longer slander against my preaching of the truth, and hindering the salvation of many.

"But, believe this: Simon is himself a magician and a slanderer. He is a minister of evil to those who know not the truth. Therefore, he has the power to bring diseases on sinners, and even to have them aid him in his exercise of power over them.

"But I am a servant of the one true God, the Creator of all things – and a disciple of His true Prophet Jesus Christ. Being His apostle, I preach the truth and drive away disease.

"I tell you now that you were stricken with disease by that evil magician called Simon, because you strayed away from the ways of God. But, if you listen to me here, and believe in my Lord and my God, you will be cured. Then, you will be able to turn to good works, and have your souls saved."

As Peter says these words, many people fall on their knees before his feet. Lifting up his hands to heaven, and praying to God sincerely, many are healed just by his simple prayer.

Peter stays only a few days because Simon has fled to Byblos, a nearby town. And after his usual teaching, healing, and baptizing sessions – and setting up a church with a bishop – he leaves for Byblos in pursuit.

In Byblos

When Peter arrives in Byblos, he learns that Simon has not even stayed there a single day, but has straightway headed for Tripolis. So, after spending a few days healing and teaching the people in the Word of God, he follows in Simon's footsteps to Tripolis, determined to track him down and repudiate his heresy in public. But a great number of people are now trailing his movements, hoping to receive healing or to learn about God.

NOTES

1. Epicurus was a Greek philosopher (341-270 BC), notable for his belief in the atomistic theory of physics, but was especially celebrated for his ethical teaching, which gave him the reputation as a savior of souls. He believed that there was no life after death, since the soul, on leaving the body was immediately dissolved into the primordial atoms of which it was made.

2. Also known as Laodicea in Canaan, Berytus was a center of Roman presence in the eastern Mediterranean. Modern-day Beirut, Lebanon, was founded on the site, where ancient Roman ruins can still be found.

3. Reference Matthew 7:13-14. The wide path is referred to as 'smooth stones' in Sirach 21:10.

4. A clear reference to Purgatory.

5. Peter rarely used the term 'born again', but here he did. Reference John 3:3-8. In some translations, 'born again' is written as 'begotten from above'.

6. This included food from dead animal carcasses, from animals which had been suffocated or caught by wild beasts, and from blood.

8 IN TRIPOLIS

Upon arrival in Tripolis, Peter and his group are met at the city gates by the 12 who had been sent ahead, and taken to various lodgings that had been prepared. When they come to the house of Maro,[1] where preparation had been made for Peter, a great assemblage of people gather in front of the house, clamoring to see Peter. So, he turns to the crowd, and tells them that he will address them the day after tomorrow, because he is too exhausted from his trip. The people leave quietly, murmuring with anticipation.

Later that evening, Clement, Nicetas, and Aquila come to the house from their nearby accommodation, and the group of disciples now numbers 16. The 12 scouts explain everything that they have learned about the proceedings of Simon, and the state of things in the city. Likewise, Peter explains what has happened on their travels. And after the fellowship and a light meal, everyone retires for the night.

IN THE GARDEN OF MARO

The next morning, some family members come to Peter and announce that crowds were already gathering outside the front gate, even though Peter had asked for another day delay. They are standing impatiently, pressing on the gate and fence, and conversing among themselves, hoping to be able to see him before the next day. And as the morning wears on, the multitude increases, as does their exuberance and expectations.

So, Peter feels obligated to address the crowd. He stands on a rock in the center of the yard, such that all may see him, and starts to greet them in a welcoming and devout manner.

Pandemonium

But suddenly, the throng of people in their enthusiasm, break through the gate. Many who are distressed by demons or afflicted with long-standing sicknesses, are shrieking with lamentation, and throw themselves on the ground, begging for healing. More keep coming and the situation starts to become chaotic. Peter retreats to the back corner of the garden and stands on the base of a broken statue. The disciples fear for his safety and form a human chain around him.

But Peter waves his arms and calms the people, rebukes the demons, comforts the sick, and restores order. Then, at his command, the demons flee and the sick revive. He motions his hand, beckoning for stillness, and the crowd becomes tranquil and settled. With that attained, he addresses the people:

Peter Addresses the Crowd

"God, who created the heavens and the whole universe, does not have a time frame for salvation. Therefore, let no one who is suffering from evil afflictions, rashly charge Him with laxity or neglect. For people do not know all the causes and issues behind those things that happen to them – they just think that it is evil. But God knows all the causes and issues.

"So it is in the case of Simon. He is a power of the left hand of God, and has authority to do harm to those who do not know God. That's why he has been able to involve you in sickness and disease. But by these very ills, which have been permitted to come upon you by the providence of God, you are driven to seek Him, hoping to find cures for the body. But, if you submit to the will of God, you may have your souls as well as your bodies restored to a healthy state.

"Now, I have been told, that after sacrificing an ox, Simon celebrated with you in the great town square. And being carried away with much meat and wine, you made friends with evil demons. In this way, many of you were seized by sicknesses and trouble. For the demons would never have had power over you, if you had not first dined with the devil.

"For a law has been imposed from the beginning by God, the Creator of all things – that on each of the two princes, seated at His right hand and at His left hand, neither can have the power to benefit or hurt anyone, unless he has first sat down at the same table with them.[2]

"Therefore, when you consume meat and wine that has been offered to idols, you become servants to the prince of evil. In like manner, if you cease from these things, and seek refuge with the prince of good – honoring Him without sacrifices – then your bodies will be healed and your souls will become healthy. For only God can both destroy and raise up the fallen.

"Know now, that you have been deceived by the one called Simon – you have become dead in your souls to God, and sick in your bodies. But now, if you repent, and submit to those things that are well-pleasing to God, you may get new strength to your bodies, and recover your soul's health.

"So listen up, here is what is well-pleasing to God:

- pray to Him and ask for forgiveness
- abstain from sitting at the table with devils [3]
  - abstain from eating food offered to idols
  - abstain from tasting dead flesh
  - abstain from drinking blood
- wash yourself from all pollution [4]
- be minded to do for your neighbor those good things that you wish he would do for you
- do not commit murder
- do not commit adultery, since you would not like your wife to be seduced by another
- do not steal, since you would not like your things to be stolen

"Friends, by understanding what is reasonable, and then properly acting on it, you will become dear to God – your soul and body will be healed. Otherwise, your body will be tormented in life, and your soul will be punished in the afterlife.

"With better understanding you can resist those things that you should not rightly desire, and the hope of immortal blessings may be restored to you. For the demons know if a person has given himself up to God. So, I say to you, the weakest believer is more powerful than the strongest demon.

"When Satan, the prince of darkness, tempted the Christ and King of Peace, by promising Him all the glory of the world, if only He would worship him as His god, our Lord promptly rebuked him, confirming the worship of only one God, by saying:

Away with you Satan! Scripture has it: 'You shall do homage to the Lord your God; Him alone shall you adore' [5]

"Terrified by this answer – fearing that belief in the one and only true God would be re-established on earth – Satan quickly moved to send false prophets, false apostles, and false teachers into this world – like Simon – who would speak as if in the name of Christ, but in reality, would accomplish the will of the devil.

"Therefore, observe the greatest caution – believe no teacher or wise-man, unless he brings testimony from James, the Lord's brother, or his successor. For no one, unless he has gone to Jerusalem, and been approved as a fit and faithful teacher for preaching the Word of Christ, should be heard or received by you.

"For there is only one true Prophet – and His words are the words we twelve apostles preach."

When Peter finishes speaking, he invites the people to come back to the same place in good time on the morrow. Then, he dismisses the crowd and they depart reluctantly, but happy. After dinner and prayers, he talks a little about the Lord's miracles to the disciples, and then retires for the night.

Four Days of Preaching and Healing

The next morning, some friends of Maro come to Peter and announce that Simon, when he heard of Peter's arrival, had departed in the middle of the night, for Antioch, in Syria. They also note that a large crowd has gathered in front of the garden, anticipating Peter's appearance.

And so, without blinking an eye, Peter goes out to speak to the people with tenderness and concern, but also with determination and spunk:

"As you know, ages ago there was a great flood, and God destroyed by water all the sinful people of old. But having found one man alone who was God-fearing and pious, caused him to be saved in an ark, with his three sons and their wives. This illustrates that the wickedness of a great multitude can still be punished by God, but the goodness of even one will be rewarded with salvation. Therefore, the greatest sin of all is forsaking the one God of the universe, and worshipping many idols, who are not gods, as if they were gods. This sin can destroy you all.

"Just as land that is neglected by the cultivator necessarily produces weeds and thistles, so also is it with religious belief. Faith that has been long neglected, produces a plentiful crop of noxious opinions on the nature of things and on the views of false science. There is now a great need to cultivate the field of your mind with the word of truth. Render obedience to it, and ignore superfluous yearnings and anxieties, lest a noxious growth choke off the good seed of the Word.

"Yes, a short and earnest diligence can sometimes repair a long time's neglect. Indeed, the time of every one's life is uncertain, and therefore we must hasten to salvation – for unhappily, sudden death may seize upon him who delays."

Then, Peter embarks on a long and all-encompassing sermon that mesmerizes the crowd, as well as the disciples. The sermon lasts four days, and every day more people come to listen. He discusses all the topics he has previously talked about, plus new material. He covers the understanding of demons, the folly of idolatry, desires of the flesh, temptations of the devil, the importance of baptism, and the immortality of the soul. He explains the concepts of evil, sin, suffering, ignorance, knowledge, faith, salvation, morality, and free-will. And he preaches about Jesus, the Savior and true Prophet, the two kingdoms, the creation of the world, the call of the Gentiles, the invisible God, the 'Golden Rule',[6] and much, much more.

Each evening after the preaching session, he asks that those who are taken with diseases or possessed by demons, be brought to him. And then, by laying his hands upon them and praying to God, he immediately heals and comforts them, while reminding them to seek out the love and mercy of the Lord through piety and good works. Both those who are cured, and those who look on in wonderment, are amazed and blessed – they rejoice and turn to God with firm conviction and new hope.

***

The transformation of Peter, from a peasant fisherman to the world's foremost evangelizer, is complete. He is now, truly, the 'Rock of the Church',[7] and will continue to be so until his death.

***

Peter and his entourage stay in Tripolis for three months. A great many people are baptized in the natural springs that are near to the sea, Maro is ordained bishop of the local church, and presbyters and deacons are appointed.

The evening before his departure, Peter speaks to his disciples and the new elders of the church:

"Our Lord and Savior, who has sent me here, declared that the devil Satan, after having tempted Him for 40 days without success,[8] promised that he would send out agents from among his subjects, their purpose being to deceive mankind. Therefore, above all else, remember to shun any teacher, apostle, or prophet who does not come with the blessing of the bishop of the church in Jerusalem. Otherwise, the agents of Satan could prevail and cause many to lose their faith and their salvation. In such a manner, Simon has been sent upon us, preaching in the name of God, under the façade of truth, and sowing error and turmoil everywhere. The Lord predicted this when He said:

Be on your guard against false prophets, who come to you in sheep's clothing, but underneath are wolves on the prowl. You will know them by their deeds.[9]

Having spoken these words, Peter selects a few good men and asks them to go to Antioch as spies, requesting that they learn whatever they can about Simon – his deeds and his whereabouts.

The next day, he bids farewell to the believers in Tripolis, and starts out on the trip to Antioch, accompanied by his core disciples, family, close friends, and ardent followers.

NOTES

1. Also called Maroones

2. This, of course, is a metaphor for giving in to carnal impulses that are driven by the devil.

3. This includes abstaining from food offered to idols, from dead carcasses, from animals which have been suffocated or caught by wild beasts, and from blood.

4. This includes washing after sexual relations, and women keeping the Mosaic law of purification (refer to Leviticus 12:1-8 for the details on women's purification after childbirth).

5. Jesus' temptation in the desert – Reference: Matthew 4:10 and Luke 4:8. Also see Deuteronomy 6:13.

6. "Treat others the way you would have them treat you". This counsel for living was repeated multiple times by Christ. One of the first principles of moral law, the 'Golden Rule' was also known to Aristotle, Confucius, and Plato.

7. Matthew 16:18

8. Mark 1:12-13; Luke 4:1-13

9. Matthew 7:15-16

9 ON THE WAY TO LAODICEA

After leaving Tripolis, Peter with his family and followers make their first stop at Ortosias, not too distant, where they spend the night. The next day, they move on to Antaradus. And many people from Tripolis, and the surrounding areas, follow him. Peter asks Nicetas and Aquila to go on ahead with half of the followers, so that the large crowd won't be met with resentment.

"Lead the way to Laodicea," he says, "and after two or three days, I will overtake you. And you alone should meet us at the city gates of the next place, so that we may enter along with you without causing any tumult. By following this plan, we should be able to enter every city of the Gentiles travelling in two smaller groups, rather than in one large group. Others can go forward in your place, by turns, to the towns and cities beyond, and arrange for lodgings accordingly."

After listening to all his sermons and discourses, and transcribing them on paper, Clement is so enamored with Peter, that he offers himself as a servant. But Peter shakes off the suggestion, saying:

"I have no wardrobe of splendid clothes, and I don't partake of gourmet meals. I lead a simple life, eating mostly just bread and olives, with some herbs from the garden. My dress is what you see, a shirt and an overcoat. Having these, I require nothing more – present and visible things don't delight me much. That is because my mind is not occupied with things in the present, but instead with things eternal. You see, my brother Andrew and I grew up from our childhood as orphans, extremely poor, and no strangers to hard work. As a result,

119

I can bear up with the fatigues of our journeys. So, rather you being my servant, I should more readily discharge the duty of a servant to you."

Clement is overawed by Peter's humility and says, "I give thanks to the providence of God, because I have merited to have you as my teacher instead of my natural parents."

And Peter will consider Clement to be his protégé for the rest of his life.

That evening, one of the followers suggests that they all take a day-off tomorrow to visit a close-by island called Aradus, so as to see the great curiosity there – a very old temple museum with enormous columns of petrified wood, like glass, at the entrance, and sculpted statues and paintings by the renown Greek artist Phidias inside.[1]

EXCURSION TO ARADUS

The next morning, a large group of people, divided into two smaller groups, takes a ferry boat to the island and slowly makes their way to the tourist site to see the marvels. They all go inside the museum except Peter.

The Beggar Woman

After admiring the columns, but not going inside, Peter notices a poor straggly woman begging for handouts near the entrance. Looking earnestly at her, he says, "Tell me, woman, what part of your body is so deficient, that you subject yourself to the indignity of begging for alms? Can you not work with the hands that God has given you, and thereby procure your daily food?"

"I wish that I had hands able to work!" groaned the woman. "But now they just look like hands, because they have been rendered feeble and without feeling by an old injury and overwork."[2]

"What is the cause of your suffering so terribly?" asks Peter.

And she answers, "Weakness of soul – want of courage – nothing more. For if I had any bravery in me, I would have thrown myself off a precipice, or drowned myself in the sea, thereby ending my grief."

Then, Peter says, "Do you think, my dear woman, that those who kill themselves are set free from torments? No, I tell you – that is not true. The souls of those who die by suicide are instead punished with an even worse torment in Hades."

"I wish that I could be sure that souls live in Hades," she says, "for I would gladly embrace the suffering of the penalty of suicide, if only I could see my darling children but for an hour."

"What is it that grieves you with such a heavy sadness?" says Peter. "If you tell me the cause, I might be able to prove to you that souls do live in Hades and the nether regions – and instead of the precipice, I could give you a remedy that would enable you to end your life without torment."[3]

Feeling the need to vent, the poor woman begins to tell her sorry story to Peter: "My name is Macidiana. Being born of noble parents, and having become the wife of a suitably powerful man, I had two twin sons, and then one more son after them."

She notices that Peter is listening intently, and so she continues with the whole story of why she had to leave Rome, the boarding of a ship, the shipwreck, the loss of her sons, her rescue on the rocks, and her friendship with another troubled widow. Then she continues, "Eventually, my hands became powerless, and she who had taken me in, fell to the palsy and now lies in bed. No one would come to our aid – we are both helpless. So now I sit here begging – and when I get anything, one meal serves two wretches.

"Now that you have heard enough of my affairs, fulfill your promise, and give me a remedy, by which both of us may end our miserable lives without pain and suffering."

After a few seconds of suspicious reflection, Peter says to her, "Please tell me the names of your children, and then I will give you the remedy."

And after hearing the names Faustinus and Faustus, he says, "Aha! I wondered if this might be a special day, thinking that you might be a certain person, whose affairs I have heard about."

To which she moans, "Tell me Sir, what woman could possibly be more wretched than myself?"

Moved with compassion, Peter replies, "There is a young man among those who follow me for the sake of understanding and faith, a Roman citizen, who told me that he had a father and mother and two twin brothers, of whom not one is left to him." After relating the full story told to him by Clement, he says, "And his father set out to search for his lost wife and sons, but he was also lost."

After hearing this from Peter and overcome by emotion, the woman swoons away and faints. But Peter catches hold of her, calms her down, and persuades her to confess what is troubling her. Being powerless in the rest of her body, as if intoxicated, she slowly turns her head, recovers her breath, wipes her brow, and appears in a state of euphoria. Finally, she manages to mumble, "Is he here, the youth of whom you speak?"

Now realizing the full implications of the affair, Peter says, "Tell me first who you are and his name, or else you shall not see him."

And then she says, "I am the mother of the youth. His name is Clement."

"Yes, it is he, and he is here now at the boat dock," replies Peter.

Seemingly in a stupor, the woman then falls down at Peter's feet and unabashedly begs him to bring her to the young man.

"I will do so," Peter assures her, "if you promise me to remain composed until we leave the island together."

To which she answers, "Sir, I will do anything – only show me my only son – for I think that I may also see in him the memory of my other two children who died here."

The First Miracles

Taking her hand, Peter leads her to the boat. Once there, upon seeing the pair maneuvering carefully to step from the dock to the boat, Clement offers his hand to help the woman. But as soon as he touches her hand, she utters a loud motherly shout, rushes into his embrace, and begins to devour him with a mother's kisses. But, being ignorant of the whole matter, Clement shakes her off as a mad woman, and she falls down.

But Peter speaks up and says, "Hey, what are you doing, my son Clement, pushing off your real mother?"

As soon as he hears these words and recognizes the familiar countenance, Clement falls down next to her, bathed in tears, and begins to kiss her profusely. The two are choked with emotion as they struggle to get to their feet.

Hearing and seeing the commotion, a large number of followers and bystanders gather together to see the beggar woman, telling one another that it is a miracle – her son, a man of means, has recognized her! And they are happy for them.

Then, when the group is about ready to sail away from the island, Macidiana says to Clement, "My darling son, it is not right for me to leave without bidding farewell to the woman who took me in; for she is poor, debilitated, and bedridden."

When Peter and all who are present hear this, they deeply admire the prudence and compassion of the woman. So, Peter orders some of his followers to go and bring the woman to the boat, in her bed as she lay.

And when she has been brought to the boat, and placed in the midst of the people, Peter touches her shoulder and says in the presence of all, "If I am a preacher of truth – in order to confirm the faith of all who stand here; that they may know and believe that there is only one God who made heaven and earth – then, in the name of Jesus Christ, His Son, let this woman arise."

And as soon as Peter has said this, the woman rises up whole and falls down at Peter's feet. In amazement, she greets her friend with kisses, and asks her what the meaning of it all is. The people are astonished, as is she when she is told everything that has happened.

Seeing her friend's whole body cured, Macidiana then begs Peter that her hands might also obtain healing. And by placing his hand upon her, Peter cures her also.

Then, Peter briefly addresses the assembled on the love of God and the basics of the faith – and adds that if anyone wishes to know more about these things, then he should come to Antioch, "where I have resolved to stay three months, teaching fully the things which pertain to salvation."

After Peter has said this, Clement gives a hefty sum of money to the woman who had comforted his mother,[4] and leaves her in the custody of a good man, who promises that he will take care of her. Then, he extends his thanks to others who had helped out and gives them a little money.

After all this, those who are set to sail board the boat, including Macidiana, and they all return to Antaradus.

JOURNEY TO LAODICEA

Arriving back at the lodging place, Macidiana asks Clement about his father – her husband. So, Clement tells her what he knows: "After a few years, my father went in search of you, and of my twin brothers, but he never returned. I fear that he probably died years ago, either by shipwreck, or being killed en-route, or just by wasting away because of grief."

When she hears this, Macidiana bursts into tears, and moans with sadness and grief. But the joy which she feels at finding Clement, mitigates to some extent the painfulness of her recollections.

Early the next morning, Peter enters the foyer where many are gathered, and says, "Clement and his mother Macidiana, and my wife,[5] must take their seats immediately on the wagon."

And in short order, the half-group of believers departs from Antaradus, bound for Laodicea.

They stop at Balaneae, where they stay for three days, and then on to Pathos for one day, and Gabala for one day, before arriving at Laodicea.

NOTES

1. Most art critics and historians today consider Phidias (c. 480-430 BC) to be one of the greatest of all ancient Greek sculptors. He is usually credited as the main instigator of the classical Greek sculptural design. He was celebrated for his statues made of bronze, and in gold and ivory (chryselephantine).

For the ancient Greeks, three of his works far outshone all the others: the colossal 'Statue of Zeus', which was erected in the Temple of Zeus at Olympia, the 'Athena Parthenos' (Athena the Virgin), a sculpture of the virgin goddess Athena, which was housed in the Parthenon in Athens, and the 'Athena Promachos', a colossal bronze which stood between the Parthenon and the monumental gateway at the entrance to the Acropolis.

In 447 BC, the Greek statesman Pericles commissioned these sculptures for Athens from Phidias, to celebrate the Greek victory against the Persians at the Battle of Marathon during the Greco-Persian War (490 BC).

2. See Endnote 2 in Chapter 2.

3. Peter has no intention of helping the woman commit suicide. The remedy he speaks of is faith, love, and understanding of God in the Christian manner, whereby she can happily live out her prescribed lifetime without torment.

4. Clement's gift was 1000 drachmas, per multiple references. This is only worth about $3.25 today, but in 50 AD it was worth much more. Because the currency standard has changed over 2000 years, it's difficult to calculate an exact conversion. But it is estimated that at the time of Christ, 1000 drachmas would cover the living expenses of a family of four, plus a slave, for a year. So, Clement's gift was very generous.

5. Peter's wife is a great comfort to Macidiana, and they travel together for the rest of the trip.

10 IN LAODICEA

Meeting Peter and his party at the gates of the city, Nicetas and Aquila give them a warm greeting, and then escort them to the place of lodging. Seeing that the city is large and splendid, Peter indicates that a stay of 10 days or longer might be worthwhile, in order to reach as many people as possible.

Nicetas and Aquila then ask who the strange woman is, that accompanies them. To which Clement answers saying, "She is my mother, who God has given back to me by means of my lord Peter."

Then Peter recaps the whole story – everything he has been told by Clement regarding the loss of his family, and everything he has been told by Macidiana regarding her experiences and troubles. And he relates how he chanced to meet her at the museum on Aradus.

THE SECOND MIRACLE

After Peter has finished with his summary narrative, Nicetas and Aquila look at each other in astonishment – their faces become pale, their fingers start to fidget, and their eyes begin to moisten. In voices quaking with emotion, and looking up to heaven, they ask in unison, "O God, Ruler and Lord of the universe, are these things true, or are we in some kind of dream?"

"Unless we are asleep or deluded, these things are certainly true," responds Peter.

After a few seconds of deep reflection, and wiping of their brows and eyes, the twins say, "We are Faustinus and Faustus. Even at the first, when you began this story, we looked at each other and were curious as to whether the incidents you spoke of might relate to us – for many coincidences take place in life – and so we remained silent, although our hearts started to beat ever faster. But when you came to the end of the story, we knew that it directly related to us, without any doubt, and we could avow who we really were."

On saying this, bathed in tears, the twins rush to see their mother, anxious to embrace her. But she is sound asleep in the wagon, and Peter interjects, saying, "Permit me first to prepare your mother's state of mind – for in consequence of this great and sudden joy, she may lose her reason, and her emotions may run wild. So, let her sleep for now."

After a few hours, Macidiana awakens from her sleep, and Peter goes to her straightaway and gives her a crash course on God, faith, and salvation. "So, I hope you won't be surprised or appalled at some of your son's behavior, because he is like a Gentile pagan no longer – he is one of us now," he says, "a Christian."

But Macidiana is unfazed. She readily accepts all the Christian tenets and asks to be baptized as soon as possible.

Hearing this from their mother, the twins can restrain themselves no longer. They rush into the room, embrace her warmly, and shower her with hugs and kisses.

Taken aback, she mutters, "What is the meaning of this – what is going on?"

Then, Peter assuredly asks for decorum, and staunchly declares, "Summon up your spirits with courage, my good woman – and be prepared to enjoy your children – for these two good men are Faustinus and Faustus, your sons, who you thought had perished in the deep on that most disastrous night. But they did not die – they survived and are alive – now one bears the name of Nicetas, and the other one is Aquila. Exactly how they escaped that horrible night, they can rightly explain to you – as well as to all of us, for even we have yet to learn how it occurred."

Not surprisingly, hearing this astounding news early in the morning while still groggy from sleep, Macidiana faints and drops to the bed.

After a few long minutes, she is revived by the housekeepers, and slowly manages to mumble, "Would you be so good, my darling children, to tell me – tell us – what happened to you during and after that dismal and cruel night."

The Survival of Nicetas and Aquila

And so, Nicetas agrees to relate the story of how they survived the shipwreck:

"On that very night when the ship went to pieces, and we were tossed all about on the sea, supported on a plank of wood from the wreck, we were rescued by some unruly men in a small boat, who were like pirates and robbers. They were not kind, caring, or helpful. Instead, they tormented us with hunger, fear, and beatings – they threatened us not to reveal the truth of what they did – and they changed our names to protect their crimes.

"At length, they took us to Caesarea Stratonis,[1] where they sold us on the slave market. And we were eventually bought by a proselyte of the Jews,[2] a very honorable widow named Justa. She adopted us as her own children, and educated us in Greek literature and liberal arts.

"We became strongly attached to her religion, often disputing with other cultures, trying to convince them of their error. We also made a thorough study of the doctrines of the pagan philosophers, with the goal of refuting them.

"As teenagers, we became friendly with a man called Simon, who was also educated and very smart. Now, in our religion, it was taught that a great prophet was coming – one who would grant joyful and eternal life to anyone who believed in him. And by his own insinuations, we thought that Simon was this prophet. But we were deceived.

"Luckily, we met a good and sincere man named Zacchaeus, a colleague of our lord Peter, and he warned us not to be duped by the magician Simon. He introduced us to Peter, who has been teaching us all the things that are good and true. And we follow him now, learning more truth every day.

"This, then, is what actually happened to us, dear mother. We really hope that you will accept the same blessings that have been given to us, and follow the same path of living that we follow on the road to everlasting life and happiness. We hope that you will be baptized into Christ, such that we can unite around the same table!"[3]

Baptism of Macidiana

Early in the morning, following a day of fasting, Peter announces, "Let Faustinus, Faustus, Clement, and the household,[4] accompany me to a secluded and sheltered spot by the sea, and there Macidiana will be baptized without attracting attention."[5]

And when they have come to the seashore and the men are sent away to pray, Macidiana is sacramentally baptized in the Name of the Father, and of the Son, and of the Holy Spirit, in a secluded spot between some large rocks.

After the ceremony, amid much rejoicing, the three brothers join the women and accompany them all back to the lodging, where Macidiana is initiated into all the mysteries of the faith in the proper order.

But Peter remains by the rocks. He has noticed a strange man lurking nearby who has seen them praying and talking, and he is curious.

THE OLD WORKMAN

After the brothers and the women have set off back to the lodging, a graying and gloomy working-man comes up to Peter and says, "For a little while now, out of curiosity, I have watched what you and the others were saying and doing. So, I have surmised your faith and worldview. Now, please don't take it the wrong way and think of me as arrogant or overbearing, but I would wish to converse with you some on this. Because I have compassion about your welfare, I don't want you to err under the appearance of truth, or be concerned with things that have no existence in reality. I feel confident enough to tell you what I think is the truth, and where you are misguided, in just a few words. But if this is unpleasant for you, then I shall leave and go on about my business."

To which Peter answers, "Speak what you think, good man, and I will gladly hear it – whether it be true or false. You are to be commended because, like a father concerned with the welfare of his children, you wish to steer us in the direction of what you regard as good."

The Astrology of the Heavens

Given the go-ahead, the man proceeds to expound on his philosophy of life: "I happened to see you praying in a secluded space, and hearing much of what was spoken, I took pity on your misunderstanding. So, I wanted to talk with you in person such that you might be persuaded not to believe in this type of thinking. You see, there is no god, nor any meaningful worship, nor is there any providence in this world. Instead, all things happen per fortuitous chance in accordance with the laws of the heavenly workings – the astrology of the heavens.[6]

"I know this because I have discovered it most clearly for myself. Therefore, it matters not whether you pray, or do not pray – so why waste your time praying? Whatever your astrology predicts, that is what will befall you.

"For if prayers could do anything good, I myself should now be in better circumstances. So don't let my shoddy garments mislead you. I was once an affluent man – I sacrificed much and often to the gods – I gave liberally to the needy – and I prayed and acted piously. Yet, I was not able to escape my destiny."

"So, what are the calamities you have endured?" asks Peter.

"No need to go into that now," replies the workman. "Perhaps later I will tell you who I am, and into what dire circumstances I have fallen. But at present, I just wish for you to fully understand that everything is subject to astrology."

Peter then goes into a concise, but highly skillful, refutation of astrology, both from the philosophical and practical standpoints. He concludes by saying, "The proof that astrology is just tomfoolery is this:[7] A person who has lost his eyesight, or use of his hands or feet, to such an extent that it cannot be cured by the medical doctors, cannot be cured by astrology – even if it has predicted the malady. But I can pray to God, and with the power of the Father, Son, and Holy Spirit, this person can be cured."

To which the old man replies, "Is it then blasphemy to say that all things are subject to astrology?"

"Most certainly it is," says Peter, "For if all the sins of men, and all their acts of impiety and wickedness, owe their origin and cause to the stars, and if the stars have been appointed by God to do this work, then the sins of all are traced up to Him who placed the astrology of things in the stars."

Faustinianus Revealed

"You have spoken wisely," counters the bitter workman, "Yet even with your logical argument, I am still prevented from believing you because of my own personal knowledge and experience. For I was once an astrologer living in Rome, and I became friends with a man who was of the family of Caesar.[8] By using astrology, I accurately determined how his life – and that of his wife – was destined to play out. And by tracing their history, I found that everything that happened in their lives was in exact accordance with their astrological predestination. Therefore, I cannot yield to your argument.

"In this case, the astrology predicted that the woman would commit adultery, fall in love with her own slave, run away with him, and perish abroad in the water. And this is exactly what actually happened. She fell in love with her slave, and not being able to bear the shame and reproach, she fled with him off to a foreign land, shared his bed, and then perished in the sea."

And Peter asks, "'How do you know that she took up residence in a foreign land, married the slave, and then died in the sea?"

To which the grizzled man replies, "I am quite sure that this is true, because after her departure, a brother of her husband told me the whole story of her passion, and how he acted as an honorable man, and did not wish to scandalize his brother's family. He told me how the wretched woman, driven by the stars, longed for him, and how she concocted a dream for disguising her actions."

He then proceeds to tell Peter the rest of the story, which closely matches the story told by Clement, the twin brothers, and Macidiana. The difference, of course, is that the workman uses a third person to substitute for himself, and the implicit trust put in the brother's twisted story that pins the blame on the wife. He finishes by saying, "Not many days after failing to find them, he died of a broken heart."

Realizing that there was more to this amazing story than first meets the eye, Peter resolves to rule out any coincidence. And so he asks the man, "What was the name of this unfortunate friend of yours?"

"Faustinianus," he replies.

"And what were the names of his twin sons?"

"Faustus and Faustinus."

"And what was the name of the third son?"

"Clement."

"And what was the wife's name?"

"Macidiana," says the despondent man.

From this short chat, Peter understands the truth. The gloomy bitter working-man is Faustinianus, the father of Clement and the twins, and the wife of Macidiana – and not merely a friend. But he plays along for a bit, knowing that the miracle would soon come to pass in the proper context.

Then Peter cunningly says, "If I could restore to you your most chaste wife and your three loving sons, will you believe that a modest mind can overcome unreasonable impulses, and that everything I have said is true, and that astrology is nothing?"

To which the strange man replies, "Since it is impossible for you to perform what you have just said, so also is it impossible that anything can take place apart from astrology – destiny is in the stars, sir, and cannot be changed by mere mortals."

Then, the two decide to part for the evening. But a seed of curiosity and questioning had been planted in the heart of the old man. After exchanging lodging information, and respectful sendoff pleasantries, Peter returns to the inn where all the others are staying. He relates his discussion with the gloomy old man to Clement's family, but does not reveal his suspicion as to his true identity. Thinking that their father is dead, there is much grief and weeping by Clement, Nicetas, Aquila, and Macidiana. A day that started joyful has ended sorrowful.

The Third Miracle

The next morning, they are all still commiserating over breakfast, when Macidiana breaks down sobbing, and laments, "O my husband! You died of a broken heart because you loved us so much. But now we are here following the path of the true God to everlasting life. But you are not here with us. It's too much to bear!"

Her moaning has not yet ended, when all of a sudden, the gloomy working man enters through the door, wondering about the reason for the wailing. He looks closely at the woman for a few seconds, and then with an expression of total incredulity, he whispers, "Who do I see here? What does this mean?"

He stares at her a bit more and she stares back at him. And then, in a fit of mutual emotion, they embrace each other warmly, like long lost lovers. There is so much sudden joy and exhilaration, that they can barely get out recognizable words. Over and over they express their love and devotion, in touches and looks as well as in words.

The brothers are dumbfounded. It takes a while for reality to sink in, and they are speechless. Finally, Macidiana manages to blurt out in a choked-up voice, "My dearest Faustinianus, you are in every way the love of my life. But how can you be alive, when we heard just last night that you were dead?"

And then she adds excitedly, but in broken emotional words, "And these are our sons, Faustinus, Faustus, and Clement – all handsome and in good health."

Of course, the three brothers then fall all over him with loving hugs and kisses. The family is reunited – and they can hardly believe it. The tenderness and affection are genuine, warm, and heartfelt.

For an hour, no one else wants to interrupt their private moments of joy, happiness, and peace.

Finally, Peter decides that he needs to formalize the identities, and so he says, "My dear sir, are you Faustinianus, the husband of this woman, and the father of her children?"

"I am," he says.

And Peter responds with, "Why then, did you relate to me your own history as if it were another's; telling me of your toils, and sorrow, and death?"

The man explains that he was afraid that the authorities would discover who he really was, and send him back to Rome, where he would be besieged with mundane trivialities and not be able to wallow in misery and self-pity – which was the debt that he felt he owed to his wife and children – his punishment, because it was his fault that they died.

The Trouble with Astrology

Peter smiles, looks around the room, and says, "You did this according to your heart-felt belief. But in regard to astrology, were you merely acting when you affirmed it, or were you sincere in asserting its existence?"

The father then says, "I will not lie to you. I was in earnest when I maintained that astrology is real. For I am not uninitiated in it – on the contrary, I associated with one of the best of the astrologers – a man by the name of Annubion, who became my friend during my travels, and disclosed to me the death of my wife and children."

And then Peter says, "Are you now convinced by facts, that astrology has no firm foundation?"

"I am unsure," replies the man, "I know that astrologers both make mistakes and speak the truth. I suspect that they speak the truth so far as they are accurately acquainted with the astronomy, and that their mistakes are the result of ignorance or clumsiness. So, I conjecture that the science has a firm foundation, but that the astrologers sometimes speak falsely, although it's unintended."

To which Peter says, "When many prophecies are uttered, it is inevitable that some of them actually come true."

The father takes a deep breath, shrugs his shoulders, and calmly says, "How then, is it possible to be fully convinced of this – the answer as to whether the science of astrology has a sure foundation or not?"

After a moment of silence, Clement speaks up, "Since I know accurately the science, but my lord Peter and my father do not, I would like it if Annubion himself were here – to have a discussion with him in the presence of all – for then would the matter be able to become public."

"Where can we find Annubion?" asks the father.

"In Antioch," answers Peter, "for I have learned that Simon Magus is there – and the two are inseparable companions. We'll be going there shortly, and if we come upon them, the discussion can take place."

THE RELUCTANCE OF FAUSTINIANUS

The next morning, Peter goes to Faustinianus and says, "I am anxious that you should become of the same mind as your wife and children, such that you may live happily with them in this world, and in the next world. After the separation of the soul from the body, you will then continue to be with them free from sorrow. Does it not grieve you exceedingly that you may not be together forever?"

"It does grieve me," says the father, "but it is not the case, my dear friend, that souls are punished in Hades or rewarded in Heaven – for the soul is dissolved into air as soon as it leaves the body."

Peter then realizes that until Faustinianus can be convinced of the reality of a future life – with potential punishment – it will be fruitless to try and convert him. In addition, his family will be troubled and upset. So, he caringly says, "What is it then, that prevents you from coming to our faith? Tell me, so that we can discuss it."

To which Faustinianus replies, "I am not hindered by obsession with material things, or public business, or cultivation of the soil, or mundane cares, much like many others. I am hindered by ideas – that the gods really exist, although you say they do not – that everything is explained by astrology, although you say it is not – and that souls are mortal, although you say they are immortal.

"I have listened to the doctrines preached by you. But I keep thinking, 'Why should I believe this new stuff instead of what the ancients taught us to believe from ages past?' How can one man be right and thousands wrong?"

Peter answers him saying, "The prophet of truth – Jesus Christ – who appeared on earth as a man, taught us that the Almighty God of all – and creator of everything – gave two kingdoms – the good and the evil – to two kings – the good king and the evil king. He granted sovereignty over the present world to the evil king, and sovereignty over the future eternal world to the good king.

"But He made each human being free to choose whether he prefers the present evil world or the future good world. Those who choose the present world can become rich, revel in luxury, indulge in pleasures, and do whatever they can. But they will possess nothing in the future world. However, those who choose the future world will have everlasting life and happiness, but they will have only a few basic things in the present world. Each person has the power to choose the present life or the future life. And he who chooses by his own individual judgment and desire, receives no injustice.

"Indeed, salvation is not attained by force, but by liberty – and not by the deeds of the individual, but by faith in the trinity of God."[9]

Faustinianus appears to be open to the new religion, but he is so steeped in the old pagan ways that he is hard to convince – and he has many questions. So, Peter relaxes the conversation, and goes off to see Clement.

Now, Clement and the twins are anxious that their new-found father become baptized as soon as possible. But Peter is cautious – he senses that there is still much trepidation in his heart. And so he says:

"I know that you have a great affection for your father, but I am afraid that you will urge him to fully embrace our faith too quickly – which he may not yet be prepared for. He may even consent, just because of his affection for you. But this is not for the best. Without true learning, the pledge of conversion may fall to pieces. Therefore, it seems to me, that you should permit him to live for a time according to his own judgment. During that time, he may travel with us, and while we are instructing others, he may hear our words and learn the truth. Then, he may request to convert to our faith on his own. And of course, we will oblige most favorably. But, if he does not, and continues to reject the faith, then he may remain with us as a friend."

The boys reluctantly agree and the matter is settled. Over the next few days, they discuss a wide range of topics, including the concepts of good and evil in depth, astrology, free-will, idolatry, pagan cosmology, polytheism, and mythology. But Faustinianus is not yet ready to convert.

THE ARRIVAL OF SIMON

Early the next morning, Peter goes outside to the courtyard, where he liked to talk to the people who were gathered. But on this day, he notices that a great multitude have assembled. Just then, one of his disciples enters and says, "Simon has come from Antioch, travelling throughout the night, having learned that you promised to speak on the topic of only one God – and he is ready, along with Athenodorus of Athens, student of Epicurus,[10] to come and hear your speech, such that he may publicly refute all the arguments that you make for the unity of God."[11]

Just then, Simon himself enters the courtyard, accompanied by Athenodorus and some other friends. And before Peter can speak at all, Simon grabs the people's attention, and announces:

"I heard yesterday, that you promised to prove to Faustinianus today, that he who is lord of the universe, is the only god who exists – and that we should neither say or think that there are other gods – because anyone who thinks and acts contrary to your belief, will be eternally punished.

"But I am especially amazed at your gall in trying to convert a wise man – one advanced in years – to your state of mind.

"But you will not succeed in your endeavor – all the more so because I am present, and can thoroughly refute your false arguments. It's possible that if I had not been here, the wise old workman might have been led astray, since he has no familiarity with the books deemed trustworthy among the Jews. But I shall omit all this religious background doctrine, in order that I may more quickly refute that which you have promised to prove.

"Therefore, speak now before us what you promised to say. But if, fearing our refutation, you are unwilling to fulfil your promise in the presence of those of us who do know the Scriptures,[12] then this of itself will be sufficient proof that you are wrong.

"And now, why should I wait for you to ramble on, when I have a most satisfactory witness of your promise in the old man who is present?"

After saying this, Simon looks at Faustinianus and points to Peter, saying, "Tell me, most excellent of all men, is not this the man who promised to prove to you today that there is only one god, and that we ought not to think or say that there is any other god – under penalty of eternal punishment for committing the most heinous sin? Is this not so?"

Faustinianus asks that a debate be undertaken, but with more decorum, letting each side make their arguments without interruption.

Simon replies, "I will abide by your proposal, but I am afraid that you may not be an impartial judge, since you may already have been prejudiced by his arguments."

To which Faustinianus answers, "I will not agree or disagree with anyone without the proper exercise of my judgment, for I am a truth-loving person. But I do have to admit, that I am somewhat pre-inclined to agree with your side of the argument, Simon. For I have always believed that there are many gods. Therefore, holding the same opinion as you beforehand, I am inclined rather in your favor. For this reason, you should have no anxiety in regard to me – but Peter rather should, because I still hold opinions contrary to his.

"And now, after this discussion, I hope that, as a truth-loving judge stripped of preconceptions, I shall be able to believe in whichever doctrine gains the victory."

Thereupon, a murmur of applause bursts forth from the crowd, commending Faustinianus for his honesty and uprightness.

More Debates with Simon

Peter commences the discussion by saying, "I am ready to do as the umpire of our discussion has said. So, without any delay, I set forth here my opinion in regard to God: I assert that there is only one God, who made the heavens and the earth, and all things that are in them. And it is not right to say or to think that there is any other."

But Simon interrupts by saying, "In dissent, I maintain that the Jewish Scriptures say that there are many gods. Furthermore, god is not angry at this because he has himself spoken of many gods in his Scriptures.

"For example, in the very first lines of the first book, he speaks of other gods as being like himself. Therein, god says, 'See! The man has become like one of us',[13] and the serpent says, 'your eyes will be opened like gods who know what is good and what is bad.'[14]" Simon goes on to give other examples of the mention of gods in the Scriptures.

Peter then takes his turn in the debate and argues the opposite view. He also cites examples from Scripture, including the big one:

Thus says the Lord: *I am the first and I am the last; there is no God but me*'[15]

He tries to explain the apparent contradictions in Scripture, but Simon counters with the well-known scriptural verse:

Then God said: *Let us make man in our image, after our likeness.*[16]

He explains this further by saying, "Now, the three words 'let us make' imply two or more – certainly not just one."

Peter responds by saying that God is referring to His 'Wisdom', where Wisdom is like the soul of God. It's a bit of a stretch for many in the crowd, and the advantage seems to be tipping toward Simon.[17]

But the debate rages on, Peter noting that other beings are often called gods, and that Christ is called the Son of God. Then, he talks about the nature, the name, and the character of God, as well as the form of God in man.

After this, Simon decides to wrap up the debate by saying, "Tomorrow I will show that your teacher, the Nazarene, asserted himself that the creator of the world was not the highest god."

And with that, Simon walks out of the courtyard.

After Simon has departed, Peter speaks to the crowd: "How I wish that the doctrines against God, which are intended to try men's souls, went no further than Simon! But there will be, as the Lord has said, false apostles, false prophets, heresies, and desires for supremacy,[18] who all find their beginning with Simon. They will blaspheme God, and they will work together in the assertion of the same sacrileges against God as those made by Simon."

And saying this with a choking voice and tears in his eyes, Peter summons the people to him by waving his hand. Once gathered together, he prays solemnly and lays hands on them for healing. And then, in a somber tone, he tells them to come back tomorrow for more debate.

The Debates with Simon Continue

The next day, the people return, and so does Simon. Early in the morning, even before Peter appears, Simon is making allegations against Peter. He accuses him of being the servant of wickedness, of having great power in magic, and as charming the souls of men in a way worse than idolatry:

"Peter deludes you while promising to make you wise," he says, "For under the pretext of proclaiming one God, he wants to free you from many lifeless images, which do not at all injure those who worship them, because they are seen by the eyes themselves to be made of stone, brass, gold, or some other lifeless material. But his image can destroy you completely. While I do not encourage or discourage you from worshipping images, Peter on the other hand, wants to free your souls from such innocuous images, and in so doing, drives mad the mind of each one of you by inventing a more terrible image, that of god in the shape of a man. And if god has a shape, how can he be unlimited? And if limited, he must be in space. But if he is in space, then he is less than the space which encloses Him. And if less than anything, how is he greater than all, or superior to all, or the highest of all? This then, is the essence of the case against Peter."

Simon goes on to claim that the teaching of Jesus is different from Peter's teaching, and that Jesus himself, was inconsistent in his teaching.

Eventually, Peter arrives in the courtyard and methodically begins to refute the accusations made by Simon, one by one. He starts by saying, "Our Lord Jesus Christ, who is the true Prophet, made concise declarations in regard to these matters brought up by Simon. Of His commandments to us, the first one is the greatest, to love the Lord God, and to serve Him only.[19] Indeed, God has shape. But His eyes are not for seeing, for He sees everything at once everywhere. His ears are not for hearing, for He instantly hears, perceives, moves, energizes, and acts on everything everywhere.

"In the greatest of all covenants, He molded the human being in His own image, such that we can receive His gifts and in return, we can give Him the honor.

"Being spirit only, God is Himself invisible, but His image is visible. Therefore, since man is made in His image, the person who wishes to worship God honors His visible image, which is like a man. In reality, the body of God is incomparably more brilliant than the visual spirit which is in us – and He is brighter and more splendid than anything else, so that in comparison with Him, even the light of the sun seems to be like darkness."

Peter goes on to talk about divine space, the heart of the universe, the nature of God, and how the evidence of the senses contrasts with that from supernatural vision. Simon interrupts a number of times, and the discussion shifts topics quickly. At the end of the day, the debate centers around the concept of acquiring knowledge through revelation. And to this, Peter says:

"The Son was revealed to me by God the Father. I know the significance of revelation, having learned about it first-hand. For at the very time when the Lord said, *Who do they say that I am?*, one follower said one thing and another follower said another thing. Then, it came into my heart to say – and I know not how I said it – 'You are the Son of the living God.'[20]

"But the Lord, pronouncing me blessed, pointed out to me that it was the Father who had revealed it to me [21] – and from that very moment, I learned that revelation is knowledge gained without instruction, and without apparition or dreams. And this is indeed the case. For in the soul, which has been placed in us by God, there is all the truth of everything. But the truth is veiled and only revealed by the hand of God. The truth hidden in the soul, is uncovered by God according the pious merit of each.

"Understand that the eyes of mortals cannot see the incorporeal form of the Father or the Son, because it is illumined by exceedingly bright light. For the power to see the Father, without undergoing any change in constitution, belongs to the Son alone. But one day, the righteous will also be able to see the Father in like manner. For in the resurrection of the dead, when their constitution has been changed, they will become like the angels, and they will be able to see Him."

With that, the day's discussion concludes, but Simon declares that he will return again tomorrow to debate more about the unrevealed god and the creator of the world.

Sure enough, the next day Simon appears early in the morning and says, "I promised to you to return today, and prove to you that he who made the world is not the highest god – but the highest god is another who alone is good, and who has remained unknown up to this time."[22] Simon believes that there is some unrevealed power, unknown to all, even to the creator himself, who reigns supreme.

The discussion quickly turns to the definitions of goodness and justice, and the work of revelation. It turns out to be mostly a rehash of what was discussed earlier in Caesarea. And there are spiteful barbs that emanate from both sides.

At the end of the day, Simon pretends to be utterly astonished at what was said, and feigning agitation, he says, "I don't know why I listen to your discourses. You cannot engage in meaningful discussion – you just say over and over the things you think you understand. For a while I endured you, and discussed with you in good faith, but now I will retire. In retrospect, I should have withdrawn earlier on, because I heard you say, 'Whoever says anything whatever against the one true God who created the world, I will not believe – whether it be angels, or prophets, or Scriptures, or priests, or teachers, or anyone else – even though they may work signs and miracles, or shine brilliantly in the air, or give a revelation obtained through visions or dreams.' It appears, then, that nothing or no one can change your predetermined opinions – it is an impossibility – so why engage in debate at all?

As Simon walks away, Peter shouts out one more thing, "Regardless of what is said, I will not give up worshipping my God alone, and doing His will. For he who does not love his own Creator, can never truly love another person who does not love his Creator. And if it seems that he does love another impious person, it is because he has been influenced by the devil. Simon, you should be aware that you are the servant of wickedness!"

Walking out the gate, Simon yells back, "Ha! You can't even explain how evil came to be, much less know what a servant of wickedness is!"

And once again, the next day Simon appears early in the morning. He quickly goes on the offensive and undertakes to prove that the creator of the world is not unblemished. In this vein, they also discuss the existence and origin of the devil.

Simon and Peter then get into a war of words, each blaming the other of unbelief in the supreme God, and each claiming the other is deluded. It starts to get very testy.

But then, Peter goes into a long-winded explanation of the theories about the origin of the devil, and about how God is entirely incomprehensible by humankind. He maintains that God created Satan, but not the concept of evil, which is caused by sin. And pain and death are the result of sin. He also discusses why Satan is entrusted with power, but not power equal to that of God.

The discussion then moves on to cover lust, anger, grief, ignorance, and the inequalities in human life. Peter seems to be getting the upper hand.

Finally, wishing to conclude the debate, Simon says, "Do not think for a minute that I agreed with you in each topic we discussed. I went from topic-to-topic yielding to your ignorance, so that you might go on to the next topic quickly, and I could become acquainted with the whole range of your ignorance. This way, I can condemn you, not through mere conjecture of individual points, but from full knowledge of the big picture. Allow me to retire now for a few days, and then I shall come back and show that you know nothing."

When Simon is at the point of exiting the gate, Faustinianus calls to him and says, "Listen to me Simon, for a moment, and then go wherever you like. I remember that before the start of the discussion, you were worried that I'd be prejudiced toward Peter, although I said that I was inclined to favor you. Well, I have now heard the entire discussion, and in my opinion, Peter has won the debate. I believe that he speaks the truth. So, do you think that my judgment is because of predisposition, or due to a fair and unbiased opinion? Can you explain to all how I have not judged correctly? I don't think you can, and I don't think you will debate with him anymore. For I think that it is plain to all that you have been defeated.

"But, of course, you won't admit to it. You will pretend not to have been bested, and you will proclaim to the people that you were chased away by ignorant fools. Simon, I fear for your soul – that you may suffer agony and pain of conscience. And if you do not hear the truth soon, your soul may be condemned and you will be lost forever."

But Simon just trudges away in a huff. Tomorrow is another day, after all. However, he does not return to further engage Peter in debate.

THE TRANSFORMATION OF FAUSTINIANUS

A few days later, when all the disciples and followers of Peter are together at the lodge and are preparing to dine, a trusted houseworker enters and announces that Appion Pleistonices, along with Annubion, have just come from Antioch, and are lodging with Simon not too far away.

When Faustinianus hears this, he becomes enthused and says to Peter, "If you permit it, I would like to go and visit Appion and Annubion, for they are friends of mine from childhood – and perhaps I can even persuade Annubion to debate with Clement on the subject of astrology."

To which Peter responds, "I consent, and you are commended for respecting your friends. But consider carefully how all things occur to you according to God's providence – for not only have your loved ones been restored to you, but also the presence of your friends is arranged."

Then, the father of Clement says, "In truth, I consider that what you say is so." And when he has said this, he gets up leisurely and departs to go see Annubion and Appion.

The next morning at the breakfast table, Peter looks at the boys and says, "I wonder what has befallen your father. He has not been seen this morning."

Just at that instant, Faustinianus comes in the room and apologizes for remaining out overnight. But when everyone looks at him, they are horrified and amazed! For appearing on his face is the face of Simon, and not his own – yet his voice is that of Faustinianus. But he looks just like Simon!!

All the assembled begin to cower and back off, except Peter. The old workman is astonished at the cold reception – he has no idea that his countenance has been changed.

"Why do you shrink away from your father?" says Peter. Peter is the only one in the room who sees the man's normal face, his natural countenance.

"He appears to us to be Simon, although he has our father's voice," reply Clement, Nicetas, and Aquila.

Macidiana agrees: "It is Simon that I see before me, with the voice of my husband."

Then Peter says, "You recognize only his voice, because it is unaffected by magic. But my eyes are not affected by the sorcerer's magic. I can see the form of his face as it really is – and he is not Simon, but your father Faustinianus."

Then, looking at him, he says, "The reason that your wife and sons are repulsed is because you do not look like yourself. Your face appears to be that of the detestable Simon."

Everyone is disconsolate but nobody knows exactly what to do.

TROUBLE IN ANTIOCH

A few minutes later, one of the advance groups that Peter had sent to Antioch to assess Simon's activities, enters the room and says to Peter, "I wish you to know, my lord, that Simon has been doing many tricks and miracles publicly in Antioch. And his sermons and public talks were solely meant to stir them up against you – calling you a magician, a sorcerer, and a murderer. He had worked them up to such a fever pitch, that every man was eager to kill you outright, if you should ever show up there.[23]

"Seeing the city raging wildly against you, we met secretly to consider what ought to be done. But we had no good ideas."

Arrival of Cornelius, the Centurion

"And then, fortunately, Cornelius the centurion arrived in Antioch. He had been sent by the emperor to the governor of the province for some public business. He is the same person who our Lord converted and baptized when he was in Caesarea.[24] We sent for him as soon as possible, and when he came, we explained to him everything that was happening because of Simon. We begged him to help us right the situation in any way he could.

"Cornelius graciously promised that he would chase Simon out of town, but we would have to aid in his plan. Of course, we readily agreed.

"And then he said, 'Caesar has ordered sorcerers to be sought out and arrested in the city of Rome and throughout the provinces, and a great number of them have already been detained. Therefore, I will spread the news that I have secretly come to apprehend that magician – that I have been sent by Caesar for this purpose – such that he may be punished with the rest of his ilk. But your people must help. Have them who are spying on him in disguise, report to him in confidence, that they have heard through the grapevine that I have been sent to apprehend him. When he hears this, he is sure to take flight and leave the city. Then, people's opinions can start to be changed.'

"Cornelius was true to his word, and we all did exactly what we had planned. And sure enough, it worked. We have heard from our confidants that he has left the city and come back here. But we believe that you should not go to Antioch just yet – not until we can determine whether the hatred of you, which he had sown among the people, is in any degree lessened by his departure."

SIMON'S DEVIOUS MAGIC

After hearing all this from the returned scout, Peter looks around the room and says, "Faustinianus, your countenance has been transformed by Simon the magician, so that you now look like him. He did this on purpose because he knows that he is being sought after by Caesar, and that when found, will be severely punished. Therefore, he has fled in terror, hoping that you will be found and apprehended in his place – thereby relieving his fugitive status. Moreover, he is also keen on punishing your sons for leaving him, and your internment would bring them great sorrow – and he would have his revenge."

Hearing this from Peter, Faustinianus is beside himself with tears and choked with emotion. Wailing and lamenting, he says, "O what a fool that I am, not to believe it when I heard that he was a magician! What a laughable old wretch I am – on one day being recognized by my wife and my sons in joy and bliss, and on the next, being rolled back to the former miseries I endured during my wandering.

"Peter, you have judged rightly. For my friend Annubion hinted to me about his devious ways, but unhappily I paid no attention, content to suffer in my misery."

At the same time, Macidiana is tearing her disheveled hair, and weeping bitterly – and the brothers are thunderstruck and beside themselves, confused and stunned at the change of their father's countenance.

In the middle of all this, Annubion enters the room to announce that Simon has fled during the night, heading for Judaea. But he finds everyone crying and grieving.

Faustinianus continues to moan, "Alas, alas! Woe is me! Miserable man that I am! Once I was happy, but now I am doomed!"

Annubion stands speechless, seeing and hearing the sorrow and gloom.

Then, Peter says to the brothers in the presence of all, "Believe me, this is Faustinianus, your father. Therefore, I urge you to treat him as your father and attend to him accordingly. I know that God will present the opportunity where we will be able to unmask him – remove the face of Simon and exhibit again the distinct face of your father."

Then, Peter turns to the old workman and says, "I gave you leave to salute Appion and Annubion, since you said that they were your friends from childhood, but I did not permit you to associate with the dark magician Simon."

"I have sinned; I confess it," moans Faustinianus.

"I also beg you to forgive this good and noble man," affirms Annubion, "for he has been unhappily tricked and imposed-upon by the magician in question. And I can tell you exactly how it happened:"

Simon's Trick Revealed

"When the good man came to visit us, it just so happened that at that very instant we were standing around Simon, listening to him tell us that he intended to flee the city that very night – for he had heard that some officials had come to Antioch, and even to Laodicea, to apprehend him by command of the emperor. Then, he indicated that he wanted to turn his anger about this against Faustinianus, who had scorned him at the recent debate.

"So, he said to us, 'Make him agree to dine with us, and while you are relaxing beforehand, I will compound a certain ointment and put it in the sauce – and when he eats, it will get on his lips and spread all over his face – and he will become woozy from the drug. From that time on, he shall seem to look like me. But first, you others must rub on your face the juice of a certain herb that I will give you – with that, you will be immune to the ointment and the deception. To everyone then, except you, he will appear to be Simon.'

"And when he said this, I said to him, 'What is it that you expect to achieve from doing such a thing?'

"Then Simon said, 'In the first place, those who are seeking me, may find him instead, and thereby stop searching for me. And if he is ever punished by Caesar, then his sons who forsook me and fled to Peter, may feel much sorrow.'

"Now I swear to you, Peter, that what I have just said is true. I did not dare tell Faustinianus then, but neither did we have any opportunity to speak with him in private, and disclose Simon's plan more fully.

"Then, sometime in the middle of the night, Simon ran away, making for Judaea. And Athenodorus and Appion have gone with him as an escort. But I pretended to be sick, such that I might remain at home, and help him return quickly to you in the morning – where he can be hidden away. I couldn't let him be seized by those bounty hunters looking for him, and then be brought before Caesar, and possibly executed for no good reason.

"Now, in my anxiety about all this, I have come to see if he is OK, and then to return before those who have gone to convoy Simon come back."

And then, Annubion turns to the brothers and says, "I, Annubion, do indeed see the true countenance of your father – I was previously given the antidote by Simon himself, as I have told you, such that the real face of Faustinianus might appear to my eyes.

"However, I am truly amazed at the magical art of Simon Magus – and astonished that you who are standing here, do not recognize your own father."

And while everyone in the family weeps on account of the calamity that has befallen them, Annubion, being moved with compassion, also weeps.

Peter's Strategy and Counterplot

Evincing much sympathy, Peter promises that he will restore the face of Faustinianus, saying to him, "Listen now my friend, you have heard how and why things are as they are. But this false face of yours can be useful to us in the near term. I have a plan that will benefit us all. So, if you assist us in doing what I tell you, then I will restore to you the true form of your countenance. And all will be well."

"I will do everything that is in my power most willingly," says the woeful father, "just please restore my face such that my family may see me as I truly am."

And so, Peter continues: "You have heard from one of my scouts who has returned from Antioch, about Simon's nefarious activities there – stirring up the multitudes against me – inflaming the whole city into hatred of me – declaring that I am a magician, a deceiver, and a murderer – so that they are eager to kill me on sight. We can remedy this situation with your help.

"Leave Clement with me, and go before us to Antioch with your wife and twin sons. And I will send others with you, who are fit to help.

"When you arrive in Antioch, you will be thought to be Simon by all the people. Stand in a public place, proclaim your repentance, and say something like this:

'I Simon declare, and confess to you, that everything I have said concerning Peter was utterly false – for he is neither a seducer, nor a magician, nor a murderer, nor any of the things that I accused him of being. Unfortunately, I said these things under a case of temporary madness. Therefore, I beg you – even I who gave you the cause for such indignation – beg you to stop thinking such things about him. Lay aside your hatred and cease from your loathing – because he is a disciple and apostle of the true Prophet, the Christ – who was sent to us by God for the salvation of the world.

'Therefore, I advise, urge, and encourage you to listen to what he has to say – and believe him when he preaches to you the truth. Otherwise, if you despise or reject him, your very city may be doomed.

'Now I wish for you to know why I have made this confession. Last night, an angel of God rebuked me for my wickedness, and scourged me terribly, because I was an enemy to the herald of truth.

'Therefore, I ask you never to listen to me again, if I should ever come to you and attempt to say anything bad against Peter. Do not receive or believe me. For I confess to you that I was a magician, a seducer, and a deceiver. But I have repented, and sincerely hope that my former sins will be wiped out by such repentance.'

"So, can you manage this little charade?"

After listening to Peter, Faustinianus replies, "I understand what you wish – do not trouble yourself further – I know what to do when I get there."

"One more thing," says Peter, "after you get there, have given your speech, and perceive that the people are persuaded by your talk – they've laid aside their hatred, and returned to their yearning to see and hear me – then send notice to me quickly, and I will come immediately. And when I arrive, I will remove the strange face-shape without delay, and restore to you your own countenance, which is well known to your family and friends."

Having said this, he motions for the wife, Macidiana, the twin sons, Faustinus and Faustus (who were previously called Nicetas and Aquila), and a few trusted followers, to accompany him to Antioch. Macidiana is reluctant because she feels awkward traveling as the wife of a man with a strange face. But Annubion convinces her to go by saying that he sees the correct face, and that he will go also for reassurance.

Around midnight, the group heads out for Antioch.

Appion and Athenodorus Return

The next morning, Simon's two companions, Appion and Athenodorus, return to Laodicea after escorting Simon to a secret destination in Judaea. They go to the lodging of Peter, looking for Faustinianus.

Peter invites them in and they ask, "Is Faustinianus here? Can we see him?"

In a crafty manner, Peter answers, "He's not here and we don't know where he is. Ever since the evening before last when he left to visit Annubion, none of us have seen him. Maybe he is still with Annubion. I do hope that he is OK.

"Funny thing though – yesterday, Simon himself came here looking for him. When we said that we hadn't seen him since he left to visit Annubion, something odd appeared to come over Simon. It was very strange because he said that he was actually Faustinianus. It was like he was in a trance.

"Of course, nobody believed him. So, he left in a very dejected mood. Moaning and groaning, he disappeared into the fog headed towards the sea. I feared the worst – the stress and strain of the debate might have taken its toll on him.

"But you are friends of Simon – do you know where he is? Is he OK? Do you know where Annubion is?"

When Appion and Athenodorus hear this from Peter, they are disturbed and agitated. "Why did you not try to stop him from going to the sea? If he was in a trance, why didn't you try to snap him out of it?" they groan.

Peter just shrugs his shoulders but says nothing.

Just then, Athenodorus is about to say that who they thought was Simon was actually Faustinianus. But Appion anticipates it and prevents him from saying anything.

"We have been told by an acquaintance that Faustinianus has gone with Simon – wherever that is. In fact, the acquaintance said that he asked to go with Simon because he didn't want to see his sons anymore, since they have become one with the Jews. We weren't sure if this was true, so we decided to come here and check if he was here.

"But since he is not, what we learned from the acquaintance must be true – they have left together. Yes, we also hope they are both OK."

Then, Clement decides that he should add to Peter's ruse by feigning a callous hard-hearted attitude. So, he says, "Listen to me, dear Appion: what we believe to be the true religion, we also wish for our father to accept. But if he does not wish to believe it, and decides to leave us because he detests our beliefs, then – making a harsh remark here – nor do we care for him."

Appion and Athenodorus are taken aback by Clement's seeming lack of compassion. After a terse farewell, they leave shaking their heads.

News from Antioch

Ten days later, another one of Peter's advance scouts returns to Laodicea from Antioch. He tells the trusted followers how Faustinianus stood in the public square and incriminated himself, in the guise of Simon, in the most shocking and scandalous deeds. He was wearing the face of Simon, visible to all. And he exalted Peter with unmeasured praises, commending him to all the people, and making them long for his presence. So convincing was his oratory that almost everyone changed their opinion of Peter, began to admire him greatly, and were eager to see him. Unfortunately, many of the people became so angry at who they thought was Simon, that they wanted to beat him up or even kill him. Consequently, the scouts had to sequester Faustinianus away from the angry crowds – and send notice to Peter to come as soon as possible.

"Therefore," he urges, "make haste before he is found and unhappily harmed by mistake. He told me to come here with great speed, since he is in fear, and asks you to come without delay. Hopefully, you will find him alive. And now is also a favorable moment for you to appear – the city growing in affection towards you."

Upon hearing this from the scout, Peter calls the greater household together and tells them that they must leave Laodicea immediately and go to Antioch. He appoints one of his trusted followers as bishop, and that very afternoon, they all hasten to the neighboring city of Antioch.

NOTES

1. Caesarea Stratonis is also known as Caesarea Maritima, Caesarea Palestina, and Strato's Tower. The city and harbor were built under Herod the Great from 22-9 BC near the site of a former Phoenician naval station known as 'Straton's Tower', probably named after the 4th century BC king of Sidon, Strato I. When Judea became a Roman province in 6 AD, Caesarea Maritima replaced Jerusalem as its civilian and military capital and became the official residence of its governors, such as the Roman procurator Antonius Felix, and prefect Pontius Pilate. The city was populated throughout the 1st to 6th centuries AD and became an important early center of Christianity.

It developed into a modern town after 1940, and was incorporated in 1977 as the municipality of Caesarea within Israel's Haifa District, about halfway between the cities of Tel Aviv and Haifa.

The ruins of the ancient city, on the coast about 1.2 miles south of modern Caesarea, were excavated in the 1950s and 1960s, and the site was incorporated into the new Caesarea National Park in 2011. This city is the location of the 1961 discovery of the Pilate Stone, the only archaeological item that mentions the Roman prefect Pontius Pilate by name, under whose order Jesus was crucified.

2. A proselyte is a person who has converted from one religion to another. Justa had converted from paganism to Judaism.

3. The early Jewish Christians believed that it was a sacrilege to eat at the same table with people who had not been baptized into Christianity. Peter was especially strong in this belief.

4. The 'household' consisted of Peter's wife plus the female servants and slaves that accompanied him on the trip.

5. Because baptism involved full-body immersion in water, the catechumen wore little, or no clothes. For the sake of propriety, this necessitated that female catechumens be attended by females only, during the sacramental ritual.

6. In the first century AD, astrology was often called 'Genesis'. It was the worldview that a person's destiny is determined by the stars, which rule the heavens at the time of each person's birth.

7. In reality, Peter probably used a slang word commonly in use at the time, and not 'tomfoolery'.

8. A royal family somehow related to the emperor

9. Peter is touching upon the concept of the Trinity, although the catechetical doctrine – the fundamental dogma – will not become official for many years.

10. See Endnote 1 to Chapter 8.

11. The unity of God is the aphorism used to describe the concept (or religion) of the existence of only one God, as opposed to the concept of the existence of many gods, as believed by the Greeks (or the pagans in general – the Greeks being the intellectual elite defending and upholding the many-God concept [polytheism]).

12. Being a Samaritan and thoroughly educated, Simon had an extremely good knowledge of the first five books of the Bible, the Pentateuch.

13. Genesis 3:22

14. Genesis 3:5

15. Isaiah 44:6; also see Isaiah 45:21

16. Genesis 1:26

17. The full doctrine of the Holy Trinity had not yet been formulated. Peter refers to 'Wisdom' as another essence of God.

18. Peter is paraphrasing from Matthew 4:24.

19.. Refer to Matthew 22:37-38.

20. Matthew 16:13-16

21. Matthew 16:17

22. This is similar to Gnostic philosophy and the concept of the Demiurge.

23. Simon had been in Antioch for a while before going to Laodicea to debate with Peter, and then returned immediately after the debate to further stir up the people. But he came back to Laodicea secretly with Appion and Annubion.

24. Refer to the entire chapter of Acts 10 for the story of Cornelius, the Roman centurion, who was converted and baptized, and received the Holy Spirit.

11 IN ANTIOCH

Faustinus and Faustus have spread the news that Peter is coming and will address the multitudes. An immense anticipation arises throughout the whole city.

On the day of his arrival, a vast number of people go to the city gates to meet him. Almost all the older men, and most of the rich men, come with ashes sprinkled on their heads, testifying to their repentance for having listened to the magician Simon, instead of the apostle Peter.

Peter addresses the crowd and blesses them, saying, "God is with us this day!"

The disciples then bring to him all those distressed with sicknesses, tormented with demons, immobilized with paralysis, and suffering from a wide range of infirmities – a large number of people all together.

And then Peter looks out at all the people and then up to heaven. He senses that they are repentant of the evil thoughts they had entertained about him by means of Simon, that they have come to believe in the one and only almighty God with all their hearts, and that they firmly believe that healing from every sort of ailment can be obtained by faith in God.

Sensing all this, he spreads out his hands towards heaven, pours out his prayers with tears, and gives thanks to God, saying: "I bless You, O Father, worthy of all praise – who has decreed that every word and promise of Your Son will be fulfilled – and I pray that every human being may know that You alone are the one God in heaven and on earth."

THE MIRACLES ON THE HILL

Then, Peter walks up to the top of a hill, orders all the multitude of sick people to be arranged before him, and then addresses them all in the following words:

"You see me now to be a man like yourself, standing here with nothing. But it is not so – for I have everything – because I believe with all my heart in the one and only almighty God – and if you believe, you also can have everything!

"So, do not think that you can recover your health from me – that can only be done through God and His only begotten Son – who, coming down from heaven, has shown to those who believe in Him, the perfect medicine for body and soul.

"Therefore, let all the people be witnesses to your declaration, that with your whole heart you believe in the Lord Jesus Christ, the only begotten Son of God – and that you know that only through Him can you be saved, and have everlasting life."

Then, in one loud voice, all the multitude of the sick cry out in unison, "We believe that the God of whom Peter preaches is the one and only true God!"

Suddenly, an immense and overpowering light of the grace of God shines down from heaven and into the midst of the people. And a great healing is poured forth on them all.

The paralytics begin to run to Peter's feet – the blind shout out on the recovery of their sight – the lame give thanks on regaining their ability to walk – the sick rejoice in having wellness restored – the possessed celebrate in having their demons exorcized – the deaf and dumb delight in regaining their senses – and the unconscious, even those barely alive, exult in being raised up to wholeness.

So great is the grace and power of the Father, and the Son, and the Holy Spirit, that every person present, from the least to the greatest, confesses the Lord with praise and love, in one mighty voice.

FAUSTINIANUS RESTORED

That evening, while Peter is resting from the day's exertion, Faustinus and Faustus tell the story to the others of what happened in Antioch before he arrived:

"As soon as our father entered the city, a great many people gathered around him, supposing him to be Simon. Immediately, he began to make a public confession to them all, according to what Peter had taught him to say. They all listened intently – both noble and common, both rich and poor – and hoped that he would deliver to them some new kind of favor. But it was not to be.

"I remember his words like they were written in stone:

'For a long time now, I have been the most unhappy of men. It is a heavy weight that bears on my shoulders. For I, Simon, have a secret to confess. All the marvels and wonders that you have seen me perform here were not done in good faith, but by the lies and tricks of demons – done such that I might subvert your faith and condemn my own soul.

'And I confess that all things that I have said about Peter were lies – for he never was either a magician or a murderer – but has been sent by God for the salvation of you all. So, if you think that he is to be despised or hated, then listen up! Such thinking is wrong – so wrong that you could be punished by the destruction of this entire city!

'Now, you may ask, what is the reason that I make this confession to you of my own accord? Well, the answer is that I was vehemently rebuked by an angel of God last night, and most severely scourged, because I was an enemy of truth.

'Therefore, I ask of you, from this very hour, that if I ever again open my mouth against Peter, you will drive me away from your sight. For that foul demon – the devil – who is an enemy to the salvation of men, speaks against him through my unwilling mouth, such that you may not attain eternal life through his teaching.

'Now, what is the usefulness to you of the magical arts I've shown you? I have made bronze dogs bark, statues move, and men change their appearance or vanish from sight. For these tricks, you should have cursed my magical arts, because they bind your souls with devilish shackles – wanting me to show you a vain miracle so that you would not believe Peter.

'But I say to you now, Peter cures the sick, expels demons, gives sight to the blind, restores health to the paralyzed, and raises the dead, in the righteous name of Him by whom he is sent. There is no magic – just unerring faith in the one true God.'

"When he made these self-incriminating statements, the people began to ridicule him – and they grieved and lamented because they had sinned against Peter, wrongly believing him to be a wicked man.

"That very evening, by the grace of God and the prayers of Peter, because he had so superbly played out the role of Simon, Faustinianus had his own face restored to him, and the appearance of Simon Magus left him. We were so overjoyed seeing our father's face restored, that we praised and thanked God the entire evening."

Simon is Driven Out

"But Simon, not being very far away in hiding, had heard through his spy network,[1] that his face on Faustinianus had actually contributed to the glory of Peter in an unforeseen manner. So, he rushed back to Antioch quickly in order to right the situation – to remove his likeness from Faustinianus, and thereby stop the unwanted admissions of wrongdoing and praises of Peter.

"But it was too late – the damage to his reputation had already been done. And our father had already been restored by our Lord Jesus Christ according to the word of His apostle.

"Undeterred, Simon began to secretly go among his friends and acquaintances, and to malign Peter even more than before, saying that it was not he who had made the confessions, but someone else who had been transformed by the magic of Peter. But so convincing was Faustinianus's performance, that no one believed him. They all rebuked him and spit in his face. And then they drove him out of the city, saying: 'If you ever return here again and speak out against Peter, then you will be killed – and no one will be found to be at fault.'

"And so, Simon left for good, and went off to Judaea. And that, my friends, is the whole story of what happened here in Antioch before you arrived. Thanks be to God."

And everyone sleeps soundly that night.

Faustinianus the Hero

One evening, a few days later, Faustinus, Faustus, Clement, and Macidiana ask Faustinianus whether any remnants of unbelief remain in him. To which he answers, "Come here, and you shall see in the presence of Peter, just how much the increase of faith has grown in me."

With that, he goes up to Peter and falls down at his feet, saying: "The seeds of your word, planted in the fertile soil of my mind, have now sprung up and blossomed to fruitful maturity. Nothing is wanting, but that you separate the fruit from the chaff using that spiritual reaping-tool of yours – and place me in the harvest of the Lord, allowing me to be a partaker at the divine table."

Grasping his hand, Peter then presents him to his wife and sons, saying to him, "As God has restored your sons to you, their father, so also your sons restore their father to God."

Peter proclaims a short fast for all the believers, and on the following Sunday, he baptizes Faustinianus in the Name of the Father, and of the Son, and of the Holy Spirit.

And over the next few weeks, Faustinianus tells his story to all the people in Antioch – relating in detail, all his tribulations and then all his fortunes – the whole story of his loss of family and self-worth, to the miraculous recovery of his family and the attainment of spiritual insight and faith in the one true God Almighty.

So emotionally stirring is his story that the whole city soon receives him as a hero – almost like an angel – and they pay him no less honor than they do to the Apostle Peter.

THE EVANGELIZATION OF ANTIOCH

Every day, Peter continues to preach, sermonize, heal, and comfort the people. Over the span of seven days, more than ten thousand men and women, believing in God, are baptized and consecrated by sanctification.[2]

One of the most rich and exalted persons in the city, and a bold believer in 'The Way',[3] is a man named Theophilus.[4] With unbounded eagerness and energy, he has his large house – almost like a palace – consecrated under the name of a church.[5] A chair is placed in it for the Apostle Peter by all the people – and great multitudes assemble daily to hear the Word of God, and the doctrines for achieving health, happiness, and eternal life.

A bishop is ordained, and deacons and presbyters appointed, such that the church of Jesus Christ in Antioch is well founded.

And for the next month, Peter preaches every day and vast multitudes come to listen. A great number of people are baptized, and all those distressed with sicknesses are restored to health through the mercy and grace of our Lord Jesus Christ.

Knowing that Simon has left the city and is bound for Judaea, Peter then leaves for Jerusalem, along with his household and trusted followers.

But Simon is still at-large, and more trouble is brewing.

NOTES

---

1. Both Simon and Peter had a network of spies – or scouts – who checked on the activities of the other and on the pulse of the people, and then promptly reported back.

2. Consecrated sanctification: an ill-defined term, generally meaning the act by which a person is separated from the general population, becomes purified from sin, and is dedicated to the service of God.

3. A slang term used to describe the early Christian movement – see Endnote 2 to Chapter 1.

4. This is the same 'Theophilus' as that mentioned in the Preface to the Gospel of Luke (Luke 1:1-4) and in the Prologue to the Book of Acts (Acts 1:1).

5. removed from general use, purified, and exclusively used as a church – later to be called a Christian church

12 IN JERUSALEM

Simon has fled from Antioch in disgrace and made his way south to Jerusalem. He knows that this is where Peter and the apostles are stationed, and he hopes to somehow be able to totally discredit them, such that they will no longer be a viable threat to his sham ministry. And if he can learn some of their 'magic' in the process, then even better. But he is low on funds and needs money – his travels throughout Palestine and Syria have depleted his resources.

SIMON AND EUBULA

Shortly after arriving in Jerusalem, Simon befriends a wealthy widow named Eubula, who owns collections of gold and expensive pearls, and convinces her that he is the 'power of god' revealed as a man. Through sweet-talking, he tells her that if she gives away much of her wealth to the poor, and also gives a substantial sum to god through his ministry (which actually will go into the pockets of Simon and his cohorts), then she will receive happiness in heaven and not be forever tormented in hell. She believes him and gratefully does what he says – and for a short time is contented and cheerful. They become close, and Simon is given free access to the house.

Then one night, using stealth and cunning, Simon and two associates sneak into the house and carry away all of Eubula's gold, without being seen by any of the household staff. Upon discovering the loss the following day, Eubula lays the blame on the staff and accuses them of the theft. She torments them by saying, "Why have you taken advantage of me and this man of god? You have previously seen him entering this house to bring me peace and comfort, and now you have used this honorable man, whose name is like the name of a lord, as a scapegoat in your vile scheme to steal my precious treasures. You will all be reported to the authorities, and you will pay a horrible price indeed." Of course, the staff deny any involvement, but the veracity of their explanation holds little credibility with the constabulary. Needless to say, Simon also disappears, and cannot be found by Eubula or the police officials.

Now, the news of the theft — and round-up of the household staff — quickly spreads throughout the city. It is a hot topic of gossip. But because the name of Simon is involved, a person who said that he was the 'power of god', this otherwise mundane news event reaches the ears of Peter and the disciples. Peter is grieved and fasts for three days, praying that the details of the matter should become clearer and surer to him.

Peter's Vision

Then on the fourth day, Peter has a vision:

Two of the young catechumens who he has instructed in the name of the Lord, named Italicus and Antulus,[1] along with a chained naked boy holding a loaf of bread,[2] come to him and say, "Peter, wait yet two more days and you will see the mighty works of God. You should know that everything lost from the house of Eubula is attributable to magic, deception, and delusion brought about by the sorcerer called Simon, and two of his associates. They have covertly stolen it, but you can catch them trying to pawn away some of it in three days at the ninth hour, at the gate which leads to Neapolis.[3] They will attempt to sell a golden idol weighing two pounds — a statue of a young satyr containing a precious stone [4]— to a goldsmith named Agrippinus.

"You will be able to see it, but don't touch it — you don't want to be defiled by the pagan idol — but go with some of Eubula's servants and show them the shop of the goldsmith to confirm his identity. In this way, the wickedness of these men will be made clear, other items they have stolen will be found, and many will come to believe in the name of the Lord."

When Peter has recovered from his vision, he hurriedly goes off to the house of Eubula, and there finds her sitting in a sorrowful melancholy of dejection. Her clothes are torn and her hair disordered. She is crestfallen and glum.

He addresses her respectfully, saying, "Eubula, rise up from your grieving, compose your face, order your hair, and put on attire befitting your station. You must pray to the Lord Jesus Christ, the invisible Son of God, who will judge every soul, and by whom you will be saved if you repent all of your sins with a whole heart. You will then receive new power and enlightenment from the Lord. For He says to you, through this humble intercessor, that you will find everything that you have lost. But listen to me closely now: After receiving back your treasures, you must properly thank the Lord for His grace. You must renounce this present world, and seek after Him for everlasting refreshment. You can be baptized and become a disciple of God."

Then, after a brief moment of reflection by both parties, Peter continues:

The Plot to Catch Simon

"So, listen to this now and take heed: Let two of your most trusted servants keep watch at the city gate that leads to Neapolis on the day after tomorrow at about the ninth hour. There, they will find two young men carrying a golden statue of yours – a satyr set with a gem and weighing two pounds. This I know because I have seen it in a vision from God – Alleluia! They will offer this statue for sale to a man named Agrippinus, who unbeknown to them, is a godly man and a faithful follower of our Lord Jesus Christ.

"This should prove to you beyond any doubt that you should believe in the almighty living God, and not in Simon the magician, the unstable devil, who only desires that you remain in sorrow, and your innocent household be tormented. By fancy words and clever speech, he has deceived you. With his mouth he speaks of godliness, but he is wholly possessed of ungodliness.

"When you once thought that you would commemorate a holy day by setting up this golden idol, veiling it behind silken curtains, and arranging it with ornaments upon a round three-legged table, Simon secretly brought in two young men and they clandestinely stole away your idol, without being seen by anyone, and then disappeared. But in the seeing-all eye of God, this act is not concealed – it is plainly visible – and He has shown it all to me.

"So, do not be deceived! Awake, and repent for those sins which you have committed that are contrary to God's Word – you will then not perish in hell. He is full of all truth, the righteous judge of the living and the dead, and there is no other hope of everlasting life but through him. He is the reason why you will recover all that you have lost. So now, do what is right to save your eternal soul, and accept Jesus Christ as your Lord and Savior."

Then, Eubula throws herself down at the feet of Peter, saying: "Dear Sir, I do not know who you are, but I tell you honestly that I had received this Simon as a servant of god, and whatever he asked me to give to the poor, and to his ministry directly, I did so happily in his name. What hurt did I do to him, that he should contrive all this larceny against my house?"

To which Peter answers, "There is no trust to be put in words, but only in acts and deeds. Now, I strongly suggest that you continue with the plan that I have laid out." And Eubula agrees to do so.

Peter then takes his leave of her, and goes together with her two trusted servants to the shop of Agrippinus, and says to him upon arrival, "Sir, please take note of these two trusted servants; for tomorrow they will come to you, shortly followed by two disreputable young men desiring to sell you a golden idol – a young satyr beset with a fancy jewel – which belongs to their mistress. Please pick up and look upon the idol and pretend to praise the work of the craftsman. Then, when these trusted servants come in, they will recognize it and declare it as stolen property – and the crime will be exposed, thanks be to God."

On the next day, the trusted servants of Eubula come shortly before the ninth hour, soon followed by the two dishonorable young men wanting to sell the golden idol to Agrippinus. And the scenario plays out as planned – the servants appear surprised at having found the idol, declare it to be owned by their mistress, and demand that it be confiscated and returned to its rightful owner. Security men are called to prevent a ruckus, and a messenger is sent to Eubula with the news.

Upon receiving notification of the incident, Eubula promptly rushes to the office of Pompeius, the deputy magistrate, and in noticeable distress of mind, explains everything that has befallen her in a loud voice. When Pompeius witnesses this respectable and prosperous matron – a pillar of the community – being so troubled and upset, he immediately rises up from his judgement seat and goes directly to the courthouse,[5] ordering that those two men be brought there and tried straight away.

The trial is quick; and while they are being questioned, the two accessories to the crime confess that they did it in the service of Simon, who had induced them with money. Furthermore, under continued rigorous questioning, they confess that everything that Eubula has lost, plus many other stolen items from others, are hidden – buried – in a cave just on the other side of the gate.

When Pompeius hears this, he immediately gets up to go to the gate along with the two accused men, who are each bound with double chains. And sure enough, Simon has also cautiously come close to the gate, seeking his two associates because they have tarried so long. But when still a distance away, he sees a throng of people approaching, including his two accomplices bound with chains. He quickly realizes what has happened, and runs away so fast that he cannot be caught by anybody.

In this way, Simon, the angel of Satan, is driven out of Judaea, where he did many evils with his magical charms, and is never seen there again. He decides to go to Rome, but first has to stop at the port city of Caesarea, where he first debated with Peter.

When Eubula has recovered all of her treasures, she gives them to charity in the service of the poor. In addition, she gives all the rest of her prized possessions to the widows, the fatherless, and the underprivileged. Sincerely believing on the Lord Jesus Christ, she withdraws from society and is comforted by spending her time in meditation and quiet prayer. And after a good long life, she receives her rest in peace.

PETER LEAVES FOR ROME

It is the year 59 AD. Peter doesn't know it, but Simon has already left Judaea and is making his way to Rome. Late one evening, he has a prophetic vision that gives him a glimpse of what will soon come to pass.

As he is fasting and quietly praying, an angel of the Lord appears to him and says, "Peter, the man called Simon the sorcerer, who you convicted of heresy and chased out of Syria and Judaea, has come again to haunt you – this time in the great city of Rome, where he is profaning your name, preaching false doctrine, and claiming that he has the 'power of god'. So convincing and astounding are his teachings and his deeds, that nearly all who were believers in our Lord have fallen away – tricked and deceived by Satan and his devious henchman Simon. So, do not delay – set forth tomorrow for Caesarea – there you will find a ship ready to set sail for Italy, and within a few days I will reveal to you a great miracle."

Inspired by the vision, Peter then relates it to all the followers and disciples without delay, saying: "It is necessary for me to go to the great city of Rome to fight with the enemy of the Lord, and to be stalwart with the believers there."[6]

And so, Peter and his wife hurriedly go down to the port of Caesarea and board the next ship destined for Rome,[7] taking only small bags of provisions with them.[8] The captain of the ship is a man named Theon – he looks straight at Peter as he is boarding and says, "Sir, whatever amenities we have here, they are all free for you to use. For what are we in the eyes of God, if we take in a holy man like yourself – who is in an obvious state of unease and worry – and we don't share with him all that we have? So, let us pray for a peaceful voyage, and let all your anxieties be quelled."

Giving him thanks for the offer, Peter, nevertheless, stays to himself and fasts, sorrowful in mind and troubled in spirit. He prays for safe passage, and consoles himself, knowing that God has accounted him worthy to be a minister in His service.

NOTES

1. or Antyllus

2. The significance of the chained naked boy holding a loaf of bread is unknown, but it could be a metaphor for the generic oppressed slave who sought freedom through belief in Christ.

3. The Roman city of Flavia Neapolis (the biblical city of Shechem – and the modern-day city of Nablus) was about 30 miles north of Jerusalem. So, the gate referred to was an ancient northern gate. Neapolis means 'New City', renamed by the Roman emperor Hadrian.

4. The satyr was an anthropomorphic woodland god having squat legs, pointed ears, and short horns like a goat.

5. In reality, Eubula went to the praetorium, the building where the Roman magistrate worked.

6. There are only a handful of 'Christians' in Rome at this time – believers who left Jerusalem after the Holy Spirit descended, or fled during the purge of Saul, travelers who met and were influenced by Paul during his missionary voyages, and friends and locals who were evangelized by these people.

7. Caesarea was the main port city for Judaea on the Mediterranean Sea.

8. It's possible that a servant or two, and his 'daughter' Petronilla accompanied Peter and his wife to Rome. It is not known whether Petronilla was a blood daughter, an adopted or foster daughter, a servant, or a convert (a 'spiritual daughter', or follower) of Saint Peter. Most scholars subscribe to the 'convert' theory. However, it's probably more likely that the servants and the 'daughter' followed Peter on a subsequent voyage.

13 ON THE WAY TO ROME

SIMON AND DRUSILLA

Staying in Caesarea for a time, on his way to Rome, Simon becomes involved in an intrigue with the Roman provincial governor Antonius Felix,[1] who has an infatuation with a woman named Drusilla[2] – the daughter of King Herod Agrippa I,[3] and sister of Herod Agrippa II.

Drusilla was a granddaughter of Herod the Great, and a niece of Herod Antipas, the son of Herod the Great. It was Herod Antipas, as the ruler of Galilee, who had John the Baptist beheaded after being deceitfully tricked by his wife Herodias and daughter Salome.[4]

For political expediency, at the age of about 15, Drusilla marries Priest King Azizus of Emesa, Syria.[5] The marriage was arranged to celebrate his conversion to Judaism (he even consented to be circumcised in order to marry the beautiful Drusilla).

But, enamored with her Oriental beauty, Felix hires Simon to 'convince' (trick) both Drusilla and Agrippa, into thinking that she should divorce Azizus and marry him, Felix, instead. To do this, an elaborate abduction scenario is staged by Simon, using some of his best magic, to make it look like she is running away from an abusive and violent husband, and is rescued in the nick of time by Felix. Drusilla willingly goes along with the ruse in order to outmaneuver her sister, Berenice, who is jealous of her beauty and covets her status – and has threatened to declare that she is an unfaithful wife.

It isn't long before she divorces Azizus and is married to Felix, the pagan Roman governor.[6] Many Jews condemn the marriage as illegitimate,[7] but they remain together for years.

In late 57 AD, Drusilla appears with Felix at a hearing in Caesarea concerning the Christian missionary and evangelizer Paul,[8] who has been charged by the Jewish high priest Ananias, and his lawyer Tertullus, of being a dangerous nuisance and riot-starter.[9] Wanting to gain favor with the Jews, and hoping to receive some bribe money, Felix keeps Paul in prison for two years.[10]

SIMON IN CORINTH

It was back in 50 AD, when Paul visited Corinth, a city just southwest of Athens, on his 'Second Missionary Tour'. He stayed there for a year and a half, preaching and debating with both Gentiles and Jews.[11] Many of the Corinthians believed in his message and were baptized, especially many of the poor and unprivileged. It was here that Paul received a vision from the Lord, that said:[12]

Do not be afraid. Go on speaking and do not be silenced, for I am with you. No one will attack you or harm you. There are many of my people in this city.

Paul left Corinth to return back to Jerusalem, thinking that a healthy seed had been planted in good soil. Among others, the eloquent and fervent Apollos, an Alexandrian Judeo-Christian, rendered great service to the Corinthian community.[13]

But the budding church would soon be scandalized by open factionalism, including moral, legal, religious, and leadership conflicts. Certain members of the community were identifying with Paul, others with Apollos, others with Peter, and others with 'the Christ'.[14] Pagan and Hellenic customs were creeping in.

Simon arrives in Corinth in late 56 AD with an assistant named Cleobius. He is on his way to Rome, but the ship has docked in Cenchreae, the port close to Corinth, for weather and maintenance delays. Simon uses his time here to preach his message of divine emanations, multiple gods, and human authority to the masses,[15] but especially to the people who have been 'confused' by Paul and Apollos.

He proclaims to be 'the power of god', and spreads dissension and disorder in the nascent Christian community – at the same time bilking many out of their money and labor. He maintains that many of the things the Corinthians had previously learned were not precisely true. He claims that only he knows the real truth – 'corrects' all the errors of the previous teachers – and performs certain magical tricks to prove his power.

He stays only for a few months, but his interference in the thinking of the new believers is so serious,[16] and the devoted church members are so distraught, that they decide to send a message to Paul in early 57 AD, asking for spiritual help.

Paul is in Philippi, Macedonia, on his 3rd Missionary Expedition, but the believers in Corinth are worried that they might never see Paul again. They don't know if he will return to visit them, go back to Jerusalem, or set off for Spain. Their worry is exacerbated by the fact that newcomers had recently arrived who preached a very different message from Paul's. There are now a lot of different opinions about everything, and church order and decorum has broken down. Nearly everyone in the Christian community has become shaken in their faith, and many have fallen away.

So, the devoted believers decide to send an express letter to Paul in Philippi, asking for help and clarification. It is carried by hand by Threptus and Eutychus, deacons in the Corinthian house-church. The letter reads as follows:

To: Paul our eternal brother
From: Stephanus and the elders, Daphnus, Eubulus, Theophilus,[17] and Zenon

Greetings in the Name of the Lord:

Two men have recently come to Corinth, Simon and his partner Cleobius, and they are overthrowing our faith with many strange and peculiar words and deeds. Many of the believers have fallen away and are now disciples of Simon. We hope that you can examine their messages and set us straight in the eyes of the Lord. We have never heard such words from you, nor from the other disciples. Everything that we have received from you, we hold fast and believe, but it is becoming increasingly difficult to counter Simon's teachings, when he was recently here in the flesh and you are far away.

If the Lord will have mercy on us, we hope to hear the real truths from you again, while you are still in the flesh. So, if at all possible, please visit us again, or write to us. For we believe that the Lord has delivered you out of the hand of Satan, and you are now on the path of righteousness.

Now, the things that these men say and teach are:

1. The ancient Hebrew prophets were not truthful, because they were enlightened by sinful angels and not by God
2. God is not One Almighty – He is composed of various god-like entities with frailties and weaknesses
3. There is no resurrection of the flesh, only that of the spirit
4. Jesus Christ was not the 'Son of God' who came down from heaven in the flesh
5. Jesus Christ was not born of a virgin named Mary – nor was he of the seed of David
6. Jesus Christ did not die by crucifixion – it was only a trick that appeared that way
7. The body of man was not created by God, but by lesser gods created by the 'thought of god'
8. The world was not made by God, but by lesser gods created by the 'thought of god'

In a nutshell, there were many things that these men taught here in Corinth, deceiving many believers and many other people. We hope that you can 'clear the air' and bring us all back to the 'Good News' of Jesus Christ as soon as possible.

The Lord be with you.
In Jesus Name, we pray.
/ signed /

After receiving this letter, Paul immediately replies with a practical letter that throws spiritual light on the many down-to-earth problems facing a newly established community in a pagan environment notorious for its immorality. This letter is the biblical 'First Epistle to the Corinthians', and it gives clear guidance on all the nagging issues. Paul follows-up with an in-person visit a few months later.[18]

Meanwhile, Simon has headed for Rome.

THE CONVERSION OF THEON

Peter and his wife are on a ship headed for Rome. After a few days at sea, the captain of the ship requests that Peter join him at the captain's table for the dinner meal, saying: "Sir, I do not know you personally, but I take you to be a servant of God. For as I was steering the ship at midnight, I perceived a voice from heaven say to me, 'Theon, Theon!' Twice it called me by name and said, 'Among those who sail with you, let Peter be greatly honored, for it is because of him that you, the crew, and the entire manifest will be preserved safe, and not encounter any violent storms.'"

Hearing this, Peter believes that God will answer his prayer for safe passage, and so he tells the captain that the trip will be without incident. Perceiving that Theon was of one mind in the faith and a worthy disciple, he then begins to tell Theon about all the mighty works of Christ, how the Lord had chosen him from among the apostles, and why he was sailing to Italy. Daily, Peter reads to him the Word of God, and they are united in fellowship.

One night, when the sea is very calm, Theon comes to Peter and says, "If you will account me worthy, there is now an opportunity to baptize me with water and the seal of the Lord.[19] For all that are in the ship have fallen asleep, and by raft and rope the sacrament is possible in the sea."

And so, in the middle of the night, Peter and Theon go down to the raft by a rope ladder, and Theon is baptized in the name of the Father and of the Son and of the Holy Spirit. As he comes up out of the water, he rejoices with great bliss, and Peter is very glad that God had accounted Theon worthy of His name.

And just then, miraculously, a shimmering image of a youth appears in the raft, shining brightly and beautiful, and says to them, *Peace be with you*. Then, it quickly fades away.

Immediately, Peter and Theon get back up on the ship and go to Peter's cabin. Then, Peter takes bread and gives thanks to the Lord, for accepting him as worthy of this holy ministry, and for the privilege of receiving the vision that had appeared to them.

And he prays: "Thank you, O one and only almighty God – and thank you my Lord Jesus Christ – for I know that it was you who appeared to us in the vision – in your name has this man now been washed and baptized with your holy seal. Therefore, in your name, do I now impart to him the Holy Eucharist, that he may follow your commandments and be your perfect servant without blame for ever."

As they partake of bread and rejoice in the Lord, there suddenly comes a fairly stiff wind into the ship's sails – not vehement but moderate – and it continues for six days and nights, until they come to the port of Puteoli in Italy.

NOTES

1. Marcus Antonius Felix was the 4th governor of the Roman province of Judaea. His name means 'fortunate', but his life was marked more by cruelty than by luck. Beginning life as a slave (then freedman), he ended up as a ruler of a Roman province. But he was duplicitous, savage, treacherous, and steeped in blood. Coupled with his penchant for bribes, his reign was marked by many internal disturbances, which he put down with severity. He hired assassins to murder Jonathan, the Jewish High Priest, shortly after he criticized Felix's governance of Jewish affairs. Porcius Festus succeeded him as governor (Refer to Acts 24:27 and 25:1-27).

2. Drusilla was a notable name among gentrified Romans. It means 'watered by the dew' or 'dewy-eyed'.

3. Herod Agrippa I was visiting Rome when the emperor Caligula was assassinated in 41 AD, and he helped Claudius solidify his claim as successor emperor. Claudius was grateful to Herod for this help and appointed him king over all of Palestine. Although Herod Agrippa was raised in Rome, he was conscious of the role of Judaism in his territory, and publicly supported the Jewish religious leaders in Jerusalem. In order to gain their favor, he started a major attack against the Jesus movement. His first high-profile victim was the apostle James, son of Zebedee and brother of the apostle John.

"About that time King Herod laid violent hands upon some who belonged to the church. He had James, the brother of John, killed with the sword. After he saw that it pleased the Jews, he proceeded to arrest Peter also." (Acts 12:1-3) Peter was delivered from prison by an angel of God (read the whole story in Acts 12:6-19), but the legacy of Herod Agrippa was solidified. As such, he was labelled the 'first royal persecutor of the Church'.

4. John the Baptist had publicly condemned Herod for engaging in an incestuous marriage. He had married his brother Philip's ex-wife, who had divorced her first husband. But this violated Jewish law since the brother was still alive (see Leviticus 20:21). Herodias hated John for this because it made both her and Herod look bad in the eyes of the people. The intriguing, but sad, story of Salome's dance, and Herodias's revenge, is told in Matthew 14:1-12, Mark 6:14-29, and Luke 9:7-9.

5. Gaius Julius Azizus was his full name – Emesa is modern-day Homs, in Syria.

6. The details of the divorce proceedings are unknown.

7 Drusilla's marriage to Felix was sinful in two ways: 1) As a Jewess, she married a heathen who did not confess the faith of her fathers, and 2) since her first husband, from whom she had not been divorced, was still alive, she married Felix illegally.

8. Acts 24:24

9. Drusilla is mentioned in the Bible in connection with Paul's second appearance before Felix, when she is about 20 years of age. It may have been because of her urging that Paul was brought back to trial again. She probably wanted to hear what he had to say about why he changed his beliefs from a Jesus-persecutor to a Jesus-follower (see Acts 24:24).

But Drusilla and Felix both heard a message they did not expect. When Paul preached about justice, self-control, and the judgment to come, Felix and Drusilla trembled with anxiety. They sat in transfixed silence as Paul plunged the two-edged sword of God's holy law into their hardened hearts. His message traumatized their consciences, for their sins would one day be exposed.

Paul's dialogue was interrupted by Felix when he became agitated. "Go away for the present," he said. "When I have an opportunity, I will send for you." (Refer to Acts 24:25) But Paul remained in custody for two years. Although he checked in on Paul many times after that, the apostle refused to pay a bribe for his release.

Drusilla may have been very beautiful, but she was also very shameless. Because her conscience was greatly disturbed by Paul's convicting truth, it's very likely that Drusilla was the impetus behind cutting short the discourse, and having the apostle sent back to prison. Many scholars believe that she was the driver for Paul remaining in prison and not being released – without Drusilla, Felix might have been converted and baptized, and Paul released. Unfortunately, the earnest conviction and mannerisms of Paul, and the power with which he presented his beliefs, failed to bring the sinful Drusilla to her senses. Instead, she saw in Paul the enemy of everything she represented, and hated him for his exposure of her private sins.

After the trial of Paul, Drusilla disappears from the pages of Christian history. But she re-emerges 22 years later in secular history (79 AD), when the terrible eruption of Mount Vesuvius occurs, and the cities of Pompeii and Herculaneum are destroyed. Underestimating the danger, she and her child, Marcus Antonius Agrippa, left their villa at the last moment. Endeavoring to escape the catastrophe by running out of the city, they were overcome by the onrushing lava flow and buried alive. Her son was one of the few people documented by name, who died in the Vesuvius eruption.

10. Acts 24:1-27

11. Acts 18:1-11

12. Acts 18:9-10

13. Acts 18:27

14. Reference 1Corinthians 1:12.

15. Simon preached on many topics, but one of his favorites was the impossibility of bodily resurrection – in other words, "live for the now, because there is no after-life".

16. All of the community ills and disorders are described in 1 Corinthians Chapters 1 through 15.

17. This is not the same Theophilus as the rich church builder in Antioch.

18. It was in Corinth at this time that Paul wrote his famous 'Epistle to the Romans', the closest of all his letters to a theological treatise. But after leaving to make his way back to Jerusalem, trouble again emerged and Titus had to be sent to Corinth to smooth things out. Titus manages to restore order and notifies Paul of such. Paul then expresses his relief, his anxiety to restore good relations, and warns and encourages the church in his 'Second Epistle to the Corinthians'.

19. Full body immersion in water was the common form of baptism in the first century. This could be done in the sea, off the side of the ship, only if the seawater was calm.

14 PETER IN ROME

It isn't long before a commotion arises in the midst of the fledgling Christian community in Rome. Some members are saying that they have heard about a man named Simon – that he has done some wonderful and amazing things – that he is now at Aricia [1] – and that he claims to have the great 'power of god'. In fact, he maintains that everything he does is because of god. "Is this man the Christ?" they wonder. "Or another Christ? Or another incarnation of Christ?" They want to believe in Jesus Christ, the one who had died and rose again – the one who Paul had preached about in Asia and Greece, and eloquently described to them in his recent Letter to the Roman Christians. [2]

But Paul is not here. And this Simon is articulate, proud, and persuasive. And he is making himself popular with the people – many Italians are becoming his disciples, and even some from the small Christian flock are leaving and following him. *Maybe, this Simon will come to Rome*, they think, *and everyone will be able to see and talk to him in person*. With much eagerness, they press him to come to Rome, saying with great acclaim, "You are a god in Italy – the savior of the Romans – make haste and come quickly." [3]

THE ARRIVAL OF SIMON

Reveling in the adoration of his followers, Simon says to them in a shrill voice, "Listen my friends! Tomorrow at about the seventh

185

hour, you will see me enter Rome by flying majestically over the gate of the city. So, if you need further convincing of my power, go to the gate at the proper time, and see for yourselves." Of course, word spreads like lightning throughout the city that the 'power of a god' is coming.

Early the next morning, many people from all over the region begin converging on the gate. When it is the seventh hour, abruptly, a dust cloud is seen in the sky afar off, like a whirling pillar of smoke, with rays of shining light emanating from all around it and stretching for a long way. Slowly, it gets closer and brighter. But when it draws near to the gate, suddenly it disappears with a puff and a flash, and evaporates into the sky. And amazingly, Simon then appears standing in the midst of the people, proclaiming his power and greatness. Naturally, the throng falls down and worships him as a god – they know that he is the same person that had been seen the day before, who had said that he would fly over the city gate.

Even the sprouting Christian believers are unnerved. Since Paul is not yet in Rome, and neither is Timothy or Barnabas, they have no immediate defender or comforter. Many begin to fall by the wayside, especially the catechumens, who have no teacher. And as Simon exalts himself yet more by his daily acts of magic, many of the people start calling Paul a fake, a deceiver, a fraud, and even a sorcerer. As Simon's popularity soars, almost all the new believers who have only recently been brought into the faith, quietly fall away. Only the church elder Narcissus, and six women who can no longer go out of the house, remain in the service of our Lord. They give themselves up to prayer day and night, pleading with the Lord for Paul or Peter to come quickly, because the wicked devil is fast at work in the city.

THE ARRIVAL OF PETER

When the ship docks at the port of Puteoli in Italy, Theon leaps out onto the pier (while the crew are still making all the preparations for disembarkation) and rushes to the inn where he usually stays, so that Peter can be properly welcomed. The proprietor of the inn is a man named Ariston – and he is a passionate believer who rightly fears the Lord. It is because of this faith that Theon has always looked up to him, trusted him, and stayed at his humble inn.

When he arrives at the inn and sees Ariston, Theon warmly says to him, "Praise be to God! The almighty One in heaven, who has accounted you worthy to serve him for all eternity,[4] has communicated his grace to me by his holy servant Peter, who has just now sailed with me from Judaea, being commanded by our Lord to come to Italy."

The Faith of Ariston

When he hears this, Ariston falls upon Theon's shoulders and embraces him – and begs him to bring him to the ship and introduce him to Peter:

"Ever since we heard from Paul by letter that he was returning to Jerusalem instead of coming here, before going on to Spain, we have all been discouraged and depressed.[5] There is no prominent preacher of the faith with whom I can stand up straight with, and refresh myself – no one with the wisdom and credibility of an apostle.

"Moreover, a certain wicked pretender has broken into the city – a man named Simon – and with his charms of sorcery and glibness of tongue, he has made all the believers here fall away this way and that. He has so stirred up the people – cursing Peter's name in the process – that the few remaining believers have had to flee from Rome for fear of persecution. I also fled from Rome, but have been confidently expecting the coming of Peter, because Paul had told us about him – and I also have seen many wonderful things in a vision.

"And so, now I am hopeful that the Lord will once again build up His ministry – and that all this deceit will be rooted out from among his servants. For our Lord Jesus Christ is faithful, and will forgive us if we falter, but then return to the fold."

When Theon hears these things from Ariston, whose eyes are misty, his spirit is raised even more and his will is strengthened, because he perceives that he has finally come to believe in the true living God.

So, Theon and Ariston quickly make their way back to the ship and go to Peter's cabin. Opening the door, Peter looks at them and smiles, being filled with the Holy Spirit. Falling on his face at Peter's feet, Ariston then blurts out:

"Brother and lord, you have taken part first-hand in the holy mysteries, and you have shown us the way of the truth and the light, which is our Lord Jesus Christ. You have restored my faith, but by the workings of Satan, we have lost all the believers who Paul had reached and delivered to the faith. But now, I put my trust back in the Lord, who has commanded you to come to us, sending you as his messenger.

"I believe that He has accounted us worthy to see and understand His great and wonderful works by means of you, Peter. Therefore, I pray that you make haste to go to the eternal city. For I have left brothers there who have stumbled; who have fallen to the temptations of the devil. And I have left others who have departed the city, saying to them, 'Brothers, stand fast in the faith, for within two months, the mercy of our Lord will result in his faithful servant being brought to us.' Then, I saw a vision of Paul, saying to me, 'Ariston, get up and flee out of the city.' When I heard it, I believed and departed without delay, even though I had a sickness at the time.

"And so, I came here to Puteoli and prayed every day. I would stand at the sea-shore asking the sailors, 'Has Peter sailed with you?' The answer was always 'No.' But now, through the abundance of the grace of God, you are here – and I beg of you, let us go to Rome without delay, before the teachings of this wicked man prevail yet further."

After Ariston says this with tears in his eyes, Peter gives him his hand and helps him up, saying with great conviction, "The devil and his fallen angels have tempted all the world through the ways of the flesh. But our loving God has the power to save his faithful servants from all evil temptations through the ways of the Spirit. He shall quench the deceits of Satan and his followers, and put him beneath the feet of those who have believed in our Lord Jesus Christ."

As they are leaving the ship, Theon pleads with Peter, saying, "You did not refresh yourself at all during the sea voyage, and now after so rigorous a journey, will you set out straightaway to Rome from the ship? Why not stay here a bit, rest, and refresh yourself? For the road to Rome is rocky and hard on the legs and feet, and I don't want you to suffer."

But Peter politely refuses, implying that he must not lose a day to the devil, who is hard at work tempting souls. His inconvenience is inconsequential to the task ahead – saving souls from the evil one – so he must stand tall with his fellow-believers at all costs. So, Theon cannot prevail on him to tarry even one day.

After unloading the cargo and verifying the manifest, Theon catches up with Peter and Ariston and follows them to Rome. Ariston brings them to the house of Narcissus, the church elder.

AT THE HOUSE OF NARCISSUS

Word spreads quickly throughout the city, and also to the believers dispersed in outlying areas, that the apostle of the Lord has come to Rome to rally them back together, preach the 'Good News', and rebuke the man called Simon, who is a grave deceiver and trickster. All the scattered believers rush back to the city to see the man who has actually been with, and personally known, the Lord and Savior, Jesus Christ.

Peter Addresses the Crowd

On the first day of the week, a great multitude assemble on the lawn in front of the house of Narcissus. And Peter begins to address them with a loud voice:

"Brothers and sisters gathered here today, always keep your trust in Christ and put your faith in Him. For there is no other – He is the Alpha and the Omega, the beginning and the end – the first and the last. And He will never desert you.

"Yes, I know that you have suffered temptations from the pagan authorities, and also from certain false teachers. But you must learn and understand why God sent his only Son into the world, doing it in such a way that He was born of a virgin, named Mary. Why else would He have done this miracle, if not to procure some divine grace or dispensation for us mortals? By this very act, He took away all sins, all ignorance, and all the contrivances of the devil – and all the minor offenses that befell people before our Lord shined forth in this world. And although His wisdom, His power, and His grace have existed since the beginning of time, sincere belief in Christ is now the key to our salvation and everlasting life.

"Whereas, in the past through ignorance, men fell into death by many and diverse infirmities, Almighty Father God, moved with compassion, sent his Son into the world to bring His children more readily into the divine kingdom. And yes, I was blessed to walk with Him – even to walk on the water.[6] I myself remain a witness to His miracles, and do testify that He ministered to the world by great signs, parables, and wonders.

"However, I do confess, dearly-beloved brethren, that although I was with Him – yet I denied Him, our Lord Jesus Christ – and not only once, but three times.[7] For there were evil doers all around me that were overcome by the sway of Satan – intolerant of hearing the truth, and embedded in the religious bureaucracy. And I crumbled before the onslaught, unable to shield myself from Satan's arrows. Later, when I was bitterly grieved, deplored my actions, and lamented the weakness of my faith – because I was fooled by the devil and did not keep the word of my Lord – He did not punish me or ignore me. Instead, He turned to me with love and had compassion on the infirmity of my flesh.

"And so now I say to you, brothers and sisters who are gathered here together in the name of Jesus Christ, against you also has the deceiver Satan aimed his deadly arrows, such that you might depart from the way of righteousness. But fear not my friends! Do not let your spirit fall – but be strong, persevere, and continue to believe without doubt in the Lord. For if Satan could cause one like me, who had actually walked with the Lord, to stumble and thrice deny that I knew Him, what do you think he will try to do to you – you who are but young in the faith? Satan tried to make me flee the true faith and put my trust in a mortal man instead. And by similar deceit, he will try to get you to turn away – make you an enemy of the kingdom of God – and by so doing, cast you down into Hades. For whoever is cast out from the grace and hope of our Lord Jesus Christ, is a son of perdition forever.

"Therefore, I urge you to turn again to our Lord Jesus Christ – resist temptation and be strong again in God the Father Almighty. No person has ever seen Him in His natural spiritual state – nor can anyone living ever see Him. Only those who believe in Him, are saved, and go to heaven, will be able to see Him.

"Now, you must understand from where this temptation comes – it comes from Satan, and all those on earth who have been deceived by his wiles and have become his malefactors. And they are unrelenting.

"But you need to know that it is not only with words by which I preach to you, but also with deeds and great shows of power that the Lord works through me. I say this now, such that none of you will be tempted to look for any other god, prophet, or messiah – for there is none – only He who was despised and mocked by the Jews – the Nazarene who was crucified and died; and on the third day rose again – Jesus Christ, our Lord and Savior."

After hearing this rousing speech from Peter, many of the fallen-away believers repent and beg Peter to fight against Simon, the usurper of holy doctrine – who claims that he is invested with the 'power of god', and makes convincing shows of magic. Simon is lodged in the house of Marcellus, a Roman senator who had previously been sympathetic to the ministry of the 'Jesus followers'.[8] But he had changed his tune because he was convinced by the charismatic charms of Simon, that he truly was the 'voice of god' and the 'power of god'.

One of the repented believers then says, "Believe us, brother Peter, there was no one among men who was more pious than this Marcellus. All the widows who put their trust in Christ turned to him for help – all the fatherless children were fed by him – all the poor called Marcellus their patron – and his house was called the 'house of the strangers and the poor'.

"Even the emperor once said to him sarcastically, 'I will certainly keep you out of every official office – otherwise, you will give everything away to the needy and the poor, and in the process, bankrupt the government.' And Marcellus would only answer, 'All my goods are also yours.' To which the emperor would reply, 'Yes, they would be mine if you had kept them for me. But now they are not mine, for you have given them away to whoever you wanted – and I don't know what vile persons you have given them all away to.'

"And so, having seen and heard all this first-hand, we feel that we must report it to you, brother Peter – how the great mercy of this man has been turned upside-down into blasphemy. Being a man of such stature, if he had not turned away from Christ, then neither would the rest of us have dismissed the holy faith of Christ our Lord.

"But the sad part of all this, is that Marcellus now laments about all the good deeds he once did. He walks about in a miserable mood, angrily complaining, 'All these riches that I have given out have been wasted. I wrongly believed that giving it in the name of God would benefit my soul, and also help bring all the beneficiaries closer to God. But nothing has happened. These nameless souls show no inclination to embrace the faith – they just greedily grab the goods. And I don't feel in my heart that the message or the hope of God, is being furthered.'

"It's gotten so bad that if a stranger now comes to the door of his house, he strikes him with a stick, and warns him to leave or be beaten further. He goes about mumbling to himself, 'I wish I had not spent so much money on those impostors,' and he speaks with curses to everyone all the time.

"O Peter, we believe that the mercy of the Lord abides in you, and the goodness of his commandments are inviolate. So, please help this man see the error of his ways. He has done many good deeds for the people in the service of God – help him to return to the true path of Christ."

When Peter hears this, he is sharply afflicted and very distraught. After a moment of silence, he addresses the crowd – with great sorrow, but also with great conviction of purpose and resolve:

"O the contrivances and manipulations of the wicked – the elaborate and intricate tricks of the evil one – the twisted and convoluted temptations of the devil! The ravening wolf who devours and scatters the seekers of eternal life, who enjoys destroying the spirit and soul! He led the first man to sin and bound him with iniquity, chained to the lusts of the flesh! He is the champion of bitterness and envy!

"It was he who compelled Judas, my fellow-disciple, to become exceedingly wicked and deliver up our Lord Jesus Christ. He hardened the heart of Herod, and inflamed the mind of Pharaoh, compelling him to fight against Moses, the holy servant of God. He gave boldness to Caiaphas, such that he delivered our Lord Jesus Christ to the unrighteous multitude. And even now, he continues to shoot poisonous arrows at innocent souls!

"O you wicked enemy – adversary of all men – let you be cursed by the church of the holy Son of God, and cast down into the fire by the servants of our Lord Jesus Christ. Let blackness and isolation encompass you and your evil followers! Let your own wickedness and depravity be turned back against you, leaving you in a bottomless pit of darkness!

"Depart from those who believe in God – depart from the servants of Christ and from those who desire to be his soldiers! Keep your garments of darkness to yourself! Stop knocking at the doors of those who do not belong to you, but belong to Christ Jesus, their shepherd. You despicable thief – you would carry off the sheep that are not yours without remorse – even the ones belonging to Jesus, who cares for them with all tenderness and love."

When the people hear these words from Peter, they are greatly comforted, and many are added to those who believe in the Lord. But many of the believers plead with Peter to join battle with Simon, so that he will no longer be able to vex the people. So, without delay,

Peter rises up and goes to the house of Marcellus, where Simon is staying – and many people follow him.

AT THE HOUSE OF MARCELLUS

When Peter arrives at the door, he calls to the servant and says to him, "Go to Simon and tell him that 'Peter, the one who cast you out of Judaea, is waiting for you at the door.' "

The servant then answers Peter, saying, "Sir, I don't know whether you are Peter or not, but I have been commanded to say that Simon is not in the house. You see, he found out yesterday that a man named Peter had entered the city, and he told me: 'Whether it be day or night, at whatever hour he comes, say that I am not at home.' "

To which Peter replies, "You have done well in reporting that which you were instructed to say." Then, he turns to the people that have followed him and says, "You will now see a great and marvelous wonder."

The Talking Dog and Statue of Caesar

Seeing a large dog bound with a strong chain, Peter goes over to it, and frees it from the chain. When it is unconstrained by the chain, the dog miraculously receives a man's voice, and says to Peter, "Servant of the unspeakable and unseeable living God, what do you bid me to do?"

Peter then speaks to it, "Go in and locate Simon. Say to him in front of everyone in the house, 'Come out of the house you most wicked deceiver of souls – for your sake I have come to Rome.' "

And immediately the dog runs into the house, rushes into the midst of those who are with Simon, lifts up his forefeet, and says in a loud voice, "I say to you Simon, that Peter, the servant of Christ, stands at the door and says to you, 'Come out of the house you most wicked deceiver of souls – for your sake I have come to Rome.' " And when Simon hears this, and beholds the incredible sight, he loses his nerve, and can find no words to say that will rebut the words of the dog. Everyone in the room is amazed.

When Marcellus witnesses all this, he runs to the door and casts himself down at Peter's feet. Sobbing and choking with shame, he says to Peter, "I embrace your feet, most holy servant of the Holy God – for I have sinned greatly. My sins are unforgiveable, but I know that the true faith of Christ is in you, and you remember his commandments to hate no man and be unkind to no man. Therefore, linger not on my faults, but pray for me to the Lord, the Holy Son of God, whom I have abandoned in disgrace. For I have turned away from Him and persecuted his servants – and for that I am in deep remorse. I pray to you and to God that I not be delivered with Simon into the eternal fire.

"That cheat and swindler, Simon – O how I regret it, that by his persuasion, I erected a statue to him on an island in the river Tiber, with the inscription: 'In Honor of Simon, the Newest God'.[9] Believe me Peter, if you could have been won over with money, then at one time I would have given you everything I owned – although I would have despised myself, trying to gain my soul with money. But I was so confused. Even if I had sons, I would have considered them as nothing, just to have believed in the living God.

"But I do confess that he would not have deceived me except for the fact that he said he was the 'power of god'. O most gentle Peter, let me tell you that at this time I was not worthy to hear you, servant of the true and almighty God. I was not yet firmly established in the faith of God, which is in Christ Jesus. I was made to stumble, and I am ashamed.

"Therefore, I beg you not to take what I am about to say the wrong way: I heard that Jesus said to you, and all the apostles, that if you have faith – like the faith one has that a tiny mustard seed will grow into a great bush – then you will be able to move mountains by simply saying 'mountain, move yourself'.[10] But Simon said that you were without faith – that you doubted – and because of that doubt, you sank and could not walk on the water.[11]

"And I have also heard that Jesus said, 'They that are with me have not understood me.'[12] Then I ask you Peter, if you did doubt – one chosen by Him and upon whom He laid His hands – then what

195

chance do I have, under the spell of the devil, to not doubt? I was weak and not strong in my faith. And so, therefore I repent, ask for forgiveness, and put myself at your mercy. I pray that you can receive the soul of one who has fallen away from our Lord and from His promise, but has returned home again. I hope and pray that He will have mercy upon my weakness – and that the Almighty is ready to forgive my sins as I am ready to repent them."

Then, Peter exclaims in a loud voice: "Glory be to Almighty God, Father of our Lord Jesus Christ. To Him be all the praise, the glory, and the honor forever, world without end. Amen.[13]

"Because you have now fully strengthened your will and confessed your trespasses in the presence of all, I ask our Holy Lord God to fortify Marcellus, and to send Your holy peace upon him and his house this day. I pray to You Lord, to turn back all those who have lost their way. You are the shepherd of the sheep that once were scattered, but now shall be gathered again in one flock. As such, receive back Marcellus as one of Your lambs, and suffer him no longer to go astray in error or in ignorance. I ask that You receive him Lord – with anguish and tears, he begs for Your forgiveness."

As Peter says this prayer, embraces Marcellus, and turns to the multitude, he notices that one man in the crowd has a sly smirk about him – he can sense that an evil spirit is lurking inside him. So, Peter calls to the man, saying, "Whoever you are who is hiding something with a sneer and a snicker, show yourself openly to all who are present, and profess your secret."

Hearing this, the young man runs into the courtyard of the house, cries out with a loud voice, and bashes his fists against the wall, shouting, "Peter, there is a great conflict between Simon and the dog that you sent – for Simon said to the dog, 'Go back and tell Peter that Simon was not here, but that you related the entire message to everyone else who was here. Then, fall down dead at his feet.' "

But Peter responds calmly, saying, "Whoever you are, young man, you are possessed by a devil – so I call on the name of our Lord

Jesus Christ – get out of that young man and bother him no more – show your evil self to all who stand here."

When the young man hears Peter's command, he runs to the impressive fountain in the center of the courtyard, in a crazed state. He then grabs the imposing marble statue of Caesar that is set behind the waterfall, and smashes it into pieces on the ground.

"O no!" cries Marcellus, slapping his forehead, "a great crime has been committed – if this damage is made known to Caesar by some rascal, miscreant, or troublemaker, there will be repercussions – he will punish me grievously. Destruction of statues of Caesar are grave offenses."

Then Peter says to him, "Are you not the same man that you were just a few moments ago? Didn't you say that you were ready to spend everything you had to save your soul? Marcellus, if you truly repent, and believe in Christ with all your heart, then take some of the water from the fountain in your hands, and pray to the Lord. In His name, sprinkle it on the broken pieces of the statue, and they will return to the unbroken state – the statue will be made whole as it was before."

No longer doubting, but believing with all of his heart, Marcellus cups some of the water in his hands, lifts them up, and prays, "I believe in you, O Lord Jesus Christ – and Your apostle Peter believes that I believe rightly in Your Holy Name. Therefore, I take water in my hands, and in Your name do I sprinkle it on these broken stones, commanding them to reassemble, so that the statue will become whole as it was before. My Lord, if it is Your will for me to continue on the path and not suffer at Caesar's hand, then let this stone be made whole as it was before."

And then he sprinkles the water on the broken stones, and the statue miraculously becomes restored. Peter is grateful that Marcellus had not doubted in asking of the Lord – and Marcellus is very lifted in spirit, because such a wondrous sign has been accomplished through his direct involvement. And from then on, he believes with his whole heart in the name of Jesus Christ, the Son of God, by whom all things impossible are made possible.

Meanwhile, inside the house of Marcellus, Simon finally says to the dog, "Tell Peter that I am not at home." Then, the dog answers in the presence of Simon's followers, "You exceedingly wicked and shameless man, enemy of all that live and believe in Christ Jesus – here before you is a dumb animal, which has received a human voice to confuse you and show you to be a deceiver and a liar. And all you can say is, 'Tell him that I am not home?' Aren't you ashamed to utter such feeble and useless words against Peter, the minister and apostle of Christ? Did you think that you could hide yourself from him who commanded me to speak against you to your face? In truth, I say this not for your sake, but for those who you are deceiving and causing to fall from grace: Cursed you are, enemy and corrupter of the ways of Truth. For the sins that you have committed, you will be condemned forever to burning fire and utter darkness."

Having said this, the dog leaves the house, and all the people inside follow him out, leaving Simon alone. The dog comes up to Peter as he sits with a group of supporters and admirers who had come to see him – and it relates everything that it had said to Simon. Then, the dog speaks prophetically: "Peter, you will soon have a great contest with the enemy of Christ and his devotees. You will turn back to the faith many that have been deceived by him, and you will receive God's reward for your good work."

After the dog has said all this, it falls down dead at Peter's feet and breathes its last. When the crowd of people see with amazement that the dog could speak, many begin to kneel down at Peter's feet in respect and reverence.

A Dead Fish Restored to Life

But some dubious men in the crowd say, "Show us another sign, so that we may believe in you instead of Simon as the true minister of God – since Simon also performed many miracles in our presence, and that is why we followed him."

Then, Peter turns around and sees an oily soft-finned fish – like a herring – laying for sale on a counter-top in the window of a meat and fish store. He buys the dead fish, and holding it up, says to the people, "If you could see this very fish swimming in the water like a live fish, would you believe in Him of whom I preach?"

And together in one voice, they reply, "Yes, we will believe you and in what you preach."

Seeing that there is a small wading pool nearby, Peter prays aloud, "Since the people here need another sign, in the name of Jesus Christ, let this dead fish live again and swim like a live fish, in the sight of all."

With that, he throws the herring into the pool, and it miraculously returns to life and begins to swim vigorously. All the people see the fish swimming, and it continues to swim for a long time, such that no one can claim that it is only an illusion. Word quickly spreads, and soon, people from all over the city begin showing up – and they see for themselves the dead fish that was made into a living fish. A number of people even throw bread crumbs to it, and see that it is indeed alive. Witnessing this, many people decide to follow Peter and believe in the Lord.

Over the next few days, through the grace of Jesus Christ, and confirmed by the continuing works of Peter, Marcellus grows ever stronger in the faith.

Finally, Marcellus runs up to Simon as he sits in the dining room of his house, and rebukes him angrily, saying, "You are the most unpleasant and irritating of men – corrupter of my soul and my house. You tried to get me to fall away from my Lord and Savior – you are evil and a tool of the devil!"

Grabbing Simon with his hands, he commands him to get out of his house. The servants, of course, back up their master, and scold him severely – some slapping his face, others striking him with sticks, and one emptying out a pitcher of wastewater on his head. Other servants, who Simon had admonished in front of Marcellus, reproach him openly. Even some servants who had fled from Marcellus in order to follow Simon, reverse their loyalty and chide him, saying, "Now by the will of God, who has mercy on us and on our master, we repay you with a penalty fitting to your wickedness."

And so, Simon leaves the house of Marcellus.

BACK AT THE HOUSE OF NARCISSUS

Harshly censured and cast out of the house of Marcellus, Simon runs to the house of Narcissus, where Peter is staying. Standing at the gate to the front yard, he cries out, "Here I am Peter – it is I, Simon – and I am here to convict you for worshipping a man who was a simple uneducated Jew, and a poor carpenter's son."

When Peter is told that Simon had said this, he sends a woman with a nursing baby out to him, saying to her, "Go down quickly to the front gate, and there you will find a man who is seeking me. Do not say anything to him at all – just keep silent and hear what the child, who you are holding, will say to him."

Dutifully, the woman goes to the front gate with the child in her arms. Suddenly, the child receives a man's voice and says to Simon, "You are detested by God and by men – you are evil and a destroyer of truth. Know that you will be seen here only for a short while. Then, eternal punishment waits for you, and is your destiny. You are the son of a shameless father, who never put down solid roots for your well-being. You became a poisoned, faithless youth, void of all hope! And look at you now – you were not even disturbed when a dog chastised you.

"Now, I am only a child, but I am compelled by God to speak to you – and look at you – and even now you are not ashamed! But hear what I have to say to you: On the coming sabbath, an official will bring you into the Forum of Julius, even against your will, such that it can be shown to all what manner of man you truly are.

"So, leave now – depart from this gate, through which the feet of the holy walk – for no longer shall you corrupt innocent souls and turn them away from Christ. Your evil nature will be revealed, and your tricks will be rendered useless. And now, I tell you one last thing: In the name of Jesus Christ, you will soon become voiceless, and you will be forced to leave Rome for a time."

When the woman returns to Peter, and tells him, and the rest of the believers, what the child had said to Simon, they are all amazed, and praise the Lord.

As foretold, Simon temporarily loses his voice and moves to the city outskirts, living alone in a stable until his voice returns.

Meanwhile, people from all over the city are coming day and night to the house of Narcissus, the pious elder,[14] hoping to see Peter perform signs and wonders. And Peter preaches to them about the prophets in the scriptures, and about the things that our Lord Jesus Christ had taught and revealed, both in word and in deeds.

Peter's Vision

When night comes, Peter has a vision. He sees Jesus illuminated in a bright white light, smiling and saying to him:

Many people who had come to the faith, but were lost because of the heretic Simon, have eagerly come back to the faith because of the signs that you have performed in My name. You are the champion of My church! But hear this: In the days ahead, you will have a demanding contest of faith, and many more of the as-yet unbelieving Gentiles and Jews can be converted to the faith in My name — even though they were the ones who just recently criticized, mocked, and spit upon My followers. But I will be present with you when you ask for signs and wonders to counter the enemy. In this contest, you will have Simon opposing you, relying on his deceits and the tricks of his father, so be alert. But remember that all of his ploys are mere deceptions, ruses, hoaxes, and contrivances of sorcery. So, do not delay, and welcome anyone who I send to you as an ally.

The next morning, Peter tells the gathered believers about his vision – and they are all nervous about the contest with Simon – but confident that he will prevail with the help of the Lord. Addressing the group, Peter speaks of the upcoming contest:

"Dearest friends and beloved believers in the Faith, let us fast together and pray to the Lord. For it is only with His help, that we were able to drive Simon out of Syria and Judaea, and only with His help, will we drive Simon out of Rome. Let us accept the help of the Lord – He will grant us the power to withstand Simon's magical charms, and prove that he is a puppet of Satan. For on a sabbath day, our Lord will bring him into the Forum of Julius for the contest. Let us therefore bow our knees to Christ, who hears our pleas even though we don't cry out. He always sees us, even though He Himself cannot be seen by our eyes – because He is yet inside us. If we are true to Him, He will not forsake us. Let us therefore purify our souls of every evil temptation, and God will not depart from us."

After this was spoken by Peter, Marcellus comes to the house, and says, "Peter, for you I have cleansed my entire house from the traces of that detestable Simon, even down to the dust of his wicked feet. Calling upon the Holy Name of Jesus Christ, my faithful servants and I have taken water and sprinkled it all over my house – in all the dining rooms, relaxing rooms, and patios – even to the front gate. And I said, 'Lord Jesus Christ, I know that you are pure and untouched of any uncleanness. Let my enemy and adversary be driven out from this place, such that it be purified of his evil.' And now, honorable Peter, I have asked all the widows and older women of the neighborhood to come to my house, such that they may pray with us. And in service to the name of Christ, I will give each of them a piece of gold, such that they indeed may be called 'servants of Christ'. Everything is now ready, so I beg you O blessed Peter, come with me back to my house so that you can pray with the women in my place. Let us go as soon as possible, and take Narcissus with us, and any of the believers here who wish to go."

Consenting to the request, Peter then goes with many of the believers back to the house of Marcellus.

BACK AT THE HOUSE OF MARCELLUS

As Peter is entering, he comes upon an old widow, who is blind and being led by her daughter into the house. Respectfully, he says to her, "Come here, mother – from this day forward Jesus gives you His right hand. It is through Him that we have light everlasting, which no darkness can hide. It is He who says to you through me, 'Open your eyes and see – and walk by yourself.' And straightaway, as the widow feels Peter laying his hand upon her, her sight is restored.

Peter's Prayer to the Faithful

Entering the fellowship-hall, Peter notices that the Gospel is being read.[15] Upon seeing him, the lector stops reading and motions Peter up to the front. So, he quietly walks up to the lectern, closes the Book gently, and says to the attendees:

"Those of you who believe and hope in Christ, you must learn the right manner in which the holy scriptures of our Lord are to be understood.[16] For it was by His grace that we wrote down the little bit that we could – and by His grace that others have written down what we have said. So, it may appear to you to be a bit feeble – a little disjointed and unclear maybe. But the writings do not capture the big picture of what we experienced. The whole story is longer, more complicated, and more wondrous than I can ever convey in words – or text on paper can ever impart – but it has been instilled into my memory and my flesh.

"First, we must understand the will of God, and accept the goodness of God. From His first covenant with humanity in the beginning,[17] error in thought and in deed, provoked by the devil, has been spread about everywhere – and because of this, many thousands of people have been cast down into hell. Only a few have been saved and gone to heaven. But God was so moved by His unfathomable love and mercy, that He decided to reveal Himself to us in a form that is in the likeness of a human being, and to make a new covenant with us, even though we were not worthy to be enlightened. This is the 'Good News' that He brought, and it is a new way to live and achieve salvation. Of course, we could not fully understand everything at the time. Every one of us saw only what he was able to see, and understood only what he was able to understand.

"Now, let me explain to you what has just been read. Although I am a man of very humble means, I confess that I am privileged to behold the majesty of Our Lord. I do not know why this is so, but I accept His grace fully.

"When I was with James and John, the sons of Zebedee, on Mount Tabor,[18] I saw the brightness of His light – and I fell to the ground as one who was dead, and shut my eyes – and I heard a majestic voice come from Him that I do not have words to aptly describe. I thought that I had been blinded by His brightness! But when I breathed again, I thought to myself, 'Has the Lord brought me here to blind me? If so, then let it be.' And at that moment I said, 'Lord, if this be Your will, then I resist not.' Then, He gave me His hand and raised me up – and when I arose my blindness was gone – and I saw Him again in such a glorious magnificent form that I was barely able to take it all in.

"Fellow brothers and sisters, our merciful Lord, Son of the Father, has suffered and died for our sins. He has given us the clear path to salvation and everlasting life, even though we didn't perceive it at the time. For He is in the Father and the Father is in Him.[19] He is the fullness of all majesty, and has shown us all His good things. For our sakes, He ate and drank with us, although He was never hungry or thirsty. For our sakes, He bore harsh criticisms and accusations. And for our sakes, He died and rose again.

"He defended me when I sinned and comforted me by his greatness – and He will comfort you also if you love Him and accept Him. This is our God – Father, Son, and Holy Spirit! He is great and He is small. He is young and He is old. He is male and He is female. He is invisible for all eternity, but He has appeared to us for a short time. No man has ever touched Him, but His servants have held His hand. He is the Word proclaimed by the prophets and the Word incarnate in the flesh. He is not subject to suffering, but He has suffered on earth for our sakes. He existed before the world was created, but He was born of a virgin and lived in our time. He is above all the angels in heaven, but He was brought down low beneath earthly despots. He is almighty in majesty, but He is humble in dignity.

"Brothers and sisters, this is our Lord, Jesus Christ. He is the door, the light, the way, the bread, the water, the life, the resurrection, the refreshment, the pearl, the treasure, the seed, the harvest, the vine, the plough, the grace, the faith, and the Word. He is all things and there is no other greater than He. To Him be all praise, world without end. Amen."

Marcellus Sets Up a Debate with Simon

After having encouraged them all to meditate on the Lord with all of their hearts, Peter, Marcellus, and the original believers, begin together to minister to the newcomers, the curious, and the onlookers.

Marcellus says to them, "Listen to me, those of you who are new to the Word, and just starting down your path of understanding – you have a place here to stay – and those things that are called mine, are yours also. Don't leave right away – refresh yourselves for a bit. For soon will come the day when Simon will have contest with Peter, the holy servant of God.

"In that regard, let it be known that I have reserved space, posted notices, and officially organized a public debate in the Forum before the governor. Even now, I understand that scaffolds are being set up and equipment being readied. There and then we will behold the ruin of Simon the magician. For as Christ the Lord has always been with Peter, so now also will the Lord stand by His apostle."

Word spreads quickly throughout the city that two Jewish religious philosophers will engage in a public debate over the doctrines of their gods, in the Forum in the near future.[20] Interest soon reaches a fever pitch when it is learned that the god of Peter is performing miracles [21]– making dogs talk, changing dead fish into living, and making the blind see again.

On the following sabbath, many sick people are brought to him, pleading that they be healed of their infirmities – usually attended by relatives who also plead for healing. They come with many different diseases – palsy, gout, breathing disorders, and all kinds of debilitating fevers. And all who sincerely believe in the name of Jesus Christ, are healed by the grace of our Lord, and added to the family of God.

Marcellus's Dream

That night, after sleeping only a short time, Marcellus awakes, goes to Peter, and says, "O Peter, apostle of Christ, let us go boldly into this debate which lies before us. For just now, when I had turned in to sleep for a little, I beheld you in a dream – sitting in a high place.

Before you were assembled a great multitude – but in front of them all was an exceedingly vulgar woman, uncouth and filthy, clothed in rags, with an iron collar about her neck, and chains upon her hands and feet – cavorting about with distasteful movements.

"When you saw me, you said in a firm voice, 'Marcellus, if the whole power of Simon and his false god is in this dreadful woman who dances before me, then you should behead her at once.'

"And then I said to you, 'Brother Peter, I am a senator of high standing – I have never defiled my hands like this – nor killed so much as a sparrow in my time.'

"But then, upon hearing this, you began to cry out loudly, 'Come to us Christ Jesus, our true sword and protector, and cut off the head of this devil – and chop all her limbs into pieces, in plain sight of the multitude here.'

"And immediately another imposing one came – one who looked just like you – and wielding a sharp sword, hacked her to pieces. I then looked closely at you both, and marveled greatly to see how alike you were.

"And then I awoke, and now have told you about these strange signs in my dream."

When Peter hears about the dream from Marcellus, he is encouraged. Strange and gruesome as it seems, he knows that it means that the Lord always cares for His own – and if called upon, will protect and support His children.

Being refreshed by these words, they all retire for the night and sleep soundly.

PETER AND SIMON BEFORE AGRIPPA

On the morning of the scheduled debate, it seems like all the people in Rome have gathered together in the Forum. All the senators, governors, and those in authority have paid an admission price, and have taken the best seats in the house.

When Peter arrives, he is made to stand in the middle of the crowd. And then they all cry out, "Show us, O Peter, just who your god is, and why you have such confidence in his greatness. Do not disappoint the Romans – we are lovers of the gods, and we are lovers of a good contest. We have seen and heard convincing evidence from Simon, so let us see and hear it from you. Convince us then, why we should believe what you say."

As they are saying this, Simon enters the arena and stands next to Peter. He appears haughty in his demeanor, and he looks disdainfully at Peter.

After a long silence, Peter is motioned to speak up first:

"Citizens of Rome," he begins, "you are here to judge between the two of us – who speaks the truth of God and who speaks the lies of the devil? So, I tell you here and now, that I have believed, and still do believe, in the living and true God – and I promise to give you proofs of His glory, which are known to me, and also to many among you.

"For you see that this man standing here has been rebuked more than once. He knows that I drove him out of Judaea because of the deceits and transgressions that he inflicted upon an honorable and simple woman named Eubula – offences using artful tricks and sorcery. Being driven out from Judaea, he has now come here – thinking that since you know nothing about his sordid past, he can be free of preconceived notions among you. And now, he stands face-to-face with me here.

"So, tell us now, Simon, did you not fall at my feet in Samaria, when you witnessed the healings that were done by my hands? Did you not say, 'Please accept some money from me – as much as I have – just teach me how to do such mighty works by simply laying hands on men.'?

"And when we heard you say this, did we not rebuke you, saying, 'Do you think that you can bribe us into teaching you the mysteries of God? Do you think that we desire to possess money? Do you think that faith in God can be bought with money? Have you no fear of God?'

"So, I tell you now that my name is Peter, because the Lord Christ wished to call me 'prepared for all things'.[22] And I trust in the living

God with all of my heart – by whom I shall expose you as a fraud and put down your sorceries.[23]

"People of Rome, ask him now to do in front of all of you, what he has previously done only in front of a few people in private rooms. Therefore, in light of what I have said about him, do you still believe in him?"

But Simon speaks up proudly, "The Lord Christ you speak of – I presume you mean Jesus of Nazareth, the son of a carpenter, and a carpenter himself – whose birth is recorded in Judaea. Now hear this, Peter: The Romans have understanding – they are not fools."

And then he turns to the crowd and says, "Honorable men and women of Rome: can a god be born of a mortal woman? Can he be crucified on a cross? Jesus was seen to pray, and call to his master. But he who has a master cannot be a god."

And when he had said this, many in the crowd shout back, "You have said well, Simon."

With that, Peter becomes irritated, and snaps back, "Cursed are your words against my Lord Jesus Christ! Do you presume to know more than the Hebrew prophets of old? For it was an ancient prophet who once said, 'He had no beauty or comeliness – he was alone and rejected by his own kind.'[24] And it was another prophet who said, 'In the last days, a child shall be born of the Holy Ghost – his mother never knew a man, and no one claims that he is his father.'[25] And another has said, 'Behold, a virgin shall conceive in the womb. Neither did we hear her voice, and neither did a midwife come in.'[26] And another prophet has said, 'Born not from the womb of a woman, but he came down from a heavenly place. Behold, I saw one like the Son of Man coming on a cloud.'[27]

"What more can I say? Everything in the sacred Scriptures points to the coming of the Messiah – Jesus of Nazareth! O, men of Rome, if you knew the Scriptures of the prophets, I could teach you more about the sacred mysteries – about how the kingdom of God is made manifest to those on earth – and how eternal life in heaven can be obtained. All these things will become known to you in the near future.

"But now, I turn to you Simon – do one of those tricks that you have done before, and by which you have deceived many people. Do it again, and by calling on the name of Jesus Christ, I will show it to be nothing but deception."

With that, Simon ratchets up his boldness, and says, "If the governor allows it, prepare yourselves and I will show you that I have the 'power of god'."

Peter Out-tricks Simon

But governor Agrippa doesn't want to show partiality to either side – so he doesn't acquiesce to Simon's offer – he is patient, and doesn't want to appear unjust. Instead, he brings forward one of his young slaves and says to Simon, "Kill this man without touching him."

And then he turns to Peter and says, "And you, bring him back to life."

Turning to look at the crowd of spectators, he says, "It is now for the people to judge which one of these two men is the more credible – and acceptable to our society and our beliefs – he who kills on command, or he who returns one to life."

Straightway, Simon whispers something in the ear of the slave, and makes him speechless. A moment later, the young man appears to drop dead. But he has only fainted by a gas that Simon has squirted into his nose, the man's face being blocked from view by Simon's body whispering in his ear.

But before Peter can say or do anything, a commotion among the standing spectators begins to overwhelm the proceedings. There is a lot of muttering and murmuring. Then, suddenly, one of the widows being cared for in the house of Marcellus, cries out from the back of the crowd, "O Peter, servant of God, my son is dead, my only son. Help me please. Help me."

The people make way for her and lead her to Peter. Once there, she falls down at his feet, saying, "I had only one son, and by the sweat of his hands he furnished me with nourishment – he raised me up and cared for me. But now that he is dead, who will give me a hand?"

Peter then motions to a few nearby spectators and says to her, "Go with these witnesses, and bring your son here – such that all may see and believe – that by the true power of God, he will be raised – and that this man Simon may witness it, and be shown to be the fraud that he is."

Then, he says to the spectators, "We have need of a few strong young men, especially those who are willing to see and believe."

And at that request, 30 young men arise, and prepare to carry her to the place of her dead son. But by now, the widow is beside herself, weeping and wailing uncontrollably, so the men pick her up and carry her to the place where her son lay. Clawing and scratching her hair and face, the woman sobs over and over, "My son, my son, the servant of Christ has sent for you."

Upon reaching the house, the young men examine the boy and determine that he is indeed dead. Having compassion for the woman, they tell her, "If you wish it, and have faith in the god of Peter, we will take him up and carry him to the Forum, and there we will see if he can be raised up and restored to you."

Meanwhile, back at the Forum, the governor looks sternly at Peter and says, "Well, what do you say Peter? My favored servant here – who is also a favored servant of the emperor – is dead. I did not spare him, even though I had with me other servants of lesser rank. You see, I really want to put you, and the god of whom you preach, to the ultimate test – to know for sure whether what you say is true or false. To that end, I am prepared to sacrifice the life of this noble servant, to find the truth."

In response, Peter quietly replies, "God is not intimidated or extorted, O Agrippa. But if he is loved and praised, he hears those who are worthy. But now, since my God and Lord Jesus Christ – who has already done so many great signs and wonders by my own hands – is being tested by you in the sight of all the people here – I ask my

Lord and my God, at my word, to raise up the one who Simon has slain. So, I say to you governor Agrippa, go and take hold of the right hand of your worthy servant and help him up – you will find him quite alive and able to walk with you."[28]

So, Agrippa goes to the lad and takes his hand – and there and then the young man is raised up alive and walks, although a bit wobbly.

Seeing this, all the multitude cry out, "There is only one mighty god, the god of Peter!"

Peter Raises a Widow's Dead Son

In the meantime, the widow's son is brought in on a makeshift bed by the young men – the people make way for them, and they are brought straight to Peter. Lifting up his eyes to heaven and stretching forth his hands, Peter serenely prays:

"O Holy Father, who has granted us the power to obtain any good thing, despite all the sorrow that is in the world, that we faithfully ask for through Your Son Jesus Christ – You who are seen by few but would be known by many. We ask that You shine Your light on us, enlighten us, and raise up the son of this faithful widow, who cannot help herself without her son.

"So, I say to you, young man, being a spokesman for Christ our Lord, arise and walk with your mother, for as long as you can do her good. And thereafter, you shall serve God with a higher calling, ministering in the role of a deacon for the bishop here."

And then, with but a touch, the dead man rises up, and all the people gasp! They marvel at the power of Peter, and cry out, "The god of Peter is the one mighty god,[29] the invisible god, the savior of us all."

And the word spreads like wildfire throughout the city – that a common man has the power over life and death, by calling upon his lord and god with but a few words and a touch – and many become neophyte believers and followers wanting to learn more.

Peter Raises Nicostratus, with Strings Attached

Later in the afternoon, after the mid-day break, the mother of a prominent young senator comes into the area where Peter, Simon, and Agrippa are gathered. She barges through the crowd and throws herself down at Peter's feet, wailing, "My friends have said that you are a servant of a merciful god, and that you can impart his grace to all those who desire the gift of life. Please, can you give this gift to my son – for I know that you disregard no one. His name is Nicostratus – please don't turn away from this matron who is begging you."

Then, Peter says to her, "Do you believe in the one true God, and the Lord Jesus Christ, by whom your son can be raised?"

In a loud weeping voice, the mother cries out, "I believe, Peter, I believe!"

And the people in the crowd shout, "Grant the mother her son!"

But Peter replies, "Let him be brought here before all the people." Then, he proclaims, "Men and women of Rome, I am a mortal person just like you – I bear a man's body and I am a sinner – but I have obtained mercy through my faith. So please, do not look at me as if I do this by my own power. What I do is only by the power of my Lord Jesus Christ, who is the final judge of the living and the dead. In Him do I believe, and by Him am I sent. I have confidence when I call upon Him to raise the dead. Therefore, I say to you woman, go and bring your son here, and he will rise again."

So, the woman passes back through the midst of the people and goes into the street, running with great joy, and hope and belief in her thoughts. When she arrives at her house, with the help of some young slaves, she picks up her son and carries him back to the Forum. She asks the slaves to put signs on their heads, indicating that they are freed men, and to walk before the open casket.[30] And everything that she had decided to burn with the body of her son, is also paraded before the casket.[31]

When the procession arrives back at the Forum, including a supporting group of senators and their wives, all the spectators moan and lament the death – they have sorrow for the woman, but they are also anxious to witness the works of Peter's god. Because Nicostratus was noble and beloved by the senate, he is set down before Peter with great fanfare – and the crowd becomes noisy and boisterous.

When Peter sees this, he has compassion for the body of Nicostratus and his mother. He calls for silence, and with a loud voice shouts out: "Men and women of Rome, let there now be a just and final judgement between Simon and me – you must decide which one of us believes in the true living God.

"Let Simon raise up the body that lies here, and we will believe in him as an angel of God. But listen to me, he will not be able to do this because he is a fake. However, if I call upon the true God and am able to restore the son alive to his mother, will you then believe that this man, who has previously tricked you with magic, is nothing but a sorcerer and a deceiver?"

After hearing this from Peter, many in the crowd try to encourage Simon, saying, "If you truly have the 'power of god', then show it to us openly! Either convince us, or you will be convicted. Why do you just stand there silently? Come now, begin!"

When Simon realizes that everyone is watching him intently, he shouts out, "Men and women of Rome, if you behold the dead man rise by my command, will you cast Peter out of the city?"

And all the people together say, "Yes, we will not only cast him out, but we will burn the demon that resides inside him with fire!"

Then, Simon goes to the head of Nicostratus and stoops down closely beside him. Three times he touches him oddly, and then commands, "Raise yourself."

And then, the dead man slightly lifts up his head, partially opens his eyes, and weakly bows to Simon! At least, that is what one might surmise. In reality, Simon has used strong smelling salts to evoke an autonomic response.

Straightway, many of the people in the crowd begin to clamor for wood and torches, such that they can burn Peter, the fraud. But calling on the strength of Christ, Peter raises his voice, and appeals to them that have cried out against him:

"People of Rome, now I understand why your eyes and your ears and your hearts have been deceived. How long shall your understanding be obscured? Can you not see that you have been beguiled by this huckster? How can a dead man be raised without lifting himself up?

"I could have uttered some nonsense in my defense and left you to your vices, but I have the unquenchable rebuke of fire in my eyes. So, to prove to you my point, let the dead man speak – let him arise if he lives – let him loosen his wrappings with his hands – let him call for his mother – let him beckon to us with his arm and fingers. Of course, he can do none of these things.

"Now, to prove to you that he really is dead, and that you have been deceived, let this man depart from his casket. But if you look closely, you will see that the dead man is just the same as he was when he was brought in here."

By this time, the patience of Agrippa has worn thin. He pushes away Simon with his own hands, and once again the dead man lay as he was before.

Now, the people are becoming impatient. They look at Agrippa and yell out, "Hail Caesar! If the dead man does not rise, then let Simon burn as well as Peter – for he has tricked us, and the Romans don't like being tricked."

But just then, Peter stretches out his hand and addresses the crowd: "Citizens of Rome, have patience! Even if I do raise the lad, it is not right that you should burn Simon."

But the people are irritated and cry out again, "Peter, we will do it, even if it goes against your wishes."

Taking a deep breath, Peter then says to them, "Brothers and sisters, if you continue in this mindset, Nicostratus will not arise. Believe me when I tell you – the followers of Christ know that it is not good – not right – to repay evil with evil. We have learned to love our enemies and pray for our persecutors. For there is a chance that even this man can repent, and find mercy with God. So, give him the chance to come into the light of Christ. But if he will not receive the light, then let him wallow in darkness – but do not let your hands become dirtied, and your soul defiled. Let him be himself."

After saying this to the people, Peter walks up next to the dead Nicostratus. But before doing anything, he says to his mother, "These young slaves who you have set free in the honor of your son, can still serve our almighty God even after your son lives again – for I know that the heart of some will be hurt if they see your son alive and well, but then see that these slaves are once again returned to bondage. So, let them all continue to be free, and receive their sustenance as they did before. For your son is about to rise again – let them be with him once more."

Then, Peter looks at the mother of Nicostratus intently for a long time, to 'see' into her heart.

And then, the mother of the lad says, "What else can I do? Of course, I hear and obey. Therefore, I say in front of the governor: Whatever I had planned to burn with the body of my son, let the freed slaves possess it."

And Peter continues, "Also, let some of the residue be distributed to the widows."

Sensing that the woman's intentions are upright and honorable, Peter then prays out loud, "O my Lord Jesus Christ, You are merciful. Show Your power to Your servant Peter who calls upon Your name – You have always shown him mercy and loving-kindness. Therefore, in the presence of all those present here, and all those who have obtained freedom to become Your servants, in the name of Jesus, let Nicostratus now arise."

Peter touches the top of the young man's head with both hands, and commands, "Nicostratus, arise!"

With that, the man slowly becomes cognizant and tears off his funeral clothes. Sitting up and loosening his jaw, he asks for clean clothes. Then, he steps down from the casket and says to Peter, "Man of God, I pray to you – let us go to our Lord Jesus Christ, who I saw and heard speaking to you. Pointing to me, He said to you, 'Bring him here to me, for he is mine.'

When Peter hears this, he is strengthened even more in confidence and in spirit. Then, he says to the people, "Honorable men and women of Rome, it is by the true power of God that the dead are raised up – they arise and walk, they talk, and they live as long as God wills. It is not by any phony 'power of god' conjured up by trick sorcery.

"Therefore, all of you who have eyes to see and ears to hear,[32] turn away from your false gods, turn away from uncleanness and sin, turn to Christ with all your heart, receive fellowship and partake in the holy prayers [33]– do this and you will obtain everlasting life."

And in that same hour, many start to worship him as a god – like another new pagan god of Rome – falling down at his feet, and begging him to heal the sick and the dead who they have at home.

Seeing that a large crowd is beginning to crush upon the small wooden stage that they occupy, governor Agrippa signals to Peter that he should quickly withdraw himself. So, Peter tells the people to come later to the house of Marcellus, and then is quickly shuffled away through a back gate under the protection of followers and Forum guards. Not surprising, Simon also manages to slip away in a similar fashion.

However, the mother of Nicostratus begs Peter to come to her house, so that she can offer more hospitality in thanksgiving. But Peter has promised to be with Marcellus this evening, to minister to the people and to comfort the widows, so he politely begs off. With that, the mother goes back to her house, giddy with happiness and joy.

But at the same time, Nicostratus is single-mindedly adamant. "I depart not from Peter – I will follow him always!" he announces. And he follows him back to the house of Marcellus.

A few hours later, when he realizes that he has given nothing tangible to Peter in thanks, he runs home and immediately returns with 4000 pieces of gold, saying to Peter, "Praise be to God! I who was raised, now give you a double offering – and from this day onward, I give myself to Christ as a humble servant in His service!"

The next day, the mother of Nicostratus comes to the house of Marcellus and brings Peter another 2000 pieces of gold, saying to him, "Divide these among those who follow Christ, and serve Him faithfully."

NOTES

1. Aricia was an outlying suburb about 16 miles from Rome.

2. In the city of Corinth in Greece at the end of his 3rd Missionary Voyage, Paul writes a letter (dictating it to an associate named Tertius) to Christians in Rome [The Epistle of Paul to the Romans]. He has startling news. He says that he has finished the work of planting house-church congregations in the eastern half of the Roman Empire. Now, he wants to head over to the western reaches of the Empire – to Spain. He says that he hopes to stop in Rome along the way to meet the Christians there, and enjoy their fellowship. However, before he goes, he must first go to Jerusalem to bring a gift to the poor among the believers there – an offering that has been given by the Gentile believers in Macedonia and Achaia [Greece] (Refer to Romans 15:25-26).

Paul has a lot of friends in Rome (more than 2 dozen), including former ministry associates (including Phoebe, a deacon of the church in Corinth, who personally delivered the letter – refer to Romans 16:1-2), people who he converted (Epaenetus was the first convert in Asia), folks who spent jail time with him (Andronicus and Junia, who became Christians even before Paul), and one couple who risked their lives for him (Priscilla and Aquila – the full list is given in Romans 16:3-15).

3. Simon had 'greased the skids' by letter and by word-of-mouth, and already had a bunch of followers in Rome, even before appearing there.

4. Ariston has been baptized.

5. Paul's Letter to the Romans (The 'Epistle of Paul to the Romans' in the Bible). This must have been disappointing to the Roman Christians, especially those who he had met on previous travels. Paul had a lot of friends in Rome, including Priscilla and Aquila, who had left Rome in 49 AD when emperor Claudius expelled the Jews, met Paul in Corinth, traveled with him to Ephesus, and had just returned to Rome after Claudius's death in 54 AD.

6. Matthew 14:28-31

7. Matthew 26:69-75; Mark 14:66-72; Luke 22:54-62; John 18:15-27

8. The term 'Christian' was still not common in the outlying regions far from Palestine.

9. It was reported by the early Church Father Justin Martyr, that a statue on an island in the Tiber River (which flows through Rome) had been erected with the inscription *Simoni Deo Sancto*, ('To Simon the Holy God').

However, in the 16th century, a statue was unearthed on the island in question, inscribed to 'Semo Sancus', a pagan deity, leading some scholars to believe that Justin Martyr confused Semoni Sancus with Simon.

10. Compare with the 'miracle of the fig tree' in Matthew 21:18-22.

11. Matthew 14:28-31

12. Marcellus may have been referring to the miracle of the feeding of the five thousand. Reference Mark 6:51-52 and John 6:26.

13 A precursor to the 'The Gloria Patri', a Catholic Hymn of Praise (also called 'The Minor Doxology').

14. Narcissus was an elder and a presbyter in the nascent Christian home-church in Rome.

15. This was not the Gospel that we know today. It was just a very early attempt by someone to write down all that the apostles, disciples, and believing witnesses had said.

16. Remember, the New Testament was not yet written. Only bits and pieces of what had actually happened had been written down. Almost all doctrine was passed on through verbal teaching and learning.

17. Peter is probably referring to God's covenant with Noah, where He promised to never destroy the world again because of the wickedness of the people in it (generally recognized as the Second Covenant, the First being with Adam and Eve, and the promise that they may eventually receive salvation if they are responsible stewards of all creation).

18. Peter is describing 'The Transfiguration' event. Reference: Matthew 17:1-8, Mark 9:2-13, and Luke 9:28-36.

19. Compare with Matthew 11:27. Only God the Father fully comprehends the mission of Jesus on earth, and only Jesus fully understands God's plan for salvation, which He gradually unveils to humanity.

20. Although Simon was a Samaritan by birth, the Romans considered him to be Jewish because of his knowledge of Hebrew scripture.

21. Most people in Rome had absolutely no concept of the nature of the true Christian God – only a few travelers from Palestine or Asia, who had witnessed events or heard accounts from eye-witnesses, had an inkling of God's being and persona.

22. Peter had not yet realized the full meaning of being called 'the Rock', and all the implications of the future role of the church. Reference: Matthew 16:18 and John 1:42.

23. Peter's recounting of events in Samaria differs slightly from the account recorded in Acts 8:9-24.

24. Isaiah 53:2-3; Mark 6:1-4; John 1:11

25. Isaiah 9:6-7; Matthew 1:18; Luke 1:30-35

26. Isaiah 7:14; Matthew 1:23

27. Daniel 7:13; Matthew 24:30; Mark 13:26; Luke 21:27

28. Peter knew that grabbing the man's hand and pulling on it would be enough to awaken him from his faint.

29. Different people had different ideas about who 'the god of Peter' actually was. Many thought it was just a new god in the overall pantheon of gods. Deeper understanding of the one true God usually required intensive teaching of the precepts of the true faith, accompanied by liturgical practice.

30. The casket was not meant for burial – it was for adoration, and movement of the body to the funeral pyre for cremation.

31.. Cremation was the most common method of interment from the formation of Rome to the mid-2nd century. The body was taken to the 'necropolis' (city of the dead) and put upon a funeral pyre. It was then burned, and the ashes and remaining fragments of bone and teeth were interred in a funerary urn. It was believed that until the body was interred, the person's 'spirit' had not yet crossed the river Styx, the river that takes one from the 'World of the Living' to the 'World of the Dead'. The body was not buried with any possessions (a very old practice used in Egypt and throughout the Mediterranean, but hardly ever used in Rome), although possessions were often burned separately from the body.

32. Jesus said many times throughout the gospels of Matthew, Mark, and Luke, "He who has ears, let him hear." This is not just short for "listen up!" Instead, He was calling for people to take careful heed of what He was saying. Peter is using the same aphorism, which had become familiar to him. For examples, reference: Matthew 11:15, Mark 4:9, and Mark 4:23.

33. Peter was not referring to the divine liturgy that we know today, but to the prayers and customs that had been taught to him by Jesus. The early house-church read verses from the Hebrew Scriptures followed by the prayers and customs associated with the 'Good News' (especially confessions, baptisms, and communion with consecrated bread and wine).

15 PETER AND PAUL IN ROME

The year is now 60 AD.

Paul has completed his three missionary journeys and is now under Roman house arrest in Jerusalem because of charges brought by the temple High Priest Ananias, supported by accusations of Jewish leaders from the Asian provinces where he had earlier visited and preached.[1] When it is learned that conspiratorial plots have been hatched to kill Paul because of his disruptive teachings, the Romans whisk Paul away under heavy guard, to Caesarea for an audience with Felix, the governor. He remains in Caesarea for two years in protective custody, presenting his case to Felix,[2] his successor Festus, and the Jewish king Agrippa.[3]

Invoking the privilege of a Roman citizen, he refuses to travel back to Jerusalem to stand trial because of the danger to his life, and appeals his case to the jurisdiction of the highest court in the empire.[4] Relenting to the situation, Festus finally says, "You have appealed to Caesar, and to Caesar you will go." And so, shortly thereafter, under guard by the Roman centurion Julius, and accompanied by fellow Christian prisoner Aristarchus,[5] Paul is finally put on a sailing ship headed for Rome.

Shipwreck on Malta

However, the ship is battered by a severe storm at sea for 14 days, and is finally wrecked on a reef just off a beach on the island of Malta. Although the ship is destroyed, all hands are saved under the wise leadership of Julius.[6] The island inhabitants are friendly, and Paul remains on Malta for about three months, healing, sermonizing, and converting the local residents.[7] During this time, a message is sent on visiting ships travelling eastward, that the crew and prisoners have survived the wreck and will continue on to Italy with another ship when it can be scheduled and readied. The news reaches Palestine and eventually to the apostles in Jerusalem. But Peter had already left for the coast in pursuit of Simon and didn't receive the message. He eventually reaches Rome just a few months before Paul reaches Italy, thinking that Paul has probably died at sea. However, the news spreads fast among the Jewish diaspora – even to those in Rome – that Paul is alive and heading for Rome.

PAUL'S ARRIVAL IN ITALY

The Jewish leaders in Rome know that Paul has appealed to the emperor, and they do not want him coming to Rome to spread his 'lies and falsehoods'. Not only are they fearful of his religious teachings, but they also believe that he will request that the emperor destroy the temple leadership in Jerusalem. Their lament goes something like this: "It's not enough for him that he has confused and afflicted all the Jewish people in Judaea, Samaria, and all of Palestine – but now he wants to bring his sacrilegious ideas and wicked preaching to the eternal city of Rome. He is certain to cause us great misery and distress. He must be stopped."

When they hear that he has already arrived in Italy, they decide to go to emperor Nero and request immediate action – that Paul not be allowed to make it to Rome. So, carrying many presents, they get an audience before the emperor, saying: "We beg you, O good and royal emperor, send orders to all the local governments in Italy telling them to stop this agitator and troublemaker before he gets to Rome."

Nero has already been notified through formal diplomatic channels that a man named Paul has requested a hearing with the emperor instead of a trial in Jerusalem – and is supposedly on his way. But to him, this is a trivial matter. If by some accident, the man never makes it to Rome, then that would be just one less irritant on his schedule.

Having heard the supplication of the Jews, Nero thinks about it and then answers them: "It will be according to your wish. I will see to it, through informal channels, that all our representative jurisdictions be on the lookout for Paul, and prevent him from reaching Rome. At the same time, they will be on the lookout for the one called Simon, whom you have often complained to me about. Hopefully, neither troublemaker will be able to reach our city. But if they do, they will have to be dealt with like any other Roman citizen, within the framework of our law."

However, unbeknown to Nero, Simon is already in Rome, and starting to cause a stir. Meanwhile, some of the Christian believers in the city,[8] (many converted and baptized by Paul in Greece or Asia) learn about the Jewish plan and the underground order of the emperor. Afraid that a personal letter would not be received, they decide to send two representatives to Paul while he is still in Malta.

They carry a letter that says:

Paul, dear servant of our Lord Jesus Christ, and brother (comrade) of Peter,[9] the leader of the apostles:

Greetings:

We have heard that the Jewish rabbis in Rome have asked the emperor to send out an order, that wherever and whenever you are found, you should be put to death, thus stopping you from ever reaching Rome. So, please be careful and discreet. We firmly believe that God has willed it for you two servants of God to follow each other and not be parted – just like God has made the two great lights in the sky. We sincerely believe in our Lord Jesus Christ, in whom we have been baptized, and give thanks that we may have the opportunity to hear your teaching.

Having received the two men with the letter, Paul becomes eager to go, and gives thanks to the Lord Jesus Christ for the comforting visit and 'heads-up'. He then sails from Malta to the city of Syracuse in Sicily, along with Aristarchus, Julius, and the two men who had been sent from Rome to greet him, and stays there for three days.

From Syracuse, they sail on a different ship to Rhegium in the toe of Italy. From Rhegium, they ferry back to Sicily across the strait of Messina to the city of Messina,[10] where Paul ordains a man named Bacchylus as bishop.

Leaving Messina, they stay overnight at a nearby dock, and the next day they sail on a new ship to Puteoli in Italy.[11]

The Death of Dioscorus

Dioscorus, the shipmaster who brought them from Malta to Syracuse, is very sympathetic toward Paul because he had healed his son from a grave sickness. And so, he had left his own ship in Syracuse and accompanied Paul all the way to Puteoli.

Now, the two messengers from Rome, who are travelling with Paul, know that there are some believers living in Puteoli, so they locate them – and they cheerfully provide hospitality. They even convince Paul to stay with them in hiding for a week because of the order of the emperor – all the police and military folks are on the lookout, hoping to seize Paul and possibly kill him, thereby gaining favor with the emperor.

Like Paul, Dioscorus is balding and of a similar height and frame. On the first day in Puteoli, wearing his shipmaster's garb, he naively goes into the town square and starts speaking boldly to the people about the 'Good News', which Paul had preached to him. He sincerely wants people to know about Paul and his new religion.

But wrongly thinking that he is the 'high-ranking' Jewish man on the emperor's 'wanted list', a fellow named Paul, a group of overzealous officials seize him, and rough him up. One thing leads to another, and in short order the decision is made to kill him by beheading, and then send the head back to the emperor in Rome for the sizable bounty. Sadly, Dioscorus loses his life that day, but Paul is still alive.

Puteoli Sinks into the Sea

When the news reaches him that Dioscorus has died, Paul is overcome with grief. Gazing into the night sky, he cries, "O God Almighty in heaven – who has appeared to me in every place that I have gone on my mission to fulfill the Holy Word of my Lord Jesus Christ – I ask that this city be punished for this heinous crime against a holy believer. Let all those who believe in You and follow Your Word, come out of the city unharmed, but let all the unbelievers be partakers in the punishment."

As the believers are exiting the city limits, Paul meets them all and somberly says to them, "Follow me." Then, Paul and all those who believe in the word of God, walk a mile or two away from the city to a promontory ridge with an overlook vista, called Baias.[12] Looking out over the panorama, they all witness the city of Puteoli sinking into the sea-shore about six feet – a just and fitting punishment for a place full of iniquity and sinfulness.[13]

Arrival at Three Taverns

Walking further north from Baias, they come to a place called Gaitas.[14] Paul and the messengers stay for three days in the house of Erasmus, whom Peter had sent from Rome a few months earlier to teach the Gospel of God.

Then, they move on to a place on the gulf of Gaeta near the main town of Fondi – a fortified castle-like village on the main road to Rome, called Taracinas (or Terracina). Here they stay for seven days in the house of Caesarius, a deacon who has been recently ordained by Peter through the 'laying-on of hands'. From Taracinas, they take a small boat to a resting or staging place for travelers about 31 miles from Rome, called Three Taverns,[15] where Paul stays for four days.

The Head of Dioscorus

Meanwhile, traveling fast, the murderers from Puteoli have made it all the way to Rome with the head of Dioscorus in a bag, and present it to the emperor, claiming that it is the wanted man Paul. They receive their reward, but when they return back to Puteoli a few days later, they find their homes underwater and ruined – a small payback for their crime.

Nero then summons the leaders of the Jewish community and announces to them, "Rejoice with great joy, for the man named Paul, your grievous enemy, is dead. See for yourself!" And he shows them the head of the dead man. But not having actually seen Paul, none of the Jewish leaders can positively ascertain that this is not the man – they are all convinced that it is. And so, both the emperor and the Jewish leaders celebrate that very day – they think that their vexation is over.

But those who had not died in the city of Puteoli, send news letters to the emperor in Rome, saying that the city has unexpectedly sunk into the water, and a great number of people have been lost. Upon learning this, the emperor is saddened, but is also apprehensive.

So, he summons again the Jewish leaders and says to them, "Now look at what has happened! Because of your petitioning, I had this enemy of yours, Paul, killed in Puteoli. But now, as a result of that action, the city of Puteoli has sunk into the sea! What is going on? The gods may be angry! Who really was this man? Have you deceived me?"

Without missing a beat, the glib-speaking representative of the Jewish religious leaders calmly replies, "Most worshipful emperor, we have not led you astray. Did we not say to you that he caused troubles in all the lands of Asia and Palestine – that he perverted our fathers and daughters? Believe me, most honorable emperor, it is a far better thing for one minor far-flung city to be destroyed, than the glorious city of Rome, the seat of the empire. Thankfully, for the sake of us all, he has been eliminated just in time."

And hearing these slick words, the emperor is appeased, and they all go back to their everyday business.

PAUL ARRIVES IN ROME

Departing from Three Taverns, the next day Paul comes to Appii Forum, where he spends the night.[16] But during the night he has a strange dream that shakes his composure:

The Sins of Bishop Juvenalius

Out of the foggy stillness, there mystically appears a majestic man sitting in a golden chair – and there are a multitude of disheveled people standing around him, all talking to him at once. One of them says, 'Today, I made a son murder his father.' Another one says, 'Today, I made a house collapse, killing all the parents and children.' And all of them at the same time are saying that they have done one kind of evil deed or another – many evil deeds altogether.

But there is one person who seems to stand out from all the others – not louder or more forceful – he just seems to override the bunch in metaphysical energy. And his report is very specific and disquieting. 'I have made bishop Juvenalius, who was recently ordained by Peter in Rome, have sexual relations with the abbess Juliana,' he states.

Awaking uncomfortably from his disturbing dream, Paul knows immediately what has to be done. So straightway, he dispatches to Rome one of the trusted believers who has followed him from Puteoli – and sends him directly to bishop Juvenalius, telling him to tell the bishop that both he and God know everything that has occurred. Dutifully, the believer promptly makes his way to Rome and delivers the message to the bishop personally.

Upon hearing this, Juvenalius is filled with shame and remorse. He is so distraught, that he immediately runs to the house of Peter, and throws himself at Peter's feet, weeping, wailing, and lamenting. He tells Peter everything – what had happened with the abbess and what the messenger had told him.

Then, after some moments of penitence, contriteness, and prayer, he says to Peter in an insightful way, "I believe that the light has come – the light that you were hoping and waiting for."

Peter is startled, but on reflection says to no one in particular, "Is it possible that it could be he, when we all thought that he was dead?"

Peter is having feelings of déjà-vu and insecurity – hadn't a similar event happened once before – with world-changing repercussions?[17] Getting giddier by the second, Peter asks if he can speak with the messenger. So, Juvenalius then brings the believer in to Peter, and he explains everything to him – the whole story of the events in Puteoli and the subsequent trip – how he had been sent by Paul – that he was alive and well – and that he was now at Appii Forum, and on his way to Rome.

Hearing the report from the messenger, Peter falls to his knees, thanking and glorifying Almighty God, the Father of our Lord Jesus Christ. Then, having summoned a few sincere believers, he tells them to go and look for Paul – and when found, give him escort and protection on the way to Rome. If necessary, they are to go as far south as Three Taverns looking for him.[18]

But just outside Appii Forum, the group sent by Peter finds the group following Paul, and there is much rejoicing by all. Embracing the warm reception, Paul gives thanks to the Lord Jesus Christ, and his courage and resolve are bolstered. They continue walking, and that night, Paul and his followers sleep soundly in the Roman suburb of Aricia.[19]

Paul Arrives in the City

Very quickly, word spreads throughout the city of Rome that Paul, fellow-preacher and friend of the apostle Peter, is coming – and the resolute Christians in the city exult with great anticipation.

But there is also much consternation among the Jews of the city. So, they seek out Simon 'the Magician' (Simon Magus), and plead with him to go to the emperor and tell him that Paul is not dead, as they have wrongly thought – and furthermore, that he is not far from Rome and coming quickly. They are just too afraid and embarrassed to do it themselves.

Like the others, Simon is curious as to whose head it was that had come to the emperor from Puteoli. But he agrees to inform the emperor as requested. However, he does not personally transmit the news. Instead, he sends a letter by messenger saying that Paul, the preacher of false gods and the enemy of the Jews, is still alive and about to enter Rome.

When Nero receives the letter, he murmurs something like "ugh – more annoying trouble from the Jews and the Christians may be coming – when will it stop?" as he throws it in the wastebin.

When Paul enters the city of Rome, he is allowed to live in a rented house by himself, along with the centurion who is guarding him.[20] Although officially under house arrest, he is otherwise free to move about – but he cannot meet with any lawyers or solicitors before his court date with the emperor. As long as he stays out of trouble, the authorities will leave Paul alone.[21] And Nero is in no rush to set the court date.

PETER AND PAUL TOGETHER

In short order, a great dread and anxiety falls upon the Jewish leaders. So, they gather together and head off to Paul's house, to confront him and his teaching. They press and prod him, saying: "You should be true to the faith in which you were born – for it is not right that you, being a Hebrew, should call yourself a teacher of Gentiles. Being yourself circumcised, you should not be an advocate for the uncircumcised – it brings to nothing our faith in the circumcision. Now, when you see Peter, you should speak out against his teaching also, because he has flouted all the principles and rules of our law. For instance, he has not always kept the sabbath and the holidays appointed by the law."

The Jewish leaders would have kept going on and on, but Paul politely cuts them off, saying: "Yes, it is true that I am a Jew – this can be proven physically. But what of the sabbath and the circumcision? You are free to continue observing those traditions – he is not telling you to stop. We all have fathers, and patriarchs, and the law. What, then, is Peter preaching to the Gentiles? They are not like us – should they be forced to be like us? So let me say this: if Peter preaches any new teaching that is contrary to our law, then send him notice, we will listen, and I will convict him in your presence. But if his teaching is true, and supported by the holy book, then we should all listen carefully to him."

Having heard what Paul had to say, the Jewish leaders then go to Peter and say, "Paul of the Hebrews has come to Rome, and requests that you come to his house, since the Romans do not permit him to wander about and speak with whomever he pleases – at least not until his appearance before Caesar."[22]

Hearing this, Peter is overwhelmed with happiness. He kneels down and rejoices – and praises God for His favor.[23] Then, he quickly gets up, readies himself, and makes straight for the house where Paul is staying.

Once arrived, the two evangelists embrace each other, commiserate profusely, and commune for a long time.[24] It is a moving moment.

And then Paul relates to Peter the whole story of everything that has happened to him since he was led out of Jerusalem to Caesarea – the hearings before the officials, the plots on his life, the ship disaster, and the travel intrigues – the whole story.

Peter then tells him the whole story of everything that has happened to him during that time – specifically, how the 'Jesus movement' has suffered from Simon the magician, and all his evil plots. The two 'men of God' bond in fraternity, and celebrate their allegiance to the Lord well into the evening. After the emotional reunion, Peter quietly returns to the house of Narcissus, where he is staying.

NOTES

1. Acts 21:27 – 23:23

2. Paul was defending himself against accusations made by the temple high priest Ananias and the Jewish elders – accompanied by a smooth-talking lawyer named Tertullus.

3. Acts 23:23 – 26:32

4. the court of the emperor in Rome

5. Aristarchus was with Paul in Ephesus at the 'riot of the silversmiths' on the 2nd Missionary Journey (Acts 19:29), and eventually became a co-prisoner with him in Rome (Colossians 4:10).

6. When the ship was run aground and being torn apart by the waves, the soldiers onboard wanted to kill the prisoners so they couldn't escape custody by swimming away. Knowing that that was not Paul's intent, Julius opposed that plan, and instead convinced the soldiers to make an orderly evacuation of all hands (Acts 27:39-44). And with Paul's help and God's grace, all hands were indeed saved. Julius stood up for Paul on a number of occasions, giving him considerable freedom of movement and speech.

7. Reference: Acts 28 – Paul may have also been in the Maltese sister island of Gozo (Gaudos).

8. As news could spread rapidly throughout the Mediterranean world under the improved Roman road system, there were novice Christian believers in Rome scant years after the Resurrection of Christ. In 57 AD, near the end of his 3rd Missionary Voyage, Paul sent a letter to the Roman believers (the biblical 'Letter of Paul to the Romans') from Corinth in Greece, explaining the tenets of the Christian faith, and saying that he hoped to visit them soon. Many believers are identified by name in the last chapter of the Letter. The letter was personally delivered to the Roman believers by Phoebe, a deacon of the church at Cenchreae, a town neighboring Corinth (Romans 16:2). Many scholars still believe today that this Letter is the most concise and eloquent statement of the Christian faith ever written.

9. A person who was a friend, companion, fellow-worker, or group member was often called a 'brother'. Christian men frequently called other Christian men 'brothers'.

10. called Messana in Paul's day

11. also called Pontiole or Pozzuoli

12. Baias was named after the helmsman of Odysseus's ship in Homer's *Odyssey*, who was supposedly buried nearby.

13. And there it is until this day, a remembrance of the injustice, partially under the sea. Scientifically speaking, the lower part of the town became submerged in the sea due to local volcanic bradyseismic activity (the gradual descent of surface land caused by the emptying of an underground magma chamber or hydrothermal vent, particularly in volcanic calderas).

14. or Gaeta – named after 'Caieta', the nurse of Aeneas, the mythical hero of Troy and Rome. As a point of interest, the U.S. Navy's 6th Fleet is headquartered there.

15. The name actually means '3 shops'.

16. Appii Forum, or the Forum of Appius, was the closest post-station and rest-stop on the way to Rome along the Appian Way – very near a place called Vicusarape. From here, there were two major roads by which travelers could journey to Rome.

17. Of course, Peter is thinking of the resurrection of Jesus Christ.

18. The distance from Rome to Three Taverns is about 38 miles.

19. Aricia is about 16 miles from Rome. The group sent by Peter returned directly to Rome.

20. Julius was replaced by other soldiers, although it's not known exactly when this occurred.

21. It was during this time that Paul wrote Letters to the Colossians, Ephesians, Philippians, and the Letter to Philemon.

22. 'Caesar' was the word commonly used for 'emperor'.

23. Peter and Paul are not the warmest of friends – they have had sharp differences of opinion in the past. Peter doesn't consider Paul to be a true apostle, but they both share the desire to spread the Gospel, and they respect each other's contributions.

24. It is said that they 'bedewed each other with their tears'.

16 BEFORE THE EMPEROR

At this time in Rome, many strange fads, crazes, and cults are spreading all throughout the city. The people are inundated everywhere with weird goings-on, and they are becoming restless.

SIMON GOES BEFORE NERO

Just at this time, Simon rouses himself, shakes off his shortfall with Peter under governor Agrippa, and moves with zeal, again claiming that he is the 'power of god' on earth – and that all people should follow him and worship him. He begins to say many evil things about Peter – that he is a wizard, a cheat, and a false prophet. And many in the populace believe him, marveling at his miracles and awed by his slick words. Many people testify that he has made a brass serpent move itself, a stone statue start to laugh – and even made himself rise into the air.

But at the same time, Peter is healing the sick, bringing sight to the blind, and sending demons to flight, all by a prayer and a command. He pleads with the people to flee from Simon's deceit, so as not to be slaves to the devil – and also to expose him for the charlatan that he is. But a great many people continue to follow Simon, awed by his illusions.

Of course, all pious men and women abhor Simon the sorcerer, and proclaim that he is heretical. But those who follow Simon strongly affirm that Peter is the sorcerer, bearing false witness against god and against Roman beliefs.

The controversy between the two soon becomes the talk-of-the-town, and when it starts interfering with normal everyday business as usual, the leaders and officials decide to intervene. The matter finally comes to the ears of Nero the emperor, and he gives an order to bring Simon before him, just to check him out for himself.

Coming in before the emperor, Simon stands directly in front of him, and suddenly begins to assume different physical personas, so that at one instance he is a child, and then a short bit later an old man, and then a bit later again, a young dashing man. He manages to change himself both in face and stature, by using a combination of magic tricks, and is giddy in his behavior – having the devil as his servant.

After watching this, Nero truly believes that Simon is a god – or 'the god' – or the 'son of the god' – but he isn't quite sure which. Simon has captured his attention, but he isn't sure what to do with him.

Simon is Raised from the Dead

To further solidify his claim of being the 'power of god', and further his standing with the emperor, Simon declares to Nero, "Order me to be beheaded in a dark place, buried in a tomb dug by my followers, and there to be left dead for three days. And if I do not rise on the third day, then you will know that I am nothing but a sham magician. But, if I rise again, then you will know that I truly am the 'power of god' – who some people call the 'son of god'.

Having ordered this to be so, Simon uses his magical arsenal of tricks to deceive the emperor. In the dark, while the executioner is distracted, a ram is smuggled into the room and its head put on the chopping block in place of Simon – while Simon quietly slips away.[1] It isn't until after the beheading that the executioner realizes that it is the head of a ram and not that of a man. So embarrassed, and fearful for his life for failing to carry out the order, that the executioner says nothing to the emperor. He just lets him think that the job has been properly done. Meanwhile, Simon's accomplices remove the head of the ram and the body, leaving the congealed blood there as evidence of the execution.

Three days later, Simon shows himself to the emperor, and announces, "O mighty emperor, you may now have my blood, that was poured out on the executioner's slab, wiped up and burned. For behold, as you are witness, after having been beheaded, I have risen again on the third day, as I promised."

Simon Seeks another Audience with the Emperor

But out in the streets, the squares, and the temples, Peter continues to call out Simon. He accuses him of being both a liar and a wizard – base, impious, and apostate – and in all things, opposed to the truth of God.

Of course, Simon continues with his wicked deceptions and illusions, roaming all over the city, claiming that he, and not Peter, is the true 'power of god'.

And Peter continues to rail against Simon, saying that nothing resides in his soul except pure wickedness and evil. And that one day, by the command and real power of God, he will be plainly shown to all, to be nothing but a sham imposter and a mere puppet of Satan.

After many months of name-calling and back-stabbing by both Simon and Peter, Simon again decides to seek the help of the emperor in his ongoing war of words with Peter. By appointment, he manages to get an audience with Nero, and pleads with him:

"Hear me again, O good and gracious emperor. I am the true 'son of god' who has come down from heaven to help the people of Rome. Until now I have patiently endured the man called Peter, who calls himself an apostle, but now he has doubled the evil persecution against me – for he has enlisted another – a man named Paul,[2] who also teaches the same unholy things – and they both have turned their minds against me and are trying to destroy the truth of what I preach. Their message is so hideous and their outreach so widespread, it is plain to see that if you cannot contrive their destruction, then the empire cannot stand – it will crumble from within."

This gets the emperor's attention.

SIMON, PETER, AND PAUL BEFORE NERO

Filled with concern, Nero orders that Peter and Paul be brought speedily before him. And on the following day, Simon, Peter, and Paul all dutifully report to the office of the emperor. After all niceties have been formally concluded, Simon announces, "These are the disciples of the Nazarene – they are not representatives of the Jews and they are not ambassadors to the Romans. They are seditious, ungodly, and a threat to the empire."

"What is a Nazarene?" asks the emperor.

In reply, Simon continues, "There is a city in Judaea that has always been opposed to the people of Samaria, where I come from. It is called Nazareth, and the teacher of these men was raised in that place. They hate all Samaritans and they hate me just for being one."

Nero turns to Peter and says, "The gods command us to love every person. Why, then, do you persecute Simon and his kind?"

But Simon interrupts before Peter can answer, saying, "This is a group of men who have turned aside all Judaea from believing in me and following me."

Looking a little exasperated, Nero then says to Peter, "Why do you and your group not believe in the ways of the Samaritans?"

But instead of answering the emperor, Peter turns to Simon and says, "You have been able to impose your false beliefs upon many, but not upon me – never – and many of those who have been deceived by you, have been enlightened by God through me. Furthermore, since you have learned by experience that you cannot get the better of me, I truly wonder if boasting yourself before the emperor is just a last gasp effort to save your reputation. Since you cannot overcome the disciples of Christ through your magic arts, you turn to the emperor for help?"

Nero is annoyed that the two adversaries are talking around him and at each other. So, he states unequivocally, "Stop disparaging each other and talk to me. Now then, who is this Christ?"

Peter speaks up first: "He is in reality what this Simon, the sorcerer, only claims to be – the 'Son of God'. But this Simon is a most wicked man, and his works are the tools of the devil. He is not the 'Son of God'.

"O good and noble emperor, if you really wish to understand all the things that have been done in Judaea surrounding the Christ, then look at the letter from Pontius Pilate which was sent to emperor Claudius, your predecessor, and then you will know much more."

The Letter from Pontius Pilate

Nero is dubious about the whole affair, but he is curious enough to order the letter be brought to him straightaway, and read in their presence. This is done, and after a few minutes the letter is retrieved and read out loud by a scribe in front of all present:

From: Your humble servant Pontius Pilate, Procurator of Judaea
To: The Honorable Tiberius Claudius Nero Germanicus
Greetings;
    There has lately happened a series of events in which I myself was involved with — and which I am compelled to report. It has happened in Judaea that, through hypocritical and jealous resentment, the Jews have inflicted dreadful judgments upon themselves, and on those coming after them.
    It seems that their fathers from ages back had promised that their god would send them his holy messiah from heaven, who according to tradition would be called their king – and who had been promised to be sent to them on earth by means of a virgin mother.
    And then, a man who many claimed to be this so-called messiah, physically came into Judaea when I was procurator. Many people claim they saw him restoring sight to the blind, cleansing lepers, healing paralytics, expelling demons, subduing the winds, walking on water, and doing many other wonders – including the raising of the dead. Many of the Jews were calling him the 'Son of God'.
    But then, the chief priests moved with envy against him, seized him, and delivered him to me. Telling one lie after another, they said that he was a wizard, and had done things contrary to their law. And they said that he wanted to be king, and was a threat to the stability of the empire.

Regretfully, I believed that these things were true, so I gave him up to the chief priests, after scourging him, to do with him as they would. However, they maintained that the only possible sentence was death by crucifixion under Roman supervision. And so, in cooperation with the Jewish leaders, the man was crucified most ignominiously. He was quietly buried and I set guards over the tomb.

But while my soldiers were guarding him, his body was removed from the tomb on the third day – supposedly, according to the local gossip, he was resurrected back to life. Yet, so inflamed was the wickedness of the chief priests against him, that they bribed the soldiers with money, saying, 'Tell Pilate that his disciples have stolen his body.' But, having taken the money, the soldiers were not able to remain silent about what had happened – they testified that they had seen him after he was risen, and that they had received money from the Jewish priests to keep silent.

These things, therefore, I have reported, such that no one should falsely speak otherwise – and so that you would not believe the falsehoods of the Jewish leaders.

With respectful regards,
Pontius Pilate

After the letter is read, Nero smiles wryly and says, "Tell me, Peter, were all these things really done by this man?"

To which Peter replies, "They were, indeed, my good emperor. Now, this Simon here is full of lies and deceit, and sometimes he seems to be what he is not – a god – but it is just all illusion.

"But in Christ there is real purpose in life – and victory over darkness. In Christ, there are two essences. He came as a man – but with incomprehensible glory –_to come to the assistance of men. But in this Simon, there are also two essences. He comes as a man, but his works are of the devil – he endeavors to ensnare men, not to assist them."

Simon then speaks up, saying, "I wonder, O good emperor, why you would ever consider this man to be of any credibility whatsoever – a man uneducated; a fisherman of the poorest kind – and endowed with authority neither by word nor by rank. But, with your permission, since I cannot endure him any longer as an enemy of god, I shall immediately order my angels to come and avenge me for his insolence."

"I am not afraid of your phony angels," replies Peter, "but they will be very afraid of me when I call upon the power and might of my Lord Jesus Christ, who you falsely declare yourself to be."

Peter 'reads' the Mind of Simon

As it happens, Nero has no understanding of the one true God, or a concept of the Godhead. He just assumes that each of these two men have their own pet god who helps him along in life. But if he could determine whose god was the more powerful, then he could also worship that god, in the hope that it would reward both himself and the empire. In addition, the two men were causing unrest in the city. Getting rid of one of them, and recognizing the god of the other, was just good politics.

So, after a few seconds, Nero says, "Peter, are you not afraid of Simon, who confirms his godhead by powerful deeds?"

In return, Peter proclaims, "Godhead is in Him who searches and finds the hidden things of the heart. Now then, here is a good test: Let him tell me what I am thinking about, or what I am doing. I will secretly disclose to your servants who are here what I am thinking – before he can tell lies, make up stories, or utter obscure generalities."

"Come here, and tell me what you are thinking about, Peter," motions Nero.

Peter then moves close to the emperor, under the watchful eyes of the guards, and whispers, "Order a loaf of bread to be brought here, and given to me secretly."

And the emperor has it done. After the bread is secretly given to him, Peter calls out, "Now tell us, Simon, what was I thinking, or what did I say, or what has just been done?"

But Nero intervenes and says to Peter, "Do you expect me to believe that Simon does not know these things? – he who was a dead man after being beheaded by my order, but rose to life again on the third day,[3] and who has otherwise done whatever he said he would do?"

And Peter replies, "But he did not do it before me, your honor."

"But he did all these before me," rejoins Nero. "For I tell you most assuredly, that he did order angels to come to him,[4] and indeed they came."

To which Peter then says, "If he can do what is very great, then why can't he do what is very small? Let him tell us what I had in my mind, and what has been done here."

Looking somewhat exasperated, Nero sighs and moans, "Between the two of you, I am at a loss at how to judge the truth."

Then Simon speaks up: "His reasoning works both ways, honorable emperor. Let Peter say what I am thinking of now, or what I am doing."

And Peter answers, "Yes, what Simon has in his mind, I will show to you that I know – I will do what he is thinking about."

Then, Simon says smugly, "Understand, O emperor, that no one – not even the 'power of god' – knows the inner thoughts of men – only god alone knows this. Is not, therefore, Peter lying?"

Again, Peter answers firmly, "You say that you are the 'son and power of god' – then say what I had in my mind – or tell us what I have just done in secret."

Annoyed that Peter keeps pressing the issue of reading his mind, Simon finally blurts out, "This charade has gone on long enough, my emperor! There is no way to prove that one knows what the other is thinking. So, I will tell you what I was thinking – then there is no guesswork, but also no power, no magic. As it is, just at that time, I was thinking that it would be very satisfying if some great dogs came forth, and chewed Peter up before the emperor."

While Simon is addressing the emperor, Peter has silently blessed the loaf of bread which he has received, and having broken it, stuffs the pieces up his sleeves.

And then suddenly, a number of large angry dogs appear out of nowhere, and they rush at Peter. But Peter stretches forth his hands as if to pray – and the dogs see and smell the pieces of bread that were hidden, but now drop from his sleeves. But when the dogs approach the blessed bread, they run away in disarray.

Then Peter says to Nero, "Behold, I have shown to you that I knew what Simon was thinking about; not by words, but by deeds. For you see, he threatened to bring angels against me – but he has brought only dogs – showing us that he had only dog-like devils, and not God-like angels, in mind. And I knew exactly how to thwart his attack."

Somewhat bewildered, Nero says to Simon, "What do you say, Simon, have you been bested by this man?"

To which Simon replies, "This man, both in Judaea, and in all Palestine and Syria, has done the same deceitful tricks against me and to the truth. From contesting with me so often, he has learned just the right things to say and do, so as to escape from me and the truth – and the truth of it is that the thoughts of men can be known to no man – only god alone."

Then, Peter says to Simon, "Certainly you pretend to be a god – if so, then, why do you not reveal the thoughts of every man?"

The Testimony of Paul

Nero then turns to Paul, and says, "Why do you say nothing, Paul?"

Answering with conviction, Paul then replies, "Know this, honorable emperor – if you permit this sorcerer Simon to do these tricks, it will bring an onset of great mischief to your country, and will bring down your empire from its position of prominence."

Nero frowns at Paul and then asks of Simon, "What do you say to that?"

Proudly, but haughtily, Simon answers, "If I do not manifestly hold myself out to be a god, then no one will want to bestow upon me the reverence that is deserved. It is just the way of things."

Finally, Nero puts it to Simon: "So now, why do you delay? Show yourself to be a god, in order that these ruffians may be punished!"

"OK," responds Simon. "Here is what should be done: Give orders that a high tower of wood be built for me. Then, I will go up to the top of it, call upon my angels, jump off, and fly above the rooftops of Rome. Then, I will order them to carry me up to my Father in heaven, in the full sight of all. And these impudent men, not being able to do the same thing, will be put to shame as uneducated and deceitful fools."

Then, Nero says to Peter, "Have you heard what Simon has said, Peter? By such a deed, it can be known positively whether his god has the superior power, or whether your god has. It will be the definitive test."

But Peter stammers, "O most mighty emperor, can't you see that he is full of demons?"

To which Nero replies, "Your talk seems to me to be nothing but just going around in circles. Soon, we will decide the issue."

Then, Simon speaks out again: "Do you believe, O good emperor, that I am just a sorcerer – the same man who you saw was dead, and then rose again to life on the third day?"

With that, Nero turns to Paul again and says, "You, Paul, why do you say nothing? I have heard all manner of things about you, but now I wonder: Just who was your teacher? Who is your god? What exactly have you taught in the cities of Asia and Greece? And what things have happened through your teaching? For it seems to me that you do not have any wisdom, and are not able to accomplish any works of power."

To answer the emperor, Paul speaks out with conviction, "Do you think that it is necessary for me to speak out against a desperate man – a sorcerer – who has sold his soul to the devil, and whose destruction and punishment will come speedily? For he willfully speaks and pretends to be what he is not, and deceives people by magic tricks. If you continue to hear his words, and protect him against the unveiling of his deceit, you will destroy your own soul and your kingdom, for he is a most vile man.

"As the Egyptian soldiers Jannes and Jambres led Pharaoh and his army astray until they were swallowed up in the sea,[5] so also will it be with you. Through the instructions of the devil, Simon persuades and deceives innocent people to do many evil things – to the peril of the empire, your kingdom on earth.

"As for the words of the devil, which I see have been poured out through this man, with a heavy heart, I turn to the Holy Spirit for guidance. For as far as this man seems to raise himself towards heaven, in reality he is sinking down into the depths of Hades, where there is only weeping and gnashing of teeth.

"As for the teaching of my God, of which you asked me, no one can attain community with Him in heaven except the pure in heart, who allow faith in Jesus Christ to come into their soul. For it is only through peace and love and faith that one can be pure in heart – and this have I taught from Jerusalem to as far as Illyria.[6]

I have taught that only in honor, should a couple love one another.[7]

I have taught that those who are rich or famous will not be lifted up if they put their hopes in riches – instead, they should place their hope in God.[8]

I have taught that those in the middle class should be content with the food, clothing, and shelter that they honestly obtain.

I have taught the poor to rejoice and be content, even in the uncomfortableness of their poverty.

I have taught fathers to teach their children in the ways of the Lord, and children to obey their parents with love and gratitude.

I have taught wives to love their husbands, and husbands to love their wives – and both to observe fidelity forever.

I have taught masters to treat their slaves with clemency, and slaves to serve their masters faithfully.[9]

I have taught the churches of the believers to worship the one and only almighty, invisible, and incomprehensible God. And this teaching ability has been given to me not from any mortal man, but from Jesus Christ,[10] our Lord and Savior, who spoke to me clearly from out of heaven – and who also has sent me out to preach the Gospel to the world, saying, 'Go forth, for I will be with you; and all the things that you say or do, I shall make just.'"[11]

Nero then turns to Peter and says, "And what do you say, Peter?"

Peter answers him by declaring, "All that Paul has said is true. For when he was a persecutor of the faith of Christ, a voice called to him from out of heaven, and showed him the way, the truth, and the life. You see, he was not an adversary of our faith from hatred, but from ignorance.

"Understand, my noble emperor, that there were many false prophets before us, like Simon – pretend apostles, sham preachers, and false messiahs – who, contrary to the sacred writings, set themselves apart to try and invalidate the truth.

"Against these phony teachers, it was necessary to have in readiness this man Paul – who from his youth, set himself up to search out the mysteries of the divine law – so that he might become a vindicator of truth and a persecutor of falsehood.

"Since his persecution of us was not on account of hatred, but on account of his faith in the law, the ultimate truth out of heaven came to him in a miraculous vision, and held sway with him, saying, 'I am the truth that you seek – stop persecuting me and believe in me.'

"When he realized that this really was the light of God and pre-eminent over the law, he departed from his previous path of persecution, and entered the path of discipleship."

But Simon then perks up and exclaims, "O good emperor, take notice that these two have conspired against me, hoping to overcome me with doublespeak. But I say to you that I am the truth – and they conspire to work evil against me."

"There is no truth in you," retorts Peter, "everything you say and do is false and corrupt."

Once again Nero turns to Paul and asks, "And what do you say to this, Paul?"

To which Paul replies, "These words you have just heard from Peter – you can believe that they have been spoken by me also, for we preach the same thing – and we have the same Lord, Jesus the Christ."

Simon then interjects, "Do you expect me, O good emperor, to hold an intelligent argument with these men, who have agreed to collude against me?"

Then he turns to the apostles of Christ and exclaims, "Listen, Peter and Paul, if I cannot convince you of my authority here, then we must go to the place where you will be judged, for all the world to see."

Then, Paul says, "O good emperor, see what threats he holds out against us!"

And Peter adds, "It is sorrowful to think that this man cannot be brought into the Light. Still, it is hard to keep from laughing outright at such a foolish man, made to be the sport of demons."

Simon stares at the two for a few seconds, and then states, "I will spare you both until I receive my full power."

But Paul snaps back, saying, "You really need to receive the full power of our Lord Jesus Christ now, before you leave here."

Nodding, Peter adds, "Simon, if you do not see the power of our Lord Jesus Christ, then you will never believe that you are not the Christ."

The Issue of Circumcision

Then suddenly, Simon comes up with a new tactic: "Most sacred emperor, do not believe them – for they are nothing but disgraced trouble-makers – and furthermore, they are circumcised Jews."

"Before we knew the truth," speaks up Paul, "we had the circumcision of the flesh, but when the truth was revealed to us – that what is important is the circumcision of the heart, the spiritual circumcision [12]– then we both believed, and do not make physical circumcision part of our faith."

Nodding, Peter then says, "If you think circumcision is a disgrace,[13] Simon, why have you been circumcised?"

Looking surprised, Nero asks the question: "Has Simon then also been circumcised?"

Quickly, Peter replies, "Yes. How could he otherwise have deceived so many souls, unless he pretended to be Jewish, and made a show of teaching the law of God."

Nero then looks at Simon and says, "Simon, do you persecute these men because of envy? I see that there is great hatred between you and their god, the Christ god – and I fear that you will be bested by them, and involved in great troubles."

"No, you are led astray, O emperor," replies Simon.

"How am I led astray?" probes Nero. "What I see in you, I say outright. I see that you are clearly an enemy of Peter and Paul, and their master, their god, the Christ god."

And Simon instantly replies, "The Christ was not Paul's master."

But Paul quickly interjects, "Yes, He is. Christ is my master through revelation. And He taught me also, although I did not know him personally. But let me backtrack here a bit – tell me what I asked you earlier – why were you circumcised?"

To which Simon retorts, "Why have you asked me this?"

"We have a good reason for asking you this," answers Paul.

Then, Nero says to Simon, "Why are you afraid to answer them?"

And Simon responds, "Understand, O emperor, that at that time, circumcision was ordered by God."[14]

But Paul interrupts again, "Did you hear, my good emperor, what has been said by Simon? If circumcision is a good thing, then why have you, Simon, given up on those who have been circumcised, and forced them, after being condemned, to be put to death?"[15]

Nero's Final Thoughts

Somewhat exasperated, Nero then states his mind: "I do not perceive anything good from either of you. You are both petty theocrats bickering over minutia that is unimportant to the glory of Rome and her gods."

In unison, Peter and Paul respond, "What you think about us really has no relevance to the matter. To us, it is necessary that what our Master has told us to do, we will do, and what He has promised that will come to pass, will in fact occur."

"And what was that promise?"

"That the old kingdom will pass away, and a new kingdom will come in glory"

"And what if I am not willing to go along with that?" enquires Nero.

Then, Peter calmly says, "Not according to your will, but according to His will, it will be done."[16]

The emperor frowns, but before he can say anything, Simon speaks up, "O good emperor, these devious men have counted on your clemency, and have thereby entrapped you."

To which Nero replies, "But neither have you yet made me sure about yourself."

So, Simon then says, "Since so many excellent deeds and signs have been shown to you by me, I wonder how it is that you could be in any doubt."

"I neither doubt nor favor any of you," answers Nero. "I'm just looking for straight clear-cut answers to my questions, that make sense."

But Simon is now getting agitated. In a haughty manner, he responds with, "Enough is enough. I won't answer any more questions if they are beneath my station."

"I think you say this because you are a deceiver," says Nero. "You say to the others, 'Even if I am unable to overcome you, then my god, who can do it, will do it.' But that tells me nothing – doesn't convince me of anything. It is all really very simple: Prove to me that your deeds and signs are not illusions."

"I have said all that I can, and all that I will – I have nothing more to say," reiterates Simon.

Shaking his head, Nero sighs and mutters, "I don't consider you to be anything special anymore. In fact, the way I see it, the three of you are all whacky – preposterous, ridiculous, and ludicrous imaginations running amok in the real world. Why do I say this? Because the three of you have shown to me that your reasoning is ambiguous, illogical, and irrational. Therefore, I can believe nothing that any of you have to say – I can give favor to none of you."

Then, Peter speaks up again, "We preach one God, the Father of our Lord Jesus Christ, who has made the heaven, the earth, the sea, and all that exists – who is the true king of the universe – and of His kingdom there shall be no end."[17]

"What kind of king is a lord?" asks Nero.

"The Savior of all the nations," replies Paul.

Just then, Simon jumps in, saying, "And I am he of whom he speaks."

But Peter and Paul snap back quickly, "May it never be well with you, Simon – you are a sorcerer, conjurer, magician – and full of bitterness."

Then Simon turns to the emperor and says, "Listen to me now, O great Caesar [18]– I tell you that these men are liars – and that I am the one who has been sent from heaven. To prove this to you, I will fly up to my place in the heavens! I will give my blessing to those who believe in me, and I will show my wrath to those who have denied me."

Peter then bewails, "Long ago God called me to His glory. But you are called by the devil, and your eternal punishment is inescapable."

But Simon scoffs at Peter and says to Nero, "O great Caesar, please listen to me. I plead with you to separate yourself from these madmen, such that when I go up to my father in heaven, we can be merciful to you and show you favor."

"And how will you prove all this," asks Nero, "that you actually go up into heaven? Will you jump off a tower and never come down?"

Then Simon answers, "Order a high tower to be made of wood, and of great beams, such that I can climb up to the very top of it. Then, I will jump off the tower, and my angels will catch me in the air – since they cannot come to me on the earth because of all the unholy sinners here. They will carry me into the highest heaven, and all my glory will be manifested."

"So be it," says Nero. "I will have the preparations started immediately. Then we will see whether you can actually do what you say."

With that, the meeting is adjourned, and Nero breathes a sigh of relief. The participants quickly disperse under guard and go back to their homes and everyday lives.

But work on the tower construction starts swiftly, and it isn't long before wild rumors start spreading across the city as to the purpose of it.

NOTES

1. It was dark, the ram was recently killed, its body was tied together like a human body, and it was covered in the same fashion as Simon had requested to be covered. The executioner wasn't overly conscientious – he just wanted to quickly get the job done and get out. He wasn't expecting anything abnormal. So, it's not hard to believe that the deception actually worked.

2. Paul has just recently been released from house arrest after his court case was dismissed.

3. Note the deviousness of Simon's sorcery. He knew the story of Christ's resurrection on the third day, and weaved that symbolism into the magic trick of returning to life on the third day after he had been beheaded – trying once more to show that he, and no one else, was the true 'power of God'.

4. The Romans believed that angels were couriers for the gods.

5. In Jewish and Christian traditions, Jannes and Jambres are the names given to magicians mentioned in the Book of Exodus. Two of the 'wise men and sorcerers' mentioned in Exodus 7:10-12 are identified with Jannes and Jambres. In Rabbinic literature, it is said that they converted to Judaism and left Egypt at the Exodus to accompany Moses and the Israelites – however, they perished on the way.

6. Romans 15:19. The Roman province of Illyria stretched from Thessaloniki [in modern Greece] to Istria [in Dalmatia], roughly corresponding to modern-day Serbia, Kosovo, north Albania, Slovenia, Montenegro, Bosnia, Herzegovina, and coastal Croatia. Paul was probably referring to his visits to Philippi and Thessalonica on his 2nd and 3rd Missionary Expeditions – on the Egnation Way, the main Roman road across Macedonia.

7. Romans 12:10

8. 1 Timothy 6:17

9. Colossians 3:18-22

10. Galatians 1:1

11. An expansion of Acts 9:15-16, Acts 13:2, Acts 22:21, and Acts 26:16-18.

12. Paul maintained that belief in Christ results in a spiritual circumcision – the cutting away of your sinful nature. See Colossians 2:11.

13. The Romans commonly believed that the Jewish tradition of circumcision was disgraceful – just one more reason why the Jews were ostracized in Roman society.

14. Genesis 17:13

15. This is a somewhat inciting accusation by Paul. There is no historical evidence that Simon ever forced any condemned circumcised Jews to be put to death, although some of his friends were clearly anti-semitic.

16. Compare with Luke 22:42

17. Luke 1:33

18. The emperor was often called the 'Caesar', although two centuries later, the 'Caesar' was the junior emperor, and the senior emperor was simply the 'Emperor'.

17 SIMON FLIES OVER ROME

After a few days have passed, Simon once again begins to cajole and sweet-talk the people. He tries to convince as many as possible that Peter does not believe in the true God, but is in reality, deceived into believing in a false god. To support his accusation, he starts to do many tricks of magic, hoping to enhance his image and reputation. In private dining rooms, he appears to make spirits of past loves and acquaintances speak through a conjurer – he makes lame men appear to walk for a bit and blind men appear to see for a bit – and one time, he even makes a dead man move a bit, like he did with Nicostratus. Those who are firm in the faith of Jesus the Christ, deride him, but many people again become believers in his doctrine, his story, and his god.

Peter tries to follow him everywhere he goes, and convict him of magic and sorcery in front of the witnesses. He meets with mixed success, but over the next few months, Simon's reputation slowly begins to wither. He becomes thought of more and more as a party magician, and less and less as a mighty god. He is still making money, but his delusions of grandeur are fading. He needs a boost – a new and spectacular hype.

Luckily, the great tower is nearing completion – and just in time too. When he learns that it will be ready in a few days, he waits until the day before the unveiling, and then goes to the main public square in the center of town. He stands on a platform in the middle, and announces:

"Citizens of Rome – you may think that Peter has prevailed over me – that his god is more powerful than the true god that I serve – but hear me now: That thinking is false! Now, if you think that it is so, then you are deceived – you have been tricked by his mystical enchantments. In reality, you have been duped into godless and impious thinking. But, do not despair my friends – you can be forgiven, and come back to the true path, the true light, and the true god.

"To prove to you that I am the true path, and my god is more powerful than Peter's god,[1] people of Rome listen up and pay heed! Tomorrow, I will leave you all for a short time. In view of everyone in the city, I will jump off the newly constructed tower and fly up to god in heaven – right before your eyes in the sky over your heads – for I am the true 'power of god'. Even though many of you have fallen away lately, I remain upright and stand strong.

"People of Rome, there is still time for you to believe in me! Yes, tomorrow I will fly up to my father in heaven and say to him, 'They have tried to tear down my power and convict me of earthly injustices, but I remain standing tall. I have kept the faith and have done my duty. But now father– now I return myself back to you.' "

AT THE CAMPUS MARTIUS

Construction has taken a few months, but a lofty tower has finally been completed in the 'Campus Martius' along the 'Sacred Way',[2] the most people-friendly public place in Rome. All the important officials and dignitaries in the city have been invited to the spectacle, and given VIP seats in the grandstand – and thousands of commoners are standing around the periphery.

After everything has been readied and all the people come together and quieted down, including Peter and Paul, who were ordered to attend, the emperor announces to the multitude, "Now the truth will be made plain – we will see if this man Simon here, really is the 'power of god' that he claims to be."

Then, Peter and Paul together say to Nero, "O good emperor, we do not wish him any harm, but we must expose him for the fake that he truly is – he has falsely declared himself to be our Lord Jesus Christ, the true Son of God."

Peter was not in Rome when Simon first entered the city and amazed the multitudes by flying – thus, he was not able to previously denounce the trick as an illusion. Unfortunately, many people were convinced of his power by this chicanery, including Marcellus, and became followers of his corrupt philosophy and his concept of God.

Turning to Peter, Paul then says softly, "It is my role to bend the knee and pray to God. It is your role to call him out before the Lord, and reveal his evil deceit before all."[3] Then, Paul kneels down and prays intently.

Looking steadfastly at Simon, Peter says to him, "Try now to accomplish what you have boasted you will do, for both your exposure and your conviction are at hand."

"And what will you do to expose this man?" asks Nero.

"Whatever our Lord has asked of us," replies Peter.

"And just who is your lord?" queries Nero.

"Jesus the Christ, whom I see calling us to Himself."

"So, do you also then intend to fly away to heaven?" Nero asks sarcastically

"If the One who calls us wishes it to be," answers Peter.

Nero shakes his head in futility, but Simon speaks up assuredly, "In order that you may know for sure, O emperor, that these two are cruel deceivers, as soon as I have ascended into heaven, I will send my angels to you, and they will let you see me in the light of heaven."

With that, Nero simply shakes his head again and commands, "Do at once what you say."

Then, crowned with shiny laurel wreaths, and dressed in a colorful sun-glinting overcoat with ruffled sparkling trousers, and a fur hat covered in flowers, Simon slowly and majestically walks over to the tower in the view of all, and climbs up to the very top.[4]

After 10 minutes, or so, Simon can be clearly seen standing upright with his hands raised in the air, on a small platform at the top of the tower, dressed in the finest regalia. Ribbons stream in the wind from his ankles, waist, and fur hat, and his multi-colored clothes are covered with mirrors and metal coins that glisten, flicker, and shimmer in the bright sunlight.

One of his assistants and his girlfriend Helena are hidden inside the tower, making ready his equipment. They have set up an intricate contraption of cables, pulleys, and a rotating mechanism. Inside his overcoat is a makeshift hot-air balloon, and the coat is connected to the rotating mechanism by a set of fine wires. The plan is to be revolved around the tower a few times, and then released to float up and away carried by the winds.[5]

But Simon is not concerned with the technical details. He doesn't check out the device or test it thoroughly. After all, he's already used the overcoat once before, and it worked fine. He has a very haughty attitude this morning – a feeling of superiority and greatness. He feels as if this is his day to shine – to be invincible and all-powerful – to show the world that he truly is a god.

He stands at the top of the tower in splendid garb, glistening in the sunlight, and waves his hands to the people. In turn, the multitude cheer him on with thunderous acclaim – and this just fuels Simon's ego and self-assurance.

"Fly away from here, Simon," they yell and shout. "Fly up to heaven and intercede for us to the gods. We believe in you! Ask them to look favorably on us and on Rome!"

"Simon! Simon! Simon!" they chant over and over.

Looking out over the masses, he spots Peter in the crowd, and shouts out to him, "Peter, I say to you now – as I am about to fly in front of all these witnesses – if your god is real and able – the god who was put to death by the Jews in Jerusalem – and because of him you were stoned and chained – then let him prove to us all that faith in him is faith in the true god. Let him prove it now by showing everyone a greater power! For by flying up over the city, and showing myself to all, I will prove that I am the 'power of god', and your Jesus Christ is a false god, who does not have the 'power of god'."

Simon Flies Over Rome

Helena is screaming something at Simon from within the tower, but he doesn't hear her.[6] He is too immersed in his own self-grandeur – basking in the adoration of the masses – that all he sees and hears are images and sounds of glory and praise. He is locked-in to his destiny.

Then, acknowledging the roar of the crowd, stretching forth his hands and taking a mighty leap, Simon jumps off the tower, and is immediately lifted up into the air in a magnificent spectacle! It appears to many on the ground that he is riding in a chariot pulled by mighty angels, and rising above the temples. He circles the tower a few times, ever getting higher.

The whole city gasp in unison and begin to praise and revere Simon – indeed he has the 'power of god'. Some fall on their knees and sprinkle dirt on their heads – others bow their heads and clasp their hands. The day is his! He has won over the people – and prevailed in his battle with Peter. The faithful Christian believers apprehensively look toward Peter.

When Nero sees him flying in the air, he says to Peter, "The claims of Simon are true – you and Paul are the deceivers!"

But Peter responds politely, "You will soon understand that we are the true disciples of Christ, and that he is nothing but a sorcerer and a scoundrel."

"Why do you still persist?" asks the emperor. "Behold, you see him flying up into heaven."

Then Peter looks at Paul, and says, "Look up, Paul, and see the outlandish sight."

Looking up from his kneeling prayer position, Paul sees Simon flying in the sky, and his face fills with tears. Then he turns to Peter and says chokingly, "Peter, why do you delay? Finish what we have begun – for already our Lord Jesus Christ is calling us."

Hearing them, Nero grimaces, shakes his head a little, and says to his queen and attendants, "These men plainly see themselves as totally bested, and have gone mad as a result."

But Peter answers back sharply, saying, "Watch now, and you will see that we are not mad."

And Paul says to Peter, "Do at once what needs to be done."

Looking directly at Simon up in the sky, Peter then cries out in prayer, "O God, if you let this heretic succeed in accomplishing this theatrical stunt, then all those who have believed in You through my teaching will now be lost or offended, and the signs and wonders which You have given them through me, will not be believed. O Lord, please extend Your grace at this critical moment. Let Simon ignominiously fall from the sky and become disabled – let him be brought down in disgrace but not die, breaking his leg in three places.

"Therefore, I command you, demons of Satan who are carrying Simon into the air, with the intent to deceive the hearts of the unbelievers – by the God that created all things, and by Jesus Christ our Lord, who on the third day was raised from the dead – I command you, from this minute, to no longer keep him aloft in the air, but to let him drop back to earth instead."

Simon Falls from the Sky

And immediately, Simon begins to fall, being let go by the forces that held him up.[7] It's not a vertical free-fall plummet, but more like a rapidly descending spiral. He falls to the ground on the Sacred Way, not far from the tower, and his leg is broken in three places. As he lay there, many of the onlookers laugh, scold, or insult him – some even throw stones. But most just groan and go home.

Quickly, one of Simon's friends and benefactors comes rushing to his aid. His name is Gemellus, and he has given Simon a good deal of money in the past few months for his teaching and ministry. Seeing that his leg is broken, he moans, "O Simon, if the 'power of god' is broken in pieces, does that mean that your god is lacking power? In that case, I'm afraid that your god will not be of any help to me when

I'm in distress. I think that the god of Peter has more power to help me."

Being in pain and semi-conscious, Simon is unable to think clearly or speak in reply. So with that, Gemellus just callously leaves him and runs after Peter.

Seeing Simon fall from flight after Peter's prayer, Nero becomes angry and indignant. He orders Peter and Paul to be put in irons, until such time that Simon dies and three days have passed, or until Simon recovers and explains the anomaly. Nero still believes that Simon may rise again after three days.

But Peter says, "If he is truly dead, then he will not rise, since he is condemned to everlasting punishment."

Then Nero says to him brusquely, "Who commanded you to do such a dreadful thing?"

"His sacrilege and blasphemy against my Lord Jesus Christ have brought him to this path of destruction," answers Peter.

Nero is not convinced or amused. "You will pay for this crime," he bellows. "I can destroy you by a simple waving of my hand."

"That kind of power you do not possess," Peter counters. "But even if you order the soldiers to kill me for this, it was absolutely necessary for me to do it – our Master's promise to us has to be fulfilled."

With that, Nero just walks away in disgust.

THE DEATH OF SIMON

Luckily for Simon, some of his other supporters reach him quickly and comfort him. They carry him home past the unruly mob of spectators. And after a few hours of rest at home, Simon begins to recover consciousness, but he is still dizzy and nauseous.

The next morning, he is semi-alert but in considerable pain. He needs medical care to treat his leg – and he may also have internal injuries. But he doesn't want to get a medical physician in Rome because it could not be kept secret. He doesn't want the word to spread that he is not infallible – to see him as just another flawed imperfect mortal. So, he seeks out a discreet doctor outside the city.

Having nowhere to go in Rome, his supporters carry him on a makeshift stretcher-bed at night from Rome to Aricia. He stays there for a few days under the care of local doctors, but is not recovering satisfactorily. So, the decision is made to bring him to Terracina for further medical treatment by 'experts'.[8]

Here he is cared for by two physicians, supposed specialists, one of who named Castor, has been banished from Rome on accusation of sorcery. But his condition deteriorates rapidly.

In an attempt to save his life by amputating his leg, Simon catches a serious infection and dies a few days later.

Thus, Simon of Samaria, the sorcerer and heretic extraordinaire – the angel of Satan – comes to his end.

The year is 62 AD.

When the Roman emperor Nero learns that Simon has died, and did not rise again after three days, he considers the whole matter to be closed. Peter and Paul are released from detention. He considers them to be just two more religious nuts running around Rome. And in any case, he has more important things to worry about in managing the empire. But he has now become familiar with Christian preachers and the doctrine of Christianity. He knows that they can be troublesome, and he is not afraid to invoke accusations of treason (usually with deadly consequences) if they disrupt the status-quo.

NOTES

1. Peter's God was commonly understood to be Jesus Christ, the 'Son of God'. This was a difficult concept for the pagan Romans to fathom. They had no concept of the Trinity or the Godhead. Many did not believe that Jesus was the 'Son of God' and many did not believe that Jesus was also God. Simon claimed that he was the 'power of god', and that the so-called 'Son of God' was not a god at all. Simon maintained that he was equivalent to Peter's 'Son of God'.

2. The 'Campus Martius' (Latin for 'Field of Mars') was a publicly owned area in ancient Rome, about 0.77 square miles in extent. In the Middle Ages, it was the most populous area of Rome. The 'Sacred Way' ('Via Sacra' in Latin) was the main street (of rock and stone), leading from the top of Capitoline Hill, through some of the most important sites of the Forum (the main center of business), to the Colosseum.

3. Paul said this because Peter was first taken in hand by the Lord.

4. The stairs were inside the tower walls, so once Simon entered the ground-floor door, he couldn't be seen again until he exited the tower to the platform at the very top.

5. The exact design of Simon's 'magical' apparatus is still unknown to historians today. This is a conjecture based on available information.

6. The thinking is that Helena had found a flaw or malfunction in the equipment at the last minute, and was trying to warn Simon.

7. Some ancient scholars believed that what appeared to be Simon's chariot, was actually just an inflated balloon, shaped like a chariot pulled by angels. For some reason – possibly associated with the intricate wire attachments – the balloon catastrophically deflated prematurely.

8. Terracina is a town about 56 miles southeast of Rome on the western coast of Italy. It came under Roman control in 329 BC, although Roman influence existed as early as 509 BC. The construction of the Via Appia in 312 BC added to the town's strategic importance. The beauty of a local promontory (about 700 feet above the main town), with its luxuriant flora and attractive view, made it frequented by Roman nobility, many of whom possessed country homes there. The picturesque modern town occupies the site of the old, but it was rebuilt after being extensively damaged during World War II.

18 THE LAST DAYS OF PETER

Because of the ongoing teachings of Peter and Paul, many people who dislike military, government, and political life, become attracted to the 'Good News' of Christianity. It isn't just the poor, the sick, and the marginalized who follow – people from all walks of life begin to listen, hear, and accept the principles and lifestyle of the 'Jesus followers'. Even from the emperor's bed-chamber they come – including Libia, the wife of Nero – to listen to Paul or Peter, and have fellowship with the one and true God. And once they become attached to the Christian way of living and thinking, they are no longer willing to return to the army, senate, or palace.

Meanwhile, Paul leaves Rome and sets sail for Spain, having received a vision that compels him to go 'to the ends of the earth' and preach the Gospel to all the unenlightened.[1]

As Peter continues to preach the 'Good News' in Rome, it so happens that a beautiful woman named Xanthippe, who is the wife of Albinus, the adjutant to the emperor, together with many other prominent women of the city, come to Peter seeking conversion and baptism. They have listened to his sermons concerning chastity and the commandments of the Lord,[2] and have forgone sexual relations with their partners, desiring to worship God in sobriety and cleanness – thinking that it is necessary for obtaining Peter's blessing.[3]

At the same time, the four concubines of the provincial governor and chief magistrate Agrippa⁴ – named Agrippina, Nicaria, Euphemia, and Doris – also become swayed by Peter's teachings of purity and chastity, and they too all agree to renounce sexual relations with the governor, remain absent from the bedchamber, and become 'brides of Christ' instead.

Naturally, both men are annoyed and upset. Agrippa hires some men to secretly follow the four women and determine where they are going. When he finds out that they are spending time listening to the sermons of Peter, he becomes incensed. He has them apprehended – and then boasts to them, "That evil man is a member of the crazed religious sect called 'Christians'. He has brainwashed you into having no intimacy with me. For this despicable act, I will punish you all, and burn him alive." Sadly, the four women suffer wicked maltreatment at the hand of Agrippa,⁵ but they are strengthened by their faith in the Lord.

When Agrippa and Albinus get together to discuss the matter, they agree that getting rid of Peter is the only way to get back their partner's sexual favors. And so, they concoct various plans to have him arrested, and then to have him executed within the law.

THE PLOT TO KILL PETER

At his next scheduled meeting with emperor Nero, Agrippa brings up the subject of the Christians, without going into details about his personal life. "I think it is right and proper that men who introduce mischievous religious observances – dealers in the mystical and sacrilegious arts ⁶– should be done away with," he states.

Nero is sympathetic. More than once, his wife Libia has gone to listen to Peter or Paul and returned with strange ideas. "Yes, these Christians are insufferable," he replies. "I think that the leaders of this vile new religion, Peter and Paul, should be thrown into the arena, given a club, and then killed in the great sea-fight spectacle that is played out in the Colosseum."⁷

However, Agrippa thinks of a different approach: "Most sacred emperor, what you have suggested may not be quite fitting for these men – they are not common criminals – and Paul seems somewhat innocent beside Peter – in any case, I believe that Paul has left Rome, and even all of Italy."

"Then, by what means should they be executed? asks Nero.

Agrippa responds assuredly, "It seems to me that Peter should be crucified – hung on a cross – since he is the direct cause of the murder of Simon.[8] As for Paul – well – since he is an accessory to murder, and a Roman citizen, it is appropriate that he be properly beheaded, if he ever returns to Rome."

"You have judged most excellently," replies Nero. "But what about all the rest of these horrible and shameful human beings they call Christians? They seem to have a hatred for the goodness of the human race, being 'infamous for their abominations'.[9]

"Yes, there needs to be a purge," suggests Agrippa. "We must find a way to eliminate them without rousing the ire of the people or the senate. All that is needed now is a good pretext, and then public outcry will be minimal."

The leaders nod in agreement, and with that, the meeting is ended and the matter is settled.

THE GREAT FIRE

A few months later,[10] a great fire ruins half of Rome,[11] and Nero tries to blame the Christians for the fire. This is just the pretext that he and Agrippa are looking for. Excessive cruelty and persecution against Christians start to ramp up. Worship services and religious practices are forced to go underground. But Peter remains stalwart, goes into hiding, and continues to evangelize whenever and however possible.

Widespread rumor has blamed the tragedy on the unpopular emperor, who wants to enlarge his palace and is looking for an excuse to do so. But he in turn, passes the buck, and accuses the Christians.

The persecution is quick and severe. A rationale for the denunciation of the Christians is circulated throughout the upper echelons of power, and it does the trick. Popular support for the Christians wanes when the notices appear.

Notice:
Thirty years ago, there lived a carpenter in Judaea who they called a 'Christ'. He was executed as a criminal by the Roman governor Pontius Pilate during the reign of emperor Tiberius. But there remained a religious cult who revered him as a god and actively followed bizarre practices that he taught. Although repressed, this destructive superstition has erupted again, not only throughout Judea, but also within the city of Rome, in which all that is horrible and shameful floods together, and is strangely celebrated by many misguided people.

Public outcry is minimal when Nero orders thousands of people suspected to be Christians, to be rounded-up.

First Martyrs

Using information extracted from the first suspects who are seized and tortured (some of them probably being slaves), a large number of Christians are arrested and convicted, ostensibly for the crime of starting the fire, but in reality, just for being followers of the detestable Christian religious cult.

Many other people are detained suspected to be Christians – rich and poor, slave and free – and many are convicted and sentenced to the most exquisite punishments imaginable. Some of those condemned are covered with the skins of animals and thrown to wild dogs, or wolves, to be torn apart. Others are crucified, and then at sunset are slathered with oil or wax, tied to posts, and burned alive – human torches – the glow of which illuminates the emperor's garden parties, and lights the path of his chariots.[12]

Nero flaunts his pompous nature by presenting the gory spectacle in the amphitheater, as if it was a sport – while he mingles with the people in the dress of a charioteer, and swaggers about the place ostentatiously.

Unscrupulous people 'rat' on the Christians,[13] but many hold firm to their convictions. The intensity of persecution continues in rippling waves in the city, and even throughout the empire to a lesser degree.[14] Women are not exempted. The fact that women are significantly represented in the persecutions clearly shows that they are active participants in the movement, and not just innocent wives, daughters, and hangers-on.

The Martyrdom of Peter's Wife

Among those caught up in the mass arrests and torment is the loyal wife of Peter. Not content to merely do some shopping and sightseeing in the big city, she is actively aiding and abetting the underground church community – she is not a simple bystander to her husband's ministry. Rather, she becomes a bona fide threat to the Roman order in her own right.[15]

Seeing his own wife led away to execution, Peter lovingly cries out to her in a consolatory but encouraging voice, addressing her by name,[16] and exhorting her to "remember the Lord!"[17] Such was the marriage of this blessed saint and his blessed wife. To the end, they were one with each other, and one with the Lord.[18]

PETER'S VISION AT THE GATE

After a few months of intense persecution of Christians, Xanthippe discovers the conspiracy to find and kill Peter by eavesdropping on her husband's daily communications with Agrippa. She secretly notifies Peter by slipping a note to a trusted friend, who gives it to Peter. Her hope is that Peter will have time to slip away and escape the punishment.

After receiving the note and discussing the whole sordid affair with his disciples, Peter reluctantly agrees to stealthily exit the city by himself and in disguise. The disciples insist, "If you temporarily leave now to escape this evil plot, then you may yet be able to serve the Lord on another day, and provide leadership to the fledgling church in Rome." So, the plan is to meet some compatriots a short way outside the city and they will escort him to safety.

But as he is leaving the city gate, he sees a hazy apparition of a figure entering the gate – and as it gets closer, it appears to be the Lord Jesus Christ.

Somewhat dumbfounded, Peter asks, "My Lord, where are You going?"

And the Lord answers, *I am coming to Rome to be crucified.*

"Lord, are You being crucified again?" queries Peter.

Yes Peter, I saw you leaving the gate to flee from death on a cross, and so I have entered the gate, such that I can be crucified instead of you, was the Lord's reply.

Peter is then overwhelmed with embarrassment and remorse. Instantly, he understands the situation, and knows exactly what he has to do. Sheepishly, he says to the Lord, "No Lord, I will go – I will stay the course – I will fulfill the command."

And then the apparition of the Lord says to Peter, *Fear not, Peter, for I am with you always.*[19]

And with that, the apparition disappears in an upward wisp of cloud, and Peter returns to the house of the disciples.

THE LAST EVENING

There and then, Peter realizes that his fate is sealed. But he is not afraid. Rather, he feels proud and triumphant – even jubilant because it is a joyous fate. Yes, he will be crucified, as was the Lord. And soon now, he will be together with the Lord, and the Father Almighty.

Of course, the disciples are saddened by the turnaround, and beg him to reconsider. But Peter is firm: "As long as the Lord wills me to be in the flesh, I do not demur. But if He wills it to be the time for taking me, then I rejoice and am glad.

"But as for you who are new to the faith, if you are willing, the Lord will educate you in the precepts. If He finds you worthy, He will ask you to spread the faith abroad. Just as He planted myself and the other apostles, so will He plant you through His name. You have a glorious mission, but it won't be easy. You must understand that there will be hardships and persecution along the way, and you will be tested. But if you remain true to the Lord in your heart and mind, then your reward in heaven is assured."

Peter goes on to explain the separation of spiritual and secular matters, and then describes the duties and expectations of the various church officials – bishop, presbyters, deacons, catechists, and lay people. And then, after saying all this, Peter lays his hands upon Clement in the presence of all, and makes him sit in his own chair.

Then, he says to him: "Clement, I ask you, in the presence of all the brothers and sisters here, that when I depart from this life, as surely I must, you send a full account of all your spiritual beliefs and reasonings to James, the 'brother' of the Lord in Jerusalem.[20] After a brief account of your early years, you should explain how you then journeyed with me, heard my sermons, and noted my deeds in every city. And finally, at the end, please describe to him the manner of my death. For he will not be overly grieved if he knows that I suffered piously, in the same manner as our Lord. Furthermore, he will be comforted in learning that an intelligent man, familiar with the words of scripture, and knowledgeable about the ways of the Church, is to be entrusted with the chair of the bishop after me."

Clement then promises to do everything that was requested of him, and Peter gives him his blessing.

And over the next few years, with all humility, honorable intent, and judicious detail, Clement describes Peter's sermons and deeds in every city in careful writing – and sends it all to James under the heading of 'Clement's Summary of the Popular Sermons of Peter.'[21]

The Sermon of the Church as a Great Ship

As the people are gathering their things together and preparing to leave for the evening, Peter hears one of the believers mutter something about 'not understanding all this business about a church'. Now, that cuts to the heart of Peter, and he has to address the problem at once. So, he stands up and announces, "My friends, please tarry a few minutes longer – I must tell you something. You should understand that this whole business of the 'church' can be likened to a great ship, sailing through a violent storm, and carrying people from all walks of life who desire to reach the city of a great kingdom. You can think of it like this:

"God the Father Almighty is your shipmaster; Jesus Christ is the pilot, the bishop is the first-mate, the deacons are the sailors, the catechists are the midshipmen, and the multitude of believers are the passengers. In this view, the world we live in is like the sea – earthly temptations, persecutions, and dangers are like the foul winds that blow in the air – all manner of afflictions that we endure are like the waves that churn the ocean – the rhetoric and pomp we hear from unholy deceivers and false prophets are like the land winds and squalls that pop up and irritate us – the pagan judges in high places threatening terrible things are like the promontories and rugged rocks of the channel separating two waters – and the unreasonable men who refuse to believe in the truth of the Word are like the wild places where all manner of beasts prowl about.

"Now, I say to you, let the hypocrites be regarded as pirates, and let the effects of our sins be thought of as swirling whirlpools, sea monsters, deadly foundering, and terrible wrecks.

"Therefore, in order to safely reach the haven of the hoped-for city, we must all pray loud and often for the fair wind and the gentle sea. But remember, prayers must be accompanied by good deeds.

"So, I say to you now, let the passengers remain quiet, sitting in their places – since if they don't, they can cause rolling or careening of the ship. Let the midshipmen give heed to the fare. Let the deacons neglect nothing that they are entrusted with. Let the presbyters, like sailors, carefully arrange everything that is needed for each ship. Let the bishop, as the first-mate, listen attentively to the words of the pilot alone. And let Christ our Savior be loved as the pilot, and He alone believed in matters of the Word.

"Now, let us all pray to God for a prosperous voyage. But those who are sailing will experience much tribulation, since they are travelling in a troubled world – like a great and restless sea. They will sometimes be disheartened, persecuted, dispersed, hungry, and thirsty, but they will also sometimes be united, congregated, fulfilled, and at rest. The key to the latter is the confessing of one's sins – like the sea-sick man who vomits out the vile. For it is through the confession of sins, whether proceeding from bitterness or the evils associated with disorderly lusts, that you are relieved of your disease, and thereby attain health and fullness of life."

With that, everyone departs with a feeling of inner peace and strength. And Peter closes his eyes for the next-to-last time.

THE MARTYRDOM OF PETER

Bright and early the next morning four soldiers arrive, barge their way in to arrest Peter, and brusquely haul him off to Agrippa.

Once at the courthouse, all the disciples, and even many citizens, speak out in defense of Peter, but to no avail – the sentence is irreversible – crucifixion on the accusation of godlessness. And there is no delay.

Soldiers march him out to a small hilltop on the outskirts of the city, where other criminals have been executed, and a cross is hastily constructed.

Desiring to see and to rescue Peter, a great multitude of disciples and believers – rich and poor, orphans and widows, weak and strong – follow along with the execution unit, yelling and shouting, "What has Peter done wrong? O Agrippa, how has he hurt you?" Other people are hollering, "We are afraid that if this man dies, his god will destroy us. His god is powerful. We must not offend him!"

When they all arrive at the hilltop, Peter quiets the people and then addresses them, "Friends, you are soldiers of Christ! And your hope is in Christ!

"Remember the signs and wonders which you have seen that were worked through me! And remember the compassion of God – how many cures and healings have blessed you!

"Wait for Him – He is coming soon –and He will reward every man according to his doings.

"And don't be overly bitter against Agrippa – for he knows not what he is doing.[22] The time has come – my destiny is assured – for the Lord has told me that this is what must occur. Therefore my friends, do not hinder my going, for already my feet are treading on the road to heaven. Do not grieve for me, but rather rejoice with me, for today I receive the fruit of my labors."

Peter is then led to the spot where the cross is to be staked. He looks up to heaven and laments:

"O the power of the cross, the hidden mystery! O the indescribable grace that is extended in the name of the cross! O the spirit of man, that cannot be separated from God! O the love indefinable and inseparable, that cannot be expressed by unclean lips!

"I seize it all, now that I am at the end of my journey. I declare it all as truth. And I will not keep silent regarding the mystery of the cross, which was hidden from my soul when I was younger.

"My friends, let not this cross of mine affect your hope in Jesus Christ the Lord, for this is a different thing – and it is per the will of Christ that it happens this way."

"And now above all, to those who have ears to hear, I say to you this, at the last and final hour of my life:

"Behold! Separate your souls from everything that is of the senses – from everything that appears to exist, but does not exist in truth. Close your eyes, cover your ears, and forget about your daily deeds that are seen by many – and then you will perceive that which really matters to God – the whole mystery of your life and your salvation.

"But now it is time for me to deliver up my body to those who wish to take it, although it is God to whom it really belongs. Therefore, I say to you all here:

Take this body then, you whose duty it is to do so. I only ask that you crucify me head downwards – in this way and no other. For I am not worthy to die like Jesus Christ, my Lord and Savior – Who came down from heaven onto the earth to lead us to salvation, but was fixed upon the cross upright because of the folly of men."

The soldiers are anxious to get on with the business at hand. They have given Peter his last words. And so, now they fasten Peter to the cross, and stake it into the ground upside down, as he has requested.

The crowd gasps and screams for clemency and compassion, but they are powerless. The soldiers keep them at bay with intimidation and threats of force.

But Peter has more to say, even in his excruciatingly painful position:

"To those of you who have ears to hear, listen to what I say to you now: You should learn the mystery of all nature, the beginning of all things. For the first human on earth, the race of whom I bear the likeness of, was formed prostrate on the ground from the clay of the earth – its head was not upwards, for it was dead, having no motion. But when God blew into its nostrils the breath of life, the creature stood up and raised his head upwards, in the image of God – and represented a whole new order of things.[23] He was the pinnacle of God's new creation.

"And this new creation was very different from His other creations – the angels, the spirits, and the heavens. Everything was changed topsy-turvy – all the attributes of the nature of things were changed. It was like He made right-hand things into left-hand things, and left-hand into right-hand – He made things that were not fair to be fair, and things that were in truth evil, to be good.

"We know this to be a great mystery, for the Lord has told us:

Unless you understand the things of the right-hand as those of the left, and things of the left as those of the right, and things that are above as those that are below, and things that are behind as those that are before, you will not have the knowledge of the Kingdom of God.

"Therefore, I have told you this as you see me hanging here in the same manner as how the first human beings came to be born. Head downwards is the representation of how a mortal man is born and should die. The reverse is reserved for the divine – for Jesus the Christ, to whom is all the glory and honor both now and for all eternity. Amen."

"My beloved friends, hear me now: Cease from your former errors and return back again to Christ. For it is not wrong to be mounted on the cross, and stretched out like the one and only Jesus Christ.

"For the Holy Spirit has said,

What else is the Christ, but the Word and the Sound of God?

"Consider the Word to be the upright beam upon which I am crucified. And consider the Sound to be the crosswise beam, the nature of man. And the nail that holds the crosswise beam to the upright beam is the conversion and repentance of humankind.

"O Tree of Life,[24] O King of Glory, now that You have revealed these things to me, I give You thanks – not with lips that are nailed to the cross, or with a tongue by which both truth and falsehood emerge, or with words on paper which appear as artistic scribblings, but with my inner voice do I give You thanks. Mine is a voice that is understood in silence and not heard openly – a voice that does not emanate from organs of the body, and does not enter into ears of flesh – a voice that does not exist in the world, does not propagate on earth, is not written in books, and is owned by only one and not by many.

"With this silent voice, O Jesus Christ, do I give You thanks. The spirit that is in me loves You, speaks to You, sees You, and praises You – my spirit perceives Your spirit. You are my father, my mother, my brother, my friend, my bondsman, and my steward. You are the alpha and the omega, the beginning and the end, the small and the big. You are everything, and there is nothing else except You.

"Take refuge in Him, my brothers and sisters. Understand that in Him alone is your real being. Then, you will receive all that He has promised – for God's wisdom is a mysterious hidden wisdom, and not the 'wisdom' of men. Of this wisdom, it is written:[25]

'Eye has not seen, ear has not heard, nor has it so much as dawned on man what God has prepared for those who love Him.'

"I thank You, good Shepherd, that the sheep which You have entrusted to me, are together with me in mind and spirit. I ask then, that they may have a part in Your glorious Kingdom.

"And so, we ask You Lord Jesus Christ, all pure and all wise, for those gifts which You have promised to give us. We praise You, we give You thanks, we confess to You, and we glorify You – even those of us who are without strength. For You are God alone, and none other!

"Glory be to the Father, and to the Son, and to the Holy Spirit – as it was in the beginning, is now, and ever shall be – world without end. Amen."[26]

Then, the crowd standing all around shout "Amen."

And when the multitude standing by have pronounced the great 'Amen' with a righteous and holy sound, Peter gives up his spirit to the Lord.

THE END OF THE STORY

Immediately, out of nowhere, three strange men, saintly in appearance, step forward and announce, "We are here from Jerusalem, on behalf of the holy apostles and chief disciples. We will make sure that our brother Peter is given the proper Christian burial. But now, you should not be sorrowful, but should rejoice and be exceedingly glad – for you have been deemed worthy to have had a great champion and defender before God. And know this also: In a short time, the evil emperor Nero will be deposed and his kingdom given to another." Hearing this, the people are contented and slowly disperse.

Together with Marcellus, the men from Jerusalem take Peter down from the cross and lay the body under a terebinth tree,[27] a short distance away from the main Forum. Then, the three men simply disappear.

Marcellus takes it upon himself to wash the body in milk and wine. He then finely grinds up some mastic,[28] myrrh, aloes, and leafy greens[29] into an oily aromatic paste, and embalms the body.[30] He places the body in an expensive marble coffin (that he had purchased for himself) lined with honey, and buries it in the ground.

Burial and Moving of the Body

But later that night, some devout followers of Simon coming from regions of the East, try to steal the body of Peter in a last-gasp attempt to desecrate his name and legacy. But just as they are in the process, an earthquake erupts in the city. Local citizens come running out of their homes for safety, and they see the vandals digging at the grave site. This is a serious offense to the Romans – incensed, they chase after them, but they manage to slip away. However, a group of loyal Christians quickly learn about the event and they search them out, fearing they might return. And within a few hours, the criminals are apprehended and turned over to police authorities.

Then, the believers move the body to a secret place about three miles outside the city – to an abandoned cement quarry.[31] There, the tomb is continually guarded by the Christian believers for a year and seven months, until they complete the construction of a proper crypt.

The Return and Death of Paul

However, within the next year or so, after traveling to Spain, Crete, Asia, Greece, and Macedonia, Paul returns to Rome under house arrest,[32] and is shortly thereafter executed by beheading – to carry-out his earlier conviction and sentence. The body is swiftly moved to the same cement quarry by ardent believers – and the crypt is expanded to a mausoleum, intended for final interment of both holy apostles.

And then, at the proper time, after all Christian believers have assembled together with glory and the singing of solemn praises, the tombs of the holy apostles Peter and Paul are placed in the graves purposefully made for them, to rest forever.[33] Thanks be to God.

Marcellus has a Vision

Meanwhile, the night after the earthquake, Marcellus has a vision of Peter standing by the gravesite, and he speaks to him: "Marcellus, haven't you heard what the Lord has said?"

Let the dead be buried of their own dead

And when Marcellus responds affirmatively, Peter says to him, "Then, what you have spent on the dead, you have lost – for although you are alive, you have cared for the dead like a dead man."

When Marcellus awakes, he tells the loyal followers about the appearance of Peter, and what he thinks is the meaning of the vision. "A Christian burial should be simple," he says. "Earthly 'kings' are nothing – the real King is in heaven – and our praise, respect, and devotion should be to Him." Hearing this from Marcellus, all the faithful believers become further strengthened in the Gospel, and the Christian way of life.

The Fate of Nero

When the emperor Nero later discovers that Peter has been executed, he is angry, and scolds magistrate Agrippa for putting Peter to death without his knowledge. He had wanted to punish and torture him longer and more severely, because Peter had made disciples of some of his servants, and they had run away and left him.

Agrippa is appropriately reprimanded, and a 'search and destroy' order is issued for all of Peter's followers and disciples.

But that night Nero has a vision of an angel saying to him, "Nero, you can no longer persecute or destroy the servants of Christ. Keep your hands away from them!"

Being greatly alarmed at the vision, Nero countermands his 'search and destroy' order, and instead, takes a 'hands-off' approach toward the followers of Peter.

But there is rising resentment in the city against Nero's reign by both the people and the senate. Nero starts eliminating men in government who he perceives as dangerous or suspicious. And the economy plummets as extravagant expenditures on bribes, payoffs, and corruption nearly empty the treasury. He becomes hated by the old ruling class, the middle class, the provincials, and even the army troops. He is denounced as 'murderer of his mother and wife, a charioteer, an actor, and an incendiary'.

In 68 AD, the people, the praetorian guard, and the senate finally rise up and start a revolt against him, causing a big ruckus in the city. Fearing an assassination by political rivals, Nero flees into the deserted areas south of the city. But without friend or ally, he is unable to sustain himself – through hunger and cold he gradually gives up the ghost – and his body becomes food for the wild beasts.[34]

The revolt sparks a series of civil wars which threaten the survival of the empire, and cause widespread misery. But the Christians rejoice and glorify God that the tyrant is gone. For a short while there is relative peace among the Christian community in Rome.

But the peace and joy will not last.[35]

NOTES

1. Paul has a vision of the Lord, who says to him:

Arise, Paul, and go in person to the west – to the ends of the earth – to Spain – and teach the Gospel to all the unenlightened people of that place.

2. The Romans at this time considered the Lord's commandments to be like the oracles of their pagan gods. A distinct theological differentiation between Christianity and paganism was still not clear in the minds of most. Many simply considered the god of Peter to be just another new god that oversaw Roman affairs.

3. The belief that absolute abstention from sexual relations was a prerequisite for salvation and eternal life, was a common misunderstanding of Christian teaching. Neither Peter or Paul preached this. They maintained that loving consensual relations within marriage were not sinful. But they emphasized that inhibition of the passions out of wedlock, or in non-consensual situations, was the best way to maintain purity and enhance the quest for a resurrection and life everlasting.

4 The provincial governor was generally an ex-high-ranking army official who already had broad experience in legal and administrative affairs.

5. The ultimate fate of the four concubines is unknown.

6. Pagan Romans considered Christianity atheistic since it didn't believe in the Roman gods. They also considered it bizarre and peculiar. And many considered it immoral because of the strange praying, baptizing, and eating customs.

7. The standard format for the Roman games was animal entertainment in the morning session, followed by an afternoon session reserved for gladiatorial combats and recreations of famous battles. The execution of criminals, deserters, and enemies of the state often took the form of the re-creation of some tragic scene from history or mythology, such as a great sea battle, with the criminal cast in the role of the victim.

8. Both Agrippa and Nero believed that Simon had crashed and died because Peter had used his 'magic' to cause it.

9. Cornelius Tacitus (trans. by J. Jackson), *The Annals of Imperial Rome and Agricola* (Book XV:44), [Cambridge: Harvard University Press, 1937]

10. The year is 64 AD.

11. Largely made up of wooden tenements, fire was a frequent occurrence in the city of Rome.

12. Christians who are martyred during Nero's persecution, allegedly in retaliation for their starting the 'great fire of 64', are later identified as the 'First Martyrs of the Church of Rome'.

The memorial feast day for these martyrs is an aggregated replacement for the memorials of dozens of unfamiliar martyred individuals, most of whom have scant historical evidence. At least 574 individual martyrs have been recognized by the Catholic church, but the exact number is of course unknown.

13. The fickle word of a snoop, meddler, gossiper, or busybody was often enough to warrant seizure and arrest.

14. The Jews of Asia (modern day Turkey) appeared frequently in leading roles advocating the persecution of Christians. The persecution under Nero may have been influenced by their political pressure.

15. Peter's wife: Her faithfulness to Jesus and His church cost her everything, yet the church barely recognizes her devotion.

16. Unfortunately, nowhere in Scripture or in any other religious or historical writing, is `the name of Peter's wife revealed.

17. Reference: A.D. Clement, presbyter of Rome, in his signature work "Stromateus", in Eric Osborn, *Clement of Alexandria* [Cambridge: University Press, 2008].

18. It is entirely likely that Peter's wife contributed to the apostolic mission by sharing her own witness of who Jesus was, and what He meant to her and to the world. It must have been a grand testimony! Surely, she knew Jesus personally. The story in Mark 1:29-31 implies that she prepared food and provided hospitality for Jesus in her own home (and probably not only on one occasion, as Jesus' Galilean ministry was centered in the area). She must have listened to Jesus' teaching and, without doubt, she was an intimate witness to his influence on her husband, and his brother Andrew.

19. Refer to Matthew 28:20 for a similar occurrence.

20. James, the 'brother' of the Lord was an early leader of the Jerusalem Church. Also known as 'James the Just', 'James, son of Alphaeus', and 'James the Less', he was most likely the son of Joseph by another wife (a half-brother of Jesus), or the son of Mary of Clopas, sister of the Mother of our Lord (a cousin of Jesus). He died as a martyr in 69 AD after being thrown off the pinnacle of the temple, and then being stoned and beaten with a club until dead. He should not be confused with James, son of Zebedee, also known as James the Great.

21. These letters exist today as "The Recognitions of Clement" and "The Homilies of Clement" (usually listed together as the "Pseudo-Clementine Recognitions and Homilies").

The authorship, date, and doctrinal character of these writings have been the subject of keen discussion in modern times. Studied and analyzed by the most renowned scholars, they may well be the single most important writings on the history of early Christianity, and the Christian Church in its formative stage.

22. Peter remembers the words of Christ on the cross. Reference Luke 23:24.

23. Peter is paraphrasing the events in Genesis 2:7.

24. Peter is saying that his cross, as well as the cross of Christ, is analogous to the 'tree of life' in the Book of Genesis. See Genesis 2:9 and Genesis 3:22.

25. In 1 Corinthians 2:7-9, Paul is referring to Isaiah 64:3.

26. The *Gloria Patri*, a Catholic Hymn of Praise (also called 'The Minor Doxology')

27. The terebinth tree is a short but wide tree of the cashew family, once used as a source of turpentine.

28. Mastic (also known as 'tears of Chios') is a resin excreted by glands of the mastic tree grown on the Greek island of Chios. The resin is produced in 'tears' or droplets and dries into pieces of brittle translucent resin. Today, it is used in skin-care products, perfume, chewing gum, varnish, and waterproof sealant/adhesive.

29. leafy vegetables, such as spinach, mustard greens, kale, and fenugreek leaves

30. Embalming in the modern sense involves the injection of various chemical solutions into the arterial network. In ancient times, it was done by drying of the body and then covering it completely with aromatic and water-resistant oils and resins, such as myrrh (a gum resin from commiphora trees), mastic, green herbs, and aloes.

31. Traditional history established at least as early as the middle of the 4th century AD, associates the shrine of Saint Peter with two specific sites in Rome: the still-surviving Church of Saint Sebastian, beside the Appian Way (in union with Saint Paul), and the great Church of Saint Peter's built on the Vatican hill. The Church of Saint Sebastian (founded by Constantine I and originally known as the Basilica of the Apostles [Peter and Paul]) was built over the remains of a Roman cemetery, which overlay the abandoned cement quarry.

32. There is good evidence that Paul returned to Rome under house arrest, after his 4th missionary journey, which included a mission to Spain, ministry on the island of Crete, and missionary work in Ephesus, Macedonia (stopping at Miletus and Troas en-route to Philippi, Thessalonica, and Berea), Corinth, and Nicopolis.

33. Somewhere between 160 and 258 AD, the tomb of Peter is moved to the Vatican hill, where there was already a cenotaph (a monument in the form of a tomb to a person buried elsewhere) erected by the early Christian community to commemorate Peter's martyrdom nearby, and a mausoleum is constructed at the site. The building of Old Saint Peter's Basilica was started on the site by emperor Constantine I in 326 AD, and finished about 35 years later. The New Saint Peter's Basilica in Vatican City was begun in 1506 and completed in 1615. The Encyclopedia Britannica has a good summary of the archeological history.

34. Some sources say that Nero committed suicide by cutting his throat.

35. Deadly persecution of Christians will continue in waves of severity until 313 AD, when the Christians are finally guaranteed freedom to practice their religion by the Edict of Milan – issued by co-emperors Licinius and Constantine ('the Great'), it proclaimed the common policy of full toleration for all religions and restitution of wrongs done to the Christians. Constantine went further, making lavish donations to the churches and granting immunities to the clergy. Designation of Christianity ('Nicene' Christianity) as the official religion of the Roman Empire occurred under emperor Theodosius I in 380 AD, by the Edict of Thessalonica.

EPILOGUE

SIMON MAGUS

The Simonians were a Gnostic sect that regarded Simon Magus as its founder, but the gnostic philosophy didn't really blossom until after his death. Simon was more of a syncretistic preacher – he amalgamated different religious thoughts into whatever suited him best at the moment.

He is sometimes referred to as 'the bad Samaritan' due to his malevolent character (as opposed to 'the good Samaritan' of Luke 10:30-37). The sect flourished in Syria, Samaria, various districts in Asia Minor, and Rome in the 2nd century. Female members of the sect were sometimes called Heleniani, after Simon's girlfriend Helena.

Followers of Simon, and believers in Simonianism or Gnosticism, did not disappear when Simon died ignominiously in Rome around 62 AD. Two of his Samaritan disciples, Menander and Saturninus (or Satornilus – originally an apprentice of Menander), remained loyal right up until when they died near the turn of the century. And many of their devotees were still preaching even into the late 4th century.

After the death of Simon, Menander became the leader of the Simonian movement. He established a school in Antioch where he announced himself as the messiah, and vowed to defeat the evil angels that were keeping the world in captivity. He held fast to the belief that as head of the sect, he was the savior and 'messenger of god'.

Other philosopher-magicians followed, including Basilides, Valentinus, Carpocrates, Marcellina, Cerinthus, Cerdo, Marcion of Sinope, Tatian, Heracleon, and the Ebionites. They were all profuse writers and speakers, and gave immense development to the Gnostic religious philosophy, each altering it slightly to meet their personal beliefs and agenda. Marcellina became famous as the female leader of the 'Marcellian Gnostics' in 2nd century Rome, embracing strong feminist teachings. Basilides became well-known in Alexandria.

The Simonians divided during the Gnostic schism between the Menandrians – followers of Menander who believed that the world was made by ignorant angels sent by a 'mother who was created by an unknown father' – and the Satornnilians – followers of Saturninus who believed that the world was made by only 7 angels (one of whom was Yahweh, the god of the Israelites) against the will of a 'father on high'.

While Menander called himself the 'messenger of god', Saturninus considered Jesus Christ to be the only 'messenger of god'. But both believed that the 'law' of the Hebrews, as preached by the Old Testament prophets, was not from God, but from 'sinister powers' (evil angels). They believed that Jesus was only a man, but saw him as a model to be emulated, or even surpassed.

###

The church of Saint Frances in Rome,[1] claims to have been built on the spot where Simon fell to earth from his catastrophic flying exhibition. Within the Church is a dented slab of marble that purports to bear the imprints of the knees of Peter and Paul during their fervent devout prayers.

In Irish legend, Simon Magus comes to the aid of the Druid Mog Ruith,[2] who was said to have helped make Simon's flying apparatus. But, the fierce denunciation of Christianity by Irish Druids is probably the real reason why Simon became associated with Druidism. The word 'druid' was sometimes translated into Latin as 'magus', and Simon Magus was known in Ireland as 'Simon the Druid'.

The fantastic stories of Simon the Sorcerer persisted into the late Middle Ages, becoming a possible inspiration for Goethe's *Faust*.[3]

SIMON PETER

He was just a poor uneducated and undistinguished fisherman. But, for the sake of the true faith and the correctness of holy doctrine, he was set apart from all others in this world, in order to be the foundation – the rock – of the Christian Church.[4]

Jesus Christ said this himself, when He re-named him Peter[5] – the 'first-fruit' of the Lord, the first of the apostles to be blessed,[6] the first to whom the Father revealed the Son,[7] and the one to whom was given the keys to the kingdom of heaven.[8]

During the ministry of Jesus, he was called to be the chosen follower, the excellent and approved disciple. Being the spiritually and energetically fittest of all, he was called to enlighten the darkest part of the world – Rome – the center of pagan power in the west – and for this task, he was given the immense strength of the Holy Spirit.

Because of his great love for mankind, the overwhelming desire for their salvation, and his faith and commitment to the Gospel of Jesus Christ, he left Jerusalem and traveled as far as the imperial city of Rome. But wherever he went, he clearly and publicly testified in opposition to all the phony doctrines, all the sham preachers, and all the false messiahs that were threatening the fabric and integrity of the Church – especially the wicked one named Simon, who vexed, bothered, and confused the true believers in Christ at every opportunity.

But he overcame Simon, all the other evil-doers, and all the fake doctrines swirling around, revealing to the world by example, the hope and grace that comes from belief in the King of Glory, the Lord Jesus Christ. He saved many people along the way on his mission of mercy, but at God's appointed time, he accepted the sentence of martyrdom, and exchanged his life on this temporary world for eternal life in heaven. He rests now in peace. God bless his soul.

Amen.

NOTES

1. The Church of Santa Francesca Romana (also called the Church of Santa Maria Nova [New Saint Mary's])

2. Mog Ruith (or Mug Ruith, or Mogh Roith, 'slave of the wheel') is a figure in Irish mythology – a powerful druid who lived in county Kerry. Some legends say he could grow to enormous size, and his breath caused storms and turned men to stone. He wore a hornless bull-hide and a bird mask, and flew in a machine called the 'roth rámach' (or 'oared wheel'). His powers and long lifespan led some to believe that he was a sun god or storm god.

Stories about him are set in various periods of Irish history. Some legends put him in Jerusalem during the time of Christ. He is said to have been a student of Simon Magus, and helped him build the flying machine that Simon used to fly over Rome.

He has also been identified as the executioner who beheaded John the Baptist, bringing a curse to the Irish people. His daughter was named Tlachtga, a powerful druidess, who gave her name to a hill in county Meath and a festival celebrated there. Supposedly, she was raped by Simon Magus while her father was studying Simon's magic.

3. Faust was the name of a magician and charlatan of the 16th century who became famous in legend and literature, although he was a shady and relatively obscure character in reality. He attained posthumous fame because of the book *Faustbuch*, written anonymously, and published by Johann Spies in Frankfurt-on-Main in 1587. It contained retold tales of ancient magicians, such as Virgil, Merlin, and Simon Magus, but whose qualities and traits were now attributed to Faust. The enchanting idea of Helen of Troy (Simon Magus' girlfriend Helena) being summoned up from Hades to ensure Faust's damnation set Christopher Marlowe's imagination aflame, and is one of the reasons why the legend acquired immortality.

4. Matthew 16:18

5. ibid

6. Matthew 16:17

7. Matthew 16:16-17

8. Reference Matthew 16:19. Being put in charge of the church by Jesus, and then preaching in Rome before his martyrdom, Peter had been given the title of 'bishop of Rome', which was later recognized as the 'Pope'. Before Peter's death, however, there were leaders of the Christian community in Rome, who were recognized informally as 'presbyters' and 'presbyter-bishops'. Two of these leaders, Linus and Anacletus (known also as Cletus), were ordained by Peter for priestly service to the community, while he devoted himself to prayer and preaching.

Nowadays, Peter is recognized as the first bishop of Rome, and therefore the first Pope, because it was during their stay in Rome, that Peter and Paul formally established the Roman church with rules, regulations, and a specified hierarchy – and made it the church founded on a 'rock'. Since Peter was given the 'keys to the kingdom of heaven', and the 'kingdom of heaven' on earth is considered to be the 'Church', it was natural that Peter should assume the status of first 'bishop of Rome' (although he probably wasn't recognized as such at the time), simply because he was the apostolic leader at the time in the city. Upon Peter's death in ~67 AD, the presbyter Linus became the recognized 'bishop of Rome', since he had been consecrated by Paul. When Linus died in ~76 AD, Anacletus became the 'bishop of Rome' until his death in ~88 AD. Clement had travelled and studied with Peter as a young man, and was Peter's top choice for leader of the church upon his death. But he was too young in 67 AD, and graciously allowed the bishopric to transfer to Linus, and later to Anacletus. However, in ~88 AD he became the 4th 'bishop of Rome' (Clement I), since he was now an elder and had been already consecrated by Peter.

Clement was a great leader and worked hard for the church. At least one Epistle is attributed to him (the Letter to the Church at Corinth – '1 Clement'), but a number of other writings exist that purport to be in his name. He is considered to be the first 'Apostolic Father of the Church', the first of early Rome's most notable bishops, and is mentioned by Paul in Philippians 4:3. The story of his final years as a prisoner under Roman emperor Trajan, sent to work in a stone quarry, and execution by being thrown into the Black Sea tied to an anchor, is a heroic story all by itself (Reference: https://www.catholic.org/saints/saint.php?saint_id=37).

About the Author:

Edward N Brown is a storyteller with a background in science, philosophy, ancient history, and theology. His technique is to blend the interesting nuggets of historical record, legend, biography, romance, scientific fact, spirituality, and personal drama – all mixed together into an informative, but easy-reading, faith-based tale of wonder and awe. An educational background of three advanced degrees (PhD + two MS) has contributed to his insights on Christianity, Religion, Antiquity, Morality, and Human Nature. Classified as 'Narrative Non-Fiction' (ancient religious history), his works represent a speculative fusion of style – facts and events in riveting story form – drama and intrigue that will inform, entertain, and inspire readers of all ages.

Other Books by Edward N Brown:

The Passion of Nino – the Enlightener
Passion of the Slave Girls
Saint, Martyr, Virgin, Slave: Faith and Freedom Forever
The Passion of Thecla: Faith and Fortitude
The Passion of Eve: Remembering the End
The Passion of Eve: Remembering the Beginning
    Revised Edition 2020
    Original Edition 2019

"I AM the ALPHA and the OMEGA," says the Lord God,
"the One Who is and Who was and Who is to come,
    the Almighty!"
"I AM the ALPHA and the OMEGA, the First and the Last, the
    Beginning and the End!
Blessed are they who wash their robes so as to have free access to
    the Tree of Life ..."

Revelation 1:8 and 22:13-14

www.ingramcontent.com/pod-product-compliance
Lightning Source LLC
Chambersburg PA
CBHW051143030726
47504CB00004B/1015